False Harbor

A San Juan Island Mystery

Michael Donnelly

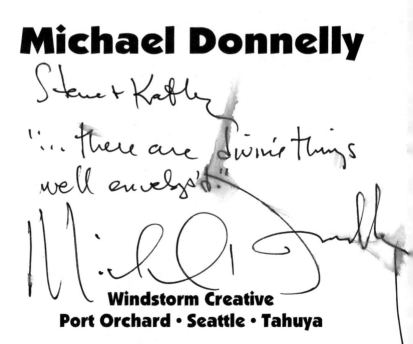

Steve + Kathey
"... there are divine things
we'll envelop".

Windstorm Creative
Port Orchard • Seattle • Tahuya

False Harbor: A San Juan Island Mystery
copyright 2006 by Michael Donnelly
published by Windstorm Creative

ISBN 1-59092-129-1
First edition August 2006
9 8 7 6 5 4 3 2

Cover image by Nancy Spaulding.
Design by Buster Blue of Blue Artisans Design.

Printed in the United States of America.

For information about film, reprint or other subsidiary rights, please contact Mari Garcia at mgarcia@windstormcreative.com.

Windstorm Creative is a multiple division, international organization involved in publishing books in all genres, including electronic publications; producing games, videos and audio cassettes as well as producing theatre, film and visual arts events. The wind with the flame center was designed by Buster Blue of Blue Artisans Design and is a trademark of Windstorm Creative.

Windstorm Creative
7419 Ebbert Dr SE
Port Orchard, WA 98367
www.windstormcreative.com
360-769-7174 ph

Windstorm Creative is a member of Orchard Creative Group, Ltd.

Library of Congress Cataloging-in-Publication data available.

For my parents, Mary Helen and Charles,
and
for Cori,
my inspiration for everything
including Egret

Acknowledgments

A shaker of Manhattans to the memory of Korczak Ziolkowski, and to Monique who allowed me to revisit his studio, now hers; warm thanks to fellow Poulsbohemian authors Alice Anderson, Cheryl Berger, Carson Farley, Celia Martin, and Sue Riddle, and to Prudence McCabe.

False Harbor

A San Juan Island Mystery

Michael Donnelly

Chapter 1

Even before the morning of the dreadful accident, I'd been intrigued by talk of Anton Gropius, how he'd turned hermit somewhere in the nearby Canadian Gulf Islands after someone bludgeoned his masterpiece sculptures. How his mail, which came to a post office box here in Friday Harbor, sometimes included *Thunderhead Island* in the address, but how the nautical charts showed no such landfall. Gropius had dropped in on my editor once, but few others in town had ever seen him during the twenty years he'd been in seclusion. Someone else picked up his mail.

The code of island living calls for respecting privacy, but sometimes a journalist's curiosity overcomes her sense of decency. My penance for this lapse of manners? Something that still jerks me awake in the night, twisted in my sheets.

I poured cream and watched it marble my second cup of coffee. Daphne's Café seemed unnaturally quiet. We'd endured Labor Day, and now the tourists were gone and the summer-cottage crowd had migrated back to wherever. The only customers besides me were two men in red plaid jackets—deck hands, from the smell of diesel. They occasionally glanced my way. When Shannon, my fellow staff writer for the *Slacktide,* arrived they'd probably bay out loud. She was twenty minutes late—the time it takes to do her lashes. I spend about twenty minutes a year on mine.

I gave up waiting and ordered breakfast. A minute later, Daphne stepped from the kitchen, the phone at the end of her saggy arm. "Someone here called Murphy?"

One of the waterfront guys took the call.

"Ah damn! Yeah." He handed the phone back. "Let's go!" he said to his comrade. "They tried swinging that crate without us and now the skipper's under it. Anton's messing his shorts." He shelled money on the table. The other guy crammed in a triple-decker bite of pancake while scraping his chair back from the table.

I had him by the sleeve before he'd straightened his legs. "Anton *Gropius*? The sculptor?"

Both men froze for a beat, looked warily at me, then scrammed without answering.

Before the door had swung shut, Shannon breezed in and

stubbed her cigarette in some scrambled eggs on the men's table. She doesn't trust any cook old enough to have lived through the Depression, and on that account suspects Daphne of re-heating leftovers. My guess is that Shannon has only a vague idea of when the Depression actually happened.

"I've already ordered. You can have it if you want. Tell Daphne to put it on my tab."

"Egret—"

"I've got a lead."

A long wooden staircase descends the embankment from the café to the marina. I'd run halfway down it when I heard clunking footsteps following me. Despite her platform shoes, Shannon wasn't far behind so I waited. From that elevation, I could see a small crowd forming on the commercial pier past the harbormaster's building. Above them, a pale disk of sun burned through the haze. I didn't mind Shannon tagging along. By disposition we didn't often compete for stories. City hall, the county commissioners, the courthouse— these were my beats. Shannon thrived on hearsay and scandal.

We hurried past trawlers and barges piled with colored nets. Near a self-service hoist people gawked at something over the railing. A siren warbled uptown as Shannon and I pushed our way to the action. A man lay on the deck of a flat-bottomed cargo transport, apparently in shock, his right leg pinned by a crate the size of a deepfreeze.

The two men from the restaurant rigged straps under the load. A stout Indian, tooled knife sheath showing below his denim vest, pushed us back from the scene.

"That's Nathan Weeping Moon," Shannon said.

"Is he connected with Anton Gropius?"

"How'd you know? He picks up supplies for Gropius." She made it her business to know who hung out on the islands and how they earned their beans.

"Who's the victim?" I called out to Weeping Moon.

He assessed me at a glance, then grabbed the hoist controls dangling from a fat wire and let out some cable. "Reese. He skippers the transport."

I scratched a note on my pad. "How'd it happen?"

"The rigging slipped," he said without looking, his voice dull as a baked oyster.

"Is he hurt bad?" Shannon asked.

Weeping Moon stole a disbelieving glance at Shannon. "Well, that's a three-ton crate. The deck plate is two-inch steel. His leg broke the fall. Yeah, he's likely dinged up a bit."

Shannon made a sympathetic noise, then grabbed my arm and pointed. "The older guy with the beard, he's—"

"Make room for the stretcher," Weeping Moon yelled.

Two medics rolled a gurney toward us. Just then Stu Broadbent, our editor's pet nephew, edged around them and jogged ahead, brandishing a camera with an elaborate flash attachment.

I ground my teeth.

"Egret! How'd you two get here so fast? Am I too late?"

Without waiting for an answer, he hustled down the ramp and found a vantage point near a floating seafood shack. Nathan Weeping Moon worked the hoist controls until the cable snapped taut. A sign on the hoist rated it at two-tons capacity; had he been guessing when he said the crate weighed three? The electric motor groaned, but the load budged from Reese's leg. His howl raised a chill at the base of my spine that nearly collapsed my knees.

While the medics did their thing, I overheard someone saying the crate had been boomed to the transport from the larger barge moored next to it. Weeping Moon wouldn't give us the destination, or explain why the crate had been lifted while the riggers were having breakfast.

A frenzied woman in a print dress arrived. "Is he all right?" After a husky wheeze, she added, "My husband?"

Before anyone could answer, Stu dashed up the ramp and pointed to his camera. "Got a prizewinner! I knew he'd come unglued the second they lifted that thing off him. Did you hear him yelp? Now if I can get a stretcher shot with the tubes and bottles..."

The distraught woman covered her mouth and hurried past us.

"The wife?" Stu guessed. "This keeps getting better."

As the medics heaved the gurney up the ramp, I stepped over to Stu and put my hand over the lens just as he fired. Reese's wife heard the click and looked up at me gratefully.

"You've got your trophy," I said to Stu. "Now leave them alone."

He puffed up the layered muscles under his polo shirt and gave me a broiling stare. When I didn't spontaneously combust, he turned away and looked for witnesses. "Did you see it happen?" he asked Nathan Weeping Moon.

"Stu, we've got it covered," I said.

Condescending smile. "This is a blue collar story. My kind of meat. Uncle will want me to handle it."

Rib Armentrout had retired from the Denver Post and, instead of working crosswords and healing his ulcers, bought the Friday

Harbor weekly—the *Slacktide*—and continued his 12-hour workdays. His one concession to advancing age was a keenly felt obligation to pass on his journalistic standards to anyone willing to endure his discipline. For the last three years, that anyone was me.

Then Stu showed up fresh out of the Navy, a yeoman trained in public affairs. He was twenty-seven, my age roughly when I'd first begged Armentrout for an apprenticeship. Rib's doting over his nephew during the past months had cost me considerable brooding—mostly about my hopes of someday owning and editing the *Slacktide*.

Nathan ignored Stu and vaulted aboard the small barge. Shannon and I moved down the ramp to watch from beside a gurgling crab tank. A man with a boxy gray beard, wearing a wrecked Stetson, commanded Nathan, in exquisitely foul language, to open the crate. The sides, stenciled *Republica Portugal*, had been jarred out of square, a corner splintered. As Nathan jimmied the top panel, the old man watched. You could have struck a match off his eyeball.

"So that's Anton Gropius."

Shannon nodded. "Our own living treasure."

This living treasure had shown more concern for his crate than for Reese's leg. "Which island does he live on?"

"Up in the Canadian Gulfs, somewhere." Unusual for Shannon not to know the details.

Nails squealed as Nathan pried the lid off, revealing a block of stone, sides lightly scored with quarry marks.

"Marble?" I asked Shannon.

"Interesting." She pursed her lips, probably wondering the same thing I was. "He used to be world class, you know—way back when. I thought he'd given it up."

Nathan knocked off the damaged side of the crate. If the sculptor's lack of profanity meant anything, the marble, a pinkish hue with a slight sparkle, had survived the fall.

"Button it up," he directed, but then something caught his attention and he grabbed the crowbar from Nathan and worked at a side panel. He jerked the panel aside, exposing something curious: a crimson blotch on the face of the stone. I had a fleeting, irrational, thought that it marked the place where Reese's leg had been smashed, but then I looked closer and made out the crude shape of something like a hand, but drooping and limp.

Whatever the symbol meant, it had a powerful effect on Anton. He stood transfixed, unsteady on his feet, then slowly deflated as if a vein had opened, coming to rest on the gunwale. He breathed deeply, then removed his hat to rub his temple.

I didn't understand his reaction and moved closer. Still, I saw only stone and the red mark—dye perhaps—a limp hand. Harmless enough.

Yet, it had caved the sculptor's broad shoulders and turned his face ashen. I knew the pose. The hollow stare, gaping mouth, palms turned upward. An appeal I understood all too well: *how the hell can this be happening?*

You would have thought someone had died.

Chapter 2

Stuart Island. Two weeks later I sat among burnished madrona trunks on the headland overlooking Turn Point lighthouse. Two hundred feet below, kelp fronds streamed northward in an ugly rip—too strong to paddle my kayak against. A tug crawled up the shipping lane towing two barges. To the west, specks of light glinted from windows on Vancouver Island. A ferry, en route there, plowed a white furrow through the Canadian Gulf Islands.

Anton Gropius lived on one of them.

It hadn't been easy finding out which; clearly he didn't want to be found. I'd finagled a radiophone number for Gropius from the firm that shipped the marble, and had been politely but firmly rebuffed by Mrs. Gropius—Clare—both times I'd called.

Finally, I'd learned the name of the island from Mrs. Reese, wife of the injured man. She'd remembered my preventing Stu Broadbent from photographing her husband and felt she owed me a favor. Reese lost his right leg just above the knee. "Another peg-legged sailor," Mrs. Reese had joked bravely.

With binoculars and chart, I found it: Thunderhead Island, though officially labeled *Rendezvous Island* on the charts.

I took a compass heading, checked my tide table. The fog had dissipated to expose an unsettled late September day, but the sun remained gauzed by the leading edge of a front. Some vertical cloud development marked where a cold front was colliding with it. The wind bumped up to around 12-15 knots. The monotone voice on channel 21-B out of Vancouver called for an afternoon squall and a small craft advisory with southerlies from 20-25 knots.

Perfect.

In an hour, the tide would change and give me a chance to cross the rip. But, as I ate a sandwich and watched seals play in the kelp, my conscience began churning. Rib Armentrout had ordered me to turn the Gropius story over to his nephew, Stu. Worse, I'd asked Shannon to cover several stories for me, knowing it would cut deeply into her play time.

Things my turned-on, dropped-out mother would do; things I found hard to forgive in either of us. Beyond the mother-revulsion trip, this job was my living and my life. I hoped my solid work at the paper had earned me some slack, but what if I'd misjudged

Armentrout's capacity for forgiveness?

I thought about the Rampling story I broke during my first year at the *Slacktide*, and recalled the gut-gnawing determination that led me to it. The series I wrote changed the San Juan Island power structure and won an award. Since then, one yawner after another. But now every phone call, every clue and detail, strengthened my hunch that the raging genius of Anton Gropius had not gone dormant in exile. If I was right, I had a hell of a story on my hands.

I returned to my kayak, a cedar lath baidarka, beached on the east side of Stuart island. I put on my bib wetsuit, spray skirt, and life jacket, then paddled past exposed oyster beds, knowing that every stroke brought me closer to being fired.

Though my arms felt heavy from the morning's long paddle from Roche Harbor, I had to consciously throttle back. Nerves. No sense burning my reserves in the protected lee of Turn Point.

I took a breath and tried to enjoy gliding past the unspoiled shore. I loved paddling at my own pace. It reminded me of the endless hours of training when I'd played competitive tennis—grinding, yet physically intoxicating—until an overhead smash to the face at the NCAA finals had detached a retina and redirected my life. I'd always made a contest of things, such as timing myself to the mailbox and back as a kid. Lilly-dippers don't enjoy paddling with me.

Nevertheless, I worried about the crossing. The two miles of open water across the shipping lane looked gnarlier from my perch than I'd pictured from the chart, and wind in this area is hard to predict. The Coast Range on Vancouver Island, and the Olympic Mountains to the south, funnel streams of air that collide here. Regardless which way the gale blew, I needed to be across the channel before the worst of it.

Shannon couldn't fathom why I didn't take a water taxi—"What if you tip over in that thing?"—but service to Thunderhead Island was restricted, and involved a detour to clear customs and immigration. They wouldn't risk alienating a regular customer like Gropius by bringing an uninvited guest. Anyway, my strategy called for arriving in a state of apparent helplessness.

The night after the accident at Friday Harbor, I'd read everything I could lay hands on about Gropius. While the wind moaned in the flue, and a cup of tea went cold beside me, I'd stared at a photograph of a heroic-sized carving of Walt Whitman, pictured before some lunatic knocked Whitman's nose off with a hammer.

I'd tried to get my mind around the idea that rock cleaved from the earth could be transformed into such a powerful symbol. I hadn't read much of Whitman's poetry, but his face was that of a great man. Gropius had pulled Whitman's interior strength and vision to the surface. It made me wonder which man was the greater. On the pedestal, an inscription:

> *The earth never tires,*
> *The earth is rude, silent,*
> *   incomprehensible at first,*
> *Nature is rude and*
> *   incomprehensible at first,*
> *Be not discouraged, keep on,*
> *   there are divine things well envelop'd,*
> *I swear to you there are divine things*
> *   more beautiful than words can tell.*

Twenty-one years had passed since the night Gropius had unveiled his Chief Sealth statue, intended for the Pike Street Market. Late that night a vandal had toured his private sculpture gallery swinging a hammer. A *Seattle Post-Intelligencer* article described Anton's subsequent withdrawal from the world, hinting at a deep depression. The crime apparently went unsolved. He sold the family home in Seattle and, as I'd confirmed through a title search, had bought the southern half of Rendezvous Island, renamed it Thunderhead, and moved there with his wife, Clare. Twice since, works of his had been vandalized. A dozen years ago, in the Library of Congress reading room, his *Johannes Gutenberg* had been chipped with an ice pick. More recently, his *Ben Franklin* in Philadelphia had been defaced with red dye. Perhaps the same stuff painted on the block at Friday Harbor. Other than the dye, there seemed to be little reason to suppose the attacks were connected. As I paddled, I pictured Gropius on the barge, face buried in his hands, and wondered.

He hadn't completely disappeared from notice. There were commissioned busts for which he charged small fortunes, but he received more attention for the jobs he'd refused—Elizabeth Taylor, Ted Turner, Billy Graham. One writer had compared his post-vandalism work to Mohammed Ali's bum-of-the-month fights, after Smokin' Joe Frazier had pummeled the greatness out of him.

But something continued to nag at me. How could a man who had produced this exquisite *Whitman*, and the others—*Luther Burbank, Isaac Newton,* the *Gymnast* with its great strength and balance, the angst-ridden *Papa Hemingway,* and my favorite, the mahogany of Father Damien among his congregation, entitled *Fellow Lepers*—be reduced to banging out uninspired likenesses, trading on his name? More to the point, why was he importing a block of fine marble tenfold larger than needed for a commissioned bust?

I had to know.

Some of it I found out from Mrs. Reese, who, after much lip biting, told me something that made the reporter in me quiver. Gropius, or somebody acting for him, had sent flowers, but flowers don't pay bills; in her bitterness, she confided that Reese had made at least two dozen trips to Thunderhead Island over the years, delivering blocks of stone such as the one that crippled him. He'd taken nothing off the island.

In the twenty minutes it took me to paddle to the Turn Point lighthouse, the wind picked up considerably. Beyond shelter of the point, it sent gobs of spindrift tumbling over the wave crests. The whitewashed lighthouse guarded the shoals: somebody's angel, but not mine. A freighter's wake rebounded off the cliffs, rising in steep pyramids where it met oncoming swells. From the lay of the kelp, the current had already reversed—sooner than I'd predicted. I let it sweep me into the channel to a wide band of broken sea where the current ran contrary to the wind—a recipe for steep waves. My focus sharpened as I rode the bucking sea, knees locked against the braces, hips rocking with the boat. A wedge of geese honked overhead, briefly quoting the Twilight Zone theme. I smiled, but not for long.

Beyond the point, the southerly whipped up trouble in the channel. Whitecaps. I should have been in position earlier. Challenge is welcome to a point, but when waves start dumping, I look for a place to put in. I have a wariness of the sea from kayaking a lot, from being in bad situations. From knowing people who didn't survive bad situations.

I fastened a leash to my paddle, widened my grip. A wave lifted and corkscrewed me, my bow slapped down on the water. In moments, my option of backtracking to the protection of Stuart Island would be cut off by the strengthening current. I don't believe in letting fate make decisions for me, so I tightened my jaw, dug my paddle blade in with purpose and committed to the channel.

At water level, it became harder to sort out the landscape. Islands melded together, and the waves horsed my boat too much for a decent compass bearing. A roaring sound mounted from a thrashing rip ahead. It looked like two currents meeting at an angle, with a stiffening wind opposing them. The arching tops of the standing waves got my attention by themselves, but their train-like rumbling turned my breath into rapid huffs. I checked the zipper on my life jacket, the flares in the pocket, the release loop on my spray skirt.

The wind built from a manageable ten-to-twelve to an uncomfortable fifteen-to-twenty, and stronger gusts darkened the water in spreading patches, ripping spume from the waves, stinging my eyes and tearing at my paddle. Because I headed broadside to the wind, it weathercocked the boat—turned its bow upwind. Having no rudder, I compensated by leaning to windward, that is, when waves weren't sweeping over my deck, slapping my chest. My right leg quivered, whether from fear or over-tensing I didn't know.

I paused to let a pair of container ships clear the channel, and tried to relax the leg, but it had a mind of its own. I acknowledged the fear but stowed it away. I'd entered a zone of bobbing logs and other flotsam, and paddled just enough to keep my distance from the big stuff. When lifted on a wave crest, I could see calmer water a mile to the west. That's where I wanted to be, and when the ship had cleared, I put my back into it.

Then, from the south, a ruffled swatch of water advanced like a dark wing. I turned upwind and prepared for the gust by holding my paddle next to the boat, knowing that if the wind got under the forward blade, it could flip the kayak or tear out a shoulder. Or both. While hunkered, I saw too late the bow wave of the first freighter sweeping toward me, sharp and dumping. Instinctively I leaned into the shoulder-high curl and reached my paddle over it in a high brace, but the blast of wind arrived and turned my paddle aside before it hit water. My body lean kept me upright as the boat scudded sideways, and perhaps I would have pulled out of the broach if my stern hadn't hit a deadhead log. I felt the bump, the sudden loss of balance, and, with a punishing swiftness that didn't even permit a breath, the wave drove me over.

Ice water streamed up my neck and under my bib wetsuit. I sculled, trying to get my face out of the water, but when I sucked for air a breaking wave exploded, forcing brine into my throat and sinuses. I regrouped underwater, feeling a panicky urge to choke, and tried to Eskimo roll up. Another wave bulldozed me before I broke the surface. Timing is everything. Out of air and panicky, I pulled off my spray skirt and did a forward roll out of the small cockpit, keeping hold of the coaming. I surfaced, coughed, and spit saltwater while trying to gather my wits.

I'd use my paddle float to make an outrigger, crawl back into the stabilized boat, and pump it out. But when I looked for the paddle float under the bungees behind the cockpit, it was gone—torn loose when my boat rolled over the deadhead. I looked downwind and saw the yellow float disappearing. The ships were shrinking into the horizon. No chance they'd notice my wimpy flares, and no telling how long before another boat would come.

I clenched my stinging eyes shut in a fit of despair, then decided to get to work. After ten minutes in these waters, even with a wetsuit, fingers stiffen making it clumsy to use safety equipment. Muscles cramp. Hypothermia fogs the mind and brings a sense of hopelessness. I decided to try re-entering the cockpit while underwater, then roll up. A few quick breaths, then I let my head go under as I tried slipping into the boat as into a pair of pants. The wetsuit and the buffeting waves made it more cumbersome than I expected and left me with only enough breath for one try. I forced my eyes open to the caustic water, and watched a green surge pass over, lifting me, trying to pull the boat off... timing... chest bursting... paddle cocked along the length of the kayak... not knowing if I'd have strength for another try... lungs on fire. As the next wave passed, I swept my paddle, arching sideways and uncoiled with a powerful hip snap. The kayak righted; my torso and then my head followed. I braced into a wave, fought to hold it together, took a relieved breath, and got pointed into the weather. Before the next dumping wake hit, I managed to attach the spray skirt to avoid a fully swamped cockpit. Still, a great deal of water sloshed inside my boat making it unstable, but I couldn't afford to stop paddling long enough to pump, needing to keep a blade in the water for balance.

I flexed the paddle with all my will, wanting only to get ashore. Any shore, any rock. Slashes of rain blotted the horizon to the south. I felt nauseous from the brine I'd swallowed, and my hands were so cold they'd lost feeling. The boat made sluggish progress, but, riding low, it caught less wind. I paddled without seeming to get anywhere and endured gust after gust, but after a minor eternity I entered sheltered water in the lee of a wooded island and relaxed my leaden arms.

I'd crossed the border into Canada.

I fought the shakes while pumping water from my cockpit. The shakes were winning. When my pump sucked more air than water, I stowed it, and rubbed my hands together for warmth. Back across the channel, the lighthouse stood witness to my recklessness. Why had I risked it for a damned headline? And why the renewed determination to go on, despite a sheltered landing within sight?

A seal dove, the slap of his flipper startling me. To get ashore before the weather worsened, I fixed my heading and paddled into the wind-strafed waters around Thunderhead Island, sweeping and ruddering with my paddle to keep straight in a following sea. I'd studied an aerial photo: the island ran maybe two-hundred yards from stem to stern with a sheltered cove opening to the west. Battling the constant tendency to broach on the overtaking waves, I drew within sight of the southeastern point, a grassy dome where three madronas posed like Balinese dancers. With the long fetch, the waves had become truly scary and I had to play each one a little differently. Finally I passed over a kelp bed which damped them a little, and I stole a look at the limestone cliffs, surf-guttered into the strangest shapes. Shores appropriate for a sculptor. An undercut became a three-fanged snake dripping sculpted venom.

Fatigue.

A man stood on a plank spanning a deep cleft. A sign nearby probably said *No Trespassing* but the sea bounced me too much to read it. He would not be greeting me with garlands. As the waves bore me toward a wrack-hung bench of rock, the man worked his way down the embankment. My boat scraped bottom and I yanked my spray skirt free between breakers and stepped into knee-deep water, trying to keep the kayak from being battered on the rocky shore. My legs, cramped from cold and from bracing in the kayak, failed and I fell over backwards.

I found my feet only to slip down on the wrack, and could do nothing but try to keep the surge from driving me and my kayak onto the rough shore. As I sputtered and ducked waves. A pair of legs waded into the water above his boots and a thick hand extended. I recognized the fancy knife at his belt and the round face above the arm. Nathan Weeping Moon.

"Private island," he said after helping me ashore. He pointed to the sign.

If he recognized me—and why should he, hair in a soggy braid, lips undoubtedly purple from cold—he didn't show it. Despite his crusty greeting, he helped me empty the water out of the kayak and hoist it above the tide line. I could see he took an interest in its workmanship. A good-looking wooden boat will make you many friends in this world.

"I don't suppose you have some dry clothes?"

I nodded yes.

"It's a bad day to be out there."

I thought Indians were supposed to say *it's a good day to die*, but I didn't feel like joking.

"Don't you have a radio?" he asked, hands on hips, weight on one leg. "There's a small craft advisory." He wore sunglasses despite the flattening light.

"My name is Egret Van Gerpin. I'm..." Somehow it seemed unnecessary to finish.

"Well, better change your clothes and shove off."

"In these conditions?" I said. "What about the mariner-in-distress rule?"

"What?"

"It's international law. Any mariner can put ashore in a life threatening situation." I gave him my helpless victim look. "That includes kayakers."

Chapter 3

Well, get your dry stuff. You're going to be plenty uncomfortable anyway when Anton finds out."

The sneer on Nathan Weeping Moon's lip, his forward posture and curved sunglasses weren't as intimidating as he probably supposed. Many of my opponents on the tennis court had affected aggression, spite, even bloodthirstiness, but I could quickly sort out the true animals. Nathan's belligerence rang hollow.

As I bent to pull gear from the rear compartment, salt water drained from my sinuses and out my nose. Turning away from Nathan to preserve a molecule of dignity, I snorted, dragged a sleeve under my nose, then scrambled up the embankment after him, dry bag in hand. Before crossing the rough-sawn planks bridging the cleft, he offered his hand and I took it. Thankfully. My legs were still rubbery from being wedged inside the kayak, and it was a twenty-foot fall from the springy planks to the rocks below.

"You know, he kept the last kayak that landed here," Nathan said. "It's still in the shed." He led me on a footpath through natural gardens of mosses, lichens, twisted manzanita and russet-colored grasses. "All the kayaker did was get out to take a leak."

"There's a moral to the story, right?"

A few drops of rain pelted us; the drops felt almost warm on my neck. Walking helped generate a little body heat.

"Then there were some yuppies anchored out who rowed their dinghy over to pick oysters—right under that sign. Me and Anton fired up the launch and circled in behind their yacht. While they baked oysters on a fire, we had leftover quiche, cornbread with real maple syrup, and salad with nuts and little oranges in it. We were just finishing up the champagne when they got back. We offered to open another bottle, but they weren't in the mood. So we took it with us, and a sack of oatmeal cookies for later. The Nootka share everything. It's our custom." He chuckled. "But it goes both ways, you know." Reverting to his watchdog snarl, he added, "Don't expect any hospitality. It ain't gonna happen."

Since my expectations rarely worked out, I generally don't bother having any. We crested a rise and dropped into an area protected from the wind; the house and a few outbuildings came into view, huddled around a cove. The old white two-story with attic dormers had green shutters and a wrap-around deck with plenty of lattice. A gull kept watch atop the guano-stained cupola. Just uphill from the house, a woman in a straw hat knelt before a raised bed of vegetables. Further up the slope stood a barn on a stone foundation; a sagging pier down at the cove ran alongside a lichen-crusted boathouse.

"He'll probably have me motor you over to Pender Island. Pain in the butt. Be prepared to beg if you want to keep your boat."

Nathan kept up the facade, but I'd seen his heart when the crate had fallen on Reese's leg. "Tell Mr. Gropius I'm here to talk to him."

He stopped and faced me with disbelief. "You don't want to complicate things. Trust me."

When we reached the cove I asked where I could change clothes. Nathan pointed to a tool shed. "I better radio Anton. Get it over with."

I closed the shed door while Nathan muttered into his walkie-talkie. Gray light filtered through a window matted with spider webs. As I stripped off my wetsuit, my stiff fingers fell on the vial hung about my neck by a thong, and I remembered the promise of protection the rose petals sealed within had once carried. My grandmother, Velva, had rescued me from my mother's commune in Iowa, and had been my lighthouse up to the day she died. Even now, really. While still coherent, she'd shown me this vial and told a strange story.

A yogi from India had come through Seattle on a lecture tour in the forties. She'd attended as a journalist, but was struck by the monk's authoritative discourse on the spiritual quest. She returned the following day because her photographs were ruined in the darkroom, and felt the same sense of intoxication. Later, in a private meeting with the yogi, she made a fine photograph of him, and he gave her seven rose petals, saying they would protect her. Though they hadn't saved her from the cancer, she'd wanted me to have them, and I'd slipped the vial from her fingers when she was gone.

I covered up when Nathan knocked briskly on the door. "He's not too happy. I didn't mention you're from the newspaper. I didn't want him to pop a blood vessel."

So he did remember me from the day of the accident. Footsteps, and another voice—a woman's.

"What have you got here, Nathan?"

"A prisoner."

"Oh heavens-to-murgatroyd! In the shed?"

"She's changing out of wet clothes."

"Oh dear God."

"She was at the wharf when Captain Reese got hurt. From the newspaper." Nathan filled her in on my arrival.

A pause. If the woman was Clare Gropius, she probably remembered my calls. "Oh, I see."

Polite rapping on the door. "You needn't change in this musty old shed, dear."

I'd finished except for my shoes, so I opened the door. The woman stood an erect six feet, and her eyes, from a face with sixty-plus years written on it, looked with curiosity into mine. A twist of hair dangling under her straw hat retained a streak of its original brown.

We introduced ourselves. Clare betrayed no hostility, just the reluctant concern of a woman who's found a mewling stray at her door. Even draped in an oversized man's shirt with gardening gloves stuffed in her back pocket, she radiated something more than simple dignity. I doubted that hostility even existed in her emotional vocabulary.

I bent to tie my shoes, and noticed Clare's lanky brown toes embedded in worn sandals. Good honest toes. I thought of the Hindu custom of taking the dust of a sage's feet. As I stood, lightning forked to the south and heavier raindrops plunked the tin roof. A gust tugged at the ribbon that kept Clare's straw hat in place.

"Ms. Van Gerpin and I will take tea on the porch," she said to Nathan, adding, perhaps with double meaning, "and wait for the squall."

"I don't care what Anton says, I'm not shipping her out in this weather and have her get seasick all over the boat."

A flock of mergansers half ran and half flew into the cove for protection.

"Yes, I know you'd rather get on with your chores."

I cautioned myself not to make too much of Clare's graciousness, but having a scare out on the water left me wanting a protector. A calico cat bounded from a pampas grass and trotted before us as we walked to the house. Clare smiled, more with her eyes than her mouth. "He never loses sight of me, nor I lose sight of him."

I took another look at the cat. I'd thought all calicos were female, and this one didn't look any different, but I let the comment pass. Nearing the house, I heard piano music, dense chords with no interplay of notes around them. We climbed the porch stairs and the same chords repeated, clearly not a recorded piece.

When Clare offered use of her restroom, I could have kissed those dusty toes. The powder room door opened off the foyer opposite a life-sized plaster replica of Michelangelo's *David*. After satisfying my urgent needs, I cupped warm water to my face to wash away the salt, then blotted dry with a towel that felt line-dried rough. I considered unbraiding my hair, as my high cheekbones would seem less severe with hair framing them, but I knew it would be a stringy mess. So I arranged the wisps that had escaped the braid and called it good. Clare returned with a tray of tea makings before I could snoop around the corner at the piano player. I held the screen door and she stepped out to the porch.

"Sit, *sit* my dear."

As I looked at the available wicker chairs and settee, the cat eyed me as if to warn against selecting her favorite. Already uncomfortable at having intruded, I didn't want to take anyone's favorite seat.

"I hope you appreciate a good Darjeeling," Clare said when we were settled. "People these days brew all manner of weeds and silage and call it tea." She poured a dab of cream for the cat, Dinah.

Still chilled from my dunking, I welcomed Darjeeling, good or indifferent.

"I suspect you came to spy on us."

I smiled. "Yes."

She poured through a strainer. "Do you ever get the feeling, Egret, that you're part of a larger scheme?" She spoke slowly, not sparing emphasis where any word might want a little of it.

Any talk about fate made me uncomfortable and I saw no reason to deny that either. "I'd like to think I'm in control of my own life."

A curtain of rain swept toward the island, blurring the boundaries of land, sky, and sea. Dried clematis rustled on the lattice. Then a rack of lightning brought thunder which silenced the piano and sent Dinah fleeing under the settee. I checked my watch: two-thirty. I feared the weather might clear before dark and spoil my plan. I might yet find myself adrift with nothing but a cup of tea for my efforts. Or worse, if Nathan could be believed.

"Clare," I said, when the heaviest weather had passed and we'd had refills. By then, not using first names would have seemed insulting. "I know about the marble shipments to Thunderhead Island."

She didn't react.

"Twenty-one years ago many people considered your husband the world's greatest living sculptor. I'm here to find out if he still is."

"Ha," Clare said, as if I'd missed the obvious.

The screen door squeaked and a man spoke in an airy, theatrical voice. "But of course he is." I supposed this short, thin-lipped man to be the piano player. Perhaps near Anton's age, he lacked the sculptor's hairiness but for some longish strands swept past his ears. No eyebrows to speak of, and so closely shaved that his impish face had a pink, scrubbed look. His veined hand gestured freely with an unlit cigarette. "Just ask him. Why, Anton's a legend in his own mind, isn't he Clare? Who's to dispute it, out here at the end of the earth?"

With a chastising glance, Clare introduced Eugene Gobi, calling him a friend of the family.

"The award-winning Hollywood composer," he said, "in case you're trying to recall where you've heard the name." He lit his thin cigarette.

The name seemed vaguely familiar. "I don't watch many movies."

"Even those who do, seldom listen—at least not consciously. So I'm a subliminal composer," he traced ovals of smoke, "who toils for subliminal rewards." Gobi gave a compact bow. "Will Ms. Van Gerpin be joining us this weekend for the... event?"

Clare didn't answer, her silence standing as a further reprimand.

"Oh dear," Gobi said. "Does Anton...?"

Clare shook her head a half-inch each way. Gobi lifted a paltry eyebrow and left it there long enough to show how very well he understood.

"I believe I'll nap before dinner." He pointed up the hill with his small chin.

There, a man on an all-terrain vehicle bounced down a trail at breakneck speed. Gobi took a last drag, dropped the butt in an old milk can, and disappeared into the house. Clare tidied the table, though it didn't need tidying.

Nathan emerged from the barn and Anton skidded the ATV to a halt just feet from Nathan's knees. I had no trouble hearing their conversation. Perhaps it was intended as entertainment.

"What the hell have you been doing?"

"Worshipping my ancestors." Nathan stood his ground as Anton climbed off the machine and approached. "I come from a big family—it's almost a full time job."

"What do you do, set out a bucket of entrails and dance the funky chicken?" Gropius bellowed with laughter so contagious I couldn't help but smile. It all had an element of showmanship to it.

But my stomach, queasy from seawater and strong tea, just wanted this to be over. Sure enough, Anton's expression darkened as he glanced at me. He spoke to Nathan again, in low tones.

Nathan pointed in the direction I'd landed, and Anton brusquely swept his hand as if to indicate I should have been repelled. Nathan stepped back for breathing room and explained, throwing in a shrug. Gropius got back in Nathan's face, jerking a thumb over his shoulder toward the barn. Nathan tried to respond, but Anton turned aside and stamped toward the porch.

Showmanship. Nathan's sparring with Anton gave me an idea.

Before leaving Friday Harbor, I'd checked the *Slacktide*'s subscriber list. The name *Gropius* didn't appear on it, but I'd asked Shannon to find out which post office box Gropius received mail at. Then I'd checked the number against the subscriber list and found a match.

His boots on the steps thumped almost as loud as my heart. But before he could say anything, I stepped forward and extended my hand.

"Egret Van Gerpin." I looked him solidly in the eye. "Perhaps you've heard of me."

Chapter 4

Gropius ignored my hand and whacked dust from his bib overalls with his hat. A person will often have an expression on the left half of their face that doesn't match the right. He had a strikingly asymmetrical face. His left side registered a look of detached curiosity; the right, belligerence. The right side spoke.

"You must be either very lost, or very stupid."

I fought the urge to be contrite. "I'm not lost."

He folded his arms and looked me over, drumming his fingers against his biceps, and muttered, "Son of a horse's bleeding ass... " Then he barked at Clare, "I'll deal with her after supper. Put her to work." In parting, I thought I saw him gesture with his eyes toward the barn.

Clare's barely perceptible nod confirmed it.

Nathan Weeping Moon climbed on the all-terrain four-wheeler behind Gropius and they motored up the trail over the ridge that bisected the island. Anton had said something about needing him at the studio.

I looked at Clare with a mixture of relief, confusion, and gratitude, and sensed she could read all this from my expressions. The squall had passed leaving a strange violet light and a double rainbow. Clare leaned against the porch post and watched. "It's been said that rainbows symbolize free will. And because no more great floods will purge the earth, so we must do our own housecleaning."

I wondered if this was an ecclesiastical or an ecological sentiment, or the ramblings of a subservient island inmate. She led me into the house and asked me to wait in the foyer. This time I mentally photographed the adjoining rooms and their furnishings so I could download it to my notebook later. Color for my article.

Clare had left through the dining room where a trestle table anchored a Chinese rug, and into the kitchen through swinging doors. The stairwell before me was furnished with a telephone table and the *David*, phone numbers penciled on his nude form. Across the foyer sprawled a large sitting room with stuffed chairs and sofas arrayed around a fireplace, walls and shelves densely appointed with all manner of artwork and collectibles. The floor space accommodated the grand piano at which Eugene Gobi had been sounding chords.

Clare returned with sheets, blanket and pillow. "All our guest rooms are made up for family, but you'll be tolerably comfortable in the attic room for the night."

I was stunned. "Are you sure this is what Mr. Gropius had in mind?"

"I'm as surprised as you are, dear. But you heard him. 'After dinner,' he said. By then it's too late for anything but staying."

I'd brought camping gear, but Clare wouldn't hear of it. "Dinner's at seven."

I asked permission to paddle my kayak around to the cove and promised to help in the kitchen. The wind had abated, leaving the air fresh and the loons laughing. After stowing my boat, I rinsed the salt water from my paddling clothes in a rain barrel under the barn's down spout. I thought I might find a place in the barn to hang them. This would also give me an excuse to look for the stray masterpiece I'd hoped to discover. I doubted Anton's hospitality would last; perhaps he simply hadn't yet conceived a punishment to fit my crime. Meanwhile, I couldn't pass up an opportunity to snoop. I didn't get the chance, however, as Clare saw me wringing my pants and insisted I use her dryer in the mudroom. I did, then asked Clare how I could be of use.

Before she could answer, her ears perked at a sound, and I followed her outside. We watched as a boat putted into the cove. It looked homemade of plywood, brushed with a coat of blue marine enamel. I could see several people in the partially enclosed wheelhouse. Aft, a canvas tarp covered a mound of something. As it drew nearer, I read the lettering on the pilothouse: Drago's Water Taxi. An air horn sounded a long blast and two shorts as the taxi drew alongside the pier.

Clare rushed to the cove. Eugene Gobi emerged from somewhere and we followed. The captain handed ashore a well-formed woman in her early forties wearing a jaunty sailor suit. She and Clare embraced warmly.

"That's Clare and Anton's daughter, Rooks," Gobi said. "I happen to be her godfather, not that she's had much use for one." A man pushing fifty stepped from the boat, slender, serious. In his pressed khaki pants, windbreaker, and polished deck shoes, he was an Eddie Bauer catalog in motion.

"Rooks' husband, Dr. Charles Underwood, vascular surgeon," Gobi said. "A vein man."

I acknowledged the joke with a sideways glance.

"His vanity may need some patching," Gobi said softly. "Last year he ran for the AMA presidency—but lost out to a plastic surgeon from Pasadena."

"Not the one who invented the prosthetic forehead?" I asked.

It was Gobi's turn to smile, a lipless, lopsided effort. "The very one." He took his turn at hugging Rooks and shaking Charles's hand. Then a third passenger disembarked—a boy of perhaps ten or eleven who had tugged a guitar case from the luggage pile. Clare made a production of being overjoyed to see him, though eyeing warily the boy's bleached flattop haircut trailing a mane of green and orange wisps.

The captain and his own lad handed off steamer trunks, garment bags, make-up cases, hat boxes, shopping bags, fishing pole tubes, boxes of groceries, even a pillow. Clare introduced me to her daughter, son-in-law, and grandson, Courtney. Looking past me, Rooks said perfunctorily "Delighted to know you," and loosely shook my fingertips. At first she'd seemed stunningly beautiful; I could see now it was an illusion created by her saucy manner, neat sailor costume and cap, carefully applied blush, eyebrows shaped into high black crescents. Her petulant lips had the look of being plumped with silicon. Beneath all that was a rather blocky face and eyes set so far apart as to give them a haunted look.

"A perfectly unendurable ride," Rooks said. "We were pulverized. Cubans escape to Florida in better boats. And those dreadful diesel fumes, Charles got seasick of course." She whispered loudly to Charles, "Don't you even think about tipping that captain."

Charles collected his notebook computer and fishing poles. He didn't look seasick to me, perhaps a bit outside his element, but not uncomfortable. Dignified, and with the exception of an upper lip double-peaked like a suspension bridge, good looking.

"And we had to go all the way to that dreadful place to clear customs."

"Bidwell Harbor," Charles said.

"Just so some fool could count life jackets."

Clare hugged Rooks again. "But I'm so glad you came today. And I wasn't expecting Courtney. Hasn't school started?"

"Ahem!" Rooks said, and glanced at Charles as if the matter fell within his purview.

Charles sucked his teeth. "The academy found Court's contribution to good order and discipline... insufficient."

"There was a misunderstanding," Rooks corrected.

"Yes," Charles said. "Court misunderstood that he was a student and not a prisoner."

Rooks lowered her chin, raising a charming little roll of baby fat. "That academy is out of touch with the world."

"Fifth graders don't get to decide who's in touch." Charles glanced at his son to make sure he'd heard the rebuke.

Rooks changed the topic. "Are we first to arrive then?"

"Your sister and Uncle Buzz are due tomorrow," Clare said. "I'm not sure about Blake."

"And where's father? He must have seen the boat when we passed the other side of the island."

"Oh, you know your father. When he gets involved..."

"So nothing has changed," Rooks said. "Mother, he owes you a better life than this... this mortification. Stuck out on this flyspeck with no society except these screeching gulls."

Clare patted Rooks' back—a calming, motherly gesture. "I'm long past the need for society, dear, and Eugene is wonderful company. Of course I don't see you kids often enough."

Nathan arrived on the ATV towing a trailer. It took us two trips to get everything onto the porch.

"If you tell me which room, I can schlep bags," I said to Clare.

"You're so thoughtful. Oh, and I've forgotten to show you your room. Top of the second flight of stairs. It probably needs airing."

"She's spending the night?" Rooks scanned me with olive-green eyes. "And what about Court? He's been expecting to have the attic room."

"It's just for the night," Clare said.

"I'll take a load upstairs," I said, thinking they could talk it over better without me. Nathan and I each grabbed what we could carry.

As I trudged up the stairs, Rooks said, "As long as Blake's not here, Court can stay in the—"

"We'll work something out," Clare said hastily.

"Well! I'd better show them where to put things." Rooks followed us upstairs, carrying only her make-up case. Probably didn't want to risk a fake nail coming unglued.

There were four bedrooms on the second floor. The one Rooks let us into was a cheery room with a gas-log fireplace, down comforter on the bed, and plenty of pillows. The window offered a fine view of the cove, where I saw Charles chatting with the boat skipper, perhaps getting some fishing tips. A jumble of cosmos, asters and nasturtiums filled a vase on the dresser. Everything carefully prepared. I realized how much Clare Gropius had been looking forward to having her family together. I guessed it didn't happen often.

The thought of belonging to a family had a beguiling draw to it. I hadn't seen my mom in a dozen years. She'd flown from Amsterdam to attend Jerry Garcia's funeral but didn't bother to make a side trip to Seattle. I had half brothers and sisters I'd never met—a lot of them.

Then I saw the carving on the dressing table and it stopped my breath. Elegantly sculpted from fine black stone, an osprey powered up from the water, holding tenuously to a fish with one talon; a decisive moment for both osprey and fish. The bird seemed about to tear free of the stone itself and take flight. The fish was more implied than rendered, more submerged in the black unworked stone than liberated by Anton's chisel.

I studied the sculpture and its reflections in the triptych mirror until I heard Rooks scold, "Mom, let the others do the grunt work."

I hurried to relieve Clare of a heavy garment and she gladly relinquished it. I hung it up, then mentioned that the water taxi hadn't left. "I can catch it if I hurry. I'd love to talk to Mr. Gropius... but I'm intruding on your family time."

She smiled appreciatively. "Thank you, but no, I'm afraid you can't. Not just yet. If Anton wanted you to leave, believe me, he would have said so." It bothered me at first that Clare apparently had no say in the matter, but as I'd detected nothing meek about her, I suspended judgment.

Later I helped get supper ready. She barbecued chicken on the back patio, but served it inside as the early northern dusk brought a chill. Anton and Nathan showed up just before seven, washed, and put on clean shirts. As Nathan brushed his thick hair back, Court stared with open mouth at the fancy knife strapped to Nathan's belt. Clare called everyone to the table and Rooks appeared in a denim jumpsuit with a bandanna scarf. I wondered how many more outfits she had in her trunks. I offered to eat in the kitchen but Clare wouldn't hear of it.

If Anton had any interest in me, he certainly didn't show it during supper. In fact, he said nothing as Rooks blathered on about her new diet until, finally, he butted in during her tofu pudding recipe.

"So, Charles, seems you'll be a plumber after all, not a politician."

Rooks answered, leaving Charles with his suspension-bridge mouth open. "He's still the top vascular surgeon in Fort Lauderdale. The tragedy is that Charles would have been just what the AMA needed. Everyone says so. If we'd been elected, we were *truly* going to raise some eyebrows. But the old bloodletters and their leaches... Cut off their noses to spite their faces."

"Maybe that's why they wanted a plastic surgeon in there," Court said. He forked a load of spuds into his mouth and swallowed like a heron gulping a smelt.

"We don't need your commentary," Rooks said, and went on about the incestuous politics of the AMA as if she had been a co-nominee for the presidency.

When I commented on the wonderful sculpture in Rooks' room, Clare explained that Anton had carved each of his offspring a gift.

"Really? Is that right father?"

Anton grunted and continued gnawing on a thigh, a stain of barbecue sauce spreading on his beard.

"Well, it's an exquisite eagle." Rooks laid a hand on her husband's arm. "We have just the perfect nook for it, don't we Charles."

Anton dropped the bone in his plate, lifted a bushy eyebrow. "It's an osprey. Nathan's idea, really. The Nootka tradition is for the chief to give gifts on his birthday, not receive them. It fits with the tradition of the island, if you can believe him. He says the coastal Indians never lived here, just canoed here to rendezvous—make treaties, trade, pass gas."

Nathan gnawed on his second cob of corn. "Yeah. It used to be a pretty nice place."

"Don't make a pig of yourself Court," Charles said as the gawky boy made a grab for the last roll.

"There's enough for two each," Clare said, and Court kept it. Both parents scrutinized him as if waiting for him to break some rule. Court sawed the bun in half and troweled on the butter. When he rattled the saltshaker over the bun halves, he'd blundered over the line.

"For heaven's sake, Courtney" Rooks said, snatching the shaker from his hand and planting it sharply on the table.

"Show some manners," Charles added.

Eugene Gobi cleared his throat. "Guilty of a-salt and buttery, I'd say."

"Off with his head," I murmured.

Rooks heard the remark and shifted her scrutiny to me. "I hope the sea isn't so hideously rough when you leave tomorrow."

I looked at Anton to see if he cared to clarify my plans. He did, though not in the way I'd expected.

"She's modeling for me. She'll stay until we're done."

I tried not to betray my shock.

Clare tidied the residue of potato salad in the bowl.

Rooks studied my face. "You're obviously not carving a Madonna, are you father."

If she'd meant to offend, it didn't work. But I hadn't heard the worst.

"No, I'm working on an old squaw," Anton said. "She's got the right bone structure."

I felt my face redden, then caught a teasing gleam in Anton's eye.

Rooks laughed. I guess it was supposed to be a laugh, but she sounded more like a demented porpoise. "Oh father. You need to get back to civilization. Whatever happened to Walt Whitman and Newton and Lincoln? You've gone native!"

Nathan stopped eating and leveled a glare at Rooks.

Anton dropped his chicken bone. He said to Rooks, "Did it ever occur to you that Indians have heroes too?"

Chapter 5

The family scattered after dinner. Nathan hurried out. Rooks retired, complaining of adjusting to west coast time. Her husband Charles, Anton, and Eugene Gobi adjourned to the sitting room for drinks. Court's bass guitar thudded irregularly from somewhere, sounding as if he'd been playing for all of a week. I helped Clare with dishes.

"Why don't you go sit with Anton? It's why you came."

She looked tired, and there were dirty dishes for eight. "It'll go fast with two people," I said. "You don't think Anton was serious about me posing?"

Clare pursed her lips in thought, shrugged.

"Can you tell me what he's been working on? Other than commissions, I mean."

She lifted an eyebrow. Clare had a way of saying much with a glance or gesture, and I smiled inwardly in small victory. The bone had meat on it. Content for the moment, I started on the pots and pans. While washing the cookie sheet we'd baked the rolls on, I realized we'd made four rows of five. Yet, she'd served only two rolls each, making sixteen. I thought it odd I didn't see the extras anywhere.

When done, Clare again offered tea. She ritually scalded the pot and cups before pouring boiling water over loose jasmine. "I can't stand a tepid cup of tea," she said, slipping a cozy on the pot.

I thought it strange to be keeping Clare company in place of her own daughter. I sat, resigned to let Anton make the move when ready to talk. I asked Clare how she'd met him. Her eyes peered back in time.

"I'd taken my degree in anthropology. It was the rage at the time because of Margaret Mead. We didn't know, of course, that she'd made up her data about promiscuity in the South Sea Islands. But it made for exciting reading. Then I got a staff job at the embassy in Vienna."

"You must have been thrilled."

"Mm." She poured tea, along with a few plump leaves. "I met Anton in a museum there. A vagabond, traveling Europe, filling notebooks with sketches of masterpieces... and, I suspect, filling his address book too." She gave a knowing glance over her half-glasses. "Our paths crossed again when the embassy got involved in a minor incident. I was able to smooth things over. You see, Anton's father manufactured fireworks, of all things. Anton supported himself abroad by soliciting orders, and he had samples of aerial shells. After rather too much kirshwasser he tried to impress a young lady by blasting off a shell in front of her father's house. Unfortunately, it ignited the excelsior in the crate and the rest of them exploded willy-nilly. There was a matter of some prize topiary to be dealt with.

"With that cleared up, we spent two delightful weeks together, exploring Austria and northern Italy before Anton decided to stay in Florence to study sculpture." Clare stirred honey into her tea longer than necessary. "Almost five years later—I'd returned to the States and took a teaching job in Boston—he looked me up. Went to the symphony, had a late dinner, and talked until sunrise. He left for Seattle later that day, and I thought I might never see him again. I'd actually given some thought to entering the convent."

She caught my surprise. "Oh yes, that was considered a career option in those days. But a week later," smile wrinkles deepened around her eyes, "came a letter with a plane ticket to Seattle. When I arrived, he drove me to his studio in a decrepit, smoking Oldsmobile, and showed me his mahogany of the gaunt child and her dead mother. Nothing I'd ever seen had so captured the horrors of the camps. I understood then about his gift.

"That same night, he proposed. You probably think I was surprised at the suddenness, but somehow I wasn't. We expect miracles at that age, don't we?"

I knew what she meant.

"Then he said, 'Before you answer, you need to understand something.' He showed me a block of marble on his work stand, and said, 'This stone will always come first in my life.'"

She paused to enjoy the effect her story was having on me. "What did you say?"

"I looked him in the eye and said, 'In my life, God comes first. Then, whatever children you're man enough to give me.'" She covered her mouth coyly. "Imagine me saying something like that. I don't know where it came from."

Then Clare cocked her head at me as if puzzled. "You have a quality it seems, Egret, that makes people want to tell you their secrets. Don't you?"

"I'm interested in things that give meaning to people's lives."

Clare nodded.

"I've been trying to imagine how Anton felt when his sculptures were damaged."

"Did you know we'd lost a son two years before that?"

A bolt of cold shot through my heart. "No."

"Our son David. A drowning accident." Clare made fists, squeezed, let go. "For Anton, seeing his creations destroyed affected him as much as losing his son. He'd breathed his life into the stone as much as he had into David. I know this must sound inhuman."

"I've heard that Charles Dickens got depressed after finishing a novel because his characters had become so real to him."

"Anton could escape David's death by working obsessively. But when the sculptures were... " Clare tensed. "And being done out of pure malice... it amounted in Anton's mind to murder."

I said nothing.

"Do you understand? He had no refuge from it."

But I didn't. I didn't understand comparing smashed stone with the loss of a child, and I told Clare how my little six-year-old, Toby, had been stung forty-one times after stumbling into a nest of ground wasps. It had been more than two years, but I still needed to cry about it occasionally, and Clare took my hand and didn't make me feel like a nincompoop.

At a quarter past eleven, with Clare and I yawning and talking about getting to bed soon, Eugene Gobi stopped by the kitchen to say that Charles had gone to bed and that Anton was ready to see me.

A Tiffany lamp and a twist of flame from the fireplace lit the sitting room just enough to bring out the muted golds of a Kashmiri rug. A clock ticked big, hollow seconds. Smell of wood pitch. Artwork everywhere: paintings, fine crystal, ceramics, bronzes, and, no surprise, carvings. Carvings in light and dark woods, and in the stone I would come to recognize as Cararra marble. In granite, rose-colored sandstone, black limestone, serpentine. Gobi seated a fresh log in the embers and it soon burst into flame. Anton Gropius, stiff in his leather chair with the look of a man refusing to capitulate to weariness, poured something from a shaker into his glass—Manhattans, I learned. Gobi and I sat at opposite ends of the sofa facing him. Anton cocked an eyebrow and studied me with that eye as if it had special powers.

"Nathan tells me you were at the pier in Friday Harbor... when we dropped the load." His voice was low and gritty.

I nodded.

"You won a national award a few years back—the Cyrus Rampling exposé?"

"Yes." It pleased me he'd known that; of course, the Rampling affair had traumatized the islands, and any subscriber who paid attention would have remembered.

"You strike me as a person who does her homework."

"I try."

"Well, based on what you saw at the marina, and your homework, let's hear your best guess about what's going on here."

Anton kept his eye fixed on me. "There's been very little in print since you moved here—the attacks on your statues in Philadelphia and in the Library of Congress, of course. Another article mentioned you do commissions, but implied you don't work up to your old standards. But that big block of Portuguese marble—the one that made Captain Reese's leg look like a cricket bat—made me curious. So I tracked it back to Stumbo's Marble and Granite in Tacoma. By the way, don't blame them for talking—somehow they got the impression I was your daughter."

Anton narrowed his eyes to slits.

"You've made at least two buying trips to Italy and Portugal and shipped stone back to Chicago. Much of it Cararra marble, from the same quarry Michelangelo used five hundred years ago. Stumbo's has stone delivered by the flatcar so you arranged to have them transport and store your marble, and ship it up as needed. They occasionally uncrate some of it to show customers—it's too expensive to inventory that kind of stone. Conclusion? You've been creating work in addition to the commissions. Work no one knows about."

"Go on."

"Then there's the red marking on the marble. You took the horrible accident in stride, and then went to pieces because somebody drew a mark on your stone. Strange. Then I read how the vandal who smashed your statues in Seattle had left some kind of red symbol, like a melting hand. Also, the Ben Franklin piece had been ruined with red dye. I'm guessing the mark reminded you of the prior attacks, or maybe even suggested a copycat crime. Stumbo's said it isn't uncommon for quarries to mark stone with chalk or spray paint. And, with the material sitting outside in their yard, anyone could have painted the red hand. They have two other blocks down there with your name stenciled on the crates. I had them opened. Stop me if you already know this."

Anton motioned like a blackjack player asking for a hit.

"Both of the blocks had the same red marking—that hand shape."

"Son of a bitch," Anton muttered, glancing at Eugene.

Encouraged, I continued. "I phoned you twice, but Clare asked me not to bother you. Finally I tried calling your two daughters and your son." I watched for anger in Anton's face but didn't see it. "Funny, none of them were home. Blake's roommate was evasive. And Charles's office mentioned a salmon fishing trip. Your brother Buzzy's hardware store said a sudden family matter had come up."

Anton cracked his knuckles.

"I'm guessing that sooner or later you're going to release some new sculpture. Maybe sooner because you're turning seventy and your family's getting together. And, by your reaction when I mentioned the other two marble blocks with red dye, you just might be worried that this vandalism thing isn't over. How am I doing?"

Anton remembered his drink, drank quite a lot of it, then looked to his friend for an opinion. Gobi twitched in a way that seemed to indicate assent.

Gropius leaned forward. "And what's wrong with doing commissions? Michelangelo did them, and at least I can tell my benefactors to bugger off. How many times do you think Michelangelo told the Pope to bugger off? After the bust I did for the JFK library, the Kennedys offered me a million dollars to add Jack to the other faces on Mt. Rushmore."

"You told them to bugger off, I assume. Otherwise someone would have noticed by now."

"I wouldn't add a footnote to someone else's masterpiece for any amount of money. Even so, had there been enough decent rock up there, somebody might have done it."

It had been a long day, and I didn't see the point of his boasting. I decided to push it a little. The worst he could do is set me adrift in my kayak. "Why don't you show me what's in your studio."

Gropius chuckled without humor. "Egret, you've done well.

You only missed one thing. This is difficult for me and I'd be very disappointed to see this in print, but I'm going to take the chance. The crimes against my sculptures were never solved. But I know something. I know they were done by a member of my own family."

I blinked a few times. Eugene Gobi confirmed it by nodding sadly. Gropius turned away, stared into the fire. It fit, yet seemed incredible.

Gobi continued on Anton's behalf. "That's why we're taking advantage of Anton's seventieth birthday to call his family together. Yes, there are major works of sculpture not known to anyone outside this household. At least we thought so until the red hand reappeared. It seems the insanity isn't over. So we're gathering everyone who could be responsible, hoping to find out who's committing these atrocities. And why."

They didn't have to spell it out. "You're thinking an extra set of eyes and ears might be useful around here for a few days," I said. "Someone who couldn't possibly have been involved."

Anton continued to look away as if shamed he must conspire with a stranger against his flesh and blood.

"Someone with an appreciation for details," Gobi continued. "Someone who can tally them up."

Chapter 6

I weighed the implications. If I stayed through Anton's birthday on Sunday, I'd be missing at least two assigned stories for next week's edition. I could radiophone Armentrout to say I had a butt-kicker coming from Thunderhead Island, but would it be the truth? Would Anton let me break the story about his new work, or use me and repatriate me to San Juan Island empty handed? He'd carved Dr. Schweitzer, but hadn't even visited Captain Reese. Would his new work be of the scope and vitality to command wide attention? Then I remembered something I'd fantasized about while paddling here, and decided to see how Anton would react to it.

"If I stay, my cover story needs work. Nobody's going to buy this 'posing for a squaw' nonsense."

Anton grunted a laugh.

"Being seventy, don't you think it's time you authorized someone to write your biography?"

This raised his eyebrow so far I thought it might get stuck.

"Jesus tits!" he said, and turned to Gobi. "Helluva demand, coming from a common trespasser, wouldn't you say, Gene? I've fed her, given her a roof, and now..." he faced me, "now you want my life. Permission to sum up my existence, and rank me against every chisel jockey in history, and pass judgment on me as a human being. What kind of reckless man would let a thirty-year-old girl interpret his life?"

I wrote off about three parts of his indignation to theatrics, but knew some of it was legit. "Consider this," I said, "I'm ten years older than you were when you carved *Walt Whitman*."

Anton bunched the muscles around his mouth as if squeezing something sour from them. "Damn it, Egret! You're a competent journalist. I read Armentrout's newspaper and I trust your byline. But a journalist and a biographer are two different beasts."

"You said you read my series—"

"It was an exposé. You destroyed him. Deservedly, but hardly the credentials I'm looking for in a biographer. A person doesn't gain the insight to understand my life by simply drawing breath for however many years." He swirled the ice in his shaker and decanted the last of the Manhattans to his glass. "And who would read the damn thing, coming from you?"

Until he said that, I'd been willing to simply pose as his

biographer for our mutual benefit. Now he'd pushed it too far. "So I'm out of my depth," I said. "It takes a genius to appreciate a genius? Right. I'd need the powers of a Melville to capture your ego. Maybe your real fear is that your life isn't worth reading about."

Other than a terse good night, that was it. I stalked out in a huff, knowing I'd be returning to Friday Harbor in the morning. I paused at the stairs, feeling hot, restless, and decided to take a walk before turning in.

The night had a Halloweenish quality. A biting chill, thin clouds dragging past the quarter moon, cornstalks rustling in the garden. I walked the rough trail to the ridge, thinking the climb would work the antagonism out of me. Now that I'd spoken aloud the idea of writing Anton's biography, I began to think I could really do it. I played out the fantasy, imagined my name on a dust jacket, bookstore readings. Then dread set in. Dread of my unfamiliarity with the genre, with the art world. Dread of what the reviewers might say: *a great life trivialized by a minor talent.* Before my fantasy became too morbid, I changed the channel.

I crested the ridge, sat on a rock, fidgeted, picked at my cuticle, got up and paced, thought of Anton's request for help. I'd been asked to do something for an old man's peace of mind, so why hadn't I just agreed? Without condition?

Too late in coming, this realization. I'd probably not get the opportunity to undo my outburst, to offer myself under whatever terms he thought best. But I'd try.

Strange, the second I let go of my headline-bagging fixation, I realized what I'd really come to Thunderhead Island for. It had lit a candle of hope in me to think Gropius had found his creative stride again. I wanted to believe in a person's capacity to rebound from disaster, but it didn't come as an article of faith for me. I wanted living proof.

So, down the hill. As I feared, the downstairs lights were off. I'd have to endure myself overnight, hold out an olive branch in the morning, and hope. Having tamed my pride, and expecting fully to be put off the island anyway, I could see little harm in indulging my curiosity to the extent of peeking into the barn. Not a large barn, it had double doors on the ground level and an outside stairway leading to a loft. The double doors were slightly ajar. I looked in and saw only tools, materials, the ATV, and plenty of dark space. No statues. I paused at the stairs, thought about my suspicions. Anton had glanced surreptitiously this way when he'd told Clare I should stay for dinner. And, when Clare and I had washed dishes, she'd pulled the curtains over the kitchen sink, blocking my view toward the barn. There was a door at the top of the stairs, and a window. Dark.

Though I'd done a fair amount of snooping in my life, it still made me uncomfortable—something akin to a bladder infection. And if Anton caught me snooping, he'd be even less inclined to accept my offer of help. On the other hand, he'd wanted another set of eyes... I can talk myself into anything—except giving up. With the conviction I had little to lose but abdominal well-being, I ascended the stairs.

Near the top, a paper-thin slit of light caught my eye. It vanished when I moved my head. From the proper angle, the light reappeared through a gap between the window casing and siding. Someone had apparently covered the window from inside to block the light. I sniffed the creosote smell of a damped-down woodstove—perhaps from the kitchen in the main house, perhaps not. Nathan's apartment? But that wouldn't account for the missing rolls. And when Rooks suggested having her son, Courtney, sleep in the barn, Clare had cut her off. I rapped. No answer.

I tried the door, it opened: lamplight, kerosene fumes, warm air on my face. I picked out features of a roughly furnished room, but no occupant and no connecting rooms. I stepped in and closed the door. Dirty plates littered a tray near a basin and pitcher. Also, a single dinner roll in a bread bag. I squeezed it—fresh—and looked around. A large wooden spool, the kind telephone cable used to come on, served as a table. On it, a sculpture of white stone striated with a dark impurity, depicting a draftsman's hands. *Anton has carved each of his offspring a gift.* The wrist of the right hand, rolled shirt cuff, back of the hand, knuckles and pencil stub were marvelously detailed, the skin alive with creases and veins. The left hand, reposed more roughly in the stone, seemed to be pressing down a straight edge before the pencil. Somehow the simple composition seemed alive, tensed. This, and the surety of its execution led me to speculate why Anton had only partially liberated the left hand.

Along the far wall, a simple platform of plywood with thin foam pad and heavy quilt sufficed as a monk's cot. Books with splayed spines were shelved above the bed; other books lay about—some face down, others bookmarked with a fly swatter or banana peel. Personal relics included a toy steam engine, a square green bottle holding a few sticks of incense. I glanced at the book titles. *Hayduke Lives* by Edward Abbey, *Greek Mythology*, a Fodor's on India and Nepal, *Foucault's Pendulum*, Dashiell Hammett, Carlos Castaneda,

Herman Hesse, Ayn Rand's *The Fountainhead,* a book of Pat O'Hara photography, Quammen's *Song of the Dodo.* Probably a man's library, and not a sniper novel in sight, so no deductions for lapse of taste. A bumper sticker pinned to the wall read *Subvert The Dominant Paradigm.*

I examined a model of an igloo-like dwelling made of plastic and foam, then thumbed a spiral notebook of sketches. Buildings: a house, a government building, church, museum, houseboat, cabins. Floor plans, elevations. Some appeared sketched from actual buildings, others may have been original designs as erasure marks showed significant alterations. The style was spare and unhurried, few non-essential lines.

Then, footfalls on the stairs. Though half-expecting to being caught, this didn't keep my heart from racing. Without a place of concealment or a back door, I continued to leaf through the sketchbook, lamplight full on my face.

The man who came in didn't seem surprised either. He hung his jacket and cap, and stood with hands on hips to look me over. Though tall, he could have pulled himself taller if he'd wanted to look threatening. Angular cheeks and chin, dark hair collected in a short pony tail, the look of a stoic warrior surveying the landscape before him, deciding if it was worth conquering.

"I'm Blake Gropius," he said dryly. "Perhaps you've heard of me."

I had to laugh. "You like that line? I've got more. Egret Van Gerpin, at your service."

He stepped forward, accepted my hand, and matched the firmness of my grip. "So, why are you in my room?" His voice had a deep texture, like pebbles grating in the surf.

"I thought your father might be storing sculptures up here. I wanted to see them."

"You were wrong."

"Except for one," I said glancing at the marble hands. "By the way, why am I not supposed to know you're here? And why, when I spoke with your roommate last week, did he act so secretive? Are you in trouble?"

He chortled deep in his chest. "Not much."

"I'm not a snitch."

He bunched his forehead muscles as if trying to see into my thoughts. I think he wanted to trust me but couldn't decide. I closed the notebook. "Forget it. I don't want to harm you or your family."

Blake caught me by the arm as I walked past. "There are certain people eager to talk to me."

From my research I knew Blake was about thirty-nine. Although his deliberate manner suggested maturity beyond that, a puppy-like curiosity made his eyes seem younger.

"That leaves me out—I'm not certain about anything."

"You strike me as someone who could be whatever she chooses."

"I'm a journalist—one who chooses to respect confidences."

"But not closed doors?"

"I wasn't going to take anything. Honest." My innocent look is intended to look none too innocent. "Can we talk awhile?" Just from searching his room I'd made up my mind to like him, perhaps even respect him.

Blake flopped his lanky self onto a sagging love seat, pulled off his boots. "I was out walking and saw you silhouetted on the ridge. I thought you might be sneaking over to Dad's studio."

"Maybe I should have."

"I don't think so. Nathan guards the place. No telling what he might do to a snoop."

"Nathan's harmless enough, I expect." Blake's little smile confirmed it. "Why do certain people want to talk to you?"

"I thought you might have heard."

"No."

"A boat sank at Neah Bay last week. People think I might know something about it."

"Oh, yes," I said. The Makah whaling boat. Sunk under mysterious circumstances. "I thought Greenpeace caught the blame for that—or the credit, depending how you look at it."

"How do *you* look at it?" The lamplight deepened the weariness lines on his face.

"Killing whales can't give dignity to the Makah."

He nodded. "I know them well. I drew the plans for their longhouse museum. There's no dignity in sinking boats either."

I sat at the table and patted the notebook I leafed through. "You're an architect?"

"I'm not credentialed. But it's what I do, mostly for barter. Sometimes I sponge off my parents and friends—just your basic scab on the ass of society."

Coming from someone else, the comment might have sounded bitter or self-effacing. "Tell me about this igloo."

He drew his legs under him, cross-legged. "My thing is low-cost housing, for all kinds of climates, combining high-tech engineering with locally available materials. Do you have any idea how many people are displaced by earthquakes and floods and war and political nonsense? So I designed a kit shelter for use in refugee camps. Sleeps eight. Can be put up in three or four hours. I've had one on my property for three years and it still keeps the rain out. You can add a little stove to burn dung or wood chips, and it costs less than a good tent." He made a palms-up gesture that meant *enough about me.* "Now, tell me how you wound up in journalism."

He cupped his hands and leaned forward for a closer look at me. I was glad of the dim light. "Would you believe I'm emulating my cigar-smoking grandmother?"

"You smoke cigars?"

"Not regularly. She wrote for the *PI* back when women weren't even allowed in the newsroom."

"When did you decide to emulate her?"

"Not all that long ago. It's a winding road."

"Take me for a drive. The scenic route."

"You must be hard up for entertainment."

"You have no idea."

"Well, then. You could say my Gram Velva honed her chops on beats no one else wanted. Mainly the black scene. Boxing, jazz. Never went anywhere without her old Speed Graphics and her photos are priceless. They've put out a book. Anyway, she rescued me—for the first time—when I was living with my mom in a commune near Ames, Iowa. The Blue Feather Farm. I was nine. Up until Gram came in her pink Thunderbird, no one had ever taken a long-term interest in me. Funny, I'd always figured it was *my* job to care for Mom, and the rest of the crowd."

"The crowd?"

"Oh, a collection of slack drifters. They orbited the farm like eccentric planets. I felt like Earth Station Egret."

"Not exactly Sesame Street."

"Nope. In those days, corporations were buying up family farms, and renting the old farmhouses for chicken scratch. We paid a hundred bucks a month for the place, which included a two-story house insulated with newspaper, a flooded quarry, and a windmill we painted like a sunflower. Firefly—my mom—would blast off for weeks at a time when the Dead were touring, so I got 'raised' by whoever was crashing there at the time."

"You didn't go to school or have any friends?"

"No. Nobody my age."

Blake simply nodded as if perhaps it had been a good thing.

"If I'd been at school or off playing, the crows would have dug up the corn seed and rabbits would have nibbled the kale to the ground and the goats would have dried up from not being milked. The propane would have run out and the lights would have gone off because Firefly spaced out paying the bills."

"Nobody helped?"

"Most of the freeloaders who came through were insulted when Mom asked them to do a little work. They were, after all, the next Crosby, Stills, & Nash, or the next Jack Kerouac, or the next Anton Gropius. Or, in the case of my father, the next Rasputin. So I became the enforcer," I said, making my best despotic face. "The miserable little tyrant with the power to make deadbeats slink into the barn, or pretend to be working. I actually threw some of the worst ones off the farm—and they went."

Blake laughed as if he had no trouble imagining it. "And what about your father?"

I looked away, mad at myself for having mentioned him. I'd never hit on a satisfactory way to explain. "He's not—I don't care to talk about him."

"Do you feel cheated of a normal childhood—being part of a regular family I mean?"

"It took me a while to realize... No, I don't feel cheated."

He nodded. "I don't have much sympathy for victim trippers. As if they're innocent bystanders spattered with misfortune they didn't deserve. Haven't we all earned exactly what we've got?"

"Karma?"

He tilted a brow.

I wanted to ask if he felt his father deserved to have his statues smashed, but didn't have the nerve. I stood up. "I owe your dad an apology, if he's still up."

"Apology for what?"

"For demanding too much."

Blake stood and got the door for me. As I was leaving, he gripped my shoulder as a friend would. "Don't apologize, Egret."

"Why?"

"My father is a man who respects people who stand for something. Change your mind if you must, but don't apologize."

Chapter 7

I crept through the darkened house, up the stairs to my room under the gables. I could scarcely believe I'd insinuated to Anton Gropius that he had an ego the size of Moby-Dick. I could only hope he didn't mind being lumped with the grand and mythical. Either way, his objection stood: I appeared too small to cope with a whale. Ironic that my idea about the biography, although it had occurred to me only yesterday, had become palpable. To have it dismissed with ridicule hurt.

I slept fitfully, rose before dawn, donned my paddling duds, and studied the tide tables. The wind whistling through the eaves had fallen off and I doubted there'd be enough breeze to keep me off the water. I wished I hadn't lost my cool with Anton; just seeing the sculptures would have made the trip worthwhile. By the clinking in the kitchen stovepipe running through my room, I guessed Clare had risen. I went downstairs to say thanks for the hospitality, and found her dicing veggies.

"You want to make biscuits while the coffee's perking?" she asked.

"Um... sure."

"Are you leaving?"

"I think so." I described my conversation with Anton.

"You should wait to see him before you go."

"I'd planned to do that." Before I could mention meeting Blake, Dinah appeared in the window. When Clare cracked the door, Dinah trotted in, clamshell clenched in her teeth. She dropped the shell on the linoleum, then somersaulted onto her back. I rubbed her belly, wet with dew. She vibrated as if I'd inserted a quarter.

"Clamshell?" I asked.

Clare added it to a terra cotta dish filled with clam and mussel shells, tube worm casings, bits of Styrofoam, and other beach flotsam, and explained they were all gifts from Dinah. She looked at me, as if judging whether to trust me with something.

"The Hindus believe that after your life's work is complete—child-raising, in my case—then comes the contemplative phase of life. Strange, I learn as much from Dinah as I ever did from raising my kids."

"Such as..."

"How to live life."

I had to laugh. "I have a cat. If I lived like Fosdick, all I'd do is eat, sleep, and shed."

"Sounds silly, doesn't it?"

"A little. But you've had more time to think about it."

"Dinah shows me how to find wonder in the commonplace. How to have a personal relationship with the all-powerful force running this universe."

I hadn't ruled out an all-powerful force, but if she existed, we weren't on the best of terms. Dinah continued writhing on her back. "Is this an example of how we should be?" I asked. "Submissive?"

"Not submission. Surrender."

"Surrender to what?"

"To something greater than ourselves."

I must have made a face.

"What?" she asked in a disarming way.

"Nothing. Maybe you need to get off this island more."

"Maybe."

She gaffed it off as a joke. But I hadn't been joking, and it really did bother me to see her up before sunrise, working like a scullery maid. "Clare, you're well educated, well traveled." I couldn't think of a way to put it delicately, but people don't seem to expect delicacy from me. "You're fit for more than cleaning your husband's boots."

Clare's thin height swayed like a cobra while she considered her answer. "My dear, I think you misunderstand me. I haven't surrendered to Anton. It would be wrong for any person to surrender to another. But each person can be, and should be, a channel through which love flows. Dinah surrenders to that flow. No matter what role an individual is called to play, doesn't it all come down to service in one way or another?"

Similar to stuff I'd heard at the Blue Feather Farm, but that didn't make it wrong. "Clare, you would have made a dandy nun."

Nathan Weeping Moon came in the back door without knocking. He looked at the woodbin next to the stove. "Down to your last stick. I suppose you expect me to fetch some."

"If you expect nothing from people, you'll never be disappointed," Clare said. "But I sure love having a thoughtful man around."

Nathan returned with split fir cradled in his arm and sat at the kitchen table with his coffee. Anton shuffled into the kitchen in slippers, heavy lidded and scowling. "God damn, Nathan, you need a haircut."

"And you need to drop about thirty pounds," Nathan said.

"That's rich coming from you, round boy." Though his spirits seemed improved by the exchange, Anton ignored me. He nuzzled Clare's shoulder, perhaps to inspect breakfast.

When Charles and Rooks arrived, we started on biscuits while the spuds and veggies sizzled in big skillets. Unsure of my welcome, I took only the smallest dab of Clare's gooseberry jam and nibbled the biscuit pensively, awaiting some indication as to whether my staying was still open for discussion. Anton seemed preoccupied with his thoughts and indifferent to his coffee. Eugene Gobi, I learned, rose late and appeared only after bathing, shaving, and pressing a shirt. Charles and Rooks wore tennis warm-ups: a satiny patchwork of pink and black and chartreuse for Rooks; Charles in the cotton variety fuzzy from many washings.

The smells of herbs and onions roused my appetite and I ventured a banana from an overflowing fruit bowl. Rooks stared as I peeled it—seems there's a food cop in every family. Court clumped down the stairs in huge athletic shoes with laces dragging, baggy black pants and a T-shirt with photos of guys in makeup. There had to be more suitable heroes for his generation, but I couldn't think who they'd be. Court stared at the floor most of the time, glancing up just enough to navigate to an open chair next to me. When he responded to my "Good morning," I could tell from his doggy breath he hadn't brushed his teeth.

"You're a mess," Rooks said, hands poised over Court as if wanting to fix him but not knowing where to start.

When he thumped his spoon on the table, she ripped it from his hand and placed it out of reach. But Court brightened when the back door opened and his uncle Blake entered, full of cheer and greetings for everyone. Clare's quick eyes saw it all, even before Blake greeted me by name, and she seemed relieved the game of hide-and-seek was over.

"Where did you come from?" Rooks said. "I didn't see a boat."

"You kick the woodwork, you never know what'll crawl out." He gave me the kind of wink that made me feel we were on the same team.

"Can I stay in the barn Uncle Blake?" Court asked, animated for the first time all morning.

Blake looked at me briefly, perhaps to see if I'd be vacating the attic. "We'll see. When are the others coming, Mom?"

"Celeste drove from Sedona in her van and called from Friday Harbor last night. Buzzy and Glenda are taking a commuter plane to

Friday Harbor this morning. They're going to meet up and share the water taxi. Everyone should be here for supper." Clare seemed radiant at the thought.

Anton asked, "Did we have to pay Buzzy's way out here?"

Clare cleared her throat.

"That's a yes. Neither one of them would turn down a free shit sandwich."

"Anton!"

He exchanged amused glances with Nathan, then drew breath to speak. All eyes went to him; such was his power to command attention just by looking as if he had something to say.

"I was going to wait for everyone before announcing this, but Egret seems particularly keen for me to get on with it."

I flushed at the unexpected use of my name.

"In recognition of my mortality I've been persuaded," he swept his hand in my direction, "to designate a biographer. She'll be staying on indefinitely."

He smiled at me rather charmingly.

I held my half-peeled banana before me, stiff as a dime store Indian.

"Oh dear," Clare said. "But the attic room is so bare and uncomfortable."

"It'll do," he said, beating me to it. "Besides, all my archives and journals are up there in the attic."

Blake nodded. "Then I suppose Court can bunk with me."

"Awesome!" Court said.

I stammered my appreciation, then remembered my responsibilities at the newspaper and asked to use the radiophone. Maybe I no longer had any responsibilities due to insubordination, but I owed Armentrout a call, and wanted him to know I hadn't failed.

"Nathan, show her how to work that contraption," Anton said.

"And I want everyone to cooperate with Egret. Give her any information she wants."

Whether Anton was serious about the biography, or meant it as a cover for my snooping, I didn't know. Either way, I felt entitled to another biscuit and this time wasn't so frugal with the jam.

When dishes were cleared, Nathan helped me raise the operator. While waiting for the call to be completed, I took a closer look at the plaster replica of Michelangelo's *David* standing next to me, and the phone numbers scrawled on his taut muscles. I couldn't help but notice a number penciled boldly on *David's* penis (it just happened to be at eye level). Just a number, no name. But I recognized it as one I had dialed just last week, belonging to Bernard Gropius, Anton's brother from Sioux Falls. Buzzy.

Nathan left, replaced by Rooks who was also anxious to place a call, and who apparently thought it would speed things up if she crossed her arms and tapped her foot. She didn't know me very well. Rib Armentrout listened to my contrite explanation—listened in silence except for the sound of an antacid being ground to chalk. I disclosed as much of the plan as I could with Rooks standing by. Then he said, "Do you have any idea of the problems you've caused here?"

"Yes, I'm—"

"No you don't."

This hit me precisely where it hurt most. I listened to the crackle on the line for a long time, knowing that if he told me to get my butt back to Friday Harbor, I'd go. I could hear ghosts of other conversations haunting our connection. Finally he said, "Call me as soon as you get a look at Anton's new stuff."

"Right."

I rang off. Rooks was getting on my nerves, but I placed another call anyway—to my colleague Shannon. After several minutes I got her on the line and asked her to collect some of my clothes, toiletries, and spare batteries for my tape recorder. I told her Drago's water taxi would be delivering the rest of the Gropius family to Thunderhead Island that afternoon. If she could get a bag ready, the taxi could bring it along. Shannon groused and said she'd try.

Rooks grabbed the phone when I got up, and turned her back to me. A dangling cocoon of hair, like Olive Oyl's, hung at the back of her long neck. Out of curiosity I pointed to the number on the penis. "Why do you suppose your uncle's number gets the place of honor?"

Rooks looked, sneered. "Buzzy? Because he's such a prick I suppose."

I forced a chuckle, thinking a moment's shared amusement might thaw the ice between us, but it didn't happen.

I looked for Anton and found he'd already gone to his studio. "Did he leave any instructions for me?" I asked Clare.

"No..."

"Maybe I should go see him."

"Perhaps you might want to start with the archives."

I wanted to see sculptures, to get to know Anton, not leaf through papers. But... "I'd be happy to get them. In the attic, right?"

"It would be easier for me."

I wondered how it could be easier for a woman well into her sixties to climb two long flights of stairs. I also wondered if Clare understood Anton had recruited me to spy on the family. I didn't ask, not wanting to be a cloud over her treasured reunion.

I waited in the sitting room. Eugene Gobi finally appeared from his ground floor bedroom. He formally greeted me, Dr. Underwood, and Courtney, then walked in short, precise steps to the porch for one of his thin cigarettes, leaving a spicy wake of aftershave.

Charles put his nose back in a medical journal, angled away from Court as if he didn't want to be interrupted. "Are you going to catch us a salmon for dinner?" I said, remembering his fishing poles.

He put a finger on the page to mark his place. "Later."

"Do you have any red and white spoons?"

Suddenly he seemed more interested. "Is that what they bite on?"

"Yup. You going fishing too, Court?"

He looked lost in a chair too big for him. "I don't care about fish."

"What do you care about?"

"Surfing."

"He means boogie boarding, not real surfing," Charles said. "Isn't that what you mean, Court?"

Court continued to look at his shoes, which he bounced off the frame of the chair.

"No boogie boarding around here," I said. "What else? Computer games?"

"I'm grounded from playing computer games until I have a good report card. That's probably forever."

"Maybe..." I started, not at all sure I wanted to finish it. "Maybe I'll teach you how to kayak—if that's something you might possibly care about."

 He looked at me with suspicion, then asked, without much enthusiasm—or hope, "Can I Dad?"

"Ask your mother."

Court looked surprised not to get a flat no and ran to the foyer to pester Rooks, who was still on the phone.

"He's bored," I said to Charles.

"He should be in school."

"What happened?"

He closed the magazine. "They caught him cutting the TV cable. It had been cut three times in a week, and they finally nabbed him in the act. They also blamed him for cutting the ends off lamp cords and other things."

"Strange. Did he do all of it?"

"It seems so." Charles pursed his peaked mouth, looking ashamed of the situation, and a little annoyed at telling me.

"But why?"

"I don't know. But if the Academy can't handle little disciplinary problems, then I think we made a bad choice of schools."

The stairs creaked as Clare descended with two green pasteboard boxes, dates neatly scribed on their labels, secured with string wound around rivets. She opened one of the boxes and showed me a collection of clippings, letters, photos, sketches, pamphlets, receipts, et cetera. From the label I calculated the box covered Anton's high school years. "When you're done with these, there're more. Some of the things are getting quite brittle."

Rooks joined us and, with the shortest of glances at me, said, "I told Court that he could go kayaking. He's at that stage where he thinks he knows everything, so if he gives you any backtalk..." Then she saw the green boxes. "Dad's records."

I understood her tone. A stranger pawing through the family treasures.

"Perhaps you'd enjoy going through them with Egret," Clare suggested.

"I'd like that," I said. Regardless of my likes and dislikes, I had a job to do and it would help to carve a toehold into Rooks' acceptance.

"I don't have time to baby-sit just now." She began walking away, then turned. "Shouldn't father have a big-time author doing his biography? Michener or someone?"

"I've got a leg up on Michener," I said, feeling quite warm in my paddling clothes. "I've got lead in my pencil."

"Huh?" Rooks said.

"He's dead, I'm not."

She flipped her hand in dismissal.

"Pity that."

Chapter 8

I spent a few minutes leafing through the archives, but couldn't concentrate. I decided both my objectives—discovering who might be threatening Anton's work, and researching a story—would best be served by talking to live people. The boxes of paper would always be there; the family members would not.

To excuse myself from wading through the clippings, I asked Clare if I might start with the most recent boxes and work backward. "But please don't go up those stairs again," I said. "I'll exchange the boxes later."

"I'm sure you know what you're doing," Clare said. She shouldered a knapsack and took Rooks for a walk. I wondered what I'd done to rub Rooks sideways, and knew it had to be more than eating her favorite banana.

As I restored papers to the box, my eye caught the name *Eugene Fedorko Gobi* on a newspaper clipping, yellowed to the same hue as the strands of his hair. He'd placed second in a piano competition. The photo showed him standing next to the great but aged pianist Emil Zatarian, under whom Gobi, according to the caption, was studying.

Gobi came from the kitchen carrying a tray with tea, sliced peaches, and English muffins. He opened a folio containing a score-in-progress. When I showed him the clipping, he smiled without showing teeth.

"So why is this in Anton's file?" I asked.

"Look again." He pointed a bitten pinkie nail at one of the other boys in the background. "Don't you recognize Anton?"

The mischievous youth with unkempt hair looked nothing like the present version, but I took Gobi's word for it. "You've known each other for a very long time then."

Gobi spread marmalade precisely to the edges of his muffin. "You might say I'm responsible for saving the world's greatest sculptor from becoming a musician."

"Mind if I tape it?" I asked, showing him my mini-cassette recorder. The smaller the recorder, the less people were intimidated by it. Being a denizen of Hollywood, Gobi seemed pleased to be in the spotlight, no matter how small.

"When we were lads about Court's age, say ten or eleven—I was a year younger than Anton, still am—we both studied with Zatarian.

The maestro was in his eighties and not up to the rigors of touring, so he devoted himself to a few promising pupils—or should I say disciples?—in varying age brackets.

"He'd had a brilliant career, you know, and didn't depend on fees for a living. His only criterion for students was musical potential. Naturally, competition was keen. My parents sacrificed a great deal by moving from Chicago to Seattle so I might study under him." Gobi quoted Zatarian in a Germanic accent, punctuated with thrusts of his index finger, "'Those who do not break the barriers are gone, poof, banished from my sight.'"

I thought I could see vestiges of trepidation still haunting his eyes. "Must have been a lot of pressure," I said. "Your parents moving and all."

"Exactly."

He seemed pleased I'd understood.

He cut his muffin precisely in half and bit a corner, baring his teeth so as not to get marmalade on his thin lips. Again he mimicked the maestro, "'I am eighty-one years old, and I have no time to waste on mamma's little genius.'"

"Anton was also a musical prodigy?"

"He had talent, and even at that age he was capable of prodigious concentration. He and I were playing at comparable levels, although I was thirteen months younger—a large difference in those days. Our lessons were scheduled back-to-back on Thursday mornings, so we were excused from school and felt very important. While one received the lesson, the other listened in the antechamber and overheard the praise or scoldings of the maestro."

"Why did Anton give up music?"

"Ah! It so happened that Zatarian had living with him his great granddaughter, Elaina." Gobi flashed one of his half-second smiles. "She made herself useful, found his spectacles, saw to his guests. Elaina was my age, very bright, a talented harpist—and more than a little conceited. But such charm... mesmerizing." He closed his eyes briefly. "So, not one, but two rivalries. We lived for the maestro's approval *and* Elaina's attentions. She had the maddening quality of aloofness, as if she were one of Zatarian's china figurines set on a high shelf away from clumsy hands. Then, when you least expected it, she could be full of the devil."

Gobi laughed. A genuine laugh with joy in it. "Such as the time she took my hand and led me to a room where Zatarian kept his papers. There, in a cigar box, which Elaina had to climb the bookshelves to reach, was a red lace undergarment, drenched in perfume, with a note to the effect, 'Emil, a memento of our friendship, lest your memory fade.' Signed 'Venus', whom Elaina informed me was Venus DeMolay, the vaudeville star. We giggled, and then she became serious and whispered to me, 'One day when you're a famous pianist, I'll give you something very personal.' And she kissed me on the cheek."

Gobi spread his hands slowly as if basking in a glorious light. "Oh, it may have been the only perfect moment of my life. We tend to forget, don't we, how powerfully in love we can be even before our bodies are equipped for it."

"Maybe love is more pure then because of it," I said. Gobi nodded, lost in his thoughts. "Then what happened?"

"She pulled the red panties over my head, then ran from the room giggling, leaving me to put them back. Of course, as I climbed the shelves, the housekeeper came and gave me the tongue lashing of my life." He shook his head. "That was Elaina: temptress and sprite."

"Anton loved her too?"

"It was impossible not to. She saw to it. She understood how competitive we were, and made herself the object of competition, playing one against the other. Just before her twelfth birthday, Anton promised her an original composition. Not to be outdone, I did too." Gobi became solemn. "I threw myself to the task. The day of the party arrived, hats and hooters, little ice cream cakes for everyone, the gifts were opened. Then we played our compositions. First Anton, then me. He'd written an amusing lyric for his piece and we all laughed. But when I played, maestro Zatarian was taken aback, perhaps a little astounded. He asked me to play it again, and then told the others—musicians, all of them, 'Do you see how the key notes of the melody are not found in the chord?' Then he said, 'This is a very clever composition,' and he himself played his interpretation, transforming it with his own genius."

"Then you've had at least two perfect moments."

He nodded grimly. "This one dissipated even more quickly than the other. Anton couldn't tolerate being upstaged. After all, it had been his idea to compose something for Elaina's birthday. When I looked for her reaction to my triumph, I found she hadn't been listening at all. Anton had posed her on the window seat, and was sketching her on the paper tablecloth. At that moment, gaining the maestro's p-praise seemed the lesser prize."

Something in his fragile stammer made me want to give him back the moment Anton had snatched away. "Can you still play it?"

"My composition? Oh yes." He slid behind the piano to play a few bars. It sounded Gershwinish. I wondered how much was as originally written, and how much subsequent embellishment.

"So that's how I rescued the great sculptor Gropius from a career at the keyboard. You see, he can't stand being bested—in art or in love." Gobi said this matter-of-factly as if intending no disparagement.

"Eugene," I asked, "do you believe someone really wants to harm Anton's work?"

His eyelids fluttered, as if jarred by his return from the past. "You can't blame him for being nervous. A man bitten by a shark does not easily return to the water."

"Is there still a shark in the water?"

Gobi turned up his palms. "My analogy is a bad one. You see, Anton himself is a shark, and like a shark, he must continue swimming or die." He had artfully avoided my question. I wondered if Gobi, in some secret, resentful place, felt that whatever befell a predator, somehow he'd earned it. Gobi appeared to enjoy Anton's full trust, but I couldn't help wondering why.

"Who does Anton suspect?" I asked.

"For what happened twenty-one years ago? It's hard to explain. As a group he suspects the family—and I include myself when I say *family*. But he can't imagine any of us, as individuals, actually doing it."

Court ran in from somewhere. "Can we go kayaking now?" He wore his sweatshirt inside out, and his fringe of orange and green hair hung out the back of his cap. I said I needed to get some work done, but when his face fell, I said okay.

Outside, I tightened my life jacket straps to fit him and spent a half-hour going over the basics. I showed him how to get in the boat using the paddle as a brace, adjusted the foot pegs, reviewed the forward stroke, and told him the plan in case he capsized.

Then we put on the water, Court in the kayak, me in an aluminum rowboat. I rowed figure-eights in the protected waters of the cove while Court followed. Even in my rather compact baidarka he looked awkwardly small in the cockpit.

When he began to get more comfortable with the tipsy feel of the boat, I took his paddle and had him lean to the gunwale of the rowboat to get a sense for how far he could put the boat on edge without capsizing. He caught on fast, so I showed him how to carve turns by leaning the kayak opposite the direction of the turn. This would save him from having to use his limited arm strength.

After that, I suggested we call it good, but he pleaded to go out beyond the cove.

We had a breeze and slight chop, but nothing that I felt would pose a threat. So I tied his bow line to the rowboat in case he needed a tow, and out we went. I'd seen Charles heading north along the shore with his casting rig, and wanted him to see how well his son was doing. "Do you and your parents visit here often?" I asked Court as we stroked.

"This is the first time. I want to have my own island some day."

"But you've met your grandparents before?"

"Grandma comes to Florida every year. We went to Disney World last year. Grandpa Anton came one time and we went to a Dolphin's game."

"So you all came just for your grandpa's birthday?"

"I don't know. Something about his will, I think."

Hmm. Had Anton used his will as bait to draw the family together on short notice?

"Have you always gone to private schools, Court?"

"Just about always."

"And you live at the school?"

"Yeah."

"How do you like that?"

"I guess it's a good way to get rid of me."

My life vest suddenly seemed too tight for me to breathe properly. "Is that how it feels to you, that you're in the way?"

Court averted his gaze and swallowed.

"I'm sure it's not true, Court. Sometimes life gets complicated for adults and they lose track of time. It doesn't necessarily mean... well, not what you might think." I realized that if my boy had lived, he'd be old enough to have a real conversation with, and I could see Rooks shipping Court off just so her new furniture wouldn't get nicked, or the nap of the carpet disturbed. My objective voice argued that maybe Court's perspective was exaggerated, unreliable, that his parents simply wanted the best for him, the best education. How would I have balanced my career with raising Toby?

"You're paddling like a pro," I said. "Maybe tomorrow we'll circumnavigate the island."

"Really? All right! Hey, there's Dad!"

Charles stood on an outcropping in his plaid shirt, fishing vest, and chinos with the crease still in them. The sea floor fell off sharply making it a good place to fish.

"He's doing wonderfully," I said to Charles.

"Court, you mind what...ah...your teacher says." Charles had started to use my name, but couldn't remember it. Then to me he said, "Sometimes Court thinks he knows everything."

"We've all been there," I said.

By the time we returned to the cove, Drago's water taxi was rounding the southern point of the island. I wondered if this next batch of Gropiuses would include the one bent on destroying their patriarch.

Chapter 9

Anton showed up to greet the boat this time. He introduced me first to his eldest, Celeste, willowy, elfin, over-decorated with fringed scarf and cummerbund, pounds of bangles, and a constellation of copper suns and moons and comets dangling at the neck of her tunic. Celestial objects. Rooks embraced her sister, called her 'Beakie', and began catching her up on all the disagreeable things in her life starting with her boat ride to Thunderhead Island. Next to the refined and supercilious Rooks, Celeste looked diffident and underfed.

Next off the boat came Anton's younger brother, Buzz, and his cringing wife, Glenda. I might have cringed, too, to be seen with a husband dressed in a canary-yellow jump suit, white loafers, and plaid slouch cap. Maybe that's how they dress in Sioux Falls, but I doubt it. Glenda's outfit looked deliberately drab.

I scanned the cargo looking for a bag that belonged to me, then heard the *zlink* of a camera shutter and whir of a motorized film advance.   Then I heard the grinding of teeth—mine—as Stu Broadbent, my editor's steroid-case nephew, appeared from behind the camera. I don't often wish ill of people, but my thoughts ran toward dismemberment.

Stu stepped to the pier carrying an overnight bag—not mine. "Egret, Uncle Rib needs to see you the minute you get back." He spread his arm toward the boat. "Your chariot awaits."

"I suppose this means my bag of clothes didn't make it."

Stu shrugged. "I figured, why bother? Since you aren't staying."

When Anton got the drift of what was going on, he broke off conversation with his brother. "Stuart Broadbent," I said to Anton. "Rib Armentrout's nephew. Stu wants to pinch-hit so I can get back to my regular job."

Anton seemed to catch the fury in my tone. His eyes lit and he shot me a wink. By the time he'd turned to face Stu, he looked like a badger after a lousy night's sleep. He ignored Stu's handshake and crowded him to the edge of the pier.

"Are you here to deliver my newspaper?" Anton asked.

"No, I'm—"

"You're looking for your lost rubber ducky?"

Stu chuckled uncomfortably. "No, the reason—"

"I know, you've just recovered from amnesia and you don't

know how the hell you got here." Anton's voice had risen steadily and he'd begun to color.

Stu sighed.

"No?" Anton pointed to the boat skipper. "Then you must have lied to that man about being invited here. Otherwise he wouldn't have brought you."

The skipper nodded vigorously.

"Well I..."

"You lied."

"Well—"

"You lied!"

"I suppose, but—"

"So you're a liar and an idiot."

"Wait a minute..."

"What, you've admitted you're a liar, and you must be dumber than a doorknob to show up on my island without an invitation."

Buzz and Glenda looked on with wide-eyed fascination, as if watching a matador being gored. Clare and her daughter Celeste simply looked embarrassed.

"Sir, I... I just want to interview you for the newspaper."

Anton turned to me. "Is this the best that Armentrout can send out here, or do they all sputter and snivel and lie like schoolboys? I could carve a better man out of a turnip."

"Look, sir," Stu said, puffing his chest, "I've had public affairs experience in the Navy. I've dealt with officials from the highest echelons, and handled extremely sensitive—"

"No, you look," Anton said, veins bulging from his temples. He inched closer until Stu was on the brink of toppling off the pier. "I don't care if you're Admiral Rickover's favorite bastard son. You're a damned trespasser, and that's all you are."

For a fleeting moment I felt sorry for Stu, and thought about intervening. Had my wish for dismemberment unleashed a terrible genie?

Anton pointed. "Do you see that shed up there?"

Stu nodded.

"In that shed is my Winchester twelve-gauge over/under shotgun. I keep one barrel loaded with rock salt for trespassers and the other loaded with bird shot for crows. It's been so long since I've had to shoot anything, I forget which barrel is which. But if you're still here when I get back, I'm just going to have to guess."

"But why are you letting her stay?" Stu pointed to me.

"Because..." Anton said, "Ms. Van Gerpin is a professional. She doesn't snivel. She doesn't lie." He fixed Stu with a cold glare, then stalked off toward the shed.

The anxious skipper herded Stu into the boat and untied the mooring lines. Buzz said something about his money being packed, so Blake rolled his eyes, fished a couple of twenties from his wallet, and paid the fare. Anton hadn't walked halfway to the shed before the motors gunned and the boat pulled away. Anton returned and laughed long and hard. "I'd say that boy just got shucked like a shallow-water oyster."

"God Almighty, Anton," Buzz said. "What did he do to you?"

"He just looked a bit too cocky to suit me." Anton winked at me again, said he had things to do at the studio, and told me to drop by when I had the chance.

As Blake and I loaded bags into the ATV trailer, Glenda apologized to Clare. "Sorry we're late. Buzzy left his ball-point pen in the phone booth and we had to go back."

"You're not late, dear."

"Oh my. Are we early then?"

Buzz surveyed the layout—the solid old house, well-tended garden, barn, shed, the crescent beach. "Didn't I tell you, Glenda? It must be worth a pile. But, of course," his tone dripped with sarcasm, "an artist needs his inspiration."

The thing that struck me about Buzz Gropius was his intensity. That, and his massive forehead. In school they teach you to sketch oval faces with the eyes in the middle of the oval. Buzz's eyes were in the bottom third. He had as much forehead as your average sperm whale.

"Don't pay any attention to him," Glenda said. "Buzzy's having trouble adjusting to a salt-free diet." In almost comic contrast to her husband's face, Glenda's was perfectly round; its shape emphasized by a bowl haircut. She squinted as if not wanting to see too much of the world at once.

"I could do with some lunch," Buzz said. "That place called itself a bed and breakfast, but all they had was muffins. I'm accustomed to meat three times a day."

As they headed for the house, Blake mounted the ATV. "Climb on," he said to me.

I hesitated.

Court piped up, "I'll ride."

"Next time," Blake said. He smiled at me and thumped the seat behind him.

Blake had more of his mother's brand of self-confidence than his father's, and he had her slender build, reserved manner, and slightly Vulcan ears. Not much of Anton in that face, except the mischief in the eyes.

It was the eyes that attracted me.

I climbed aboard. Having lived a nun's life for more than a year, the sensation of him fitted between my thighs raised a little shudder. I suppose I could have scooted back, but I didn't. He drove slowly. More slowly than necessary, I thought, and he turned often to see that the bags were secure. When we reached the house, he put it in neutral and dismounted, telling me to stay put. I did. He pulled the pin on the trailer, and climbed back on the machine.

"Hold on," he said.

I searched for handholds under the seat.

"Not there." He placed my hands around his middle, ran the four-wheeler up to third gear and we bounced recklessly up the same ridge path I'd walked the previous night. When on top, he stopped at the best viewpoint, turned off the machine. I loosened my grip on him. We absorbed the vistas: the treeless ridge running south; to the east, four rooftops—one of tin, two of weathered shakes, another of freshly split shakes; a mixed forest of fir, hemlock, and cedar blocked our view of the island's north end. Gleaming waterways and islands by the dozen receded into haze.

"How big is Thunderhead Island?"

"Dad only owns what we can see from here. Around two-hundred acres. Just past the trees there's an isthmus and some flatlands, a salt marsh, and an old homestead by another cove. It's abandoned now. Nathan says it's been in litigation for fifteen years. The heirs, the Tribe, the Canadian government, creditors... it's a mess."

It looked inviting to explore. "Is there a trail?"

"A footpath. And you can see there's a path around the south end from the house to the studio. It's longer, but easier than climbing over the ridge if you're on foot."

I showed him where I'd landed my kayak the day before. "I'm not sure I'd want to cross that plank bridge at night."

He shrugged. "You get used to it. Now that you've met the whole family, what do you think?"

"Too soon to tell." I trusted my first impressions, but they weren't infallible.

"Together we create a strange energy. A force field of weirdness."

I thought about my upbringing at the Blue Feather Farm.

Weaned on the weird; nurtured on the bizarre. "We're all crazy, just in different ways."

"If we're not, we should be," Blake said. "It would be crazy not to be crazy." He made a face resembling a magnified mosquito. It looked well practiced, but it made me laugh.

"You're nuts."

"So when's the other time your granny rescued you? Taking you away from the commune was the first time, you said."

"You were paying attention," I said, flattered. "Well, there were two more times altogether. After I started school in Seattle... it was awkward, a big adjustment. I just wanted out of there until she got me started in sports. Then, when I got to the seventh grade, she threatened a lawsuit when the local rink tried to keep me off the boys hockey team, and her newspaper covered it."

"What happened?"

"The team got themselves a damn good goalie. Then, when the season was over, I took up tennis with a vengeance. I'd grown tall and lean, and could cover a lot of court. And, anyway, I preferred individual competition."

"That's two rescues."

"The third was from my own short-sightedness. She forced me to get my degree—loaned me the money for college—before I could join the pro tennis circuit."

"But the tennis thing didn't work out?"

"Injury. And without the education, I probably wouldn't have got my newspaper job." I didn't mention my stint as a mother.

Blake drove us down the east flank to Anton's studio. At the shoreline we passed a large structure clad in rusting sheet metal. Blackberry vines rambled over a tractor with disintegrating tires, and over a stack of oil drums colored like dingy crayons. Blake explained this had been a cannery. Two rows of rotten pilings were all that remained of a pier. In contrast to this ruin stood Anton's studio, a keyhole-shaped building comprised of a windowless rectangle attached to a larger octagonal room.

A third building, under construction, lay beyond in a clutter of logs, hand tools, and scrap piles. I'd seen pictures of Indian longhouses before, but never a real one. Constructed of split old-growth cedar, longhouses had, in the old days, sheltered entire tribes: dark, smelly, smoky, but dry. Above the construction site, a shack. "Nathan's place," Blake said.

We dismounted at the studio. "Your dad didn't spend much time with his guests," I remarked.

"No."

The studio windows were set higher than eye level so I couldn't see inside. Blake reached for the door handle, paused, knocked. Anton opened the door and blocked the entrance with his husky body.

"You took off just in time," Blake said. "Before your brother could mooch the price of his boat ride."

Anton chuckled. "He already cost me a pair of plane tickets. But I want the family together, and when you're seventy, you do what's necessary."

"Do we get to see what you're working on?" I asked, craning my neck above Blake's shoulder.

Anton cleared his throat. "I'll be taking a project over to the house—I want everyone to see it at the same time."

"Need help?" Blake offered.

"No. Nathan's here."

"You want me to bring the four-wheeler around with the trailer?"

"Appreciate it."

Their civility seemed obligatory, without warmth.

"Mom's making clam chowder."

"Good."

Blake started to say something else but stopped. "Later then." He turned away.

"Stick around, Egret," Anton said. I thanked Blake for the ride, but felt a little indecent accepting privileged treatment from his father. The reporter in me, though, champed to see Anton's sanctum. I stepped inside just as Nathan snugged a canvas over something the size of a large television. I presumed the something to be a sculpture.

"Thanks for getting rid of Stu," I said to Anton.

"I didn't like the cut of his jib."

"I don't think you'd care much for the state of his Jockey shorts, either."

Anton heaved up a chuckle. "Have a look around."

I did. Heavy workbenches lined the octagonal walls. In the center of the studio, amid an assortment of tools, was a partially finished bust on a rotating worktable. A photograph of a woman in the same pose was tacked to the table. I recognized the face from somewhere.

"She's a big shot on Wall Street," Anton said.

I couldn't help feeling disappointed. The figure had been rendered faithfully from the photograph, competent, but without artistic interpretation. If this was all Anton Gropius had been doing, I was wasting my time.

Anton explained how air from a small compressor ran through a pneumatic line to an air hammer holstered on the workbench, and showed me an array of quick-release tool heads that made me think of a dentist office from hell. In fact, the entire studio had the cachet of a torture chamber littered with the gore of use: unfinished works (perhaps failed or abandoned), rumpled sketches, a pencil snapped in half. I sensed Anton had set the windows high, not so much for privacy, but to deprive himself of a distracting view.

A dozen hammers and mallets, the butt of each handle wrapped with yellow tape, lay in a cluster on the workbench.

Anton showed me a diamond-bladed circular saw for cutting stone, an array of hand chisels and a grinder for keeping the edges gleaming sharp, spoon-shaped rasps, a wall of calipers including a large wooden instrument whose jaws could take the measure of a horse.

Photographs of sculptures.

A human skeleton displayed in a glass case; on top of the case, a model of a human head showed dissected musculature.

Beside the doorway to the adjoining room stood another Michelangelo plaster—one of his unfinished slaves. The *Rebellious Slave*, Anton said, pleased I at least recognized the maker.

Nathan Weeping Moon stepped away from the canvas-draped object. "Ready." A strand of monofilament fish line trailed under the canvas.

Anton's eyes gleamed boyishly. "We're going to spring a trap," he explained, nodding toward the covered object. "First I want to hear what you make of my family, now that you've met them all."

I'd been asked that twice in twenty minutes. A self-conscious bunch, these Gropiuses. "They all seem so different," I said. "It's hard to imagine you're all from the same family."

"The hospitals just hand you the first brat they lay their mitts on."

It sent a stone to the pit of my stomach, as if he were denying his own children. Maybe he had reason to. I walked around the wrapped object. "And this is the bait?" I said. "To attract whoever might want to harm your carvings?"

"Nathan's bright idea," Anton said. "He's got more white blood in him than he admits."

"What do you mean? Us redskins invented sneakiness."

"Including the quarterback sneak?" I asked.

The two of them joined eyes for a second and something passed between them. I couldn't tell if they took me for an idiot or for someone who could join their game. I tried to purge the effects of my bad joke by returning to business. "Am I right in thinking that everybody on this island attended the party in Seattle when your statues were attacked? Except Court and Nathan, of course."

"Charles wasn't in the picture yet. Celeste had a boyfriend then, named Hornbeak, but he got his feelings hurt and went off to lick himself like a broke-leg dog. I only saw him once after that, when we found out Celeste was actually married to the twerp. It lasted a month, which was about thirty days too long. For a while I thought Hornbeak might have done it but it turned out he had an alibi."

"You apparently trust Eugene Gobi."

"Gene was playing piano when it happened."

"So you're ruling out your son-in-law Charles, Eugene, Clare—I assume—and Nathan?"

Anton nodded.

"That leaves your brother Buzz, his wife Glenda, and your kids: Blake, Celeste, and Rooks." I ticked them off on my fingers. "But why are you so sure it was one of them? I understand there were close to a hundred people at the party."

Anton smoothed his tangled mass of beard, picked out a marble chip. "You already know about the symbol drawn on the sidewalk in red chalk."

"Like the one on the marble block at Friday Harbor."

He nodded. "It wasn't there when we discovered the damage. The guests were cleared out and the police guarded the courtyard gate all night. Someone staying in the house drew the mark during the night."

"How do you know it was the same person who destroyed the statues?"

"Who else would take the risk? Terrorists want credit for their bombings, and that goddamned mark is supposed to be a clue, or is meant to mock me somehow. As if it's not enough to destroy my life's work." His cheeks flushed with rage.

"What does the sign mean?" I asked.

He shook his head. "Nothing, to me."

"My first impression was of a hand," I said. "Sort of an atrophied hand."

He seemed interested in my impression. "Could be. I suspect there's some crude symbolism to it."

I thought about the carved draftsman's hands in the barn loft, and the osprey in Rooks' room. "Those carvings you did for your guests—you didn't intend any symbolism, did you?"

Anton smiled grimly. "Clare would say everything is symbolic."

As I looked over the bulky object Nathan had been working at, something occurred to me. "What if the second mark wasn't drawn by the same person? Somebody could be playing a bad joke."

Anton removed his dusty safety glasses. His eyes, the color of string beans blanched too long, were narrowed by a fold of skin above them. The face looked tired, but the eyes were alert. "I'd like to believe that, but I can't take the chance. I *can't* take the chance. With a little luck, you and Nate and I are going to have someone by the collar before breakfast."

Nathan was on the balls of his feet with conspiratorial glee.

I felt it, too. "What do you want me to do?"

Chapter 10

My walk back to the house along the south trail began at exercise speed. I wondered if Anton was stringing me along just to get what he wanted; however, I knew my motives needed weighing too. But the path sucked the anxiety from my legs, slowing me, starving the future and past to nourish the present, making a gift of itself. I fell into a new rhythm, letting the earth push me along and feeling wealthy at owning it for the moment, my only responsibility being to do it no harm, this trail laid out for my pleasure along the land's contours, bending unnecessarily to pass through a glen lush with butterbur and asters. A lichen-plastered boulder offered a seat with a view of the Balinese-dancer madronas. The route continued over the plank bridge, where water surged into the crevasse below with the sound of a huge umbrella opening. BOOOF!

The trail seemed both ancient and temporary. At first human visitation, this land had borne a half-mile thickness of ice, the sea withdrawn hundreds of feet lower. If the melt continues, the sea might someday erase the footsteps that made this path.

At the house, I found Buzz adjusting a TV antenna mounted on a nearby knoll, beer bottle upright at his feet. "Better?" he shouted to his wife, Glenda. From under the sitting room window, she relayed the question to Clare inside.

Glenda called, "Worse. Turn it back a little."

"Son of a buck!" Buzz said.

Clare stuck her head out the window. "That's the best we're going to do, Glenda." She filled me in with amused concern, "The National League playoffs start tonight. I'm afraid we only get a Vancouver station, and not very clear at that."

When Glenda consolingly broke the bad news to Buzz, he shouted, "What did I tell you? So Anton's turning seventy. Big deal. You think he'll come to Sioux Falls when I turn seventy?"

Glenda scuttled back to the window as if her feet had been bound at childhood. "Sorry," she said to Clare. "You know how he is about his games."

As Buzz approached, Clare explained to me, "He used to pitch in the big leagues for the Cincinnati Reds."

"I'll tell you, it was a different game in those days," Buzz said. "You look around the infield these days and you're lucky if you can pronounce one or two names. Used to be baseball was the national sport of America. Now there's a couple of token Americans on each team, and that's it. We can't import Cuban cigars, but we sure as hell let their little banty-rooster ballplayers in. I could have pitched another ten years if we'd kept the game pure."

Clare slammed the window shut. The corners of Glenda's mouth sagged. She said to me, "Buzzy always gets nostalgic around World Series time."

Yeah, and he probably got choked up at the sight of pillowcases with eyeholes.

We migrated to the porch and interrupted Celeste from her book of incantations for dealing with menopause. Though the eldest of Clare and Anton's children, she seemed the least grown up. In her lap rested two seashells the size of her tiny fists. I settled into a rattan rocker. Clare brought tea, and Glenda opened beers for Buzzy and herself. When Clare queried Buzz about his hardware store, even that seemed to agitate him.

"Let's just say I'd rather be sucking down brewskis on my own island than peddling nuts and bolts to Bohunk farmers."

I realized my hands had tightened on the arms of my chair and I'd begun rocking briskly. I took a deep breath, remembering my job was to gather information and help Anton protect his work—not to express opinions or to let my suspicions run ahead of themselves.

My opinion wasn't needed anyway, as Celeste offered her own. "Uncle Buzzy, if you're prejudiced against a certain nationality, you'll probably be reincarnated as one of them." She sounded earnest as a young Shirley Temple. Celeste looked anemic, the veins beneath her eyes showing through transparent skin. Her childlike features had been corrupted by forty-some years, and she hid nothing with makeup. Her flat cheeks, lack of much chin, and nose a bit thickened at the end gave her a decidedly gnomish appearance, yet she seemed cheery enough and she dressed with panache in a billowy silk outfit, turquoise with burgundy marks in the shape of chromosomes. She wore a scarf about her neck, a sash at her waist, a glittering ribbon twisted through her unruly russet hair, and any number of rings, bangles, beads, and crystals about her fingers, ears, wrist, elbows, and ankles. A leather pouch hung from her neck by a cord, as did a small tube of ointment. Celeste produced her own tea bag from the pouch, something with runic lettering on the tag. She put the seashells on the table and brewed her tea.

"Sugar?" Clare offered.

Celeste recoiled. "Poison, you mean."

Glenda exclaimed, "Oh! Did that shell move?"

I'd noticed one of the shells lifting up slightly. As we watched, it moved an inch sideways.

"How does it do that?" Glenda asked, as if witnessing the miraculous.

"May I introduce Moon and Sixpence," Celeste said, stroking each shell with a finger. I'd seen plenty of hermit crabs, but none that big. "My life has totally changed since I've acknowledged my birth under the sign of Cancer. I understand all the weird things in my life. I can even embrace my lesbian witchcraft predilections."

Clare handled the disclosure in stride. Maybe just another in a series of disclosures. Buzz, who'd been puzzling over the reincarnation comment, jerked his head as if something had shorted out. Curiosity overcame Glenda and she timidly picked up Moon or Sixpence—I couldn't tell which—and looked inside. When a big pincher came out, she gave a little scream and dropped the shell on the table. Celeste came fussing to its aid.

"The little monster attacked me," Glenda said, and her mouth puckered like a sphincter.

Celeste clouded up. Before her emotions could get the better of her, some protective instinct prompted me to intervene. "I wonder, Celeste, if you've found a carving in your room?"

She blinked. "Well, yes. It's a big grasshopper, actually. Green and shiny. Not the kind of thing you'd expect from father."

"He's made a carving for Blake and Rooks also," I said.

Glenda's gaze rose above her half-glasses and her pucker tightened, as if to whistle.

"May I see it?" I asked, thinking perhaps she'd spill some useful information in private.

She led me upstairs and we examined the sleek grasshopper-like creature, rendered in fine detail in green serpentine. "It's really a katydid," Celeste remarked. "We have them in Sedona. You're quite sure this is for me? Whatever made him think I'd want a bug? What did the others get?"

I told her about Rooks' osprey and Blake's hands of a draftsman.

"I'm afraid papa doesn't know any of us very well. He's never bothered to find out who we've become. I think he's the most self-centered person on the planet."

"I have to warn you, I'm collecting information for your father's biography."

"So I've heard." She rotated her mouth comically until it stood nearly vertical. "Rooks thinks papa has an unhealthy attraction to you."

I smiled in disbelief. "Does he have a history of unhealthy attractions?"

Celeste gave a watery laugh. "Maybe Rooks is right, that we should be careful around you. But no, he does not have a history. In fact, he despises Rodin for his... appetites. Rodin would have been a much greater sculptor had he not dissipated himself on a daily, sometimes hourly, basis. I at least respect my father for that."

"I wonder if Anton carved a gift for his brother."

My prompting worked, as Celeste immediately said, "Let's find out, shall we?" We crossed the hall into Buzzy's and Glenda's room. I used the opportunity to look about, seeing their clothes neatly hung, personal items in order on the vanity, a bag of golf clubs by the door. And indeed a sculpture—this time a bronze head. Even before Celeste said anything, I recognized the subject as Buzz himself, but as a young man with an infectious smile, every line on his face depicting a devil-may-care scamp. He wore a collarless baseball uniform.

"It's a casting of a clay head daddy made a long time ago. It's hard to imagine Uncle Buzzy ever being that happy."

As I helped Clare in the kitchen, Nathan and Anton wheeled in the canvas-covered thing on a hand truck. They hefted it to an end table in the foyer and fiddled with it for a while, leaving the cover on. When done, Nathan washed in the utility sink off the kitchen and combed wood shavings out of his long black hair. Swiped a string bean out of the steamer. The aromatic smell of cedar hung on his jeans and hickory shirt, and mingled with the smells of fresh bread, corn, squash, onions, and black pepper.

"I'll serve some of your wonderful smoked salmon as an appetizer, Nathan, if you don't mind," Clare said.

"Suit yourself, but I'll have to take a day off pretty soon and smoke more."

"Mmm, I suppose. By the way, I don't think the dinner table's big enough to fit you in tonight, Nathan. That is, unless somebody adds a leaf."

"I suppose I better do it then, if I'm going to get fed."

"How thoughtful of you."

I helped Nathan install two leaves in the table. No one else could hear, so I asked about the trap he and Anton had set. "I learned it from my grandfather. He used to catch otters." Beyond that, he wouldn't elaborate. We set the table and Clare called everyone to supper. Court grabbed the chair next to mine, eager to tell how Uncle

Blake had let him drive the four-wheeler. Curiously, a red rosebud had been placed across the plate.

"Don't sit there," Rooks said.

"Why not?" Court's shoulders slumped. Though he looked beaten down, his jaw was set in defiance.

"Because when the family is together, your grandmother sets a place for your uncle David, who died when he was just a little older than you."

"We call it the missing man formation," Blake said dryly.

Anton scowled, but said nothing.

Clare brought a slab of Nathan's alder-smoked salmon, batted away hands that reached out to pick at it, then lugged out an enormous crock of clam chowder, thick as stew. She made a point of saying I'd made the salad and cornbread, making me feel less out-of-place at their reunion dinner.

Clare asked Buzzy to say grace, and he recited the bless-us-o-Lord thing. Anton didn't close his eyes or bow his head—I knew because I didn't either. After the amens, everyone passed their plates to Blake for salmon. Except Celeste.

"I don't eat flesh," she said, hands over her plate.

"Even fish?" Blake asked.

"Meat is murder!" Celeste passed on the clam chowder as well, and took only small portions of salad and bread. She trimmed a lettuce leaf to a size that pleased her and collected a few bits of vegetable, pear, and walnut in the center, rolled it into a pellet and placed it in her mouth.

Blake asked Nathan how the longhouse was coming. They looked about the same age and seemed to get along well.

"I got the roof on and most of the siding. There's the floor and the fire pit left."

"But why are you building a longhouse?" Celeste asked.

"It's a long story," Eugene Gobi said, smiling at his pun.

"I'd like to hear it," Charles said. In the short time he and Rooks had been here, he'd visibly mellowed from the tense surgeon to something nearly human. Islands do that to people. Another week and he'd be wearing cutoffs and chewing on a stalk of grass.

Nathan's eyes defocused. "Many generations ago this island became a ceremonial ground for the Nootka nations. It began with a canoe of Bella Bella warriors heading south to attack another tribe and take slaves. A storm swamped their boat, and forced them ashore here. The lead warrior, Crooked Hoop, was drawn to a place where the rock drops off to deep waters." Nathan pointed toward the point beyond the boathouse. "There he prayed for a sign their raid would be successful. The storm lasted five days, and for five days Crooked Hoop fasted and waited for a vision. A song came to him and as he sang it, an old bull orca with a bent dorsal swam up and spoke. The whale said, 'Do you see how my people, like your own people, live in many tribes? And we all hunt the salmon. The Great Spirit has given enough salmon for all the water people and the two-legged people and the four-legged people.' By four-legged people he meant the bears."

Nathan had a smoky voice, well suited to story telling. "The orca with the bent fin then told Crooked Hoop, 'My tribes are many, and our history stretches from the beginning of time, yet no legend speaks of warfare between us. And no tribe has ever made slaves of another. At the moon of the red fish, when all my tribes gather, it is a time of sharing and celebration.' Crooked Hoop then saw a vision of many canoes and campfires and a longhouse with many chiefs. None of the chiefs bore weapons, in honor of the spirit whale."

I looked at the brick-colored salmon on the table, and wondered about its power to draw people together.

"After his vision, Crooked Hoop could no longer keep war in his heart, and when good weather returned, he turned his war party back. He told others of his vision, and because of its power, in time it came to pass. After Crooked Hoop dropped his body and returned to spirit, many have seen him in sweat lodge visions, sometimes as a young man, sometimes old, as he lived to be very wrinkled, but he always wears a robe of black and white to honor the orca. So when the red fish had all been smoked and the first frost came, the leaders of many tribes came to this island to trade and make alliances and give offerings to the orcas for showing them the right spirit of living."

Nathan looked at Celeste, who seemed enraptured.

"That's why I'm rebuilding the longhouse, to restore what's been taken away and to remember what's been forgotten. Crooked Hoop has given this island to all tribes, including the Europeans. Visions leave their power on a place and make it forever sacred. No law, no government, no piece of paper can change that."

Clare sighed. "That's a beautiful story. I've never heard you tell it quite like that."

"This is a special night," he said.

Part of me wanted to buy the story, but I decided to file it under parables, wondering if Nathan told it to invoke a healing medicine over the family. "What happened to the original longhouse?" I asked.

Nathan sighed. "In one century, European diseases—smallpox,

flu, measles—killed four out of every five coastal Indians. The tribes formed secret societies to figure out what to do. Sometimes, the delegates met here on this island. The soldiers came to burn down the longhouse and break up the meetings."

Glenda asked, "How did you get the name 'Half Moon'?"

"*Weeping* Moon," Nathan said. "I made it up—do you like it?" He laughed. "I wanted a traditional name."

"That's the way it is with Indians," Buzz said. "They change their history when it suits them. Nobody ever writes it down. That's so they can change it. Especially if they want a particular piece of real estate, then someone remembers a story about sacred ground."

Glenda blushed. "I'm sure Nathan didn't mean it that way. He was just giving us some history."

Anton laughed heartily. "Of course that's what he meant. He wants this island—and he may jolly well get it. I'm considering adopting him!" Anton laughed even harder. "I appreciate a lad who can tell a good story, especially when it gets better every time."

All of us laughed, Nathan included.

"I think it's time to toast our reunion," Clare said, raising her water glass.

"Mom," Rooks said disapprovingly. "Let's do it right. I brought some champagne from our trip to South Africa." She sent Charles after a chilled magnum and Rooks asked her father to do the honors. Clare distributed goblets from the breakfront while Anton twisted the wire and bounced the cork off the ceiling.

Clare made the first toast, thanking God for bringing the family together. Celeste toasted Anton's birthday in advance. Blake toasted Crooked Hoop. When it appeared we could resume eating, Eugene Gobi hoisted one to himself. "Having drunk to both the mortal and the immortal—I won't say who falls in each category—I risk the wrath of the latter for my hubris. My agent assures me the box office success of *The Sirens of Tunis* all but guarantees my score will be nominated for,"—dramatic pause—"an Academy Award!"

We congratulated him and sipped our champagne. "Let's hope this one pans out," Anton said, resuming his supper. Gobi seemed a bit crestfallen at the lack of fuss over his announcement. Though an agent's assurance didn't sew up a nomination, it still seemed worth a toast. Charles stood to refill our depleted chowder bowls. "I think this clam is still in the shell," he remarked when something thunked as he emptied the ladle into Court's bowl. "My compliments to the cooks, by the way. And to the sculptor who has placed such a remarkable piece of work in each of our bedrooms."

Anton cleared his throat. "They're my gifts—yours to take with you."

Rooks clapped her hands in feigned surprise. "We shall treasure it, won't we Charles?"

"So Dad, what's this mysteriously veiled creation?" Blake asked, pointing to the covered object visible in the foyer.

"Another masterpiece, I expect," Gobi said, still sulking.

"All will be revealed Sunday, on my birthday," Anton said.

"Should be quite the soiree," Rooks said. "And what did you find in your room, Beakie?"

"Something quite... odd. A giant insect. A katydid we decided, right Egret?"

"Oh how bizarre, father," Rooks scolded. "A bug?"

Blake said, "Katydids are really very interesting creatures. Did you know the female devours the male during copulation?"

"Hardly in keeping with Beakie's vegetarianism," Rooks said.

Court laughed explosively to show he understood the joke.

Celeste—'Beakie' to her sister—seemed to withdraw into herself. She wrapped another pellet.

"Whoa, check this out," Court said displaying a lump of something in his soupspoon.

"Son, don't play with your food," Rooks said.

"But Mom!" Court dumped the thing on his salad plate. Rooks leaned closer, picked up the thing, which didn't look like any clamshell I'd ever seen, and washed it in her water glass. She squinted at it, drew a gasping breath, then, with a pensive glance at her father, she replaced it on the salad plate and pushed it away.

Even before Anton reacted, I felt a sensor trip in my mind and became keenly alert to what followed. Anton stood suddenly, upsetting his champagne. His face the color of freezer-burnt cod, he pressed his napkin to his mouth as if about to retch, looked around the table accusingly, then fled the house by the front door.

The fragment of sculpted marble on the plate appeared to be the larger portion of a nose. As champagne wicked through the linen, the blood in my veins became too heavy for my heart to pump it, and through the whirl of my thoughts came the understanding that this fragment was the nose struck twenty-one years ago from Anton's award-winning carving of Walt Whitman.

Chapter 11

Until that moment, I hadn't firmly believed Anton's fears were justified.

No one broke the awful silence as we sat around the table. Shocked—except for one of us. One of us was bitter-hearted enough to be drawing some warped and cowardly satisfaction. I wondered how any grudge could remain vital after so many years. What injury could Anton have inflicted to warrant not only the defacing of his masterworks, but this sadistic renewal of his anguish?

Hasty of me, I realized, to ascribe motive and causation; but the thought arrived as a fully-formed conviction, so I accepted it for the moment.

I scanned everyone's reactions, hoping one of the faces would betray its bile, but saw only the right things: concern-corrugated brows, gaping mouths, heads oscillating in disbelief, self-conscious glances at me. Someone had to be more than just a little bit wicked to pull this off. Anton, too, had looked at each face before leaving. Had he seen something I couldn't?

Clare ran out to look for Anton, but returned. He'd disappeared into the dusk. Many hands pitched in to clear the table, dessert forgotten. I followed Eugene Gobi and Charles Underwood to the sitting room, and allowed Gobi to pour me a Cognac. He slipped before the keyboard of the Steinway and softly played a measured progression of chords as if testing the chemistry between them. I watched over his shoulder and sensed he didn't mind—perhaps even welcomed—an audience, no matter how uncultured. Indeed, he began explaining the music to me, even as he played it.

"One of the films I'm scoring is a political thriller. While under tremendous stress due to a world crisis, the President has been seduced by a beautiful woman, who happens to be the Israeli Ambassador. The President learns that Israel has provoked the crisis, and is now torn between love and duty. He climbs to the White House roof and walks there alone, nearly irrational with fatigue. It begins to snow. So I mix the harmonically pleasing chords with the piquant. F-sharp major seventh, C-sharp minor seventh, B-major ninth, F-sharp, back to B-major ninth, diminished G, A-seventh, F-sharp major seventh. I vary the time to suggest the struggle between his conscious mind and his subconscious, which pleads for sleep. And I add a mystic quality—hear?—by substituting the major second for the tonic. The mind resonates with uncertainty. A muted trumpet comes in." He vocally imitated its plaintive line. I couldn't tell whether he was escaping the unpleasantness of dinner, or if he simply lacked any true sympathy for Anton. The music offered an alternative universe that I wanted to fall into, but knew I mustn't. Then Buzz tried tuning in the ball game. Gobi stopped playing, glared, and when that did no good, roughly dropped the fallboard over the keys.

Glenda hovered over her husband, giving advice on which buttons to tweak. Eventually Buzz gave up in frustration and turned the noisy thing off. "Oh Buzzy," she said. "I know how much you wanted to see that game."

"This trip better be worth it," Buzz said.

"I'm sure it will be." She brightened. "Why not try the radio?"

As Buzz fiddled with it, Glenda retrieved her book and reading glasses. Rooks appeared with matching decks of bridge cards, recruiting for a foursome. Charles and Blake quickly agreed, Eugene didn't play bridge, and Rooks looked between Glenda and me. "You'll play, Glenda? Of course you will."

"Well, I suppose," Glenda consented. "If nobody minds. I always seem to wind up at one no-trump or something."

I was just as happy not to be asked. Although I love to compete at practically anything, I wanted to be free to talk to Anton when he returned. I noted that Nathan had slipped away after the Whitman nose was spooned from the chowder, and had not returned.

I studied family photos on the wall, trying to match up the youthful faces with their adult versions. Celeste was easy, her young countenance always appeared shiny as a fire truck. Rooks tended to look poised, sophisticated, and thoroughly bored. I couldn't always distinguish Blake from his younger brother David, now dead. I also kept an ear tuned for any discussion about the incident at the dinner table. I'm sure comments were made, but they were uttered in low voices I couldn't make out.

After some time, Celeste flowed down the stairs, freshly bathed, in a floor-length velour robe, embroidered crenulations at the hems. Midnight blue—perhaps standard witchcraft garb. She joined us in the sitting room, and with everyone else occupied, she asked for my help. From her capacious pockets came Moon and Sixpence, and some curious paraphernalia. She turned the hermit crabs loose to roam under the piano, where presumably they'd be safe from careless feet, though Dinah the cat sniffed at them cautiously. With a distrusting eye on Dinah, Celeste sat on the edge of the sofa and began shaping a piece of foil to conform to the side of her head. She complained that the altitude change from Sedona had given her an unshakable headache. She poked a hole in the foil, then displayed something she called an ear candle and explained my role in the process. She handed me a book of matches and the ear candle—a long, narrow funnel made of wax-impregnated muslin, the small end of which is inserted into the ear. I was to set fire to the other end. She reclined on the sofa, covered the side of her face and hair with the foil, and had me hold the funnel in her ear.

"Your job is to take that little scissors and trim away the ash as the candle burns down."

"What's this thing supposed to do?" I asked, not sure I really wanted to know.

"The smoke circulates and softens things up and creates a mild suction which draws out the wax and the impurities from the Eustachian tube and the sinus cavities. That's what's causing the headache. Of course, that horrible joke at dinner didn't help."

The bridge players seemed more annoyed at Celeste's treatment than interested or concerned. They played in earnest with little discussion other than to dissect each other's bidding and card play after each hand. When smoke from the ear candle drifted their way, Rooks said, "Really, Beakie. Can't you do that in the privacy of your own room? Court, make yourself useful and get your mother a glass of wine."

Celeste turned her head a bit toward Rooks, knocking loose a glowing ash. I batted it away before it landed in her hair. "Beakie?" I asked Celeste. "A term of endearment?"

"My former husband's name was Hornbeak. Julian Hornbeak. So she calls me Beakie. He spoke thirteen languages, including two dead ones. He had our marriage annulled when I told him I wouldn't bear his child. I couldn't, in good conscience, bring a child onto this doomed planet."

"Really," Rooks admonished, "we needn't trot *all* our family skeletons out."

Blake glanced toward me. "I'm sure Dad wouldn't want a dull bio." He sorted a new hand of cards. "He couldn't stand dying if he thought no one would notice."

"Pass," Rooks said. "Then why did he abandon civilization for this bitty island at the end of the Earth? When I tell people who my father is, they don't recognize the name anymore."

"Oh, that must be so hard on you, glamour puss," Blake said.

"Sit on it!"

I was growing weary of tending the smelly ear candle. At this rate I wouldn't have the material for a news article, much less a biography. My attention fell on a piece of carved marble on the end table—a study of old hands kneading bread dough. I found the carving somewhat stiff and awkward, and the polished surfaces were marred in places, perhaps by errant chisel blows. I asked Celeste if it was one of Anton's early works.

"*The Breadmaker*? Heavens no. That's father's prize possession. You see, our brother David carved it when he was only twelve and gave it to Dad for Christmas."

I thought about the rose on the dinner plate.

"Ahhhhh!"

I looked down to see an ash sizzling in Celeste's hair. I licked my fingers and quickly picked the ember out, fanned away the burnt-hair stench. She had so much of the unruly stuff nobody would see those little melted globs. "Sorry," I said. "No harm done."

Celeste wasn't so easily consoled and grumbled rather a lot. So I turned the job over to Court. I certainly didn't care to stick around to see what, if anything, got sucked out of her head. Clare had ascended the stairs earlier so I went up to her room and found her rummaging through some drawers in a private study off their bedroom. She welcomed me in.

"I'm gathering all our photo albums. I thought it'd be nice to set them out. You're welcome to look through them." Clare seemed to be functioning on automatic pilot, shocked at the cruelty within her family, or ashamed that an outsider should be privy to it—an outsider who could be expected to put it in writing.

I wanted her to understand I'd do my best to expose the person threatening Anton's art. But then, maybe she didn't really want to know, didn't want to believe one of them capable of such a horror. "Yes, I'd like to see them," I said. "Clare, do you think Anton is okay?"

She shook her head no. "How can any of us be okay?"

"What can I do?"

Clare smiled sweetly. I could tell it took some effort. "Anton is a great man. When you tell his story, look for the greatness in him."

"Great men aren't always easy to live with."

"Neither are losers."

I conceded the point with a smile, then asked, "Who's doing this terrible thing, Clare?" I didn't expect her to tell me, but I thought if she knew—or suspected—I'd be able to tell.

Her eyes became watery and she shook her head.

I put my hand on the stack of albums. "Are there photos of the party the night the statues were damaged?"

"Blake shot some home movies that night. It's been years since we've looked at any of those old films. Some things are too painful to remember."

"Like your son, David?"

She dabbed at her eyes with a tissue kept in her sleeve. "I've never gotten over that bruised feeling in my heart, and the joy of life has never fully returned."

My blood sank to my extremities, rooted my feet to the floor, made me lightheaded, unbalanced. Clare, I knew, would understand those days when I felt trapped in a wickedly barbed bramble that twined about me and kept me from doing anything useful, even the laundry. Only work, endless work, and a few friends, could keep the brambles away. Clare's grief made my own, at losing a son, feel less neurotic. It had been such a long time ago, and she still had three children.

"David's carving of the *Breadmaker*—quite impressive for such a young boy," I said, still trying to regain my equilibrium.

"Oh yes. All of the children had talents in one area or another. But David's talent came from his father and that made it special to Anton."

I looked through an album until I found a picture of David. He was a plucky-looking kid, muscular, shaggy hair.

"We lost him the summer after he carved the *Breadmaker*, drowned in the creek at my parent's cabin." A door opened and closed downstairs. Clare went to the head of the stairs to see if Anton had returned. I followed with the photo albums.

As we descended, Anton came from the dining room with a large drink in hand. "Get yourself something if you want," he said in passing. He stalked into the sitting room and snarled at Court to get out of his chair. "Play something, Gene," he said to Gobi. "Anything. Scriabin."

When the music began, Buzz jerked the cord on the radio and headed out. Glenda jumped up from the bridge table to tag after him. "Who's winning, dear?"

"Braves are down four to one in the seventh."

"Oh. They'll get back in it, I'm sure."

"I'm going up to the room. Too much racket down here."

"Braves fan?" I asked Glenda when Buzz had disappeared up the stairs.

"Oh, *fanatical.*" She leaned close, harfing beer-breath on me. "There's more players on the Braves that he can, uh, identify with." She covered her round mouth as though she'd let something slip. The back of her hand was spotted as a trout. When Clare passed near, Glenda asked her to sit in at the bridge table for a hand or two. "I need my evening cigarette. Such a filthy habit; I've been trying to cut down."

I said I could use some air and asked Glenda if I might join her. She seemed pleased. Under the harsh porch light her complexion looked slaggy, troweled on. Somewhere a bullfrog croaked. Glenda lit a Salem and I asked her how she liked Sioux Falls.

"I was raised in Los Angeles," she said, as if that explained everything.

"The winters are hard to take?" I guessed.

"The winters, everything. We have friends in LA, including some of Buzzy's former teammates. Names you'd recognize." She named them and I pretended to recognize. "Two of my sisters live there, and some friends from school. But we gave up any thought of living in gentility when our fortunes reversed." She used the word *gentility* as if she'd read it in a Harlequin novel and had a certain idea of what it meant.

"Los Angeles is genteel living?" I asked. The beer had made her garrulous. I'd learned that word—garrulous—in a book somewhere, and it seemed to apply.

"Buzzy's star was on the rise when I married him, and his team was winning. We had a flashy lifestyle, and thought it would go on forever. Then Buzzy got sent to the minors. The team wanted to bring up some lefty pitching. They told him it would be temporary and he should work on developing another pitch—a slider or a forkball or something. But it wasn't temporary. The rosters were filling up with minorities."

I don't have much stomach for hearing people blame others for their own position in life, so I changed the subject. "How'd he wind up in the hardware business?"

"He started in the off-season to keep us going. When the club let him go, the owner of the hardware store said he wanted to retire and he made us a deal on the inventory."

"Do you have children?"

"Two girls and a boy." She told me what they did. Most mothers would have bragged more, but I got the impression she didn't see much to brag about. I asked Glenda how she spent her time.

"I've got a corner booth at the flea market. There's a big flea market at the fairgrounds. People come from all over. I specialize in carnival glass. And I do a lot of church work, you know, bingo, choir. And I read constantly. I just absorb crime stories and mysteries."

So much for my guess about Harlequins. "Sounds like you've got a full life."

She stared at me, having perhaps picked up the nuance I had a hard time keeping out of my voice: a lack of sympathy for those paralyzed by small losses. I saw my own judgment reflected uncomfortably in her eyes, and I knew it was a flaw I needed to work on.

"Like I say, it's not gentility. But in the old days, we had nothing to apologize for. I told Buzzy on the plane maybe we're being punished." Her voice had an edge I hadn't heard before.

"Punished? For what?"

She blew a jet of smoke to one side as if expelling a ghost. "For flying too high. Thinking we were some kind of DiMaggio and Marilyn."

I nodded, though my most fevered imagining couldn't blend Glenda with Marilyn Monroe. "Hmm. What did Buzzy mean when he said this trip better be worth it?"

Glenda stubbed out the Salem, though it had a good inch of smoking left in it. Her round mouth started to form answers a couple of times. I thought I could smell a lie coming, but she regrouped and trumped with the indignant card.

"The problem with eavesdropping is you get things out of context."

Chapter 12

Anton brooded in his big chair, letting Gobi's music wash over him, occasionally remembering to sip some Bourbon. As he didn't appear to want company, I retired to my room.

There were two brick chimneys rising through my attic apartment. The one next to the bed came from the kitchen stove and was pleasantly warm. The other, nearer the center of the house, probably served the back-to-back fireplaces in the master bedroom and the room occupied by Rooks and Charles. I'd noticed both these upstairs fireplaces had been converted to gas. Sitting on my cot, surrounded by opened photo albums, I wanted to understand what happened twenty-one years ago in Seattle, and wondered if I could piece it together. Perhaps by getting everyone's recollections and examining the movies shot that evening, I could pick up a clue. It would help if I could eliminate some of the family members from suspicion by getting a bead on exactly when the sculptures had been smashed and where all the suspects were. Others had surely done this before me, but until tonight it had been preferable to hope someone outside the family had hammered the statues. Now there seemed no other explanation.

The other half of the attic was used for storage. It's door creaked when I eased it open. My teeth on edge, I stepped in to do a little snooping, smelled mothballs and moldering leather, groped for a light switch, slapped at something crawling on my forehead—just a string dangling from a light bulb. The bulb switched on when I pulled the string. I watched for any movement—rodents, insects, whatever—but saw just the shadow of the swinging light cord. Cobwebs stretched between trunks, boxes, racks of old clothes. I used a coat hanger to clear them away. I checked for bats hanging from the trusses, but there were only a few abandoned wasp's nests and electric wires strung knob to knob. The contents of the attic were well ordered. A row of green pasteboard boxes, mates of the ones Clare had given me that morning, were shelved against the wall. I felt a sense of history, as when I read the old newspapers used to insulate the farmhouse I was raised in. Dust-covered answers to lingering questions. Past those were rows of cardboard cartons marked with red grease pencil. I slid out a bulky box marked *Projector/Movies*. The yellow packing tape, which sealed the box, pulled off easily, as its gum had deteriorated.

The newspaper wadded at the top—a *Seattle Times*—was over twenty years old. I removed the paper, pulled the box under the light bulb, found an 8mm projector in a gray metal case, a machine with two hand-cranked reels used to edit and splice film, a camera in a leather case, a blue metal box, light bar, some empty reels. I opened the blue box. As expected, it contained reels of 8mm film in metal cans, twelve reels in all, plus a half-dozen smaller plastic reels, and three boxes from Kodak, the same size as the small reels. The yellow boxes were addressed to the Gropius' Queen Anne Hill house and had never been unsealed. The film cans were numbered sequentially and labeled with dates and events. Birthdays, Christmases, trips, cabin. Each large reel no doubt comprised several smaller reels spliced together. The most recent label was dated three years before the attack on the sculptures. But the postmarks on the Kodak mailers were *after* the date of the vandalism.

Clare had invited me to go through the photo albums and had mentioned the movies so... Battling my conscience to a draw, I lugged the projector to my room, set it up on my nightstand. I held one of the yellow boxes, realizing that in breaking the seal, I might be violating the family's trust; worse, I'd be tearing a scab off a hideous wound that had never fully healed. The directions on the removable projector housing were easy to follow. I opened the mailer, mounted the reel, and threaded the film. The projector lamp still worked, though the machine clattered so loudly, I feared someone would hear it. I focused the frame on the white wall over the dresser, numbers flickered. I felt a sense of vertigo, as if on the edge of a place where ghosts came to whisper terrible secrets.

The film had indeed been shot during a party, the night Anton had presented Seattle with a statue of Chief Sealth, for whom the city was named. Clare must have been correct in remembering Blake as the cinematographer, as everyone else appeared in one shot or another. I could recognize them easily from having studied their old photos. There were a few jerky seconds of a jocular Anton delivering his remarks, the unveiling, a zoom on the statue, a pan of the applauding guests, and a shot of a string quartet launching into a piece. The screen went white and the tail of the film flicked on the take-up reel.

It had lasted about three minutes. If the other two sealed reels contained footage from the party, that would make a total of nine minutes recorded out of the entire evening. It dawned on me how unlikely it would be to find clues from so little film.

There were other small reels lying loose in the blue box. I looked at their inscriptions: *Reunion, Graduation, Christmas/ Sledding,* and two marked *Cabin.* I threaded one of the latter. It documented a snowball fight in a wooded area next to a cabin. Boys against girls with the girls holding their own until the youngest— David—charged, hurled snowballs, took shots to the body, threw himself into the girls' snow fort, destroying it. He paid the price when the girls—Rooks and Celeste—held him down and buried him in snow. End of reel.

I decided to try the other *Cabin* reel before hitting the rack. This one had been shot in summer. It showed a broad creek dammed with rocks to create a swimming hole, with a gap in the rocks forming a swift-flowing spillway. Short takes showed the kids swinging from a rope with a tire on the end. They would swoop out over the water, let go, and splash into the deep water.

The camera zoomed on someone standing on a bridge just upstream. It was David, hair plastered to his head, arms waving. He climbed over the wooden guardrail, made sure the camera was on him, beat his chest Tarzan-like, and leaped from the bridge. His trunks appeared to snag on something, causing him to twist and fall backward. The camera looked for him in the water. An icy premonition spread outward from my heart, and I found myself clutching the pillow to my chest. When the boy surfaced, he gasped for air, and appeared to have difficulty righting himself in the water. Someone on the tire swing came briefly into view. Seconds later, an arm reached to help as David floated downstream—it must have been the person on the swing. The picture went abruptly black.

I shivered violently as the projector chattered. There was nothing on the rest of the reel. I turned the machine off.

What Clare had said about losing a child was true. It is the worse thing that can happen to a mother. I buried my face in the pillow, and a movie far more vivid than Kodak replayed in my mind.

In the movie imprinted on every cell in my body he runs from the woods, bony knees flashing below his shorts. Screaming, swatting at wasps on his face and legs. I open the screen door and gather him into my arms. He looks through his tears for my protection and I crush wasps with my bare hands. His upper lip is already horribly swollen, and he insists hysterically there are more 'bees' in his hair. I pick through his thick mop, assure him they're gone. He continues to scream and swat at himself. Then I discover he's right: there is another. His last plea unheeded.

I didn't want to look at any more film. I'd been clutching my pillow as if it were a life preserver. I let go and turned back the bedding. My watch said one-thirty; I set it on the nightstand and switched off the light, remembering to open my door partially as Anton had requested. The chimney by the bed had cooled and even with the comforter pulled up around my neck I couldn't get warm.

It took me a long time to find an uneasy sleep, but I must have been out when I heard the piercing wail because I mistook it for an alarm clock. Then I remembered I didn't have an alarm clock. Stiffening with panic, I knew it was a smoke detector. The air smelled like my laundry room after I iron clothes, only worse. I tried to orient myself—how would I get out of the house? I heard footsteps and shouts from the hallway below.

Then I remembered Anton and Nathan's trap. But was it supposed to involve fire?

I slammed into my pants, tucked in my nightshirt, flew down a flight of stairs to post myself there as Anton had requested, to keep track of who was moving about. As I saw no glow of flame, I felt safe for the moment. The hall light came on, a haze of smoke around it. Charles and Anton rushed down the stairs. The alarm stopped. I descended to the ground floor. There, Eugene Gobi and Charles Underwood stood before the shrouded 'sculpture' hauled in earlier that evening, watching the remnants of the canvas shroud smolder. Eugene had apparently beaten the flames out with a throw rug. Anton hurried from the kitchen with a fire extinguisher and gave a burst to the scorched wall paneling. In his boxer shorts, Anton looked fitter than most men twenty years younger; only his gnarly white toes looked their age.

The air seemed to crackle. It could have been the table varnish cooling, or the sound of my nerves.

Buzz showed up, looking bleary-eyed. His hair had thinned in irregular patches, going from black to bald without bothering to gray. His remaining bristles stood out against his scalp like a burnt forest in winter. Celeste appeared, clutching Moon and Sixpence to her bosom. Her sister, Rooks, arrived last, having selected a long red bathrobe with black-trimmed hood, and matching slippers for the occasion.

Someone opened the front door to clear the smoke. Clare brought a garbage can to collect the charred bits of canvas laying about. Although we could see a polished stone pedestal, the sculpture itself stood within a charred wooden frame, still concealed by the remains of the burnt cover. Buzz stepped forward to dismantle the debris. Anton tried to stop him, but too late. I didn't see exactly what happened in the smoky light, but Buzz threw up his arms in surprise. "Christ Almighty!" He reached for his leg, clearly in pain.

Nathan's otter trap.

Someone turned on more lights and Glenda fell to her knees before Buzz. "Oh good gracious. Hold still dear." She tugged at a line wrapped around his leg.

"Owwww!"

Glenda recoiled. "I'm sorry I'm sorry I'm sorry. Does it really hurt that bad?"

Anton reached for a brick used as a weight to spring the trap. A closer look revealed why Buzz was in such discomfort. One tine of a sizable treble fishhook had pierced deeply into his calf.

Charles bounded up the stairs and returned with his medical kit. And his tackle box. He used the wire cutter on his needle nose pliers to nip the tine off the hook. He patiently sterilized the hook, pliers, and area around the wound, then told Buzz to grit his teeth. He pinched Buzz's calf near the wound, and pushed the hook through with the pliers until the barbed end broke through the skin. Charles then grabbed the barb with the pliers and pulled the rest of the hook through.

The others comforted Buzz while Charles dressed the wound. Anton looked at me anxiously to see if I had seen the culprit. I shook my head.

Court was licking his finger and thumb and putting out a few live sparks burning on the edges of the canvas, as he'd seen me do to Celeste's hair.

"Get away from there, Court," Charles said.

"I'm just trying to help."

"That's a royal laugh," Rooks said.

It felt like a fishhook had been jammed through my heart; I could only imagine how it felt to Court. I helped pick burnt canvas bits off the floor, certain that Rooks considered scullery duties to be my rightful role. I paused to examine a line of wax splashed on the hardwood. A stub of red candle lay in the corner, probably knocked there when Eugene beat the flames with the rug. A candle? Puzzlingly, the wax had dripped several inches out from the edge of the table. Quite a lot of wax. I got Court's attention. "Do you suppose you can find any more candles like this? Whole ones."

He dashed off, pleased to have a job. In less than a minute he returned with a mate to the red stub, still in a crystal holder. "I found it in the dining room on that sideboard thing. There's another candle holder that's empty."

"Excellent work, Court," I said. He puffed up.

The new candle was long, perhaps fourteen inches. With it I tried to visualize how someone might have used it to set fire to the canvas. I reasoned a candle could have served as a slow fuse so the arsonist could be in bed when the fire started. By setting the candle at an angle, the flame would work in toward the canvas and eventually set it afire. This would produce more wax drips than a candle burning upright. But I could find nothing used to prop the candle at an angle, until I examined the butt of the burnt candle and found two indentations on opposite sides of the stub, one an inch higher than the other. I massaged my jaw for a moment before noticing the table had a small drawer. I opened it partially and positioned the new candle where, if lit, it would produce drips directly over those on the floor. By now everyone was watching. The indentations the drawer left on the new candle matched those on the stub. We'd found the drawer closed, but Gobi might have nudged it shut when he beat the flames, or Buzz when he grabbed the table after being snagged in Nathan's trap.

Clare surveyed us sternly, hands on hips. "Who did this?"

No one spoke.

Anton stepped forward. "Whoever did it wasted their time." He tore apart the blackened wooden framework that had supported the canvas and concealed the brick, pulley and fish line contraption. The sculpture beneath was not damaged by the fire—could not have been. It was a simple irregular granite slab, engraved on one polished surface. A headstone.

Anton Bosch Gropius
October 7, 1931—
Born a Man,
Died a Sculptor

As the others exchanged glances, I noticed Clare removing a piece of paper taped to the wall, far enough away as to not be damaged by the flames. She hesitated, then tried to conceal it, but Anton had noticed. He took the paper, tried to find the right distance to focus without his reading glasses.

Then his face curdled with fury and he crushed the page in his hands.

Then in a composed, almost nonchalant manner, he unballed the paper and handed it to me. "For your file. One of life's irritating little footnotes."

Chapter 13

I felt the world resume its proper course the moment I entered Anton's studio in the morning. Not because of anything he said—he ignored me. His air hammer rattled as bits of marble flew from the bust he was carving. Anton seemed in his own world behind safety glasses and dust mask, perhaps earplugs as well, though I couldn't tell because of his unruly hair. Coated head to toe with talc-like dust. Here life progressed forward. In this light-saturated studio all things were possible. Let the destroyers sodomize their own souls.

I helped myself to oily coffee from a pot on a hot plate. I didn't mind being ignored; I preferred it. It's what I'd most wanted to do in the first place—watch him sculpt. After some brisk work on the hair, he seemed tuned up to tackle the fine detail on the face. He snapped on a drill head, installed a fine, cone-shaped rasp, hit the bust with a blast of compressed air and studied the face. He'd made considerable progress on it since yesterday afternoon, probably working last evening after fleeing the house. The face had come to life. Somehow he'd found the qualities—the tilt of the head, the angle of the brow, the set of the jaw—suggesting the cocky self-assurance, irreverent wit, and perhaps a temper, that had made her a celebrity as well as a successful investment analyst.

Were I to sculpt, my subjects would probably look as if they belonged on Easter Island. But Anton deciphered the personality—no, the character—as expressed in the hieroglyphs of the face, emphasizing the qualities that interested him without distorting the whole. Impressive, but destined after all for the lobby of a brokerage house, not a museum.

Anton studied the photos of his subject, positioned a magnifying lens before the face, and went to work on an eye. I watched, made notes, forgot my coffee. After a considerable time, Anton pulled back from the stone, laid down his tool, and took a deep breath. I realized that I, too, had been scarcely breathing. He lowered his dust mask and stretched as if his back ached.

"Goddamn. My attention span isn't what it used to be. But it doesn't matter. I've only got one more rock to carve." He pointed to the red-blotched marble I'd first seen in Friday Harbor. "Then it's over. Unless I outlive my money. Stick around a few days and you'll see me wipe the final wisp of marble dust off an Anton Gropius statue."

"Is that what the tombstone is all about?" I asked. "A retirement announcement?"

He rotated his shoulders to loosen them. "No sculptor in history has done any significant work past the age of seventy. I don't want to be the Grandma Moses of marble."

"How do you know when a sculpture is done?" I asked. "Some of your work seems... unfinished, like the draftsman's hands you did for Blake. But it seems the illusion of life is somehow more vivid that way."

Anton tapped his head with a thick forefinger. "The difference between man and the other beasts is that we each have a critic living up here. Every time we say or do something, the critic pipes up with an opinion. My critic is a spoiled child who's become emperor: laughing when I amuse him, yawning when I tell the same story twice. When he finally shuts up, that's when the piece is done." He waited while I made notes. "Clare says my art critic has strangled my social critic."

I unfolded the paper from my pocket—the one he'd given me after the fire. "Speaking of critics..." It was a photocopy of an undated newspaper review by someone named Clement Ely. A vicious review: mangled kinetics... clotted textures... blighted realism in an age of quantum dismemberment... belonging not to the pantheon of Greek and Italian masters, but to the ilk of those who make garden dwarfs.

Anton took a foil pouch from his coveralls and a packet of rolling papers. As he tapped shreds of moist tobacco into a paper, he explained, "Clement Ely wrote for the *Boston Globe* and the *New Yorker*, and was living proof there're more horse's asses in the world than there are horses." He chortled into his beard. "I once created a likeness of him out of fresh cow dung and displayed it in a show he attended. Never was much of a fan of realism."

"Was?"

He tucked in an edge of the rolling paper with a thumbnail grown long, licked the edge, and with a twist of his fingers created a cigarette that looked machine rolled.

"Clement died eating puffer fish in Georgetown." He put the short cigarette in his mouth, lit it with a stick match and blew the flame out with blue smoke that smelled like roofing tar. "Apropos, don't you think, that he should be killed by an expensive venom? I can only hope he paid the check before taking ill."

Anton's mood seemed elevated at the thought of Clement Ely's suffering.

"It's a good story," I said. "Can I use it in the book?"

He cocked an eye, knowing he was being tested. "I'm a sculptor, not a censor."

"When are we going to talk about your life?" I turned on my recorder and set it aside unobtrusively.

"When I'm ready."

His first answer kindled hope we'd proceed with the biography; the next doused me with doubt. I reminded myself that negativity is a losing strategy. "Why did someone post this review on the wall?"

"It hurt me once. Now I'm supposed to be tormented, wondering who hates me. I'm supposed to feel sorry for something I did. But mostly, I'm supposed to be wracked with fear for my sculptures."

Anton spoke matter-of-factly, and I used the same tone. "Are you wracked with fear?"

"No, I'm just pissed off."

"Why?"

"People think I have a great artistic gift. And I do. But they think it's as easy for me to knock off a masterpiece as it is for them to wax the car. They don't understand that every statue is the hardest damn thing I've ever done."

"Creation always looks fun from a distance."

Anton looked mildly surprised at my comment. "Without setting harsh priorities, I couldn't have accomplished a fraction of my life's work."

"Clare told me about your marriage proposal." The stone comes first...

A glimmer of smile straightened Anton lips. "I kept my end of the bargain. Four kids."

"You expected a lot from them, didn't you?"

"Not half what I expected of myself."

"Except maybe David?"

Anton rubbed the bridge of his nose. "If I didn't trust Clare to the death, I'd swear someone else fathered the rest of them. But I knew David was mine. He was *mine*."

I thought Anton might reveal more of his thoughts if I kept quiet, but the silence deepened.

He smoked the cigarette down to where his blunt fingers could barely pluck the butt from his nest of whiskers.

I noticed my fists were tight, relaxed them, and risked the question that needed asking.

"Anton, who's doing it?"

He ground the butt on the floor. "I don't know," he said, emphasizing each word.

"Tell me about Eugene Gobi. You've known him a long time."

"His dad was my dad's lawyer. Gene was what you call a prodigy. He won his first big piano competition at fourteen, and had composed a full concerto by sixteen. Degree from Julliard and all that. One day Isaac Stern's accompanist toppled into the orchestra pit during rehearsal at the Met, ruptured some goddamn thing or other. Gene got the call. With only three days of rehearsal, he pulled it off..." Anton snapped his fingers. "Stern's agent signed Gene and arranged a debut tour of the European capitals. Solo piano. Gene worked sixteen-hour days. School, practicing, composing, playing small venues. His mother worked him like a Mexican mule. By the time she and Gene boarded the plane for London, his nerves had been hammered thin. I hadn't seen him during those years but I hear he struggled with his confidence."

"Something that's never troubled you," I said.

Anton glanced at me sideways. "What the hell have I got to be unconfident about? Anyway, she trundled him off to Europe. Gene's nerves weren't up to it and he blew the Albert Hall performance, and went over the hill. They found him in an abandoned rail car on a siding in Bristol, some tramps taking care of him. His mother took him to a rest home, one of those aristocratic places in the country named Rustling Oaks or something. He missed the Paris concert. To his mother it was unthinkable for Gene not to resume the tour at Amsterdam. But he wasn't ready. The head of the clinic convinced his mom that a session of electroshock therapy would brighten his disposition. So... she approved it."

I wavered as if my strength had drained away. "What happened?"

"Everyone's disposition was sunnier. Until they discovered Gene's entire repertoire had been erased from his brain. Every goddamned note." Anton wiped something from the corner of his eye with a handkerchief. "He never toured again."

The coffee I'd drunk burned like acid in my stomach.

Anton slapped his curled Stetson against his pant leg to knock the dust off. Rings marked where his hat and goggles had been. "Gene's my closest friend. He's made a name for himself in Hollywood, but I only see the movies he brings here on tape. Egret, there's a genius in there trying to get out, and he's never given up trying. That's what I respect about him. But the truth is, he's a studio hack—no, that's too strong a word. His scores are good; they get the job done, but they always sound like something you've heard before. I prefer to remember when his playing was fiery and original. That I won't forget."

"You said he was playing piano the night your statues were wrecked," I said. "You've ruled him out for sure?"

"I... the problem is I can't rule anyone *in*."

"Your brother seems terribly bitter."

"Buzzy thinks the world, including me, owes him something. He could have had Dad's business—Gropius Pyrotechnics—because I had no interest in it. But Buzzy wanted to play ball. A few years in the bush leagues, with Dad bankrolling him so he could have a nice car and spending money. He liked good living, not traveling by bus, staying in cheap dives with the rest of the team. He came up with a pitch he called a *buzzbomb*, something like a screwball, that got him a contract with the Reds. He had four or five good years before they brought in a lefty from Venezuela who knocked Buzzy out of the rotation. He refused to pitch relief." Anton snorted and said, "Big egos run in the family and no bullpen could hold his. So there was a falling out with the owner. Buzzy made some comments that got printed, and before he knew it, no team in the bigs would touch him. He wound up playing out his contract at the Reds' farm club in Sioux Falls—the Canaries. He'd married Glenda a couple years earlier, and they were known for their high living."

Glenda's reference to DiMaggio and Marilyn.

"So he borrowed against his inheritance, expecting teams would come begging, all the while maintaining the highlife as if nothing had happened. When the money ran out, he had to stoop to getting a job. One of Dad's friends was in the hardware business, and Dad set up a franchise store in Sioux Falls for Buzzy. Covered his debt."

Screwballs to screwdrivers. I noted that Glenda had omitted a few details from her version of the story—such as where the money had come from for the business. "He's done all right, it seems. Why the attitude?"

"When our mother died—Dad was already gone—what remained of the estate passed to me. The house on Queen Anne and some income. It gave me a place to work and a chance to devote myself to sculpture without worrying about putting beans on the table. Buzz thought I should have split it down the middle with him, as if he'd never nursed on that teat."

"That explains some of the cracks he's made," I said.

"He's all mouth."

All mouth? I wondered. Maybe words hadn't been enough.

A gust of wind moaned through the eaves and the daylight diminished rather abruptly. I asked Anton if he and Nathan had other plans for exposing the vandal. They didn't. I explained my idea of trying to eliminate suspects by reconstructing the night the statues were smashed, and I mentioned the home movies. He okayed the idea, but didn't sound hopeful. I asked if he'd narrowed down the time when the carvings had been damaged. I'd taken a program from a scrapbook and showed it to him:

PROGRAM

Drinks/Heavy Hors D'Ouvres...*7:00 p.m.*
Dvorak Quartet in F Major, Op. 96 'American'...................*8:00 p.m.*
  Woodrose String Quartet

Mendelssohn Trio in D Minor for Piano and Strings, Op. 49
  Featuring Eugene Gobi

INTERMISSION

Unveiling Ceremony..*10:00 p.m.*
  Chief Sealth, a Sculpture in Marble
  by Anton Gropius

Gobi Sonata for Piano and Cello in A Major ....*10:45 p.m.*
  Eugene Gobi

Beethoven Quartet in C Major, Op. 59 No. 3, "Razumovsky"
  WoodRose String Quartet

Anton studied the program thoughtfully. "Yes, the Dvorak. The one with the folk melodies. I'd forgotten."

"When were the carvings last seen intact?"

He looked away, exhaled deeply.

"Anton... this might not help, but isn't it better than doing nothing? Waiting?" Uneasily, I realized I'd been lecturing him, and felt relieved when he didn't blow up. Perhaps the energy fueling his despotism had its limits.

"Yes," he conceded. "Everything was still okay as of intermission. Guests were still arriving. The mayor came. We routed incoming visitors through the courtyard where the carvings were displayed."

"And who discovered the damage?"

"It was Gobi. He'd gone out for a smoke, as I recall, about a quarter to twelve. Clare had all the departing guests leaving by the front door, so no one went through the courtyard from ten o'clock on."

I scratched a note in my pad. "Did everything stay on schedule?"

"Ask Clare. She wields the baton."

"What time did the family get to bed that night?"

"Late. The police talked to everyone."

"But the red mark on the flagstone, you're sure it wasn't there when everyone went to bed?"

He scraped his thumb over the sharp edge of marble chip. "The police said it wasn't there. I didn't go back after the first time. Never again did I go out there. I saw a photograph of the red mark. When we sold the place, the sculptures were moved to the civic center."

"I hear they did a good restoration."

"Yes, and for the rest of history no one will be able to view them without looking for the cracks, the missing chips, the hammer marks. There's no recovery from tragedy."

"At least Whitman will get his nose back."

"Let them do with Whitman what they please." I heard a passionless anger in his voice. An old, habitual anger, and I realized I shouldn't have tried to make light of it.

I studied the similar scarlet mark, twice the diameter of my own hand, on the big marble block. "This looks more like ink than paint," I said. The color looked absorbed into the stone rather than caked on.

"It's a penetrating dye. See that drill hole? It's permeated almost an inch deep."

"The same stuff that ruined the *Ben Franklin*?"

Anton nodded.

"Where can you get it? What's it used for?"

"We're not sure exactly. The chemical carrier that draws the dye into the stone evaporates quickly. It could be stuff for coloring concrete, and you can get that at any big hardware store."

"Applied with a brush?" I asked.

"Looks that way. It was done in a hurry; you can see the drips and ragged lines. But the strokes are practiced."

"How close is it to the one on the flagstone?"

"Too close for coincidence. The first mark was in red chalk. This one is more stylized, but it's the same shape."

I held out my hand, trying to imitate its limp appearance. I have exceptionally long fingers and I came close. "If it's a hand, it's a left. A right-hander would naturally look at their left for a model, I suppose. You already said Buzz didn't throw southpaw."

Anton seemed more interested in how the failing light fell on his marble than on continuing our conversation. Through the skylights I could see heavy clouds unfurling. Fine drops of rain speckled the glass.

"When can I see your other work? Your new statues?"

He gnarled his brows as if trying to decide how far to humor me. "Sunday," he said. "If you're still here."

I stepped outside Anton's studio into an impending bluster; gusts swirled ahead of a storm front that bruised the southwestern sky. My thoughts were equally unsettled, with Anton's parting comment making me wonder whether I'd overstepped the line. But rather than worry, I'd take my inquiry as far as I could in whatever time I had. Anton hadn't vetoed me snooping further into the original statue bashings, and I was eager to study the three film reels from the party. But as I zipped my jacket I saw Nathan Weeping Moon working at the longhouse, and walked over for a snoop.

The longhouse stretched probably a hundred feet with a shed roof and no windows, lapped cedar planks over a pole framework. An unfinished end was closed with a spread of patched fabric, probably a sun-rotted sail. Nathan drove wedges to split a plank from a twenty-foot cedar log. The outside of the log was stripped of bark and quite weathered, but inside the wood was toffee-colored and aromatic.

"It's old growth," he said. His tank top stretched over the meaty curves of his chest, sweat-damp skin the same color as the cedar. "No knots. You can't get second growth to split this clean." He spoke with a measured cadence, the same way he worked—no wasted effort. "A log float busted loose a long time ago and a bunch of these cedar logs washed up on Gooch Island and we towed them over here. The planks are attached the old way—with twisted cedar twigs."

"What's inside?"

Nathan looked at the longhouse—I had the impression he wanted to make sure I couldn't see anything. "Nothing. Just some wood and stuff."

"Mind if I look?"

He sidestepped to cut me off. "Not a good idea," he said before he could think of something more convincing.

"Okay," I said brightly, and stepped back as if my idle curiosity had passed. "Where was Crooked Hoop's longhouse?"

"Over where the old cannery is. The Army burned it down back when Crazy Horse was a pup. They said it was infested with disease, but the real reason was to break up the secret society meetings."

"Tell me about these secret societies."

Nathan resumed his measured swings against the wedges. "When the tribes acted together, they had too much power. So the Army destroyed the traditional meeting places."

I listened for bitterness in his voice but heard none. "What do you mean they had too much power?"

"In the days when the Europeans came by ship, relations were pretty good. Both sides learned from experience that treachery was bad for business, so a code of honor sort of evolved. But after awhile the tribes figured out they could bargain harder if they stuck together. They understood the ships had to trade. They couldn't haul their trade goods back home, and they had no place to store stuff. The Indians didn't need to trade, so if they didn't like the offer, they took their otter pelts and went home."

"How much was a pelt worth?"

"Oh, at first, the ships could buy one with an ax or a blanket. But later, a prime pelt would bring a lot more. You might get several blankets, a cask of molasses, a bucket of rice, a dozen loaves of bread, and a musket, maybe a pair of shoes. All for one pelt."

"So the secret societies were a price-fixing cartel?"

Nathan shook his head. "No, they were desperate. The diseases the ships brought—the epidemics were wiping out the People."

"So the whites figured the Indians were plotting war, and they sent the Army to burn the longhouse."

"Something like that."

"How did you wind up here, Nathan?"

"It's a long story."

"Do you mind if I turn on the recorder?"

He looked up sharply. "Is everything on the record with you?"

"You seem to have played a significant part in Anton's life since he went into exile. How can I tell his story without understanding yours?"

Nathan tapped the wedges, satisfied with liberating the plank by the inch.

"Okay, it's off the record."

He thought for a moment. "I don't think you give your word lightly."

"I don't."

For a long moment it seemed he'd decided not to tell his story, but then it came out. "When I was nineteen or twenty I got hired by the State Highway Department to work with a patch crew out of Spokane. I had some trouble with a guy on the crew, a smart-ass ranch kid whose old man was a party chairman or something. He thought I ought to be called 'Tonto' or, if he was feeling especially funny, he called me 'Chief Weeping Womb.' Some of the others thought it was funny, too, after he started it. One morning we were fueling our trucks. We started the gas pumps and backed away a little to smoke. Funny Boy started flicking lighted matches toward my truck. He stopped laughing when the fumes from my belly tank caught fire. You pump gas into a tank, it forces fumes out. Well, Funny Boy ran for his life. If I'd had any brains I would have run too, but it was my truck so I turned off the pump and smothered the flame with my jacket. By then Funny Boy was headed back with the crew boss, blaming me for the whole thing."

Nathan pried up the end of a plank; I added my muscle to his and as we bent the plank up it began tearing free from the log. When it popped off, he inspected its uniform thickness.

"I damn near got fired. I should have took my two weeks off without pay and lumped it. Instead I spent the rest of the summer waiting for my chance to get even. One day we hauled some gravel to repair a washout. I drove the most busted-down truck in the whole yard—a gutless old International that you had to double clutch. Funny Boy got upgraded to one of the new Ford six-speed automatics. Well, that day I was the last truck to dump. Funny Boy had to haul his load back to the yard. That's when I got my bright idea. He thought he was the king-shit driver of the crew, so I told him I was going to beat his honky-ass back to the yard by a good five minutes, even driving the International. We had a stretch of curvy road through some hills, and there's one curve in particular where I'd almost lost it one day. I'd been hauling sand and my load started shifting. When my duels came off the ground, I thought it was all over but the crying. I got the thing down, but I learned a lesson about shifting loads. I thought maybe it was time Funny Boy learned, too."

Nathan began putting more of his shoulder beef into the sledge blows for the next plank. "I took off first but he caught up. I ran full out on the straight-aways, but he kept up, even with the load. Into the curves, I knew just how far to push it. Being empty, I knew I could handle the bad place at forty-five. When I got through it, I looked in my mirror. He was streaking after me like a raped ape. For a couple seconds I thought he'd made it. But when a load starts shifting, it goes all at once and the weight swings to one side. His left wheels came up. The guardrail couldn't hold all that weight and the truck must have rolled three or four times before it landed in the river. I put on my brakes then decided I'd better just drive into the shop like nothing had happened. All the way in I thought about seeing the dust clearing, and that truck upside down, half in the water, with those front wheels still spinning. We never bothered with seat belts in them days."

I snugged the last inch of my jacket zipper and crossed my arms. "How was he?" I asked.

"Dead. He was dead."

Nathan needed to regroup before going on. He pried another plank loose with a burst of strength as if not caring whether it broke.

"Did you get blamed?"

"No. Funny, huh? First time in my life I *didn't* get blamed. But I didn't know what to do. It never even occurred to me he might get hurt bad or die. I started drinking pretty steady, came back out here and did some fishing. But I couldn't shake it. Then my cousin told me about a tribal elder, Wounded Head, who helped him once with some good advice. So I took a gift of tobacco and groceries and went to see him."

"What did he say?"

"He said that for such a serious thing, only a vision could give me the answer. He told me the things I must do to purify myself and I did them. He told me where to look for certain things, medicine and sacred objects and I went to find them. I spent a month in the fjords up north looking for a rare fern. The root has healing properties. When everything was done, I came to this island as the old man instructed, and built a sweat lodge. For three days I fasted and purified myself in the sweat lodge and ate a paste made from the fern root. But I had no vision. I went back to the old man and told him I had no vision. He asked if I'd noticed anything strange during that time. I said, 'Well, yes, there was something a little strange.'"

Nathan stopped working and searched my eyes. After a long pause, he said, "Wounded Head says it weakens an experience to talk about it."

"Then maybe you shouldn't." I knew he wanted to tell it at least as much as I wanted to hear it.

"But he also said I would know when it's all right to speak of these things. Maybe my story has the power to heal others in some way. It wants to go somewhere, and maybe you will help it to find its place."

The cedar planks and the cold mist beading my face and

Nathan's talk of power drew me into a past that seemed near enough to touch, into a comforting feeling of closeness to one's shelter and food and land, into a disorienting world where symbolism dwells within events.

"I told Wounded Head, 'Father, when I went to bathe in the sea after a sweat, I saw an old gray whale with many barnacles on his back washed up on the shore. I looked in his eye and touched him, and I knew he was tired of being a whale. But I told him he must be a whale and return to the water. I told him I would care for him until the tide returned, but then he must swim away. I carried water to keep his skin wet, especially his eyes and blowhole. Seven white swans flew over in a V from the north. When the tide came in, the whale returned to the sea.' I asked Wounded Head, 'Does this mean something?'

"He smoked for a long time and then told me the meaning of the whale and the swans. He said, 'You are responsible for taking a white man's life, therefore you must give your life to a white man who is in bad trouble until the snow flies seven times.'

"I thought about this, and asked, 'But which white man? Do you mean the family of the one I killed?'

"He said, 'They are all of one family. Do you not know of one who needs help?'

"I said, 'There is a white man who has come to Thunderhead Island. I think he might be in trouble.'"

Nathan propped a hand on his hip, just above his bone-handled knife. His brown eyes challenged me to understand.

"Anton," I said.

He nodded.

"It doesn't snow here very often."

Nathan smiled. "It took eleven years for the snow to fly seven times."

"Yet you continue to serve?"

"No, I don't serve. My time is up." He paused to give me a chance to work it out, then explained, his pockmarked cheeks puffing when he smiled, "Now he serves me."

"Anton?" I didn't get it. The idea of Anton serving anyone seemed ludicrous.

Nathan's enigmatic smile declared he did not intend to make it any clearer. Perhaps he'd already said more than Anton would have approved of. He read the sky in a glance as we felt the first serious drops of rain. "I need to get my tools in. Take cover in my shack if you want."

"I think I can make it back to the house."

I hurried along the southern path because, though longer, it would take about the same time and I didn't want to risk being cooked by lightning on the shortcut over the ridge. But I'd gone only part way when I heard a sound like a waterfall. Where the storm advanced over the sea, hail pummeled the water, raising a band of froth two feet high. I watched for a full minute, holding back the sensible urge to find shelter.

Then an idea came.

I turned and saw Nathan running in a short-legged gait toward his cabin. I began hoofing it back toward the longhouse.

By the time I'd made it, marble-sized hailstones were tattooing my back. The rain and hail fell so heavily that Nathan's cabin became an outline in the gray.

I fumbled with a tie-down on the tarpaulin covering the unfinished end of the longhouse, then ducked inside as the hailstones became painfully large.

I caught my breath, and let my eyes adjust to the dark. The freshly split cedar, strong as incense, mixed with the wormy smell of earth. Hail battering the shake roof made me think of being inside my boss's typewriter. My eyes strained to make do with what light passed through the canvas and through an open-sided cupola in the roof—a place for fire smoke to escape.

From Nathan's refusal to let me inside, there had to be something here worth seeing.

Then, in a flash of lightning, I saw a massive upright figure clad in a shroud and felt a prickle of vestigial fear. Silliness. I searched the mesh pocket of my paddling jacket for waterproof matches but found only my three emergency flares. They were the kind that launched into the air, so I gave up on the fire idea. I couldn't raise the canvas wall for more light, as the brunt of the weather pummeled it.

Another lightning flash illuminated a totem pole, three feet in diameter, lying prone on blocks before me. A pop-eyed face with a long beak stared back at me.

Tympani rolls of thunder resonated in my chest. The hail redoubled its fury; wind snapped the canvas in and out. Then ragged bursts of lightning illuminated the length of the totem pole, and the spectral upright object that loomed beyond it. As the thunder rumbled menacingly, an after-image of the object persisted.

Wrapped in what may have been sailcloth, it shifted and billowed with disturbed air, and I imagined some primitive force stirring under that shroud, a lightning strike away from taking on monstrous life.

But the lightning didn't repeat and the object, twice my height, remained a ghostly glow at the far end of the longhouse. The hail also passed, but the rain continued. I wanted to investigate the sculpture—for what else could it be?—but I recalled the painful trap Nathan had set earlier and decided to keep my distance.

When the pelting abated, I resumed my walk toward the house. Patches of rain strafed the nearby islands and a glowing light found thin spots in the clouds, painting the landscape in ever-changing strokes of amber, indigo, smoky green.

I wanted nothing more than to get a flashlight and return to the longhouse and tear the wrapper off that new carving by Anton Gropius.

I went in the kitchen entrance. Clare helped me peel off my soaked clothes in the mudroom, and she threw them in the dryer as I shivered in a towel. Blake stood over the sink cleaning geoducks while Celeste scraped guts from a pumpkin.

When I caught Blake sneaking a peak at me, he quickly averted his eyes. But he knew I'd caught him so he looked back, holding up a prize geoduck—an enormous clam that wears its shell as an obese Shriner wears a vest.

Clare gave me a terrycloth robe to wear while my things dried. I hurried up to my attic room to change into my extra clothes—not stylish, but dry—and re-plait my hair. There, hanging on my door, I found a pair of gabardine slacks, cashmere sweater, and a thick pair of socks.

A note pinned to the sweater said:

> *Egret,*
> *Thought you might appreciate a change of clothes.*
> —*Rooks*

Chapter 14

Rooks' clothes fit well enough, though without a pair of mirrors, I couldn't tell if certain less-than-flattering curves showed too much. I felt grateful just to have something clean and dry and not made for camping. A few minutes preening and I went downstairs. At the foot of the stairs, I overheard Eugene Gobi complaining petulantly over the radiophone to someone I deduced was in Hollywood. Something about composers being paid worst and paid last. I looked for Rooks to thank her for the clothes. In the sitting room, Buzz racked up fortunes on his hand-held poker machine while his wife Glenda read a crime novel— a different book than yesterday's. But no Rooks. In the kitchen, Celeste incised the face of an imp onto her pumpkin, while the hermit crabs—Moon and Sixpence—grazed on stringy bits of pumpkin innards. Clare thumped the geoduck steaks tender with a serrated mallet. The mallet had yellow tape around the base of the handle, same as the hammers in Anton's studio.

Blake looked up at me from the food-crusted pages of a *Joy of Cooking*. "I almost didn't recognize you in clothes," he said.

I scowled out of general principle and explained where they'd come from.

"Hmmm. Something wrong with them?" He inspected the outfit. "Button loose? Moth hole? Wrinkle? Speck of dirt?"

"She's just being kind," I said.

"She'll regret it when she finds out you look better in her pants than she does."

"You've been cooped up on an island too long," I said. He met my accusing stare full on and I felt a warmth pass through me. "Don't tell me that you're cooking dinner," I said hastily, breaking eye contact.

He tapped a finger on the cookbook. "Would you believe there's nothing about preparing geoduck in this thing—though there is a bit about hermit crabs." He spoke loud enough so Celeste could hear. "Page three-seventy-one: 'Tiny hermit crabs are found in vacated univalve shells and respond to deep-fat frying and sautéing, but not to being eaten raw.'"

Celeste reddened. "Liar! You're disgusting."

"I bet you say that to all the guys."

Celeste looked at her brother as if puzzling out the real meaning of his comment. Before she could react, the lights blinked out and the clothes dryer groaned to a stop. Only the fading daylight remained, and the blue flames of the stove burners. Clare didn't seem fazed. "It's the generator. Probably out of fuel." She tried to raise Anton on a walkie-talkie, at the same time telling Blake where to find the kerosene lamps.

Buzz rushed to the kitchen with Glenda on his heels. "What the hell," he said, his enormous forehead an expanse of pleats. "What happened to the lights? Game six is on in another forty-five minutes. If I'd of known this was a foreign country, I would of told Anton to stuff his lousy birthday."

Glenda soothed Buzz with petting motions. With her smallish head and ample flanks, she looked pigeon-like. "Dear, we're here and we have to make the best of it. If I could just twitch my nose and have us back in Sioux Falls, I would." She tried it but the population of Sioux Falls remained the same.

"Anton must not have his ears on," Clare said, bumping the walkie-talkie with the heel of her hand. "Or the storm, maybe. Buzzy, you must know a thing or two about generators."

Buzz frowned. "I'm a businessman, not a mechanic."

"No matter," Clare said. "We've got kerosene and propane and wood heat and we're not likely to starve."

Buzz stomped out with Glenda a pace behind, saying, "At least it's not the World Series."

Celeste rolled her eyes and shook her filleting knife menacingly toward them. Probably trying to think of some lesbian-witchcraft incantation.

While Blake lit a lamp, I asked nobody in particular if Charles had caught any fish, and learned we'd be having ling cod and snapper with our geoducks—except for Celeste, of course, who would be having miso soup with garden vegetables. Blake folded a white napkin into a tent and set it on a geoduck. "A special dish just for Buzz: Ku Klux Clam."

Clare tried the walkie-talkie again, raised Anton, and told him about the generator. A half-hour later, with darkness fallen and dinner nearly ready, the power had not come on. We heard Anton and Nathan approaching the house. Blake had opened the windows to vent the lamp fumes, and we could hear them bantering loudly.

"You ought to put that frigging Hercules generator on a chain," Nathan said. "All it's good for is an anchor."

"It'd run like a sewing machine if it wasn't for that cut rate diesel I buy from your uncle. Full of Indian piss."

"You gets what you pays for. If you didn't spend nickels like they were manhole covers..."

Anton roared back, "Nathan, if you had ten bucks to your name, which you don't, you'd spend the first five on a grunt and the rest on penicillin."

"Money well spent compared to Uncle's diesel fuel."

They burst into the mudroom in high spirits, and had started pulling their boots off when they both were frozen by a stern look from Clare.

Anton removed his hat and exchanged sheepish grins with Nathan. "Mr. Weeping Moon believes there might be water in the fuel. We'll check it after supper."

Buzz returned to the kitchen, Glenda still in tow, and tapped at his watch at Anton. "My game's already started."

Anton steepled his eyebrows. "Life is for playing, Buzzy, not spectating. You used to know that."

Rigor mortis couldn't have made Buzz any stiffer. Glenda tried to disarm the tension with a little humor. "You have to understand, sports is a religion with Buzzy, and the Stations of the Cross are ESPN and FOX and NBC." She gave a mousy little laugh.

Anton put his hat back on. "Well, me and Nathan will go take a quick look at that generator. And don't throw those fish heads out. Nathan's favorite part. You know, sharks won't eat the head of a cod, and by the time the heads float to shore they're just about ripe enough for him."

"No you don't," Clare said. "Supper's ready now. Nathan, off with those boots."

He stood on one leg and wrenched off a cowboy boot. "Lucky for us you white guys destroyed the salmon runs. We'd still be savages, instead of getting diabetes and heart-disease at McDonalds."

Buzz made some noises about taking the boat into town to watch the game at a bar, but Anton dismissed the idea. "I'm not risking my boat in a gale."

I, too, regretted the power outage, as I'd planned to study film that evening. Then I had an idea. It would mean exposing my interest in the films to Blake, but Anton had made it clear to everyone I'd be doing research. So after supper I asked Blake for help in rigging a flashlight to the film editor. Ordinarily it worked with a small electric light. The reels cranked by hand. He said a flashlight wouldn't be bright enough, but had a thought. When I'd hauled the films and editor to his barn room, I found him tinkering with a tarnished brass lamp. A carbide lamp, he explained, left from the days of the cannery. He added fresh pellets of carbide from a can, added water to a reservoir, and polished the reflector. He moved a stiff lever and struck a match. The gas jet lit with a pop, producing a fine white light, much brighter than a flashlight. By angling a mirror under the film editor, we were able to cast a workable image on the viewing screen.

While I went to work on the films, Blake started a fire in the barrel stove and put a kettle of water on. He arranged some pillows against the headboard of his bed, got comfortable, and began sketching in a notebook.

"You don't have to stick around on my account," I said.

"I've had enough family for one day. Besides, mother needs the encouragement."

"Oh?" I asked.

"I don't want her to think I'm disinterested in women. She's not at all happy about having only one grandchild. Celeste is hopeless and Charles is out of commission. Dad feels he did his bit by whelping four kids, now it's our turn. So, they watch my personal life with crossed fingers." Blake didn't look up from his sketchpad. The tip of his tongue emerged like the siphon of a clam.

"You've never married?"

"It hasn't been practical."

"What's practicality got to do with it?"

He shrugged. "I went with a girl—Ann—for almost twelve years. But I didn't even have an apartment most of the time. Just a pickup truck and a storage locker. I met her in Mongolia, so she was no Barbie doll. But she opened a physical therapy clinic and married a psychologist and they spend a fortune on wine and talk about socialism and live in a place full of carvings from Tanzania and penis gourds from Irian Jaya. Despite that, I enjoy the guy—he's got a streak of wildness in him. What about you?"

My domestic life was a sore subject, but I'd raised the topic. "I don't know if I'm married or not," I admitted. "I want to be, but John is a practicing anarchist."

"What does that mean?"

"No rules; no expectations. My idea of a charming guy, actually. But, inevitably I suppose, he decided marriage is both these things and off he went to study philosophy under some goateed professor at Duke." Then, before I could do anything about it, my face tightened. "Maybe it would have been different if our son had lived." Blake asked, and I told him about how it took ten wasp stings per pound of body weight to kill the average person. "But if you're allergic..." I squeegeed some tears with my fingertips.

I was glad Blake didn't say how sorry he was. We remained silent for a while, looking somewhere other than at each other. Then, at each other.

I couldn't think of anything to say. Just then the kettle coughed water out the spout, raising a steam cloud off the stovetop. Blake moved it to a cooler part of the stove, and spooned coffee into a filter.

"You really think Anton wants grandkids? He doesn't seem close to Court."

"Court's hard to warm up to. I think Dad always enjoyed us kids when we were little. He just doesn't like what we've grown into. Now, in his advanced years, I think he'd love to have grandchildren huddled at his feet, absorbing his hard-won wisdom. If David had lived, he would have made up for the rest of us, I'm sure."

"What hard-won wisdom?"

"We've all got some, don't we? He believes in work. If you don't go to work every day, you're a bum."

I felt the pain in Blake's comment.

He gave a quick, self-conscious smile. "You can quote that in the biography."

"This isn't easy," I said, "the biography. It seems very important to him, how he's remembered."

Boiling water released a singed aroma from the coffee grounds. "Historical recognition is Dad's way of excusing his failure to discover something greater than art."

"Has your mother found something greater?"

"Maybe. Dad always pokes at her spiritual beliefs, though I think he ultimately respects them."

"Who do you side with?" Blake gave me coffee and, as I blew on it, I had second thoughts about asking, as it would be fair game for Blake to reverse the question. And I didn't know how to answer.

He laughed it off. "I'd live the same whether I believed in eternity or not. Mom says if you live fully in the present, the future takes care of itself. It seems to work." He arched a dense eyebrow at me. "Living in the present includes appreciating beauty wherever I find it."

Before I could blush, there were footsteps on the barn stairs. Court came in without knocking.

"We're going to be busy in here for a while, Court," Blake said. "How about finding something at the house to do?"

"They're playing cards again, Uncle Blake. They don't even want me watching. Mother says I swallow too loud." Court stuck his nose in front of the film editor and began turning the crank. "Whatcha doing? Hey, are we going to kayak around the island tomorrow?"

I made some half-promises to Court, pulled the Sherlock Holmes off the shelf, and pointed him back toward the house to read it. With hanging head, he trudged down the stairs, and carelessly dropped the heavy book. It must have seemed just another adult tactic to get rid of him, and he was right. I felt icy-hearted.

Nevertheless, I went to work, running all three of the short films through the editor to put them in chronological order. The earliest showed a buffet table with its splendid array of hors d'oeuvres. Shots of Clare taking wraps from guests, strictly black-tie. The second film included shots of the string quartet sawing vigorously and Anton slapping backs and laughing, always conscious of the camera. The third reel recorded the unveiling ceremony. I planned to go through each reel again, frame-by-frame if need be, for clues.

Blake fed the fire and paused to look over my shoulder. "The party," he said in a tone so flat he might have used it to recall a funeral. "None of us has any stomach for watching these old movies. When you shoot them, you think you're creating an heirloom. A time capsule. Something to be nostalgic about in our dotage. Nobody thought the movies would capture our tragedies, too. You know, not all of us think you should be looking at them."

"Oh? I've only mentioned it to Anton. He approved it."

"He must have told Mom, because she brought it up. Celeste came unglued. Family privacy and all that. Rooks too. They don't want others passing judgment on us."

"What did you say?"

"I said I didn't think you needed to see them either. I know what's on the films. Easter-egg hunts and birthdays and cheerleader tryouts. Stuff like that."

"Did you shoot the movies at the unveiling party?"

He shrugged. "What does it matter what happened twenty years ago? Are you researching, or investigating?"

His piercing stare activated an alarm in some ancient stem of my brain. "An interesting distinction," I said. "Can't we just call it curiosity?"

He nodded almost imperceptibly, narrowed his eyes, and I knew he took my evasion to be his answer—as I took his evasion to be mine.

"I'm curious whether you've seen your father's new work."

Blake sipped his coffee. "Oh, I've seen the commissioned pieces, but other times the studio is off limits." He cranked some film through the editor, viewing it absently as if it were a stranger's life. "Even Mom won't say what he's up to. Big hush-hush. Nathan doesn't want my help on the longhouse. Of the three kids, I'm the only one that visits on a regular basis, yet..."

"Yet you don't feel included."

"Dad's dug a moat around himself."

"How long have you felt that way?"

"A long time."

I pointed to the picture on the film editor. "Before this?"

"I don't know," Blake said quickly. He clearly didn't want to go there.

"Maybe that's what your father wants to do this week. Bring the family together."

"No Egret, not Anton Gropius. He's a castle without a drawbridge." Blake took up his sketchpad and retreated to his cot.

I spent a couple minutes thinking about the monumental object in the longhouse. With the hail and thunder and raging wind, I'd seemed on the threshold of a secret world. I resolved to satisfy my curiosity at the next opportunity, then I put my nose back to the viewfinder and went to work, listing details: the appearance of a family member, glimpses of the grandfather clock showing the passage of time, the dimming of daylight through the French doors leading to the courtyard in which Anton's masterpieces were displayed.

I noted that Rooks, at age nineteen, had already become a chic dresser, posing in a black sweater with a cowl collar in an off-center orbit around her neck. A felt bowler hat balanced her thick jaw and made her appear elegant. A neat lozenge of brunette hair hung at the back of her neck, similar to the way she wore it even now. The camera caught her looking coyly into the eyes of several different men during the course of the evening.

On the other hand, there was Celeste, two years older than Rooks, in a maroon beret, frizzy hair, and cape. She appeared in the first reel beside a man even more dreadfully skinny than she, wearing a leather vest and bell-bottomed pants, and wincing at the harsh floodlights from the camera. A later scene recorded Celeste trying to keep up with her friend as he knifed through the guests toward the front door. Blake, his hand on my shoulder as he looked at the screen, identified the skinny man for me as Julian Hornbeak, the guy Celeste had married briefly. He said he didn't know any details of the annulment.

For two hours I hunched over the editor, going through the films again and again, making notes, occasionally asking Blake to name someone or describe the layout of the house. His replies became less informative as we went, and I had a passing thought that he'd been hoping for a greater share of my attention that evening. I put the thought aside and focused even more intently on the smallest of details captured on the film. Buzz and Glenda, looking far less frumpy in those days, watching the bartender pour something red into their beers. The cellist rosining her bow. A cat curled on the piano bench. Each scene more crowded than the last. A shot of the courtyard filled with people milling, discussing the statues set among plantings of chrysanthemums.

I took particular note of a fit-looking man in his forties, elegantly turned out in whites with a yellow rosebud in his lapel, fancy handkerchief. Blake identified him as Clement Ely, the syndicated critic much detested by Anton.

"He once wrote that Dad's sculptures were harmless enough, if you could avoid being head-butted by the sculptor, who didn't know when to stop taking his bows."

"Whatever it takes to sell newspapers," I said with an undertone of mock evil.

Blake smiled faintly and patted a yawn. "Aren't you about done with that?"

"Pretty close."

The unveiling itself was preceded by a speech from Anton, camera flashes popping. When he pulled the cloth from the carving, I felt again the sense of wonder I'd had when looking at photos of Anton's works. I turned the crank slowly to look at each frame as the camera zoomed on the heroic carving of Chief Sealth, then veered off at an angle as if jostled. The next shot found Gobi at the piano.

I rolled the film in reverse through the unveiling sequence, then forward, seeing what I'd missed before: Clare standing in the background with her hand behind the curtain. The room lights dimmed until only the veiled carving remained brightly lit. The curtains had been drawn over the French doors, so that the statues in the courtyard were out-of-sight from the house.

I turned off the carbide lamp, and became aware of Blake snoring softly on the bed, notebook on his chest. I made more coffee and went through my notes:

7:14 (grandfather clock) guests arriving; lady in fur is Barb Shork—
    husband WA state senator; still some daylight

7:?? guests milling thru courtyard viewing sculptures
(undamaged); floodlights on; Gobi in tux smoking alone;
lights off in north wing where bedrooms are

8:?? quartet playing—according to program started at 8.00—
Dvorak

?   Barb Shork posing with Anton (draped on him)
before veiled statue—tipsy? (Anton uncomfortable?)
French doors to courtyard open, lights on

8:40 Clement Ely (Globe critic) arrives in white tux
(grandfather clock)

?   Buzz and Glenda hit buffet and bar. Barb Shork
offers punch and plenty of cleavage to camera (Blake?)—
definitely tipsy

9:?? Gobi at piano (Mendelssohn, according to program)
one champagne flute on piano
Rooks trying out Clement Ely's thin cheroot
Anton holding court w/guests
Hornbeak and Celeste seated in corner alone
Buzz guzzles beer for the camera

9:55 pan of room (to use up end of roll before unveiling?)
75+ people—haze of smoke (French doors closed?)
Hornbeak and Celeste pushing through guests (upset?)
Clare and Rooks rearranging chairs for unveiling
Clement Ely cheroot smoked down from five
inches to three

10:00? Unveiling (scheduled in program for 10:00--late?)
courtyard lights off; French doors shut; Gobi
with champagne
Clare standing near light switch
Chief Sealth unveiled; zoom of carving; camera jostled

11:?? Gobi playing + cello (new sonata?)—people talking in
background, not listening; three champagne flutes on piano
camera work choppy (Blake drunk?)
Gobi takes bow, seems rushed

French doors opened (ventilation?) outdoor floods still off
Rooks has Clement Ely's rosebud in lapel of her jacket
no Buzz/Glenda (did they go home? when?)
bedroom light visible through French doors (whose?)

"Tired of that damned party yet?" Blake said, practically in my ear.

I sucked a lungful of breath.

"Maybe you've figured it all out for us."

My chest tightened. "Figured what out?"

"Who smashed Dad's work. That's what all these notes are about, isn't it?"

I tried to put a palatable slant on it. "It occurred to me, of course—I've got a mutant curiosity gene. None of my business, I suppose."

"Go on."

I heard curiosity in his tone, possibly even support, though it might have been wishful thinking. "It does seem the attack must have occurred after the unveiling." At this point I had little to conceal—and I wanted to ask Blake something. "Someone turned out the courtyard lights before then, and drew the curtains, but it seems any hammering would have been heard during the ceremony."

"But when the music started back up—"

"Yes. And it appears everyone in the family had an opportunity to slip away. Celeste and her boyfriend left early, but they could have stolen back to the courtyard. And there's a rather long gap in the film between the unveiling and the end of Gobi's sonata. Makes me wonder where the camera man was."

"Maybe he didn't want to distract the musicians with the lights. They're rather blinding, you know."

"True enough. Or maybe one of the drunken wives needed some... special attention? In one of the bedrooms? Perhaps the wife of a state senator?"

He blinked a couple of times then tilted his head as if trying to explain something complicated. "Do you think adolescence ever transcends the bittersweet, for anyone?" Blake said.

A flush of embarrassment made my skin clammy. "That must have sounded judgmental," I said. "I'd better call it a night." I tidied up, thanked Blake for his help, and headed to the house.

To my surprise, the front doorknob wouldn't turn. Locked. Why would anyone lock a door on a remote island? My watch said a quarter to twelve. I walked around to check the kitchen door and found the screen door hooked securely. I stood there a moment, fatigued, arms crossed over my chest for warmth, not willing to wake anyone up, and wondering if someone had deliberately shut me out. I had a tent and sleeping bag stashed in my kayak, but it would be a pain to set up in the dark. I did retrieve my sleeping bag, but headed back to the barn with it. When I reached the steps, Blake stepped out on the landing wearing a jacket.

"Where you going?" I asked.

"Jeez!" he said. "You startled me. Just going out to squeeze my pickle."

"Pickle? Oh... pickle. Well, I'm locked out. Can I crash?"

"Locked? Nobody ever locks the house. Well I guess Court found somewhere else to sleep, so you can have the foam pad or the hammock, whatever's comfortable."

"Are you okay sleeping in the hammock?"

"I always sleep in one when I go to Guatemala."

"Where does one, ah, squeeze one's pickle around here— assuming one has a pickle?"

"The beach, of course. It flushes twice a day." He switched on a flashlight and trudged down the steps in untied sneakers.

I went upstairs. On a shelf next to the bed I found sweat pants and a flannel shirt two sizes too big for me, and slipped into them (he'd told me to get comfortable, hadn't he?). When he returned, he assessed my pajamas without comment, then offered something to drink: hot chocolate, Scotch. I took a small Scotch and water. "Cutty Sark," I commented as he poured. "I've never known anyone who drinks Cutty Sark."

"Me neither, but there's something earthy about it, like tasting an ancient rain forest."

We sat at his wire spool table. "Death to the dominant paradigm," I said, paraphrasing the bumper sticker on his wall.

"God bless our pointy little heads," he answered, and we clinked glasses. I held the rim of my glass to his for too long and the candle on the table nearly set the sleeve of my borrowed shirt afire, and we both laughed. The dim light made it seem safe for me to look into his eyes. They struck me as eyes that had seen much and assumed little.

I tasted some ancient rain forest. "Tell me about Guatemala."

He drew circles on the table with his thumb. "I go down once a year to build brick ovens in the Mayan villages. Myself and a few others."

"Uh huh."

"The highland people are extremely poor. They make fires on

their dirt floors for heating and cooking because they can't afford eight cents a brick to build ovens. For fifty bucks we can buy the bricks, mortar, and sheet metal to build a traditional oven for a family. It makes a huge improvement in their standard of living."

He told me more as I finished my drink. He had the hardened face of a fisherman and the quiet voice of a monk. Listening to him made me think about how my husband John always had an impressive rap about making the world a better place. I pictured him in his wool vest, in a neon-lit coffee shop, asserting truths around the stem of a pipe. I felt my own jaw tighten and tried to let the Scotch relax it. Maybe someday John would put his convictions into practice, but I wasn't going to hold my breath. The world needed fewer big plans and more small action.

Neither of us spoke. The time for it was over. I knew a thing or two about lost opportunities. I'd made my share of decisions at midnight, and wished I had some of them back, but there were more voices in my head than there used to be, and they were all talking at once so I couldn't understand any of them. Except for one thing: all it would take was for me to inch my hand forward and place it on his. When the tension in my chest became unbearable, I knew the question had hung long enough.

"I'm married," I said. It came out more as an apology than I'd intended.

Blake looked at me with steady, concerned eyes. "Life is about letting go of things that aren't working."

My mom—Firefly, as she liked to be called—had a love-the-one-you're-with philosophy that had stopped working for her a long time ago. I got up and rinsed the glasses and dried them. Blake began hanging the hammock but I stopped him. "If you were more comfortable in that thing, you wouldn't be sleeping on the foam pad. We can share the pad—head to toe. I have my own sleeping bag."

I made a trip to the beach. When I got back, he was in his sleeping bag—in the hammock. "It's better this way," he said. "If I have to get up in the night, I won't wake you."

He'd unzipped my bag and draped it over a chair to warm by the fire. When I had blown out the candle and crawled in the bunk, only my feet were cold. John had never objected to me pressing my cold feet against his legs—one of the things I missed most, now that I lived alone. Part of John's protective nature I guess, and maybe part of what drove him away. He couldn't reconcile his guard dog mentality with his need to be unfenced. Sad thing is, I didn't need protecting... just someone to be my friend and warm my feet.

Chapter 15

Athin, piercing scream woke me.

I sat up, tried to remember where I was. Sound of a sleeping bag zipper, Blake's feet hitting the floor. I gave my brains a shake and rushed outside to the landing, and in the gray dawn, I saw Blake racing toward a spindly figure on the front porch of the house, hands clapped over her mouth as if to keep more screams from coming out. Blake took his sister, Celeste, in his arms. I followed barefooted down the frosty steps. They were staring at the jack-o'-lantern Celeste had carved and placed on the porch, now destroyed, a hammer lodged in it. Blake pulled the hammer out, delicately, like an artifact, a stout tool, with double blunt faces angled slightly toward the shaft, the handle marked with Anton's yellow tape.

Anton and some of the others arrived, disheveled.

"This is yours, I think," Blake said to his father.

Anton took the hammer, put his wrist through the thong, found his grip, and, grimacing, hefted it as if he wanted to use it on something—or someone.

A sense of dread undermined my equilibrium and I felt unsteady on my feet.

Anton turned away from his family, perhaps not wanting them to hear the quaver of fury in his voice as he brandished the hammer. "Like shaking hands with the dead."

Anton insisted the family take breakfast together though I think most of us would rather have done without. Clare set places for everyone, including me and Nathan, who had yet to arrive. When I thanked Rooks for the clothes she'd loaned me, she joked about not wanting to sound like a witch in her father's biography, then said that Court had been behaving better since I'd taken him kayaking. I took it as a peace offering, not a bribe. Charles descended the stairs groggily oblivious to the morning's event until Gobi, up earlier than usual, served him coffee and led him to the porch to view the crime.

By the time Clare and I brought out the food, my appetite had staged a recovery, but faltered when Anton chucked the hammer on the table between the fruit and the scrambled eggs, denting the tabletop. Celeste, still gray from her shock, pressed back in her chair.

Court's young eyes opened wide, trying to understand what had gone wrong. Anton waited until all were seated, looked at Nathan's empty chair with narrowed eyes, then sat.

"Let's eat."

"We shall say grace first," Clare said. An unthankful meal would not be served in her house. No exceptions. And she didn't recite a canned prayer, but improvised something about rising above delusion that, for me at least, helped elevate my thoughts above the recent outrage. If only the effects had lasted past the amen.

Blake said, "Thank you Mom," and helped himself to the fried spuds with an enthusiasm that seemed to infuriate Anton. As he squirted a puddle of ketchup, Anton snatched up the hammer and glared at him.

"What do you know about this?"

Blake glanced up briefly, then tilted the peppershaker and tapped out a hail of specks with a forefinger. "It seems to be the one that went missing in Seattle."

"I want to know if you used it." Anton's question sounded choked by the bile in his throat.

Blake glanced at me as if suspecting a betrayal.

My mouth dropped open; my tongue felt coated with lint.

Blake turned back to meet his father's stare. "Am I the lead suspect then?"

"That's no answer."

Blake swallowed a bite of something I'm sure he didn't taste, and said, "Do you respect me enough to believe my answer?"

Anton jabbed a finger. "I can see inside stone. Don't think I can't see inside you."

Anton's intensity froze time into a gray-toned snapshot that I didn't want to remain in, because it frightened and repulsed me.

Blake dropped his fork and leaned his forearms on the table. "Then take a long look. I wonder if you can stand it."

"Stop it, you two!" Rooks said. "Let's not turn this into an inquisition."

Buzz tilted his chair back and crossed his arms. "Why not? Otherwise it seems we're just waiting for the next shoe to drop." He added with a smug look, "I think my big brother is finding out what it's like to be dumped on by his family."

Clare said, "This family has never dumped on anyone, and never will."

"Buzzy didn't mean it quite that way," Glenda said.

"I'm sure he didn't. Now, can anyone offer any information

about this hammer." Clare looked at each person in turn. Rooks shook her head no. Charles shrugged. Celeste had been shredding her napkin, but sat up, composed, at her mother's attention. Gobi averted his gaze, perhaps to offer the family a gesture of privacy. Buzz rocked on the back legs of his chair.

"Then let's finish our breakfast." Clare wrapped the hammer in a napkin and laid it on the breadboard behind her.

"Well, if no one else is going to mention it," Celeste said, her chipmunk mouth twitching, "It-it's highly possible my brother has an alibi."

She didn't look at me, but I knew what was coming.

"I think you'd better explain, Celeste," Clare said.

"After I screamed, and Blake came... well, he wasn't alone."

Court snapped a look at me. Anton caught it and asked me, "Is that so?"

Before answering, I looked at Clare. She didn't say anything, but my heart sank at her silent look of censure. She belonged to an era where appearances mattered as much as deeds.

Court piped up, "They were looking at old home movies of when Grandpa's statues were cracked. That's why I had to come back and sleep on the couch."

Payback for brushing him off. Now the whole family knew what I'd been up to with the films, as if things didn't look bad enough already. "I was locked out of the house," I explained.

Clare's face looked slack and troubled. "We don't ever lock the house."

Anton placed both his massive fists on the table. "Whatever. Can you give Blake his alibi?"

I started to give an unqualified *yes* when I remembered he'd gone out during the night. I hedged. "Except for when I was asleep."

"I'm glad to hear you got *some* sleep," Rooks said, and gave a staccato bridge-club laugh.

Blake said, "She got a full night's sleep—in her own sleeping bag. And I did go out once. I thought I heard a boat. I went to the cove, didn't see anything, took a leak, and went back to bed. To continue sleeping."

Anton seemed lost in other thoughts. He pushed away from the table. "Where is that damned Nathan?"

"Probably working on the generator," Clare said. "You know our Nathan."

Anton left his food untouched, grabbed his hat and vest on his way out the door. I tried to help clean up the dishes, but Celeste said,

"We can handle it," and Clare wouldn't even look at me, so I slipped away, dejectedly, to look for Anton. I climbed the ridge trail and paused at the crest as I entered the early morning sunshine. Spider webs strung with dewdrops bulged in the breeze. A chickadee harvested seeds from a dried wildflower. I continued down the trail toward Anton's studio. When I approached the shore, a flotilla of widgeons burst into flight and some heavier buffleheads ran across the water, feet slapping like tabla drumming. A shadow skimmed the ground and I knew what had scared them. A bald eagle drifted over the shoreline in a watchful trance. I, too, felt the shadow of a circling predator. One who'd planted the marble nose in the chowder, started the fire, and had now produced the long-lost hammer used to strike the nose from the Whitman carving. I tried to focus on what this meant for Anton and for the safety of his works, but couldn't shake the burn of rejection at being shooed from the kitchen. And worse, Blake probably suspected me of turning his father against him. I looked over the sea, eyes defocused, body leaden. I'd stopped, it occurred to me, because I didn't really want to see Anton. The sight of the carved pumpkin, symbolically destroyed with that particular hammer, must have staggered him; nonetheless, I couldn't forgive his treatment of Blake. Not that he cared a fig for anyone's forgiveness anyway. But I was carved of softer stone. Somehow I'd gotten used to the idea that I belonged here on the island, and the family's feelings mattered to me. As I'd done before in troubling times, I tensed and relaxed, and touched the vial of rose petals at my neck, and told myself I had a job to do. But which job: reporter? biographer? spy? friend?

Anton came around the side of the abandoned cannery; I walked over.

"Have you seen Nathan?" he asked, voice burred with anxiety.

"No."

He rattled the brass padlock on the cannery door. "He's changed the blasted lock."

I thought for a second. "So this is where your work is stored?"

He nodded.

I felt ill as I pictured defaced statues standing in a litter of their own fragments. "Is everything okay in there?"

"That would be nice to know, but I don't have a goddamn key."

"But why...?"

"Don't ask me."

"What's this?" I picked up a dusty blue aerosol can lying on the ground near the door. "Freon," I said, reading the can. There was still some liquid sloshing in it and I sprayed a short burst on my finger.

"You'll give yourself frostbite," he said, taking the can away from me.

"I don't get it."

"This can's been in the barn for years."

"Did Nathan have a key to the old padlock?"

"He's got keys to everything."

I remembered Blake saying he'd heard a boat in the night. "Including the boat? Have you checked?"

Anton smoothed his beard. "No, the damned kid is apt to do anything. Maybe he's getting a part for the generator. Anyway, I need a hacksaw."

"You don't think he would have harmed anything?"

"I'm sure as hell going to find out."

When we got to the studio, he rummaged through his tools. I looked at his array of hammers and had an idea. Something I'd seen an Iowa farmer do once. I selected one, and told Anton I wanted to try something. We walked back to the cannery, its sheet metal dulled to the color of the sea. Anton watched as I iced the padlock with the can of Freon. When the can was empty, I dropped it and quickly swung the hammer with both hands. I hit it squarely twice and the hasp fractured. Mouth agape, Anton twisted at the padlock. It fell to the ground.

"Maybe Nathan lost his key," I said.

Anton frowned. "Just like Nate. Too far out of his way to come borrow my key."

"Almost as far to the barn for the Freon," I said, but Anton didn't seem to hear. He swung open the door to the cavernous building. Pigeons bolted through broken panes of a high bank of windows. The air inside felt cold and smelled like a birdcage. A metal-clad sliming table, running the length of the building against one wall, sagged under boxes and machine parts and odd pieces of stone. On the slab floor stood some two-dozen objects—sculptures I assumed—protected with sheaths of heavy cloth. So many of them! It staggered me to imagine the creative effort involved, and I had a lunging urge to see them. Many of the objects were tall as a man and some much broader. Bird droppings spotted some of the covers, and it knotted my guts to think these precious things were locked in here out of fear for what someone might do to them. I stepped in, followed Anton past a forklift.

"You've been busy."

He nodded, but didn't seem inclined to inspect under the covers. "You'd better look," I said.

He let an exhalation puff his cheeks, then lifted a sheet without letting me see more than a glimpse of white marble. He checked a few more.

"Maybe you should call off this birthday thing, send everyone away."

"No, damn it all! I've lived seventy years now, and I've smoked cigarettes for damn near sixty of them. While I can still draw breath..." He sighed, a weariness in the slump of his shoulders. "I can't protect them any more, you understand? And I don't want to spend my last days fretting about it."

"Tell me, do you really suspect Blake?"

He flicked a hand. "Of all of them, he's the most capable. That's why I hope it's not him. You hope not, too, I suppose."

I nodded, and smiled with embarrassment.

Anton took a last look around. "If we don't get that goddamn generator running, we'll need lamps in here. Let's go check on the miserable thing."

We headed up the ridge trail, the sun knifing through chilly air onto our backs. It felt good after being in that desolate place built on the ashes of Crooked Hoop's longhouse, redolent of spirits, visions lost and visions persisting. At the ridge top, Anton stopped to catch his breath and roll a smoke. From our view we could see any number of islands rising from the ruffled sea, some forested in dark green, some rocky, some merged where interlacing waterways were blocked from view. In the strait, a sailboat beat into the breeze.

"You've been keeping your eyes open, I suppose."

"Yes," I said.

"So what can you tell me about my family that I don't already know?"

I raised my eyes in thought. "Everyone seems to have had their troubles, except perhaps Clare. Several think you could have been more helpful."

"If my calling was to be a wet nurse, I would have been born with tits."

My fuse must have been lit during Anton's tirade at the breakfast table, and been smoldering ever since, because before I could control myself, it hit powder. "You know, Anton, you've had your share of trouble, but it wouldn't hurt to show a little sympathy when people need it. Coming from you, it would mean a lot."

"Is that right?"

"For example, you could have done something for Captain Reese. You remember, the guy who lost his leg—"

"I know who he is. Clare sent flowers."

"That's a start."

"It was his own damn fault, what happened."

"So what? It's not an admission of guilt to stop by and ask an injured man how he's doing and find out how you can help. You have no idea..." I gritted my teeth.

He turned away and smoked his cigarette. When he was done, he crushed the butt on his boot sole and tucked it in the cuff of his overalls. "Come on," he said, and we started walking again. "All right, I'm an insensitive lout. So far, so good. Now, what else have you observed?"

I took a breath and told Anton about the films and a few of my observations. I asked if something had happened at the unveiling party between him and the critic Clement Ely.

Anton twisted his mouth. "Clement was your classic overcompensating eunuch cheap-shot artist. I'm glad he showed up just so I could have the pleasure of throwing him out."

"So you asked him to leave? Why?"

"The little piss-ant made some lewd suggestions."

"About what?"

"Gloating over Rooks being stuck to him all evening. Getting his jollies by pretending to compliment the catering: not expecting such a sumptuous spread. I didn't want to disturb the guests by flattening his nose, so I let it pass. Then he commented on the wine and how he enjoyed sampling a young vintage occasionally. I suggested that perhaps his corkscrew couldn't open a mature bottle. He said, 'Someone has to pop the first cork to see if the new wine is ready.'"

"So, you popped your cork."

"I should have put out his lights."

"Did he say anything about your new carving?"

"Yeah. With the mayor and the others listening, he said it might have even been relevant, if it had been knocked out in the time of Caesar. He compared carving faces on rocks to learning Latin, and said all preppies should have a whack at it."

"You have a clear recollection."

"He said the same thing, verbatim, in a dozen Sunday newspapers. No doubt he'd scripted it before coming to the party. Gene was a trifle unhappy that I ran the piss-ant off. He was debuting a sonata, you see, and wanted the coverage. The way things turned out, it was the best possible thing for Gene not to have a critic in the crowd."

"Why's that?"

"His piece was a disaster." Anton stopped, removed his hat to wipe a line of sweat from his forehead. "It wasn't a good evening for either of us. Gene fell apart. After the unveiling, he tried to beg off altogether from playing, but I didn't give him a choice. So it was partially my fault. I thought he was over his problems. And my parlor wasn't exactly the Albert Hall." Anton scratched his scalp through thinning hair, squinted into the sun.

"So he doesn't do concerts—ever?"

"I told you what happened in Europe. The shock therapy. It was Clare's idea for him to play at the unveiling—and it was a good idea. An opportunity to trot out one of his compositions before a small group, not much pressure. And Gene was happy as a clam about it. But when the time came, he got a case of the nerves. I'd even done the introduction and—" He made a poofing gesture with his fingers. "No Gene. Nowhere to be found. We got the quartet back while I tracked him down and found him in the library trimming his nails as if nothing had happened. I gave him a pep talk and he went back out ready to set the world on its ear. He'd written a nice little sonata, nothing to be ashamed of. But he had trouble, right off, finding the tempo, and the cello was struggling to follow. And he was just hitting notes, as if someone else had composed them—not putting any eyebrows on them. Then, the piano or cello lost track, and it took a few awkward bars to connect up. Gene was so rattled, he took his bow after the third movement. The fourth was a virtuoso movement and he'd lost his confidence."

The picture of Gobi ensconced behind the piano on this rocky island, happily experimenting with chords and orchestrations, writing anonymous subliminal music for the screen, now made sense to me. "It must have been a terrible experience for him."

"He'll always make the worst of things. That's Gene. Not five people in that room had the ear to notice. And if they did, in a matter of minutes we discovered my statues... mutilated. Even if he'd been brilliant, no one would have remembered."

"I suppose he would have remembered."

"You can't be great every time out of the box."

"Do you know if he was taking any medication at the time, maybe antidepressants?"

Anton thought. "He was always consulting some head doctor or another. It's likely he was popping something."

"He was drinking that evening," I said. "In one of the films he was holding a champagne glass and I saw three empties on the piano. Mood elevators and booze can make your brain think it's on a roller coaster."

Anton began walking. "A man needs to lick his wounds and go on."

We arrived at the generator shed. Anton inspected the fuel tank, then tried to turn the flywheel by hand. It was locked up. Puzzled, he tried it again without success. He pulled the dipstick and took it outside to inspect it in the light. His lips tightened and his eyes narrowed. He hurled the dipstick on the ground, cursed.

"What is it?"

"Look for yourself." He stepped back in the shed and unscrewed the oil cap.

I dropped to one knee for a closer look. The dull oil caked near the filler hole sparkled with fine beach sand.

Chapter 16

Clare pressed her knuckles into a wad of dough, arms floured to the elbows, wedding ring on the corner of the table. She stopped humming when I came in.

The look she'd given me that morning upon learning I'd slept in the barn had persisted like nettle stings. She'd earned my respect and it pained me to think I'd lost hers. But it also troubled me that she'd sweat the morals of her thirty-eight year old son and thirty-two year old houseguest—particularly since neither of us had locked me out of the house. People are entitled to their flaws, but somehow I'd wanted Clare to be perfect.

"I know it didn't sit well—me spending the night in the barn. I'm sorry."

She glanced up only briefly and resumed working the dough. "Guess I'm an old stick-in-the-mud. We were raised to assume the worst." A pause. "Apology accepted." She sounded as if she'd expected the apology and was glad to have it out of the way. If Clare knew I'd been raised in a commune, where the goats and the people shared the same values regarding sex, she'd probably invite me to launch my kayak posthaste. The camaraderie I'd felt with Clare didn't feel fully restored, but I'd done what I could.

"I saw Anton. He's okay. The statues are okay, but someone changed the lock on the cannery. The generator's been sabotaged with sand in the oil."

She buried her fists in dough, reminding me of the carving her young son, David, had done. "But why?" she said. "What's the point?"

"I can think of two possibilities: to shut off radiophone communication, or perhaps someone didn't want me looking at the home movies."

"Oh, I can hardly..." She straightened up and looked into the distance. "But we still have the ship-to-shore radio in the boat. In fact Buzzy's down there right now, thinking of motoring to Bidwell Harbor to watch the next game."

"No, it's gone—the boat. I checked just a few minutes ago. Anton thinks Nathan went after some parts."

She frowned and picked up the pace of her kneading.

"Clare, after I asked your permission to review the film, did you let anyone else know?" I already knew she'd mentioned it to her kids, but I thought Clare might add something to what Blake had told me.

She nodded. "Well, yes. Celeste happened to say we should look at home movies. Of them all, she's the one for family things, like a Monopoly tournament tonight. I told her about your access to the family archives, and that you'd found some movies still sealed up from that last party in Seattle."

"How'd she react?"

"Ahh... you have to understand Celeste always looks for the symbolism. She doesn't believe in coincidences or random occurrences. She felt the films were forgotten for a reason."

"What reason?"

"She feels we disintegrated as a family around that time, with David's death, and the attack. She wants to look at the older films, the ones that show us behaving like a family." Clare glanced at a sun-yellowed group picture on the refrigerator. Blake looked only six or seven. With their long tousled hair, it was hard to tell girls from boys.

"How did things change when David died?"

She rolled dough over on itself with the heels of her hands, her lanky arms stronger than they looked. "Thinking back, it does seem we had a proper life before then. Anton never took much time from work, but he enjoyed having the kids hang around the studio. They were so proud of their papa. He was becoming quite famous then. But things were starting to change. Blake talked of going into the Peace Corps. Rooks was growing up, becoming more interested in her friends... well, boys. Anton's success meant less time for other things. Of course, I was a basket case for a year after David died." She looked up at me and blinked. "A mother's prerogative."

"Yes." We would always have that bond, no matter what came between us.

I thought back to the film. "The night of the party—Celeste is there with her beau, Julian Hornbeak, and there's a clip showing them leaving, with Hornbeak looking mad. Do you recall what happened?"

"Ahem!" Celeste stood in the doorway, toes pointed apart, arms at her sides, hands balled in little fists. "If you want to know things, then you should ask me."

"Thank you, I will," I said, and Celeste shrunk back a bit, looking as if she'd used up her supply of boldness for the week. I thought it best to level with her, at least partly. "Your father is worried about the strange things going on. I thought as long as I'm researching his history, I'd go back to the party, thinking there might be a connection."

Celeste stepped in, pinched some dough and nibbled at it. I waited, my way of getting people to talk. She looked at her mother and perhaps received some mother-duck gesture of reassurance I couldn't detect. She began speaking in a detached monotone that seemed to conceal strong feelings.

"Julian was, and probably still is, a petulant juvenile who considered himself a leader of the underground 'cognoscenti'." With two fingers on each hand she made quotation marks. "Julian had asked Dad to do a bust of Richard Brautigan for his bookstore in the U District. The bookstore was called *Watermelon Sugar* after one of Brautigan's novels. Julian had an espresso stand in there too, and wanted to expand into the adjoining florist shop, which closed. He planned to put in some tables and a microphone for poetry readings. Like the City Lights in San Francisco. Big plans; no money. But he'd found someone maybe interested in financing the expansion and Julian had told everyone about getting an Anton Gropius bust of Brautigan. I suppose any carving by Dad would have been worth more than the entire shop at the time. Anyway, the guy with the money figured the Brautigan carving would give the business some sort of legitimacy and would bring people in the door. But it didn't work out."

"Your father didn't do the carving?"

"No."

"He and Julian talked about it the night of the party?"

Celeste nodded. "Julian had given Dad a copy of Brautigan's *Trout Fishing in America* to read. Dad read a few pages and called it drivel. I don't think he ever promised to do the bust. But when someone tells Julian they'll think about it, he interprets that as: how soon do you want it?"

"Julian was angry?"

"Distraught."

"And how did you feel?"

She shrugged and watched her mother dust the dough ball. "I was twenty-one years old."

I wasn't sure what her age had to do with it. "Where did you and Julian go after you left the party?"

The skin of Celeste's face always looked thin as tissue paper; now it had that wadded-up look of having been used.

"Moon and Sixpence want some dough; they love anything with yeast in it." She rolled a pinch into two small pellets, then noticed me waiting for an answer.

"We went to an art gallery uptown," she said, adding an

exasperated huff. "Someone was dipping insects in liquid nitrogen and electroplating them with gold. It was revolting."

"And did you go back to the house?"

"I don't remember."

"You don't remember the police?" I'd rather have grilled Celeste privately, but feared I couldn't get her started again if I put it off.

"Of course. Yes."

"What happened to the bookstore?"

Celeste's face uncrinkled a bit, relieved, probably, to move on past the night of the vandalism. "Julian held on a couple more years before he lost his lease. Then he rented an old church and started a Celtic band."

"Were you two engaged at the time of the party, or married?"

Celeste went stiff. "It's not a subject I care to talk about, thank you."

She opened one fist to look at her flattened hermit crab pellets, and left without another word. I was leaving, too, when Buzz showed up eager to tell us something.

"I guess we know what happened to that damn Indian."

Clare stood erect, dusted off her hands. "You couldn't possibly be referring to Nathan!"

"I catch one or two of 'em every week at the store looking to slip something in their pockets when I'm not looking. This one of yours is no better than the rest, it seems. He's run off in the night with your motorboat." For emphasis he ratcheted his great forehead closer with every word.

"I'm sure if he did, he had a good reason. I'm not going to worry about it."

"He knew I was keeping an eye on him and figured he'd grab what he could and scram. You'd better check your valuables. It's obvious that's why he wrecked the generator, so he could get away without us calling the Coast Guard. Your boat's going to show up in some fishing village next year so shelled out you're not going to want it back."

Clare quartered the dough with a long knife, shaped each piece, plopped them into pans and covered them with a cloth. Without looking up from her work, she muttered, "It doesn't pay to argue with experts or idiots."

I found Eugene Gobi in the parlor, marking up his orchestral score in short, precise strokes, as if plucking cactus spines from it. I took a chair by the far window to keep out of his light, and reviewed my film notes.

The sculptures in the courtyard had been intact until the unveiling at around ten p.m. The courtyard lights had been on and the curtains open until then. According to Anton, Eugene discovered the damage when he went to the courtyard for a smoke at about 11:45 p.m. Celeste and her volatile boyfriend, Julian Hornbeak, had left the party by then, and could easily have waited in the garden for their opportunity to pay Anton back for their disappointment. But would this anger persist for twenty-one years, especially considering their feelings were so changeable that they'd managed less than a month of marriage?

Rooks had seemed in high spirits in the films, unlike someone about to destroy the fruits of her father's genius. She'd appeared in the last few seconds of film—wearing Clement Ely's rosebud in her lapel—after Gobi had rushed away from the piano. Ely himself had been evicted by then, to meet his fate with a puffer fish some years later, removing him from current suspicion. Charles Underwood, Rooks' future husband, hadn't arrived on the scene, so I put him on the long shot list for the current terror campaign, along with Nathan, Gobi, and Clare. Could Rooks have been angry over the way her father treated Ely? Again, not an enduring motive. Blake all but admitted being seduced by the legislator's wife, and the gap in the filming supported it, but he might well have been hammering statues instead. He'd recorded the unveiling, and resumed filming near the end of Gobi's performance, plenty of time for more than one kind of mischief. Buzz and Glenda had spent the evening ensconced before the fireplace with their free food and beer, Buzz slumped in sleep by the third reel. Anton said the program had been altered due to Gobi's attack of nerves. The sonata, instead of being played immediately after the unveiling, came after the Beethoven Quartet. Plenty of time for Gobi, as well as Blake, to do the bashing. Hm. Despite Anton's trust of Gobi, perhaps I shouldn't give him a free pass.

I wondered how long Blake had been gone last night. He'd mentioned hearing something at the beach. Could he have been out long enough to know something about the missing padlock, the smashed pumpkin, and the motorboat? Had he been colluding with Nathan?

Could Nathan, after all, be behind the torment, perhaps to alienate Anton from his children? Had Nathan come to regard Anton as a father figure, arousing expectations regarding Thunderhead Island? If he was responsible, why would he have left suddenly when the plan seemed to be working? And why change the lock?—unless to terrify Anton with a sense of vulnerability. It didn't quite add up.

As Gobi hunched over the score, I thought about the electro-shock therapy, the unfulfilled promise of his early talent. I'd seen how hard he worked at his music, and admired him for it. He looked up, caught me watching, and reached inside his sweater for a package of cigarettes. He pulled one from the pack with his thin lips and left it there unlit, slammed the folio closed and pushed it away from him. His cigarette wagged as he said, "This hack would need a stepladder just to kiss my ass."

"That's not your music?"

"The studio owns the music. They paid André Houseman a small fortune eight or ten years ago to score the *Hounds of Hell*."

I remembered hearing about the movie. "A big flop, wasn't it?"

"Never has Hollywood spent so much for so little. The studio almost went bust. And Houseman..." Gobi shook his head. "He fled to Italy just ahead of the lawsuits—the parents of several choirboys. Now the studio wants me to recycle this trash for an African adventure. Throw in a few drums and no one will notice. Right. The cheap sons-of-bitches. If I make something decent out of this, then Houseman's the genius. If I simply re-orchestrate as they want, then Gobi's lost his touch—time to drop him from the A-list."

"Tough business."

"If this Oscar nomination comes through, that'll make the phone ring. They can stuff these whoring retread jobs."

"Mind if I ask, Gene, why haven't you composed more orchestral music?"

"Child," he said shaking his head. "When is the last time you heard an orchestra play a living composer? The patrons of the arts would have to, by God, decide for themselves if something is good; but it's so much safer to genuflect before the alter of convention. Even Stravinsky, they don't play the stuff he wrote after, what, 1920?"

Did Gobi think life was fair for people other than composers? "But you've written more than movie scores. The program for the unveiling party has you down for a sonata."

He nodded. "The piano and cello piece. I cannibalized it for one of those *film-noir* things a few years back, *Avalon Ballroom*."

"Do you ever perform it in its original form?"

He answered with quick shakes of the head. "My performing days are over. I lack the temperament, as they say." He plucked the cigarette from his mouth and studied it.

"I hear you were the one who discovered the damage in the

courtyard. Do you remember the exact time?"

Gobi twitched one shoulder and scrunched the opposite eye as if a spasm had shot through him. "I don't recall... I wasn't feeling well. Do you mind?" He held up his thin cigarette and looked toward the front door.

I joined him outside. He sat on the rail, and while dipping his cigarette into the lighter flame, he saw the ruined jack-o'-lantern on the stoop. He stared at it, his face gone chalky, cigarette burning idly in his hand propped against the rail.

"A bit of déjà vu?" I asked.

"All over again," he said, smiling self-consciously at his little joke.

"You were feeling sick that night?"

"Sick? Disoriented maybe, or... trouble concentrating. Just wanted some quiet and a smoke. The music sounded like river rapids. No oxygen in the air. Someone had closed the windows."

"So you went outside after you played."

He nodded. "I didn't pay attention to the statues. I must have walked right by the *Whitman*. Of course, the lights were off. I remember the sickeningly sweet wisteria, and the crickets were too loud, almost painfully loud. In the moonlight, the statue of Isaac Newton seemed alive, holding his orb, engrossed in some mystical revelation there in the garden. I wanted to talk to him, because he seemed like the kind of fellow who'd listen, then I noticed something wrong with his profile. I didn't know whether to believe my eyes. I picked up some pieces, a section of arm. At first I didn't understand what had happened."

Gobi and I sat quietly. I wanted to believe him. I stared absently at the clematis threaded through the trellis, the feathery seed heads backlit by midmorning sun. My eyes slipped out of focus as I tried to make sense of the mystery, wondering who to talk to, what to ask. When I pulled my mind back to the present, I saw Gobi again staring at the pumpkin. I could stand its crumpled face no longer, salvaged the candle, and carted the rest of it to the compost heap. By the time I'd returned, Gobi had gone inside and I met Charles Underwood coming out the door with his tackle box and pole. His chinos had blood on them.

"Nathan was going to take me out fishing," he said, his double-peaked mouth drooping. "He knows a place where the old halibut go. The grandfathers, he calls them."

"They call them barn doors if they're big enough," I said. "Maybe Nathan went to borrow a generator."

"Hope so. The battery on my laptop is shot and I've got an article due for the *Lancet*. And I need to phone for messages."

"Now Charles," I teased, "I thought you were starting to relax, get a little fish slime on your new pants."

He inspected the stain and chuckled.

"It must have been tough maintaining a surgical practice and leading a revolt in the AMA." You build trust, Gram Velva had told me, by meeting people on their own turf. "I've been curious, Charles, what bothers you about the AMA?"

He shrugged. "A lot of things. Their attitudes about managed care, alternative medicine. But mostly they duck the moral issues, such as deciding when to let people die because it costs too much to treat them. Did you know only a third of American doctors even bother belonging to the AMA?"

"How long do you expect to practice? Vascular surgery must be... exacting."

He nodded as if I'd hit on some truth beyond the grasp of most people. "Don't tell Rooks," he said with mock secrecy, "I don't want to work past fifty. If I never cut open anything but a fish belly again, I'd be a happy man. Before I married Rooks, I spent a fair amount of time in the outback. If I look a little stooped, it's because I hurt my back packing out two hundred pounds of moose meat in the Yukon."

Though Charles did look a bit stooped, he didn't look near fifty. "So you don't mind being sequestered on Thunderhead Island."

"I could live out here. I think Anton has it made."

"And Rooks?"

"I'd give her a month. She'd take up with the first sunbelt poodle vet that would have her."

"Sounds rather ruthless."

He chuckled. "I understand what her needs are. I always have. We're both satisfied with our choices."

"Did she mind coming here this week?"

Charles paused. I could see he understood the implications of my question. "We agreed we should come for the family's sake. At the same time, she seemed... apprehensive about it. She seems to have settled in, wouldn't you say?"

To be agreeable I agreed.

Court flung the screen door open, banging it against the siding. "Are we going to kayak around the island now?" His hair remained orange but he'd lost the spikes.

"A little later," I said. He looked down. "What's that flour on your gob?"

"Nothin'. I've been helping Grandma mix up a cake for Grandpa's birthday. She made me read the recipe and measure everything out."

"I promise we'll go kayaking, but I have some things to do right now. Why don't you go fishing with your dad?"

"Court doesn't like to fish," Charles said quickly. "Anyway, he doesn't have a rod."

I saw Court's face cloud up and I felt an uncomfortable pressure building in my chest. "There're three or four rods in the shed. Surely you can spare a rubber worm for your son."

"Can I Dad!"

Charles flashed me a dirty look, but I didn't care. I helped Court pick out a pole and sent him off at his dad's side. Then I took a long walk and thought about where Nathan might have gone.

Chapter 17

Nathan's cabin could have come from the mind of Dr. Seuss: tall and leaning, sided with wavy rows of shakes, stove pipe crooking from a hole in the wall upward to a pointy cap. I looked for a line of blue smoke above the chimney, but, of course, there wasn't one.

Inside, the cabin felt tiny but not claustrophobic. A sleeping loft allowed open floor space below. Oil drum stove, heat-warped door propped shut with a whale vertebrae. I moved the prop and checked the firebox for embers. Cold. Work gloves and shapeless wool socks hung from wires over the stove. Plywood counter with cast iron burner connected to a propane bottle. Dirty frying pan and coffee cup in a sink. Cracked wafer of soap in an oyster shell. Nectarines breeding fruit flies. A shelf of books. Nathan's taste ran to thrillers and westerns, thickened from reading, and some how-to construction and woodworking books. A deck of cards lay next to a kerosene lantern on the table. And a knife. The fancy sheathed blade that Nathan wore as others would wear a wristwatch.

I pulled out the only chair and sat, thinking. Either Nathan had left the island on the boat, or had appeared to leave, taking the boat out then ducking back in where he could hide and keep an eye on things. Another of his traps designed to draw the vandal into making a move? But under either scenario, wouldn't he have taken his knife? And why change the lock on the cannery building? Something must have come up unexpectedly. I felt Nathan could be trusted, but I didn't know how to help without knowing his plan.

I checked the cedar longhouse next. As I loosened the canvas over the unfinished end, I again had the sensation of leaving my familiar world for another. Light slashed through the smoke vent and between the siding planks, the noon sun baked a smell, rich as gingerbread, from the cedar planks.

"Nathan?" I called, my eyes not yet able to see into the dark corners of the lodge. Alone except for the totem pole and what had to be a huge sculpture. My skin felt charged with electricity. This is what I'd come for: to see whether Anton Gropius had brought his genius with him into exile, or left it in the talus of his masterpieces in Seattle.

I picked my way past tools and boards and sawhorses to the far end of the longhouse where the looming object stood, wound in sailcloth. A line passed through several grommets and was drawn together at the bottom and knotted. I picked at the knot until I tore a nail then reached for my penknife—another gift from my grandmother. She'd probably used it to trim cigars. I'd never sharpened it, and if the rope had been made of banana, it might have cut. As it was, I knelt and sawed away at the line making scant progress, hoping Nathan hadn't rigged one of his otter traps, biting my lip at the thought of what Anton would think if he found out. The light improved for a moment—probably a cloud passing from the sun—and I could see the rope was nearly parted.

Then I heard a footstep, and a broad knife blade gleamed above me.

I nearly lost my balance and put a hand down to keep from toppling over. I looked up to see Anton and froze in place, trying to read his eyes. He stared down at me for a few seconds, then severed the cord with one swipe. He folded the knife, slid it into his pocket, and extended his hand. I looked past it and, to my relief, saw no anger in his face.

His hand was impossibly broad and hard, and felt rough as barnacles. He said nothing. Somewhat sheepishly I unwound the sailcloth. Then, as I was being overly cautious, he grabbed fistfuls of shroud and yanked it back from his creation.

I gasped and stepped back, then stopped breathing altogether. The statue, rising twice my height, would have been intimidating by its bulk alone. But when I began to comprehend the scope of the achievement, it left me swaying on my legs like a newborn fawn. Anton had depicted a human form, meticulously muscled, undergoing a wrenching transformation to a majestic bird of prey. I felt puny and at its mercy, and at the same time blinking at the impossibility of it. I knew this stone had once been of the material world, but no longer. From whatever hell Anton had journeyed to, he had stolen fire.

No doubt this creation had been inspired by coastal Indian mythology, and I imagined a longhouse ripe with the smell of fish grease and a hundred bodies, firelight bouncing against a layer of smoke overhead. A medicine man dons a power mask and plumage of an eagle, and in his heart becomes the eagle, his spirit mixing in the stream of spirit running through all creatures. By firelight he performs the eagle's sacred myth, sings its totemic song. Obscured by darkness and smoke, heightened by ritual preparation, the spirit of the raptor must have been palpable to those who swayed with the drums.

The carving depicted not merely a quaint ritual, performed by a shaman costumed in feathers and beaked wooden mask; Anton had evoked the transcendent moment as it must have felt in the days before the ceremonies had lost their magic, their power to transform.

I felt a rolling shiver, a passing nausea that came with the sloughing off of my own too-small concept of reality. The bust Anton had been carving for his paying customer had prepared me for the mediocre. But this was not the work of a craftsman, or a mere artist, or a hidebound atheist, or dim-eyed old man. The longer I stared, the more I felt drawn into another space—summoned—and a trance wove itself around me, as a spider wraps a fly. I imagined this raptor-man leading me away from my physical body, forever, to a place from which I would not want to return.

But I shook myself from the trance because I needed to look again upon the man who had accomplished this miracle. My mouth hung open and my eyes felt buggy. Anton nodded knowingly. Perhaps he took satisfaction in my silent acknowledgment. He had pushed beyond anything he'd ever done, and he knew it. And I understood the longhouse. It would serve as museum and milieu for this otherworldly figure. Anton bent stiffly for the old sail and, with the aid of a pole, I helped him replace it over the statue. Walking back to the studio, we didn't talk about the carving. I didn't want to gush, and he'd said it all with his chisel. I offered to help with preparations for Sunday's birthday celebration.

"Light," he said. "We'll need lanterns, candles, anything that will throw light."

"Can't you do it while there's daylight?"

"No! The world must be gone. I want only the sculptures to remain."

The tautness of his voice, the hone of his focus made me fear for his health, or at least for his state of mind. He seemed to burn with irreplaceable energy. I thought of salmon borrowing against the flesh to leap rapids, only to spawn and die. Since my arrival, he'd worked every day to the point of exhaustion, slept little, picked at his meals.

"You're not expecting Nathan to bring another generator?"

"No telling."

"Maybe he's still on the island," I ventured, wondering if Nathan might even now be watching us from the lichen-covered rocks.

Anton looked at me questioningly. "Do you know where he is?" His tone confused me, as if he dared not hope for good news.

"No," I said. "Unless he's here with you."

Anton shook his head. I sensed his worry and it amplified mine.

I certainly didn't care to hear Buzzy gloat about pegging Nathan as a sneak thief.

"But wouldn't he have left a note for you?"

Again Anton shook his head. "He's got his own way."

"You're proud of Nathan, aren't you?"

"Proud? I didn't make him what he is." We approached the studio, windblown clouds reflected in the big windows. "You saw his totem pole, didn't you?"

Sounded like pride to me. "Anton, if Nathan decided to go somewhere last night, wouldn't he have taken his knife? I found it in his cabin."

Anton paused, then shrugged. "He's got other knives. When he sees one of his girlfriends, he sometimes wears a certain knife with chrome and studs and whiz-gidgets on it—his dress knife."

I suggested he go through Nathan's things and he nodded noncommittally, then led me to the studio, violin music playing softly inside. I stopped in surprise before the block of Portuguese marble—the one marred with the red blotch—now positioned on his large workbench. Anton poured us some oily coffee, vile and only lukewarm as his morning fire had burned down. The hammer we'd found in the jack-o'-lantern lay on the bench.

"So this is the one used to destroy your statues," I said, handling it.

Anton tasted his coffee, spat on the floor. "You can make some fresh if you like." He drank again anyway and hefted the hammer. "This, Egret, is a three-pound mason's hammer. A man with a steel chisel, a strong arm and a good eye can cleave a brick squarely to within a sixteenth inch with one blow." He brushed dust off the stool, positioned it near the marble block, and faced me. "I'm an old man who's only got the will to carve one last rock, and I want you to see me do it."

My eyes widened. "Nothing would please me more."

He handed me safety glasses. I put them on and followed his gaze to the seven-foot cast of Michelangelo's *Rebellious Slave*.

"Every time I start thinking I'm pretty good, I look at that and say: you're not there yet, Anton."

He circled the marble block. Without taking his eyes from it, he sharpened a carpenter's pencil with his knife, licked the lead and began slashing at the stone with confident strokes, working his way around it until all the surfaces were marked. Satisfied, he took up the hammer and a hefty pointed chisel, its end mushroomed from a million hammer blows. He squared to the stone like a pugilist. Finally, he placed the point, tapped it lightly with the hammer, then swung on it with force, striking the corner off cleanly. Then he worked on getting rid of the red stain, finding a cadence of alternating taps and strikes that rang the tempered steel. As he had said, the dye had penetrated well into the marble.

Without changing cadence he aimed a series of aggressive blows at what I took to be the front face of the stone, producing a deepening gouge. Though I sat ten feet from it, I was glad of the safety glasses as chips sprayed out from beneath his chisel. Far from the surgical tapping I'd expected, his assault became possessed fury as he moved continuously around, chisel and hammer chiming the end of the world. As bits flew off, I feared he'd ruin the stone out of reckless despondency. When finally he moderated his blows, I breathed more easily.

Then, whether he'd accomplished some purpose unclear to me, or whether his arms, thick and hard as they were, had given way to fatigue, he stepped away, dropped the hammer on the workbench. His intensity receded, leaving a spent seventy-year old man. Not yet taking his eyes from the stone, he backed away, almost staggering, until finding his stool. There he sat, gathering himself.

"I'm surprised you didn't shiver it into gravel," I said.

"If the goddamn thing had a flaw in it, I needed to find out now, not later. There's no more time. No time to recover from betrayal."

I hoped whatever I would write about Anton—and it would be no puff piece—would not seem a betrayal to him. "What will it be?" I gestured at the stone.

"It already is. I've seen the face inside, more times than I can tell. A set of eyes to look upon the centuries undimmed."

I walked around the carving. Though I could get no sense of what Anton had in mind, already the emerging shapes had energy and a feeling of purpose. I picked up his tools, still warm from use. "Do you have a scrap of stone I could have a whack at?"

He pressed dust off his lips as he looked around, then heaved a block of stone to the sandbag on the smaller workbench. The block, lightly mottled with lavender and gray, must have weighed well over a hundred pounds.

"Tennessee marble. Each type has its own crystal pattern, you see. One stone you can hit hard, another you can't."

He showed me how to stand and how to keep the hammer close to the body to save arm strength. "You'd be better off with the air hammer, but with the power out, there's the old-fashioned way. Now, if you don't want your thumb pulped, wrap it around the chisel in the same direction as the fingers." I gave a few knocks on the pointed chisel before he stopped me. "Hold it at forty-five degrees, otherwise you'll bruise the stone."

"Bruise it?"

"If you aim a chisel directly into the piece, you compress the stone inside. This could break later, or leave a blemish on the carving. Remember, compared to granite, marble is soft."

"Really? How is marble formed?"

"It's metamorphic—essentially sedimentary rock cooked under pressure until it crystalizes. It's like soapstone and alabaster and onyx, but harder."

After I had knocked off a few chunks, he had me try what he called a bullset—a toothed chisel for shaping—then a smaller flat chisel for removing the scoring left by the bullset. In five minutes, my hammer arm was too sore to go on. Anton took up the tools and went back to work, this time enlarging the deep gouge at the front with a broad bullset. I watched, made notes, composed purple phrases I'd probably throw out before submitting the story, trying for tempered-edged words that would convey Anton's intensity. An hour passed and I began to see an eye emerge. He did some fine work with a small flat chisel before collapsing for a rest. Remarkably, from the roughed out eye, I could almost infer the entire three-foot tall head.

"It's a self portrait, isn't it?"

Anton chuckled. "Rembrandt did a hundred self portraits. I guess that makes me a hundred times more humble than Rembrandt."

"There's a reason you didn't choose Cararra marble for your own likeness."

He glanced again at *The Rebellious Slave* and nodded. "Out of respect."

Chapter 18

nton nodded approvingly as I scribbled his comments in my notebook. I closed it and offered to get started setting up some lights.

We collected a number of old kerosene lanterns, a Coleman lantern with damaged mantles, and more of the tarnished brass carbide lamps. Anton said they'd been used in the cannery when the slimers were kept buried to the elbows in fish guts through the night. He shook a can of carbide pellets, satisfied there were plenty, and told me to clean and fill the lamps. He explained where the fuel, wicks, mantles, and spare glass chimneys were for the other lamps. I gathered them up, and sealed a couple pounds of carbide pellets into a plastic bag, planning to haul everything in the four-wheeler back to the barn. I hoped Blake might be willing to help rehab the lamps—especially the carbides, as I hadn't paid much attention when he'd done it last evening, and didn't care to blow myself up. I started the four-wheeler and powered up the ridge trail. At the top I stopped at a mossy ledge in a fern grotto where I could do some thinking. Out of the wind, the day had become generously warm.

Anton's marvelous statue in the longhouse had changed everything, erased my fears that he'd become a lightweight pummeled into triviality by the damage done his earlier works. If the rest of his new sculpture approached the genius of the longhouse statue, he would create an explosion in the art world. From my ill-informed viewpoint, I had to think he'd rank with the greatest.

And it made me feel small. Too small to write Anton's story. And, of course, he knew it. He had no intention of trusting me with his biography. Once an exhibit was arranged, once the photos of his new work circulated, there would be TV documentaries, interviews, a traveling exhibition to the major cities. Publishers would offer their best 'co-authors', those who had ghosted the autobiographies of leaders and celebrities. I'd have my little exclusive read by a few thousand subscribers, and that would be that. Maybe I'd peddle a slug to the wire services.

Then, abruptly, another voice piped up in my head and said I should be appalled at this sniveling. Anton hadn't popped out of the womb a world-class sculptor. His own epitaph read *Born a Man...*, telling us all something about hard work and believing in ourselves and not giving up. I stood, made sure I was alone, and shouted in paraphrase of Anton, "What the hell have you, Egret Van Gerpin, got to be unconfident about?"

The glen that enclosed me amplified and deepened my voice, made it powerful. Regardless of what Anton's intentions were, I felt—for the moment anyway—I had the power to shape things to my liking. I could start by helping to prevent harm to his work. From what I'd seen, it was worth my effort. Anton was worth it too, despite his shortcomings.

My thoughts went back to the smashed carvings, to the hour-long gap in the film record between the unveiling and Gobi's hurried bow. The hour during which the vandalism had almost certainly occurred. With the music playing, the French doors closed, and the courtyard lights off, no one had heard the thudding hammer blows. Unless Blake heard them from the bedroom as Barb Shork—the predatory state senator's wife—took advantage of his youthful thirst for experience.

Took advantage, my butt! Blake had been seventeen. He probably enjoyed the hell out of it.

I needed to think about something else. Glenda for starters. Anton's brother Buzz appeared to have snored through Gobi's sonata—and perhaps the attack—with Glenda watching over him like a spaniel. I wondered if she had the mustard to do the dirty work, possibly without Buzzy knowing, jealous over Anton's triumph in the house that she imagined was rightfully hers.

And what about Eugene Gobi, fretting over his nails in the library before Anton pressured him into playing. Could he have already done the deed and was awaiting discovery? Is that why he was too upset to play?

I couldn't positively eliminate anyone. Had I been wasting my time trying? Or maybe if I looked at the film even more closely...

I drove down the track toward the barn. Before arriving, I glimpsed Blake striding on the path to the north woods. I parked the vehicle, grabbed one of the carbide lamps and hurried after him. In the forest, the trail became carpeted with needles. I crested a rise and looked ahead for Blake. Not seeing him, I picked up my pace and nor, to my confusion, could I see him at the next vantage. I stood with hands on hips in frustration.

Then I heard soft laughter behind me.

"Lose something?" he said, sitting cross-legged on the hillside above the trail.

"Blake!" I took some panting breaths. "I was hoping you could help me with this stupid old carbide lamp." Gads! Was that me playing damsel in distress? He didn't seem to notice, and crooked a finger at me. When I got close he pointed to a grouping of orange trumpet-shaped mushrooms. Chanterelles. Beside them lay a fat book that looked almost as old as its subject: Medieval Europe. Blake twisted a chanterelle off at ground level and placed it on his bandanna. This triggered my hunter-gatherer instinct and I spent a pleasant quarter-hour searching for more of them. Blake made me stop when we had plenty for a meal. With both his cap and bandanna full, he set them next to the trail.

"We'll pick them up on the way back," he said.

"Are we going somewhere?"

"Unless you don't want to see my favorite place."

"I'm honored. Is it a secret?"

"It's not hard to find, but I'm the only one who ever seems to go there."

"I suppose most people have their favorite place."

"Mom found a grotto that opens up at low tide. Nathan has a place to watch whales. Celeste does her tai chi at the end of the pier— she's always been drawn to water. Rooks' favorite place is the Nordstrom shoe department." He laughed.

"And what about your dad?"

"Oh, there's a gnarly madrona north of the fish plant. He goes up there to think. There's a dilapidated truck seat. He thinks that's where old Crooked Hoop had his vision. Bring your lamp and let's walk."

We took an overgrown trail across an isthmus low enough to be breached by spring tides. Blake said this marked the end of his father's land. We continued north a ways before coming to a long inlet bordered by an apron of tall grasses, patches of browned bracken, and a dozen lichen-covered fruit trees dotted with scabby apples and pears. The trail ended at an abandoned shack, loose tarpaper flapping in the breeze. North of the inlet, a derelict trawler had been winched out on a dolly resting on tracks leading to deep water. The section of track exposed to the tides had been rusted to brittle ribbons. The boat's starboard hull was splintered, repairs started but not finished. The boat looked stripped of anything useful.

Blake led me to a patch of sandy beach where a huge driftwood log offered shelter from the fitful wind and a view of the oyster-studded tidelands. He showed me three channels where rocks had been cleared by Indians to make canoe runs through the shallows. More rocks had been arranged to enclose large areas of tideland.

Fish traps, Blake explained. A flock of yellow-legged sandpipers ran past, beaks piercing the beach like sewing machine needles. I nestled in a curve of the weathered drift log and let warm sand run through the hole in my fist, watched gulls drop clams on the rocks.

"It feels wild here. Full of nature spirits."

Blake, sitting cross-legged beside me, said, "Yup." After we sat in silence for a while, he took up the carbide lamp, dismantled it methodically, tapped out the clumpy powder from the spent carbide, and showed me how to clean the gas jet with the copper wire attached to the lamp. We inspected the seals, filled the water reservoir from the bottle he carried, and charged the lower chamber with fresh carbide from the plastic bag I had stuffed in my pocket. He worked the lever which let water drip slowly on the carbide, creating the flammable gas.

"The water reacts with the calcium carbide to make acetylene," he explained, holding the lamp out for me to sniff. I recoiled from the acrid gas. "Quite explosive," he said and switched off the water. I flicked a butane lighter and the lamp lit with a pop, the flame eye-spottingly bright even in daylight. I sealed the lighter in with the pellets as the flame burned down.

I hefted Blake's thick volume, impressed to see a bookmark a third of the way through. "It's a good place to read here."

"And to nap. There's no better way to digest lunch than to doze in the sun like an iguana. Want to try it?" He produced a can of smoked tuna from his knapsack, two thick slices of Clare's brown bread, string cheese, figs, garden carrots with the tops left on, and a bottle of ale.

I rubbed my hands together in unfeigned glee. "I'm starved." While he made a tuna sandwich, I collected a few apples from the trees and cut out the wormy parts. As we ate, I asked, "What's so interesting about medieval Europe?"

"I'm curious about where we've come from as a species, where we're going. We think the twentieth century was brutal, and it was, but in comparison to the dark ages... The superstition, the cruelty, the suffering. We have no concept. Then leaders began to emerge who boosted things up a notch. Lost ideas were rediscovered. I'm reading now about William the Conqueror."

"When did he show up?"

"Eleventh century. He founded London, and created a central government that enabled peace, order, law, commerce... general prosperity. He was this stocky, robust man who could shoot an accurate arrow from a galloping horse."

"Why don't people pay more attention to history?"

Blake shrugged. "You talk to somebody just out of college, they think the world started during the Reagan administration, and know nothing about the price others have paid—even in recent generations—to end slavery and child labor, to win voting rights, decent working conditions, to defeat Hitler, to end the Viet Nam war. It seems the main struggle of the new generation is to remember their PIN numbers."

I swallowed the last of my apple. "I think every generation is faced with their own special evil. Maybe when self-absorption reaches a certain level, a Nazi comes along to take advantage of it."

He stopped in mid-bite and gave an appreciative nod.

I didn't mind feeling appreciated. And I began to zone out his discourse and tune in his expressions—his enthusiasm and puzzlement and speculation, the caring in his eyes about how things were and how they could be better, his optimism about humanity. I tucked my jacket behind the small of my back and reclined against the log. Since I had taken the most comfortable spot, I let Blake use my thigh for a pillow. He told me more things about William the Conqueror, some of which I heard.

I woke up at the sound of Blake snoring lightly. He had shaded each eye with a clamshell, making him look like a giant insect, making me smile. I enjoyed having him in my lap, and I didn't move. I studied the strong lines of his face, the carved lips that seemed incapable of uttering banalities, the hollow cheeks and narrow jaw, a strand or two of early gray hair mixed with the wavy brown, just long enough to bind in a careless pony tail. I touched his hair. Cool as feathers.

I realized how much it bothered me to live alone, and I wondered if Blake had become habituated to it. I wondered if he'd make a pass. After the smoked tuna, I'd taste like a cat after a Friskies dinner. But we both would.

Then, blinking, I pushed away the desire and, feeling short of breath, wondered why I'd let myself bask in it. But I knew exactly why—and why it frightened me. Intimacy with another man would amount to giving up on my relationship with John. I'd never allowed myself to think very far along that path, fearing the wound would rip open and the pain would be intolerable. Yet I found I could bear it and I allowed myself to inch ahead.

He breathed more deeply and I saw his mouth broaden ever so slightly into a smile, and I continued stroking his hair. He took the clamshells from his eyes and looked briefly into mine before sighing contentedly and rolling onto his side, his head still on my lap, so close to me that if I were to so much as hiccup he'd have a breast in his eye.

"This is better than a hammock any day," he murmured, voice resonating on my belly.

I sat still, thinking, the autumn sun just keeping the chill off my bare feet and arms. There's something special in being just warm enough, just safe enough. To have a slim edge of control in a dangerous world.

"How're things going with the old grouch," Blake asked, sounding half asleep.

"Your dad? We're making progress."

"That's good."

"Must be rough on you—the way he practically accused you at the breakfast table this morning."

Blake didn't say anything.

"When you were talking about William the Conqueror, it occurred to me that you have pretty high standards for your heroes. Maybe William wasn't an easy man to live with, either."

He rolled onto his back, started to say something, then shook his head.

"Blake, your father is frightened by something he can't see, and gravely disappointed by someone close to him. Don't take it too personally." Then I thought about all the things my parents had done which I still took personally, and knew my advice had been stupid. After a silence, I asked, "Are you worried about Nathan?"

"No. I think he and Dad have something cooked up."

"I don't think so, Blake. I've talked to your dad about it, and it's just an impression, but... You know, I didn't hear you get up last night. You said the sound of the boat motor woke you, and that's why you went outside?"

"Either that or your snoring."

"I don't snore," I said. "Much. About what time did you get up?"

He drummed his fingers on his belly. "Let's see, the moon wasn't quite down. It never occurred to me it was Dad's boat I heard. You can't see into the boat house from the beach."

"Did you see anyone?"

He sat up and looked at me sharply.

"No."

"How long were you out there?"

"I thought the journalist was off duty. I liked it better that way."

Maybe so, but something in his brusque tone brought the

journalist in me to full alert. I waited for an answer, knowing full well I was irreparably spoiling the moment.

"I know what you're asking, Egret." With steady eyes, he added, "It's bad enough to have Dad accuse me in front of everyone. I didn't expect the rubber hose treatment from you."

"If you don't end this madness, how can any of you ever trust each other?

"Maybe the trust has to come first."

He got up, stuffed his hands into his pockets and walked down one of the canoe paths toward the water's edge. The increasing void between us filled with a cold fog and I knew he felt it too. I took a few steps after him, stopped, battled my impulse to fix his problems, and headed back toward the house. I needed to think.

I forgot my lamp and bag of carbide at the beach, but remembered to pick up the chanterelles on the path. Back at the barn, I climbed the stairs to look at the films one more time, feeling furtive, as if stealing something. Why had I taken it on myself to sort out the family skeletons? Why the drive to have my name on a story? In a Podunk island weekly? Maybe I should be more of a person, less a journalist. I stood motionless in Blake's room for a few seconds, noticed his shaving things next to a basin and damp towel, and found I had no stomach for studying the films.

Halfway down the stairs something registered in my mind's eye and I hurried back. The film editor remained where I'd left it. But the three small reels with the party shots were missing. Fearing the worst, I looked for my notes.

Gone.

Chapter 19

I sat on the barn stairs, knocking my teeth together at my carelessness. Being too open with Celeste and Blake about my interest in the films. Leaving notes lying about. On the tennis court, I often had to raise the level of my game to exceed my opponent's. Someone now was playing over everyone's head, a game of malicious torment. Someone had curated their own museum of hate against Anton, hoarding artifacts for two decades against the day they might injure him anew: a wicked review, the nose from the Whitman carving, and the mason's hammer that had done the damage. Where would it stop? The thought kept coming that sane people don't stay angry that long. Now the generator had been trashed, the films and my notes stolen. Stolen out of general principle, or because of something I'd noticed in them?

Someone was paying attention to me and it gave me a case of the jitters.

Then I noticed Clare kneeling in the garden with her cat Dinah perched on her shoulder like a hairy parrot. I needed to tell her about the films she'd entrusted to me. The path passed under a rose arbor and I felt somehow blessed by it as I entered the garden. There's something sumptuously rich about a garden past tending except for the harvest. Spent vines on beanpoles, sprawling pumpkin and zucchini, browned corn stalks, purple cosmos arching over coppery chrysanthemums. Jays tossing the compost pile for treats.

"Sorry to have the garden season end?" I asked Clare.

She shook dirt from a clump of radishes. "The soil needs a rest—not to mention the gardener. But we'll both be ready again in the spring. In the meanwhile, there's the fireplace and the seed catalogues, and Nathan makes a trip to the library for me once a week." There was an affirmation of hope in her voice when she mentioned Nathan, and it reminded me of my notion that he might still be hiding on the island.

"Blake says everyone has their own secret place here."

"I suppose we do."

"You too?"

"Well, the garden isn't terribly secret, although if I were to keel over in the kale, they probably wouldn't find me until spring." She lowered her voice in a mock whisper. "There is one place that's so secret that I have to show it to *everyone*." She smiled. "At low tide there's a grotto with the most wonderful starfish and perfectly white sea anemones. It amplifies the wave sounds so you feel immersed, like the sound of a hundred monks chanting OM."

"I'd love to see it," I said, pleased to have returned to her good graces after her disapproval of me bunking with her son. "Blake mentioned a place Nathan goes to watch whales. Would you know where that is?"

"He must mean where Nathan used to have his sweat lodge."

"Is it possible he could be hiding there—keeping watch on things from a distance?"

Clare and Dinah both blinked at me simultaneously. Clare thrust her garden fork in the ground, used it to steady herself as she got up, and we struck out immediately. While walking past the cove, Clare stopped to listen, and scan the water with shaded eyes.

"I believe there's a boat coming in."

When the small cruiser had drawn closer, the red hull and beige upper deck told me it was Canadian Coast Guard. It motored in a smooth arc and entered our lagoon. One of the officers on the craft leaped ashore with the bowline and snugged it to a cleat. I knew he hadn't come to sell tickets to the circus.

"Mrs. Gropius?"

"Yes?"

"I'm Commander Carver. There's a runabout by the name of *Itchy Fleet*, eh? registered to Anton Gropius. Do you and your husband still own the boat?"

"Why yes," Clare said, stiffening.

"Well, she's had a near miss with the Sidney Ferry before piling on the rocks at Saltspring Island. The hull is rather worse for it I'm afraid."

"Oh dear! You didn't find anyone in the boat?"

"No ma'am. Can you tell me who was operating it?"

"Just a minute." She raised Anton on her walkie-talkie and asked him to come, then said, "We think our helper—Nathan Weeping Moon—went to get a generator. Ours is broken. But he left without saying exactly where he was going."

"Ma'am, there was no sign of anyone on the boat, but the engine was still running, with the throttle set on low. He might have been trawling, or doing something in the stern and possibly fell overboard. You'd be surprised how many people go over while relieving themselves, eh? How many life vests do you keep onboard?"

Clare thought. "Three? Yes, three."

Carver glanced at his mate who remained standing at the helm. The mate said, "There were three PFD's stowed under the seat."

Clare covered her mouth.

She didn't hear the question Carver asked next. He asked it again. "Ma'am, had Mr. Weeping Moon been drinking last night?"

Clare threw her shoulders back. "Would you be asking that question if he didn't have an Indian name?"

Carver didn't flinch. "Yes ma'am. Most boating accidents are alcohol related, eh?"

"Well," she said, toning it down, "he wasn't drinking."

Anton's four-wheeler scooted over the hill and down the trail at his customary breakneck pace. The brakes squealed and he sprang from the vehicle, hustled out on the pier. I got out of his way. Carver explained they'd alerted all vessel traffic in the area and cruised the coastline for several miles in either direction from the accident site. The investigation team asked at the only house near the site but nobody had seen anything.

Anton nodded grimly. "And the boat's destroyed?"

"I expect it can be repaired, sir. There's a couple salvage yards out of Sidney, eh? I can give you their phone numbers."

Anton explained the phone was down because of the generator. Carver offered to let Anton call in the order on his ship-to-shore radio. "We've towed your boat off the rocks and winched it above the tide line, so it's not going anywhere."

While Anton shook his head as if he didn't want to deal with it, I asked, "Commander, the steering wheel—was it tied or jammed in any way?"

Carver lit a cigarette and scrutinized me, brows drawn together.

"Didn't I mention it? The wheel had been bungee-corded to hold a straight-ahead course." He continued looking at me until certain I wasn't going to volunteer how I'd guessed. "It's not that unusual," he added, "when someone's out trawling alone."

"Was there any fishing gear out?" Anton asked.

Carver picked a strand of tobacco off his tongue.

"No."

Anton said, "I want to come with you to help search for Nate."

Carver shifted uneasily. "I'm afraid we've done all we can sir. As I've said, we've put out a notice on the radio. If there's anything, we'll let you know."

"But our radiophone is down," Clare reminded him. "And no way off the island."

"I can transport you to any nearby landing."

"No, by God," Anton said. "This family's got business before anyone else leaves this island." He started to turn away, then paused to embrace Clare and pat her back reassuringly. When he trudged down the pier, the planks rang hollow under his boots.

Carver took a description of Nathan and promised to stop back if they found anything, then the cruiser maneuvered away from the pier and returned to open water. Clare took my arm and we walked. "Let's check Nathan's old sweat lodge anyway," she said without enthusiasm. With Dinah following, we took the main path south. At a Y, she pointed left and explained where her starfish grotto was. It seemed important to her to carry on as if nothing was wrong. We took the right fork leading to a prominence jutting to the southwest.

"How much noise did your motorboat make?" I asked. "Did it have an inboard motor like that Coast Guard boat?"

"An inboard, yes. When Anton bought it, he thought the kids would be out to go skiing. You're wondering if Nathan could have taken the boat without waking us up. I suppose so—the boathouse would have muffled the sound. Anyway, Blake said he heard a boat."

I hadn't heard it, but I was raised sleeping through all-night parties. "Where did you keep the boat key?"

"In the boat. There's no one here to steal it, is there?"

Dinah bounded in front of us, then sat in the trail. Clare scooped her up and draped her over a shoulder. Dinah purred like the take-up action on a salmon reel. "You intrepid little dearie. You set out on the path, full of faith that you'll be lifted over great obstacles."

I wanted to believe what Clare was trying to tell me.

The trail climbed a knob to an overlook. Following Clare's lead, I looked over the edge to a level outcropping just big enough for a frame of bent sticks and a fire ring. No sign of Nathan.

"He hasn't used this sweat lodge in years—he built another one over by his cabin." Clare descended to the ledge, picking her footholds carefully. I followed and we sat with legs dangling over the edge and let the sea breeze blow our hair back. "This is the best place to see orcas because the currents bring up food from deep down and the salmon come to feed, you see. By the way, did you have any luck with the films?"

I took a deep breath. "Yes and no. Blake helped me figure out a way to look at them without power, but... they've gone missing. Somebody took them from the barn this morning."

"Not your fault, I'm sure." Clare tilted her head in thought. "It must have been the girls. They were asking about the scrapbook earlier and I thought you'd borrowed it. They probably decided to look at the films, not thinking about the generator. I firmly think the middle-aged are more nostalgic than the elderly. But you had a look at the films, did they tell you anything?"

"Not a lot, I'm afraid." I nearly mentioned my missing notebook, but didn't want to sound accusing. "Do you and Anton miss not seeing the kids more often?"

"Oh, I rarely go a year without seeing them all. If they don't come here, I fly out. Anton has his work, of course."

"He showed me his carving in the longhouse this morning."

"The *Spirit Dancer*," Clare said, nodding.

"It still takes my breath away to think of it. I wouldn't hesitate to call it genius, though I'm no expert."

"He doesn't carve for the sake of experts, dear."

I wondered for whose sake he did carve, and fidgeted—partly the hard rock, partly nervous energy. Clare's placid manner made me conscious of my own restlessness. Maybe I squirmed with the difficult questions I wanted to ask.

"I hope you don't mind me saying this, Clare. I get the impression Anton rather expected his children to be geniuses too."

"He doesn't understand genetics. He expected them to be little reproductions of himself, with a few inert genes from me thrown in as filler. If he could have grown them direct from sperm, I believe he would have." She chuckled, then added soberly, "Sometimes he makes them feel that to the extent they're unlike him, they've failed."

I found this matter-of-fact indictment chilling, and as I stared down to the water I felt a moment of vertigo. I shook my head. "But how can you live with that?"

Clare leaned back on her hands and looked out over the dancing waves. She'd clearly never used the estrogens and creams that keep skin looking youthful, yet in her sharp-eyed, tanned face I could see what she must have looked like as a young girl. "I'll tell you, Egret, it's taken me a very long time to learn this: it's far less important to change the circumstances of our lives than to change ourselves." A gull rode a wind current up the cliff and hovered eye-to-eye with Dinah for a few seconds. "Our souls were bound into this family because we have something to learn from each other. That's what I believe."

I watched the sea cast up the occasional whitecap. I wondered if she'd taken it as an omen that I arrived on this shore in a gale.

"Forgive this question," I said. "Which of your children is capable of destroying their father?"

It was cruel to ask, and Clare scrutinized me as if looking for something elusive. "You're the one who understands people."

I cringed at the sharpness of her tone. "Do I?"

Then, a glint of moisture in her eyes. She tossed a stone and watched it arc to the sea. "I'm sorry, you're just trying to help. Of course I've thought about it. Even the best of us is subject to delusion." She tossed another pebble. "I remember how Charles Lindbergh was such a great American hero—but he became a fascist. You know, Anton made news when he refused a commission to do a huge sculpture of him."

Dinah climbed on my lap, rolled into a ball, and purred. The second member of Clare's family to do so that day. Progress? Clare blew her nose and stood.

"Are you okay?" I asked.

She tried to sound hopeful. "I always say excellent posture and a brisk stride will get a lady through most anything."

We strode briskly back to the cove, and I parted from Clare, saying I wanted to check something. I retrieved the nautical charts and tide tables from my kayak. I assumed the motorboat left the lagoon near two a.m. last night, which would have been shortly before the moon set. Blake said the moon was almost gone when he went out. I guessed that the boat, throttled low, would run at three or four knots, roughly at kayaking speed. Then I took a compass bearing on the line from the boathouse to the cove's entrance. If the boat left the cove at four knots, and kept the same speed and bearing, what kind of current would push the boat up to Saltspring Island? By my rough calculations, I figured an ebb current averaging two knots would do it. I checked the tide changes in the table, made a correction for the area, and consulted the current book. The current would have been running in the proper direction and speed during the peak of the ebb, midway between half-past midnight and six a.m.

Sonofabitch!

I closed the tide book and watched a black cormorant glide over the choppy gray sea. And I knew why the steering wheel had been bungeed in place.

When that boat left Thunderhead Island, there was no one aboard.

Chapter 20

busied myself in the tool shed trimming wicks and cleaning chimney glass for the kerosene lamps, cleaning carbide lamps, polishing reflectors. I hoped Blake would bring the lamp and carbide pellets I'd left at the north inlet. It would save me a trip. Maybe he'd decide we could still be friends despite me lumping him on the suspect list with the rest of his family. How could I ask him about the missing films and notes without it sounding like an accusation?

To keep from dwelling on it, I focused on my hunch about the boat. It had run aground in a place it might well have reached if Nathan had simply lashed the wheel, aimed the pointy end toward the mouth of the cove and given it a little throttle. But why? To create an impression he'd left the island? Or—my polishing rag slowed to a stop—to prevent others from leaving?

Court jarred me from my speculations.

"There you are. I've been looking all over."

"Your grandpa put me to work. Did you catch any mud sharks?"

"Naw, just a little sunfish. Dad said we should throw him back 'cause he wasn't worth cleaning."

"Sound's like you had a good time."

Court shrugged. "Are we going to kayak around the island now?"

"Too much wind, I'm afraid."

"There's not much wind."

"Not here, maybe. But outside the cove it's pretty rough."

Court slumped.

"I made you a promise," I said, "and I won't forget it. Now, how about helping me here? I understand you're pretty handy with tools." I remembered the story of Court being expelled from boarding school for cutting TV cables and power cords. I handed him the wire clippers. "Especially these." He didn't get the connection at first, but it sunk in. He bit his lip. "I'm wondering why a guy would cut a perfectly good TV cable."

He jammed his hands deep in his pockets.

"I suppose if a person gets sent to a new place where he doesn't know anybody, that person would probably get homesick."

Court twitched a shoulder, looked away.

"It might even make a guy do things that he wouldn't ordinarily do."

Silence.

"It wouldn't mean there's anything wrong with that person. It's normal to feel homesick. People a lot older get homesick and do strange things. Big tough soldiers for example."

Court seemed to be trying to get his feet comfortable inside his floppy sneakers.

"Egret, what does it mean to be strained through a rubber?"

"What? Where did you hear that?"

"I heard my dad tell his friends at a party."

I felt almost shaky with anger. "He was talking about you?"

"Yeah."

"Well, Court," I put an arm around his shoulder, "It means that you're tough, strong-willed. You're a survivor."

"Oh," he said, sounding pleased.

I thumped him on the back. "I'll show you what to do, and afterward we can play a game."

When finished with the lamps, I explained the rules. "Give me a fifteen-minute head start, then you practice your wilderness tracking skills to find me."

"But I don't have any wilderness tracking skills."

I laughed. "You will after today. I'll leave some signs, but you'll have to look closely. Like arrows on the ground, or broken twigs on bushes, or footprints in mud." I piled some rocks to teach him about cairns. He looked at his watch. "Go!"

I made him turn his back, scratched an arrow in the dirt with my toe, and angled up the ridge behind the tool shed. I piled rocks every so often so he'd have plenty of clues at first. I'd make it harder as I went. I headed for an area of rugged outcroppings, small ravines and manzanita thickets, leaving a wide variety of signs. If Court missed one, he'd surely see another. I intended to blaze a route to Clare's starfish grotto, if I could find it. With the tide being out, it would make a good ending for the tracking exercise. The double plank bridge across the crevasse, though perfectly safe, had a little bit of bounce to it and I didn't care to look down. I left a pointer on the other side directing Court toward the cliffs, and with a little scouting, found a narrow ledge slanting down to an area where I thought Clare's grotto might be. My signs became subtler. Court would have to look for them. He'd be nervous about taking this ledge, but it would give him a sense of accomplishment when he'd done it.

Sure enough, I eased around the next outcropping on barnacle-studded rocks and found the entrance to a small cave. I boulder-hopped to it, trying to keep my feet dry, and looked in. A still pool filled the grotto, its basin enameled with a pink growth making a splendid backdrop for blades of iridescent seaweed, jellybean-colored sea stars, crabs, limpets, chitons, Chinese hats, and a colony of white sea anemones, tentacles unfurled. A steady drip, drip, drip from the ceiling echoed in the chamber, rippled the water. A few rocks in the pool served as stepping-stones, and crouching, I entered. As Clare had said, the grotto amplified the sounds of the waves rolling up just outside. I checked my watch and estimated the tide had already turned. I hoped Court would get here in time to see the cave without having to wade.

I watched sculpins dart and hermit crabs skulk, tiny compared to Moon and Sixpence. A clump of gooseneck barnacles drooped from the cave wall. A starfish flowed, slow as a bubble through honey, from one side of the pool toward the other. I checked my watch again. Where was Court? I eased out of the grotto hoping to catch sight of him.

Then I heard his shout.

"Egret! Egret!"

The urgency in his voice allowed no hesitation. As I scrambled up the face of the rock, I saw him peering from above. He looked panicked, but safe.

"Egret!"

"I'm here. Did you get lost?"

"Hurry! I found something."

I hurried. He led me almost to the crevasse.

"I couldn't figure out which way you went," he said. "So I went down here."

I followed as he descended an easy route to where the crevasse opened to the sea. When we reached a landing littered with otter scat, he pointed into the chasm. It took a second for my eye to pick out the shape that didn't belong there.

A boot, a human leg.

Oh bloody hell!

It was Nathan.

Had it not been for the late-afternoon sun shining directly into the deep recess, I could not have distinguished his limbs and torso from the battered driftwood wedged in the crevasse. When a swell lifted the water level, Nathan's hair streamed about his blanched features.

I took a step back and steadied myself against a rock. "Court, go get your father. Quick! Run! Be careful crossing that bridge."

By the time Court returned with Charles, I'd been wet to the chest for a long time. I knew from his horrible rigidity that Nathan had been beyond medical help for quite a while. I watched while Charles waded in looking somber and pale. "I c-couldn't move him by myself," I said between chattering teeth. Then I saw Clare standing above near the bridge, one hand over her mouth, the other holding Court. If only she could have been spared the sight.

I worked my way back to Nathan's body, and by waiting for a big wave to provide lift, Charles and I were able to free him. I cringed as barnacles rasped at Nathan's swollen arm, though I knew he couldn't feel it. When the light fell on his face I saw horrible black rings around his eyes and a place where his skull looked dented. At the same time, I caught the smell of decomposing seaweed. I felt lightheaded and knew I was going to be sick and turned away from Charles just in time. After I rinsed my mouth with salt water we struggled with the sodden corpse. I turned into the breeze every time I needed a breath, but couldn't get the smell of rot out of my nostrils. Charles and I were both panting by the time we pulled him to where I'd landed my kayak. The place Nathan had stood to warn me off. Blake and Rooks arrived. Blake helped us drag Nathan up to the path while Rooks hustled her son away from the scene.

While Clare averted her gaze, Charles caught his breath and began methodically pressing Nathan's skull, examining his scalp, muttering his findings aloud. He'd learned to cope with death by focusing on his job.

"We have a forehead laceration consistent with a fall on sharp rocks."

His fingers probed. The grind of bone on bone made the base of my spine crawl.

"Crepitation at the left parietal. A depressed skull fracture." He checked in both ears. "No cerebral-spinal fluid, though it may have been washed out by the waves."

I tried to focus on his voice, to follow his meaning, wanting his professionalism to insulate me, too, from the dead human being before us, but his words faded in and out.

"Ecchymosis around the eyes and behind the ears," Charles said, pointing something out to me, and I went down on one knee and looked at the discolorations. "They call it raccoon eyes where the blood settles after a head trauma. I'm afraid this means death may not have been instantaneous."

Chapter 21

Somehow I had the notion that when Anton arrived, Nathan would sit up and they would trade insults and laugh about it all, and the horror and the suffering would be just a joke. But Anton shambled like an old bear over to his companion, and the two of them reminded me of the tipped and broken statues in Anton's Seattle courtyard. He seemed only numbly aware of people speaking to him, and his hollow eyes were made of the same dark and hopeless matter that filled my chest. I heard, as if from a drive-in theater speaker, somebody asking who took the boat, if not Nathan, then watched Anton stumble and nearly fall. Clare steadied him, stifling her own grief to shoulder some of his. Charles asked about a cool place to store the body. Anton stared blankly for a moment. He tried to say something, but his lip quivered and Clare turned him away toward the water and they wrapped their arms tightly around each other, Clare looking fragile in his embrace, her tears wetting his woolly beard.

Blake left and returned with the four-wheeler. Charles and I helped him lift the body into the cart. Clare let loose her hold on Anton, and folded her sweater to pad where Nathan's head rested on the edge of the box. Then everyone looked to Anton for direction. Though his face remained drawn, his eyes had regained some focus. He brushed Blake aside and drove the vehicle away himself—inland over broken terrain around the crevasse, then east toward the studio. I turned away from the sight of Nathan's form bouncing roughly in the cart, limbs mimicking the Balinese dancer madronas.

I walked apart from the others to the house, wondering what compelled people like Nathan and Clare and me to rally around Anton to protect him. I changed from my wet clothes into the outfit Rooks had loaned me. Downstairs, I went to the sitting room and offered to kayak to the nearest phone, then left the others to decide how best to contact the authorities. I rather expected my offer to be accepted; however, I wasn't inclined to venture out until the wind settled. The touch of stiff, clammy flesh had made the water seem possessed of a malevolent spirit. Perhaps later in the evening, or next morning. I swiped a six-pack of Buzzy's beer and walked over the ridge to Anton's studio.

I found him aboard his old air-tired forklift stacking drift logs on the beach. He drove so recklessly, I feared a second accident. He built a mound that must have contained two cords of wood. When finished, he motioned me to help move Nathan's body to a pallet.

I gestured toward the pyre. "Don't we need a medical examiner first?"

"Charles can write out a death certificate."

"I wouldn't think he's licensed in Canada."

"Screw Canada."

"What about Nathan's family? They'd probably want a service."

"His parents are dead. We are his family." Anton tried to blink away exhaustion. "We're going to do it here, where he would have wanted it. And we're going to do it tonight."

End of discussion, I thought. Not my decision, thankfully.

"I can't make myself touch him again," I said. Anton nodded and as he maneuvered the body out of the cart, something fell from Nathan's pocket and clanked heavily. A padlock with a cracked hasp and numerous hammer marks on it.

I sank to one knee, held my breath, and forced my hand into Nathan's wet jeans pockets. I knew Anton's hands were too big to fit. I found some partly dissolved cinnamon candies and a pair of small keys. The keys did not fit the padlock. I guessed they'd open the one I'd broken from the cannery door that morning. Nathan was not wearing a knife.

Anton mounted the forklift and lifted the pallet atop the mound. He backed away, lowered the fork slowly in what seemed a bow before the pyre, and killed the motor. He dismounted and walked stiffly over to me. I offered him a beer.

"Bring one for Nate?"

"Yeah." I gave him the beers and he put one on the pyre. I opened one for myself. Our eyes met for a long, sober moment. I felt him searching within me and I tried to hide the stump field of my own losses. I recalled Anton telling Blake *I can see inside a block of stone...*

"I hope I haven't intruded."

He didn't answer, just watched the relentless waves come, the wind parting his beard. In time, he said, "You just grab what remains of life and make something of it. Anything else would be cowardice."

He didn't have to tell me that.

"Everything I think of... a bunch of goddammed clichés."

As I turned to leave, he said, "Egret, tell the others to come at sundown. And tell Clare to bring my will."

* * *

I forced myself to return via the south path, past where Nathan had died. The sun, approaching the western horizon, had lost its warmth. I imagined walking the path by moonlight, as Nathan had, perhaps awakened from a sound sleep, too rushed to strap on his knife. When I came to the plank bridge, I shuddered at the thought of Nathan lying wedged in the rocks and driftwood, unable to move. Hopefully, if still alive, he would have been unconscious. Charles had said that even with prompt medical help the cerebral swelling would have been too severe for Nathan to have lived long. The angle of the sun had restored the cleft to deep shadow.

What did the shattered padlock in his pocket mean? The hammer blows must have wakened Nathan, and he'd confronted or frightened the intruder before any harm could be done. He would have found another padlock for the cannery before rushing toward the house, hoping to identify the culprit by a bed check, or—if he already knew—he would simply tell Anton.

I eased across the planks. They seemed narrower, springier, and the crevasse deeper. Had they been slick with frost at that early hour? I had a chilling thought that Nathan may have been pushed, but his stocky build would have made him as hard to topple as an oil drum. And there was no place for an attacker to hide... unless in the crevasse itself. I peered down, looking for a ledge or foothold, but saw nothing suitable, particularly considering it would have been dark and there couldn't have been much time.

Could Nathan have passed here, gone to the house in time to see someone escaping by boat, then decided there was nothing to be gained by waking everyone? He may have assumed the intruder had left for good, not thinking that he or she might fake an escape, put ashore, send the boat away empty, then quietly crawl back into bed. Nathan could have plugged the jack-o'-lantern with the hammer out of frustration, and simply got careless on the way back to his shack. Maybe he *had* been drinking. Charles needed to talk Anton out of incinerating the body, or, at least he should draw some blood.

My mind struggled to make the pieces fit, but one thing seemed clear: this cruel vendetta against Anton had taken a tragic turn, and even if Nathan's death had not been intended, the blame rested nonetheless with the perpetrator. Whoever had the films and my notes must be at least partly to blame. I tried not to let outrage get the best of me.

* * *

I heard Buzz ranting in the sitting room as I entered the house.

"This is supposed to be a vacation. Two crummy weeks off a year and this is what I get."

Glenda grabbed at his pitching arm, which flailed about like a loose fire hose.

"None of you run a business so you can't appreciate that. Stuck here on some chicken blister of an island with no TV or radio. I'm missing the frickin' playoffs."

Glenda captured the arm. Buzz tried to flail the other but couldn't because of the beer bottle in his grip. After a moment's frustration, he banged the bottle down on the piano hard enough to invoke a flow of foam. Eugene Gobi somehow got there before the foam hit the polish, and mopped the suds with a handkerchief—*voila!*—from his sleeve. The family shifted in discomfort, except Celeste, who continued pushing a needle through a quilt-in-progress, seemingly determined not to give her uncle so much as a scrap of attention.

"Can't get a cold beer. Can't get a hot shower. Can't flush the frickin' toilet. We could have burned up in our beds the other night." Buzzy's forehead was red as a hydrant. "Then somebody thieves the only boat on the island. And now what, a drunken Indian falls on his head and kills himself? Well, we want out of here. Right Glenda?"

She turned an appealing face to Clare. "He's just upset. He hasn't been sleeping well."

"Clare, I don't care how you do it, just get us a boat to the nearest place with a golf course." Buzz turned on Glenda, muttering, "I'd rather be in Cleveland with my frickin' in-laws."

Glenda huffed a grumpy breath at him, her round face a period next to his exclamation point. She turned loose his arm and asked, "Does anybody have any fresh batteries for his poker machine?"

"Oh for God's sakes, Glenda, shut up about the poker machine. I'm going to pack."

As he turned toward the stairs I heard a grating sound.

"Son of a buck." Buzz struggled to keep his balance.

Celeste screamed. She threw aside her quilt and needle and rushed to where bits of shell remained on the floor.

"Sixpence! Move you brute," she cried, pounding on Buzz's leg.

"Jesus H. Christ, what now?"

"You've killed her, that's what."

"He didn't mean to," Glenda said. She knelt, picked up shell fragments.

"Oh Sixpence, are you alive?" Celeste extricated the fleshy

spider-like creature from the wreckage. "Oh thank heaven. You're alive. We'll get you another shell to live in and we'll keep you away from those oafish men."

"Oh, Gawd," Rooks groaned, clasping a hand to her forehead.

Clare endured all this with half-closed eyes from her rocker by the window. I wanted to pass along—privately—Anton's plans, but Rooks and Court and Charles had her surrounded. Then she blinked her puffy eyes and pushed out of the chair, saying, "We need something to calm everyone's nerves." She seemed anxious to be alone so I didn't follow her to the kitchen. Instead, I picked up the scattered quilt squares. Celeste gradually calmed down and returned to the sofa, still cupping Sixpence, the homeless hermit crab, in her hand. I made some soothing noises to the crab, then spread the quilt over my knees to examine it. "A birthday present for your dad?" I guessed.

Celeste needed a buddy, and she opened up to me. "Do you like it? It's a collage of fabrics from his life. This green velvet is from the curtains at Queen Anne Hill; some hound's tooth from a jacket he used to wear; here's Mom's wedding dress; upholstery from his favorite chair. I've been saving these squares for years. Now with all this commotion, father probably won't even appreciate it." Celeste's manner of talking from one corner of her mouth made everything sound slightly cartoonish.

"I think this birthday is a big deal to him," I said. "He'll be pleased."

Celeste's twitched a smile. "I just hope I can get it done."

"I can do a credible loop stitch, if that'll help. I used to mend my own tennis outfits when I traveled to tournaments."

She seemed ready to accept, then must have remembered how I'd sizzled her hair with the ear candle. "Thanks, but I can handle it." Just then Blake came in the front door carrying a daypack and life vest.

"There you are, Egret. We've decided, if it's okay with you, that I should borrow your kayak and paddle it to Moresby Island to report Nathan's death."

"You can call a boat for Buzzy too," Celeste said without looking up.

"And just how much paddling have you done?" I asked, suspecting misguided gallantry.

"Some canoeing."

I shook my head. "This isn't the time to learn sea kayaking. If anyone goes, I'll go. And I'm not going until the whitecaps are gone."

His mouth opened as if to argue, but nothing came out. "Besides, your father has other plans. He's getting ready for a cremation on the beach at dusk and wants everyone there."

"But he can't—"

Clare brought in a tray. "Mint tea and cookies everyone." She looked out the window as she announced it. "Just what we can use around here. Is anyone else chilly? Blake, would you consider making a fire?" Blake gave his mom a hug and she began crying again. Fire-making had been Nathan's job. When she released him, Blake headed to the woodpile.

I took some tea and told Clare about the cremation and how I'd tried to talk Anton out of it. She stirred honey into hers, and watched bits of mint swirl around, and said nothing. I said, "Anton wants you to bring his will." She glanced up in puzzlement, then nodded as if it had become clear. But my curiosity deepened.

When Blake returned with the wood, I took the opportunity to ask him about the missing films and notes.

"Is that all you can think about?" He looked long, hard at me, and when I didn't back off or apologize, he said, "I have no idea. Celeste, do you know what happened to the films that were in my room? And some notes?"

"Ouch! Naughty Sixpence," Celeste scolded. "Don't you pinch me. Notes? What were her notes doing in your room anyway?" She seemed to find the thought distasteful. "Well I for one haven't been up to your room. In case you're blind, I've been slaving away on this quilt almost constantly."

"Someone just grabbed them by mistake," I said, not believing it for an instant. While Blake splintered some kindling, I tried to be of help by holding the quilt straight. Buzzy and Glenda had left, so I took the opportunity to ask Celeste something. "I'll bet you're a light sleeper."

She answered cautiously, "Sometimes."

"Glenda said something about Buzzy having trouble sleeping, and your room is next to theirs. I wondered if you heard him go downstairs last night."

Her face wrinkled in thought.

"Why don't you ask me?" The voice came from Eugene Gobi who had been sitting in his chair by the piano, nearly invisible in his black turtleneck and jacket. "I often can't sleep and I came out here last night to read. I dozed off, but someone rummaging in the liquor cabinet woke me. Whoever it was poured a drink and went upstairs. The third stair has an F-sharp squeak."

"Did you hear the squeak when the person came *down* the stairs?" I asked.

"Down? I don't—"

Gobi's answer was cut short by an exclamation from Blake. "What the... who's been using the fireplace for an incinerator?" He collected several blackened items in the ash shovel. "There's two little brass hinges and some burnt leather thong, a board with lettering on it—"

A teacup fell to the floor and smashed.

Clare's hand remained poised in midair as if still holding the cup. "Oh, not that!" she said. "Please, not David's scrapbook."

That evening, I sat on a drift log a respectful distance from the family as Anton eulogized Nathan. The wind felt Octoberish, cold-hearted. Anton however wore only a white shirt and dark wool pants held up with suspenders. He told the story about meeting Nathan at a time when they had each come to Thunderhead Island in self-imposed exile. Despite Anton's obvious fondness for Nathan, and shock at losing him, I heard an undertone of resentfulness at him for being careless at a time when most needed. When Anton read from his will, I understood.

"I bequeath all my assets and possessions to my wife Clare, provided she survives me by at least thirty days, knowing that she is aware of my intentions regarding my sculptures as outlined below. Otherwise I bequeath full interest in my real estate holdings on Thunderhead Island, British Columbia, to the Gropius Trust to be administered by Nathan Weeping Moon, my son in spirit, my protégé, and in a sense my landlord,"—here Anton glanced over his reading glasses as if checking for a reaction—"with the condition that all my sculptures present on Thunderhead Island at the time of my death remain there in perpetuity for public display, and that the cost for each adult member of the public for visiting the island and viewing the sculptures shall not exceed the prevailing minimum hourly wage in the State of Washington, USA, except for members of Native American tribes who shall be admitted without charge. Nathan Weeping Moon shall disburse proceeds generated by admission charges to fulfill the terms of the Gropius Trust, and shall retain any residual from these proceeds for use as his conscience dictates."

The will didn't surprise me. It seemed a perfectly logical piece of business. But it also didn't surprise me that it left the family buzzing like a swatted hive. All of them were there except Buzz who'd remained at the house. Among the murmuring, I heard Glenda say to Celeste, "My golly, that tells you who counts and who doesn't." Celeste set her mouth on edge and mimicked Glenda's tone to no one in particular. Anton shook his head piteously at something, perhaps everything, then rolled the document into a torch, lit it, and thrust it the length of his arm into the pyre.

Earlier Blake and Charles had taken turns advising Anton of the reasons why he shouldn't do this; he'd endured them as an eagle endures crows, but hadn't budged. The flames climbed through the dry driftwood, increasing in ferocity, yellowed from salt. I flinched when Nathan's beer bottle exploded, and all of us but Anton turned away from the blaze. Even from where I sat, the radiant heat warmed me.

I might have kept my distance from the family anyway, but I felt particularly unwelcome because of the burnt scrapbook. I didn't feel accused, exactly, but sensed they connected the loss with my presence. I think we all dreaded the moment Anton learned of this latest outrage: the destruction of the gift made by his dead son, David, and of the memorabilia bound up in it. However, one of these grim faces half-painted by flames must be taking perverse pleasure in all of this.

And Blake had found more than the scrapbook in the fireplace. Without a word to anyone, he'd showed me a spiral of wire that had once bound a small notebook.

"Any lumps of plastic?"

"No."

Film might burn completely, but I thought the reels might melt into lumps. Small matter. The wind was dying. In the morning, I would paddle to Moresby Island to make phone calls. Then I would have to decide if I would be coming back. Was it worth getting sucked into these family miseries just for a newspaper article? Did I have other reasons for staying? Ochre flame swaddled Nathan's corpse like a monk's robe, and I searched for meaning in what I knew of his life, in the irony that he'd come here to atone for the death of a youth who had set his fuel tank afire. His immolation flames echoed those which destroyed Crooked Hoop's original longhouse. Despite my skepticism of gods and scripted lives, I needed to impose sense on a senseless landscape. He'd intuitively felt right about telling me his story, his experience with the whale, and his intuition had proven correct, for he would have no other chance to tell it except through me.

I wondered, too, about the burnt scrapbook. I'd scarcely had a chance to thumb through the bulging folio of clippings, letters, photographs, awards. Had it been destroyed just to torment Anton? It couldn't have held any clues because it predated all the trouble. Was it paranoid of me to wonder if it had been burned, in part, to discredit me? It certainly felt that way—Blake's wry comment about not showing anything to Egret unless it was insured; Rooks, her petulance accentuated by the little roll of baby-fat under her chin, asking, while looking askance at me, if she might have a key so she could lock her room; Clare's sharp gaze. I thought at first she wanted answers from me, but no, there was blame in her eyes. I understood: the shock of Nathan's death, Buzz's tirade, then the destruction of a prized heirloom; the thought of one of her own being responsible must have been too painful to accept, and by default her weary judgment swayed against me. I'd come to expect, perhaps unfairly, more of Clare. Likely, I had imagined some of the censure, but something needed to change or I wouldn't be able to return.

Something else burst in the fire—a muffled boom like an eggplant exploding in an oven. My stomach queased and I turned into the breeze for air.

"For christsake!" Rooks said. "Haven't we had enough? Charles, are you coming? Court's going to have nightmares for a month."

I looked at Rooks and shook my head in disbelief at the smart black outfit she'd managed for the occasion, her dress flats hardly suitable for the rough path. The others—Charles, Court, Glenda, Celeste, Eugene—took their cue from her and headed back. Blake, being most familiar with the trail, led the way with a lantern. Clare remained on the log next to Anton, unaware, I suspected, of my presence. She said something to him; his face dropped to his hands, and his shoulders shook, the unruly white mass of his beard backlit by the fire.

An undertow of grief pulled at my breath, and without a hand to grip I thought I might be washed away. Yet I couldn't intrude, so I started back in darkness. Anton and Clare would take the four-wheeler home.

The path wound through a copse of madrona, whose trunks agonized toward the sea as if flayed of skin, no mouth to scream, with forever to die. I wondered if they were expressing some trauma hidden in the earth, cankers of a syphilitic core. I hurried through by the meager light of a little toenail of moon, then, with relief, saw someone with a flashlight returning on the path toward me. The beam found me and painted me with light, and as it did I unaccountably became afraid—afraid of who might be at the other end of the beam.

"Hi Egret," came a reedy, frightened voice.

"Court," I answered, with a relieved laugh.

"Uncle Blake sent me back with one of our flashlights. He didn't want you walking alone in the dark."

"Very thoughtful of both of you," I said, meaning it.

"Mom didn't think I could handle it, but Uncle Blake said I would do okay."

"You did great. Lead on, Court."

When we reached the plank bridge, dank air rose from the crevasse, dropping the bottom out of my stomach which remained uneasy from retching that afternoon. It must have been even worse for Court—he'd found the body. Why had Blake sent the boy instead of coming himself? I concentrated on crossing the planks, thankful they were firmly seated in the earth to prevent them rocking side to side. My quivering knees and the springiness of the boards provided all the unsteadiness I could deal with. When safely across, I felt even more firmly resolved to get off the island. We hurried fifty yards further down the trail.

Then I tripped on a rock and nearly fell. Court played his light on the loosened stone which had caught my foot. "Did you hurt yourself?"

"I'm okay." But suddenly I wasn't okay. "We need to go back."

I collared Court and headed him back to the bridge, against his will I knew, but he was proving to be a gutsy little fifth-grader. The hill's outline slanted against the penumbra of the pyre. Back at the bridge, I knelt, repulsed by the vapors of rotting sea life. I took the flashlight and examined the ends of the paired two-by-ten planks. I scrutinized the places where the boards had been notched into the rocky soil, then looked carefully about the area and saw what I dreaded seeing: a rounded hole in the soil the size of a potato. The surrounding moss and roots retained perfectly the shape of the rock that had, until recently, been embedded there. After a minute of searching, I found a likely rock several yards away resting on some live vegetation. I tried it dirty side down and it fit the depression perfectly. Then I lifted the end of one plank, and slid the rock beneath so that the plank would teeter if someone stepped on it.

Court asked a string of questions but I ignored him. I replaced the rock where I found it, made sure the plank was solid, and hustled Court back to the house, my thoughts in a jumble. What if Nathan had confronted whoever was hammering on the padlock? While

Nathan found a new lock for the cannery, the person headed back to the house, knowing the game was up. Then came the idea, when crossing the planks, that if Nathan failed to make it back to the house...

But if Nathan's fall was engineered, how could someone have reasonably expected him to hit his head, to die? The macabre thought occurred to me that whoever set the trap could have waited in hiding and finished the job with the hammer while Nathan lay unconscious, or as he struggled to free himself from where he lay wedged below.

I debated whether I should warn the others of my suspicions. Then I reasoned that Nathan died because he knew the identity of the vandal, and that as long as no one else knew, we were not in immediate danger. Still, the back of my neck crawled with the realization that somewhere in the darkness a predator's calculating mind wondered if I'd guessed his or her identity.

Chapter 22

I made Court take my hand, thinking we could both use the reassurance. I felt even more the intruder on this stony island, wearing borrowed clothes, feeling less a journalist and more an impostor all the time. I wished I could call my friend Shannon and go to a noisy place for drinks.

Through the sitting room window I could see the family gathered about the fireplace. Odd they'd left one fire for another. Take away television, phones, automobiles and how quickly we revert to a tribal mode. That's what the elemental forces of death, dark, and cold will do. How much better would we all know each other if the power were to go out forever? Would we become less capable of violence, or more?

"Whatever happened to that pumpkin," Eugene Gobi said in his precise voice. He sat on the porch, legs crossed at the knees, rolling his thin cigarette back and forth between thumb and middle finger. "I've been thinking we should impale it on a pike. *Lord of the Flies.*"

Court and I left him to his morbid thoughts. The room smelled of kerosene from the lamps; the semi-circle around the fireplace expanded grudgingly to accommodate us. I crouched to warm my hands and noticed the conversation had lagged. They'd been talking about the will, but that was family-only business.

Buzz held a beer bottle by the neck and took big swallows. "It's typical Anton. We're all supposed to be his cheering section, as if it's some great privilege to bask in his glory. Used to be, people'd ask him if he was related to *Buzzy* Gropius."

I could tell from his blunt vowels Buzz had been drinking for a while. Blake pulled up a rocker for me. He seemed just as comfortable sitting cross-legged on the rug, so I took the chair.

After Buzz had made his point several more times, Blake responded edgily, "So he's got an ego. Is that so unusual for a great artist?"

Buzz snorted derisively. "You're quick to stick up for him, but I don't see him returning the favor. Can you picture Anton saying: My boy Blake, he marches to a different drummer and I sure respect him for it? Not on your life. It goes more like this: His sights couldn't be any lower if he was kissing a well digger's ass."

"Buzzy!" Glenda's button eyes glared. She said to Blake, sheepishly, "We've all had a lot to think about today."

Buzz scowled. "No amount of thinking changes the fact that my brother prefers Indians to his own flesh and blood. And don't give me any crap about sacred lands. It's heap-big sacred until they get their mitts on it, then up goes a casino or a fireworks stand." His look challenged anyone to argue, and when no one did, he drank off the last of his beer and set it clumsily on the end table. "Another dead soldier. Get me another, will you Glenda?"

To my surprise, Glenda said, "That'll be enough for tonight." She had a firmness in her look that Buzz didn't try to contest.

Then Dr. Charles Underwood spoke, choosing his words carefully. "It would seem Anton has a dilemma. His final intentions have been reduced to ashes. He'll have to write another will. My question is, is it fair to burden Clare with maintaining some kind of gallery on Thunderhead Island? If she outlives Anton we'll want her to join us in Florida. Maybe it's time someone in the family stepped forward to be Anton's representative. To help him make plans for displaying his works." He added, "Assuming he has works that people will want to see."

Celeste said, "I don't want to clean seagull crap off his statues for the rest of my life."

"Why can't Anton move everything to a gallery somewhere," Glenda said. "He could sell the island and pay someone to look after the gallery. Friday Harbor seems like such a nice little town—doesn't it Buzzy?—and the winters are a lot warmer than Sioux Falls."

Rooks, who'd been patrolling her black outfit for lint and cat hairs, said, "Glenda's right. Nobody's going to come here to look at statues. But Friday Harbor? Can't you think any bigger than that? If Daddy has made some wonderful things, top museums would cut each other's throats for them. Public buildings. Collectors." Her eyes blinked rapidly. "Or if Sotheby's were to auction one piece a year, think of the publicity."

"Maybe there's nothing worth selling," Buzz said. "Maybe my genius brother has gone off his rocker and carved nothing but Napoleon heads for the last twenty years."

"Wouldn't that be a joke on whoever's trying to wreck them?" Blake said.

"You can't believe that, Uncle Buzzy," Rooks said, then turned to her brother, "And I think your practical jokes have gone too far—you know what I'm talking about."

Blake craned his neck back and arched his eyebrows.

"How many statues has he made?" Celeste asked before Blake could respond. "Does anyone know?"

"Why don't you ask her?" Rooks said, thrusting her thick chin at me.

I didn't think a *carte blanche* denial would be convincing. "I've seen only one." They all waited for more information. "It's as good as anything he's ever done. Better."

Heads nodded. Buzz stared at me as if just noticing my presence. "When are you getting us rescued anyway? I thought you were going to take that kayak and get help."

Blake said, "It's too dangerous at night."

Then Rooks' eyes widened and she inhaled sharply. "What have you done to my gabardine pants?"

I looked down at myself and saw that both knees were soiled. I brushed them off.

"It must be because of kneeling at the bridge," Court said.

"Never mind, Court." I looked at Rooks. "Sorry about the pants."

To my relief, nobody asked about the bridge. The conversation turned back to Anton. Celeste faulted him for sequestering her mother on the island. "Women need psychic nourishment from each other—something men are metaphysically incapable of providing." Rooks lamented Anton's missed opportunities for cashing in on his talents. I wanted to remark that if one of them hadn't driven him to a hermit's existence... Finally, Buzz did a traffic cop thing with his hand until everyone stopped talking. He gave a pathetic little laugh, shook his head as if we were all missing the point, then told us what the point was.

"Anton's an asshole!"

Satisfied with his crowning insight, he slouched into his approaching coma.

Charles sent Court to bed in the barn, then hauled warm water upstairs so Rooks could wash. Glenda yawned and shook Buzz, who'd begun snoring like a chain saw that wouldn't start. She got him on his feet and pushed him upstairs. I stayed to help Celeste stitch the last of the quilt squares together, and before long we heard the four-wheeler; Clare had come home alone. Eyes bleary, smelling of wood smoke, she said Anton had remained at the beach, and asked Blake to check on him before going to bed. Clare sat and soon nodded off. I pushed the needle in and out meditatively until jarred by the weariness-induced illusion that my stitching had spelled out the name *NATHAN*.

Blake crouched next to me. "You don't look so good, Egret."

"I didn't get a chance to freshen my makeup."

"You know that's not what I meant. I'm going to see if Dad's okay. Feel like riding along?"

Did he want to confront me about the questions I'd asked him at the beach, or simply avoid facing his father alone? "Sure," I said. "These lamp fumes are getting to me." Blake brought me an old jacket, too big, and off we went on the four-wheeler, leaning into the steep parts of the hill. On top Blake stopped at our lookout. When he switched the motor off, silence closed in. Starlight frosted our breaths.

"I'll be able to kayak tomorrow," I said.

"I suppose Dad has to answer for cremating Nathan without a death certificate."

"There'll be a police inquiry."

"Just bureaucratic routine, I should think. Charles did an exam and drew fluids. Besides, this island, arguably, is tribal jurisdiction."

Lights winked from the city of Victoria on Vancouver Island. "Any inquiry means you're going to wind up answering questions about sinking that whaling boat."

Blake shrugged. "I'll have to show my face eventually. But maybe we should let Dad celebrate his birthday before things get complicated legally."

"You're saying you don't think I should go in the morning?"

He slowly pulled me toward him. I let his lips explore mine, awkwardly at first. I didn't make it easy, and felt like a rusty lock being picked, but he kept at it and somehow got the lock open. When he finally pulled away, we both made little smacking sounds that made me giggle.

"What's so funny," he said, cupping my hands inside his.

"We sounded like cold macaroni being spooned out of a pot."

We both laughed and our clouds of hot breath mingled. It had been so long since I felt passion and its force caught me off guard. That I could still feel that reckless depth of passion at all surprised me. I savored the expansive glow, and wondered if I was wrong for letting down my guard.

Blake started the machine and we descended the ridge, with me holding on more tightly than necessary. Nathan's pyre still burned, though now just a mound of glowing coals several feet high. The bones were gone. It took a few minutes to find Anton. We were checking Nathan's shack when Blake pointed his flashlight toward the sweat lodge. There we saw a pile of clothes next to Anton's boots and hat.

"Dad?" Blake pulled back a flap that served as a door. Aromatic steam rolled out. "Are you okay?"

My heart stopped for a moment when no response came. Then Anton answered in a gravelly voice, "Tell your mother I'm spending the night at the studio. Don't mention the sweat lodge. Go, you're letting the steam out."

Blake closed the flap and rocked uncertainly on his heels. He pushed a button on his watch to light the numbers. "Good night Dad. Take care." When no response came, he retreated slowly.

I followed, and when we were far enough away for the lapping sea to cover our voices, I said, "What if he suffocates in there, or bakes himself to death?"

"How can I stop him?"

"I don't know."

"I suppose I could sit by the fire all night and check on him every so often."

"There must be room for two in that sweat lodge."

"I didn't hear an invite."

"Blake, just because your father won't investigate your world, don't assume he doesn't want you in his." Our kiss had somehow given me the right to say it. Blake crossed his arms tightly and dropped his head in thought. "How many more chances will you have?"

"I was thinking the same thing, Egret." He fumbled to find my hands—I'd withdrawn them up the long coat sleeves and pushed them out far enough to lock fingers. "Are you sure you don't want me to go back with you tonight?"

"I can drive that four-wheeler," I said, though I knew that wasn't what he'd meant.

"Yeah," he said finally. "Tell Mom, will you?"

Shielding his face with a forearm, Blake used a stick to roll a football-sized rock from the coals. He borrowed the old padded jacket from me, wrapped the rock, and carried it to the sweat lodge. As he began to undress, I put the toasty warm jacket back on and drove back to the house.

I found Clare awake, sitting alone, scolded her gently for not being in bed, and told her about Anton and Blake. She nodded approvingly, then sharpened her attention on me as if detecting the lingering intoxication of Blake's attentions. My face felt warm and I turned away. Partly to preserve my privacy, and partly driven by the burden of a secret heavier than I could hold, I confided my suspicions about Nathan's death.

Clare listened, gripping my arm ever tighter, then said, "Egret—good God—Nathan was sure-footed as a billy goat. I had a horrible feeling about it the second Court brought the news." The hushed urgency of her tone frightened me.

My whispered reply carried the force of a demand. "Who?"

In the indistinct shapes beyond the throw of the kerosene lamp, there were no rules, no barriers against the wolves, not even air to breathe. Clare hugged herself and peered into the shadows, panting.

I made sure my words would carry no further than the amber light. "What if someone else gets hurt because you're too protective?" I hated to be so rough after her terrible day, but I needed help. "Tell me what you know."

She squeezed her veined eyelids shut. "But I don't know."

"Then I'm afraid for us all."

"I'm afraid, too." Her eyes opened to me, bottomless. "You must find who it is Egret. Please!"

Chapter 23

We ate a late breakfast the next morning. I don't believe Anton slept at all that night. He anchored the head of the table, every movement slow as if underwater, watching us without speaking, fishes nibbling on coral. Blake, heavy lidded, shuffled in after everyone else had started. His T-shirt said *Instant Human: Just Add Coffee.* Anton acknowledged him minimally, a nudge of the waffle plate in his direction.

Blake met my eyes briefly and gave a subtle smile and nod, signaling that things had gone well in the sweat lodge.

Glenda had apparently been waiting for a quorum before speaking her mind. "Everyone, I have something to say." As if startled by her own boldness, her neck retracted until her round head sat directly on her shoulders.

Clare closed her eyes briefly, as if expecting the worst. "Go ahead, dear."

"We've all had a terrible shock. And I know Anton isn't going to feel much like celebrating his birthday. But when a man turns seventy, it shouldn't pass unnoticed, so, I think we should try and put this tragedy behind us the best we can, and... you know..."

Confused looks. Celeste, veins darkening the latex skin under her eyes, said, "I think you mean we must give ourselves permission to go on."

"But," Glenda added, "Whoever goes to phone the authorities, I want them to call the water taxi so Buzzy and I can stay in town tonight. We'll come back out tomorrow, because tomorrow is Anton's birthday." Glenda turned to her husband for assurance she'd covered it properly.

"Mm," Buzz said.

Clare started to answer but Charles interjected, "I have a thought. Why not move the birthday celebration up one day?—do it this afternoon. What do you say, Anton?"

Summoned back to the surface, Anton looked at Charles and worked his jaw as if suspicious of his motives. "Things aren't ready. And without Nathan..."

Court raised his hand as if in school. He'd rinsed all the orange and green color from his hair. Had he been sobered by events, or could he possibly be feeling better about himself? "I can help, Grandpa," he said.

Anton turned his hoary head to the boy. "I appreciate the offer, Courtney."

Rooks put a hand on her son's thin shoulder. "Thank you Court, but you can help most by keeping out of Grandpa's way."

Charles said, "It would be cleaner from a legal perspective if we report the death at the first opportunity. It would make our lives—"

Anton crashed a fist on the table. "Nobody leaves the island until Monday morning." He looked around the table. His fierce eyes stopped on me long enough to convey that I was not exempt. "This family needs to get some things settled."

Buzz sat up tall, forehead deeply ridged. "You can't keep us hostage. You're nobody's warden. Someone needs to cut you down a few pegs, Anton."

I stopped chewing, unable to swallow, and looked around the table. Were we all thinking the same thing?

Anton glared. "Just how short do I need to be cut down, Buzzy, to make you feel like a man?"

I came away from breakfast tense, jumpy, underfed. I knew a workout would help clear my mind—pop a good sweat—and I needed to make a decision. Then it hit me: no electricity, no hot water, no pump, no shower. Okay, a sponge bath from the rain barrel would have to do. So I took myself for a trot around the island, north past the agate beach to the rocks where Charles liked to fish, on to the intersection with the ridge trail, up the ridge, down to the studio, around the south end of the island and back to the house. Three times.

While running, it struck me that Anton wasn't our warden: whoever trashed the generator and the boat was. I strongly doubted Nathan had anything to do with either. The sea had calmed and I considered defying Anton by paddling off to summon the authorities. But I doubted it would solve anything. Nathan's death would be ruled accidental, and Anton would have lost his chance to expose his tormentor. Not to mention it would cost me my chance to work with him on his biography.

Each time I jogged past the cremation fire, the tide had advanced, hissing against embers still live under the thick ash. By my third circuit, all that remained were bits of charcoal bobbing in the water and a wavy black line on the beach. I paused to say my farewell to Nathan. Near this spot, he'd let down his guard and trusted me with the important details of his life, and though I'd known him but a few days, I'd felt his sensitive, generous heart. My pulse drummed in my ears and I imagined a circle of dancers. I spread my arms to broadcast fond regards to wherever he'd gone.

While bathing in the open air behind the barn, I heard a *whoosh-thwack* coming from the front yard. Every thirty seconds or so, *whoosh-thwack*. I dressed and emerged to find Buzzy driving salvaged golf balls. He hit one squarely, held his pose until well after the ball had lost momentum and arced into the sea. Just then Celeste climbed the bluff from the agate beach. Perhaps she'd been house-hunting for Sixpence: a new shell. In any case, she strode indignantly in front of Buzz as he prepared to knock another ball into the drink. For a moment I feared he hadn't seen her, or if he had, that he wouldn't stop.

"You shouldn't do that," she scolded.

Buzz took off his plaid cap, waved it in open-mouthed disbelief, and put it firmly back on.

"Seals might eat those balls and it would block their digestive tract."

Buzz clenched his jaw, positioned his club behind the ball, drew the club back, and turned forcefully.

I gasped as Celeste stepped away just in time to avoid being whoosh-thwacked. It was her turn to give the gaping-mouth treatment, and she propped her hands on her boyish hips to register even greater indignation. "I mean it, Uncle Buzzy."

He teed another ball. He had a hundred of them in his bag. "Why don't you go pester Charles," he said. "He's the one killing the fish."

Flushed with earnestness, Celeste said, "I will not stand by and let you defile this ecosystem."

The standoff owed much, I thought, to Buzzy's comment at breakfast, and to Anton's emasculating reply.

"Leave him be." The voice came from Celeste's younger sister, Rooks, who had come to the porch with an armload of glossy brochures.

"But he's hurting the seals!"

"I don't think so," Rooks said. In a lowered voice, she added, "It's not the seals that need protection, anyway."

"What do you mean by that?"

"Good grief, Beakie, don't be so naive."

It sounded more a plea than a scolding. A dark recognition that we'd all become victims.

Whoosh-thwack.

"Well, I can't stand here and watch this." Celeste stomped off. Nobody tried to stop her.

I thought about following Celeste, but guessed Rooks might have more to tell me about Nathan's mysterious death—if she would talk to me. Yes, she'd loaned me the sweater and pants, and had been somewhat less prickly lately. Yet... I marked up her aloofness to a sense of family sanctity, and approached her, towel over my shoulder, with a comment about Celeste. "She has some strongly-held opinions."

"She's a mule," Rooks said, shaking her head. She made brief eye contact with me as I climbed the three steps to the porch, then looked away quickly as if realizing she'd broken her own rule.

"Has she always been strong-willed?"

Rooks leaned against the railing. "Oh, gawd!" She watched another golf ball fly away. "When she was a little girl—I kid you not—she used to hold her breath until she turned purple. Dad had to hold her head under the faucet to make her breathe."

I chuckled appreciatively as Rooks again glanced my way, and I turned in profile to look less threatening, like letting a wild animal get accustomed to my presence. After a moment she sat down before the travel brochures.

"I was going to wash your pants," I said, "but the label says dry clean only."

She scarcely looked up. "Forget it."

I sat in one of the wicker chairs and toweled my hair. "Planning a trip?"

She turned a few pages then decided to answer. "I'm taking Charles to the Australian Open in January. And since it's so far, we may as well take some side trips. Cairns, maybe Papeete."

After her sobering comment to Celeste about needing protection, it jarred me to hear her casually discussing a vacation. But people react differently under stress. Maybe she needed some emotional distance from Thunderhead Island. "Tennis fans?" I asked.

"Enormous tennis fans." It seemed Rooks could get enthused, even to me, provided the topic was her own special life. "We've been to all the majors except the Australian."

"Any trouble getting tickets?"

"Not for Australia. For the others we know a black market guy, a broker. The ushers like to make some unofficial income, you see." She seemed proud of the arrangement, as if it made her appear urbane, privileged. I didn't mention my tennis background and how I'd dreamed of playing on the red clay of Roland Garros, the lawns of Wimbledon... and the rubberized cement of Melbourne. Expected to play. I didn't think I could stomach attending as a spectator.

"Of course, we'll snorkel the reef. And we've been invited to stay at a fishing cabin in New Zealand with a friend of Charles's who is a *famous* famous cardiologist." She looked up. "Open heart surgery on Boris Yeltsin."

"Can't pass that up," I said, trying to make it sound sincere.

She held up two brochures and looked back and forth at them. "I can't make up my mind where to shop for gemstones: Hong Kong or Singapore."

She didn't really expect an opinion. I gave one anyway, hoping to find some level I could connect with her. "Singapore is too clean and orderly for my taste, but I suspect you'd like it. Don't miss the jade museum and the Tiger Balm Gardens. For star sapphires, Colombo, Sri Lanka is the place to go."

Rooks looked at me with open mouth, as if deciding whether I'd made this up. She cleared her throat but didn't say anything.

"Will you be taking Courtney?" I asked, knowing the answer.

"He'd be bored, and he can't afford to miss any more school after that stunt he pulled at the Bates Academy."

"How's he doing since yesterday? Finding Nathan's body."

Rooks shrugged. "A little shook up, I suppose. But, you know, he seems to be coming out of his shell. He can't stop talking about kayaking."

I waited. She was trying to give me some credit for Court's change, but couldn't quite say it. "What kind of a shell is he in?" I asked.

"Oh..." She rolled her hand a few times. "He tries to be shocking to make up for being timid. The hair job. He has a hard time making friends. What he did at Bates is... troubling... but there's nothing *really* wrong with him."

Denial? "I haven't noticed anything wrong with Court."

"No, of course not."

"Certainly nothing that compares with whoever's tormenting your dad."

Rooks stiffened and her glare of superiority returned. "That's none of your business, is it? For a second I forgot you were a reporter." She said *reporter* like it was a social disease.

"The last thing I want to write about is trouble."

"I'll bet."

She wore her moral indignation like a halo. But my tendency as a journalist, as it had been as a tennis player, was attack, and her sharp manner made me drop any pretense of chumminess. "Okay, Rooks, maybe you can clear up something for me. Looking at those old films of the unveiling party made me curious. Why were you flirting with Clement Ely? You must have known your father despised him."

It took Rooks a moment to find traction on that one, but then she let me have it. "I didn't need father's permission to talk to people then, and I certainly don't want your approval now."

The fact that she didn't banish me from the porch encouraged me. "I didn't mean to sound judgmental. It's just a matter of how you'd like to see things portrayed in the book."

She hesitated. When the hesitation lasted too long I could see she needed more persuading.

"Biographers usually make... judicious mention of the family. For example, people love to read about plastic surgery—don't ask me why."

That turned her red enough. I'd studied her early photos sufficiently to notice the blockier jaw and thicker nose.

She placed her knuckles on the table and leaned forward like a lineman awaiting the snap of the ball. "You'd better be careful. We're talking invasion of privacy. And how would your editor like a gigantic lawsuit?"

Rooks' acceptance of the idea of me authoring her father's bio inspired me to believe it myself. "I wouldn't say anything without documentation," I said in a reassuring voice. "But, naturally, readers tend to fill in the gaps with their own imaginations. That's why it's best not to leave something like Clement Ely unexplained—it just encourages wild speculation. If you can clear things up... well, it's not likely to arise later."

Rooks regarded me with a kind of respect she'd never shown me before, as if extortion was a quality she admired in a person. "If you must know," she said, "Mr. Ely made a very charming first impression."

"No doubt he found you charming, as well," I said. "But he had to have been using you to spite your father. Do you know that? Anton told me that Ely even bragged about seducing you."

"I will sue if you print that."

"Then what's the truth?"

"Clement tried to seduce me, but not until the next day. And he didn't get very far."

"You said he made a charming first impression. What kind of second impression did he make?"

She grimaced. "A slimeball."

"What happened?"

She hesitated. "Only if it doesn't go in the book."

I pretended to think it over. "Okay, you have my word."

"Well, he sent a cab to bring me to his hotel. When he tried to get me to take Quaaludes—he said it was a sex-enhancer—I got out of there in a *huge* huge hurry."

"Hmm. So at the party, were you just flattered by this older, sophisticated man? Or, trying to get your father's attention?" I had readily excused Blake's roll-in-the-hay with Congressman Shork's gin-soaked wife. Yet... rarely is a woman's outing a mere physical adventure.

Rooks shrugged. "A little of this; a little of that."

She didn't like the interrogation, but once you get someone in the rhythm of answering questions, it's hard for them to stop. "So your relationship with your father was strained even before that evening." She didn't contradict me so I took it as true. "When did things start going bad?"

From the way her ivy green eyes looked straight ahead, I could tell she wasn't trying to remember. Just calculating how much to tell me.

"Father never had much time for any of us."

"How did David's death affect things?"

She stared again, this time directly at me. Sometimes an educated guess can make a person think you have ESP.

"That was the end of us as a family." She raked the travel brochures into a pile.

"It must have been dreadful," I said. "I watched the film where David jumped off the bridge. That's when it happened, isn't it?"

Her mouth sagged, and she seemed genuinely stricken.

"It looked like he snagged on something and fell awkwardly and hurt himself."

Rooks started to rub the bridge of her nose, marring her makeup. "There's a deep spot in the middle of the creek. A channel. But he went off to the side and his legs flew out from under him. We found an ugly bruise on his tailbone, a knot like an egg. His legs must have been paralyzed, at least temporarily, Charles says. He couldn't swim or even stand up."

"When did you realize he'd been hurt?"

"We didn't, really. Not until afterwards. We all thought he was clowning around. David was such a huge showoff. I was swinging on the tire and he floated under." Rooks swallowed a lump. "He reached up and I screamed because I thought he was trying to pull me off. Then I saw by his face something was wrong. I reached for him but then I heard father yelling and I looked up and David had floated past by the time..."

Rooks seemed in a trance as she recalled the scene. I asked gently, "What about Blake and Celeste?"

"Blake was building up the dam with rocks, and Beakie, she was swimming—she liked to swim. Beakie heard Dad and tried to catch David, but the water was deep... Blake couldn't hear, I don't think, because of the spillway. He finally got the idea, and tried to grab David as he went over, but the current... it took him and..."

I covered my mouth.

Rooks pressed her eyelids shut until they quivered. A thick tear ran down each side of her nose. "Dad ran through the poison ivy and into the creek with his clothes on. He and Blake got to David about the same time. In those days, none of us had CPR. Maybe we could have saved him, I don't know."

I wanted to reach over and take her hands, but couldn't quite do it. "Children aren't supposed to die," I said, the words sticking in my throat. "And we don't believe it, even when it's happening before our eyes."

Rooks nodded and sniffed.

"It sounds like you all did the best you could."

She looked old and I could see something of Clare in her face. "We all did our best. It was a *terrible* terrible accident, nobody was to blame."

Chapter 24

In the few days I'd been on Thunderhead Island, the south path to the studio had become familiar. Vignettes of lichen-splashed rocks, ripening rose hips, twining manzanita branches, the hollow drumming of a grouse. Full of lunch, I walked slowly, absorbing reflected warmth from the ground, air rich with the smell of curing grass. Since Nathan's fall, I now skirted the crevasse inland, though there was no detour around the horror of it. The land, however, seemed to have a capacity for absorbing tragedy, making it seem a natural part of things. The wildflower lived out its measured span, leaving only a seed rattle. The land had suffered, too, but in glacial spans. Our niche lay in between.

Anton admitted me to his studio. I had some things to discuss, but they could wait until he was done working. As he had told Clare during his marriage proposal, the stone came first. And it was for the stone that I'd come to Thunderhead Island. With a soft-bristled hand broom he brushed dust off the hulking self-portrait-in-progress, then stood back to regard it, motioning me to his side. Though the features were not fully released, the essence of Anton Gropius, sculptor, lived already in the stone. When pregnant, I'd known the instant the heart began beating, transforming a fish-like embryo into my living son. Anton had fine-carved and polished his pistol-butt of a nose, and the eyes overhung with brows like anvils. Just below the blocked-in beard, Anton had detailed the left hand curled around a chisel, thumb in the same direction as fingers, as he'd taught me, the hand thick, joints arthritic. But the singular point of attention was the clenched brow, his storehouse of energy, the seat of concentration, the place from which his vision and will flowed.

"You could almost leave it like it is," I said. "The important things are all there."

He nodded. "It's a matter of balancing the masses to create the illusion of movement. It's the secret of sculpture: setting stone in motion." Anton motioned toward my recorder. "You can turn it on."

Though he'd seemed stooped with weariness at breakfast, he now rippled with a vigor both euphoric and final, spawning grounds at the near. I started the tape.

"It's a hard morning," he said. "Each time I lay down a particular chisel or rasp, I wonder if it's the last time. Every tool I sharpen." He looked at the clock over the door. "These, Egret, are my final hours of work. Tomorrow, my life belongs to anyone who might give a damn for it."

I hadn't heard the ticking of the clock before. It sounded like footsteps to the gallows.

"But why stop?"

He shook his head as if I'd failed to grasp something. "You don't know how hard it is to make these things. I've worked twelve-hour days, six, sometimes seven days a week, every week of every year. For fifty years, and more, I've done this." He exhaled deeply, worked his fingers. "There's nothing left. I barely have the concentration to chisel my own face." He studied the carving for a while. "You can't help the face you're born with, but by my age, you've got what you deserve."

I knew he was serious about this being his last sculpture. Anton did nothing in a half-hearted way, and easing into retirement would seem an ungropius-like compromise. "I've been wondering what mood you'd choose for yourself. I was afraid, because of..." Anton looked at me, interested. "Well, I don't see you as a morose man, and it wouldn't be right to leave a morose expression to remember you by. But somehow you've avoided the whole issue of mood. When you're working, there is no mood, is there? Only intensity."

He took off his safety glasses, looked directly in my eyes, and winked, and I knew I'd been promoted to another level of trust. When I smiled, he chuckled.

"Has it been a good life?" I asked.

His gaze flicked down at the tape recorder then back to me. "I've learned some things, and if there's one lesson I want to pass on to my children, it's this: In the darkest hours, you can find great satisfaction and strength, even in your mundane duties, if you live for something greater than yourself."

Clare had said something similar. Had she, after all, changed Anton in some fundamental way? "Is that the big answer then?"

He turned his palms up. "I have more big questions than big answers." I waited, realizing I had come to Thunderhead Island in part to find out if individual achievement led to happiness, hoping that Anton Gropius had discovered some ineffable truth.

"And what is the bigger thing you've lived for? Art in general?"

"No."

No explanation seemed forthcoming. "Okay, be that way." I laughed. "But tell me, why does living for something greater lead to satisfaction? Does it work for everyone?"

Anton's turn to laugh. "Questions to ponder in my dotage."

"So it seems more a big clue than a big answer. But maybe the lesson is more important than the stone, do you suppose?"

He smoothed his moustache away from the corners of his mouth and said, "Dammit, Egret, do you badger Armentrout like this?"

There must be a chamber of the heart reserved exclusively for the gifts of a father to a daughter, and for the first time I felt something warm and glowing in there. I felt his respect, even fondness, within his gruff words, as he knew I would. As hard a father as Anton had been to his own children, I doubted my own father had ever bothered to tally up his offspring. Most of us, I assumed, would prefer anyway not to acknowledge being sired by the Rapid City Rasputin.

"You said you wanted your children to know. But why tell me and not them?"

"I've been telling them my whole life."

Some people need to hear it in words, I thought. "Anton, when you write your next will, what's it going to say about the statues?"

"Oh, Lord," he rolled his head slowly. "I felt as if I'd carved Nathan and brought him to life to carry on for me." He huffed at the irony of it.

"Geppetto and Pinocchio." I'd seen it, but hadn't expected Anton to admit it.

"Something like that. He was my bridge to the world."

An ironic word choice. "There's something I need to tell you about Nathan," I said haltingly. "I examined the planks over the crevice. I think someone rigged them to tip so he'd fall."

Anton froze, then made the gasping sound of a fish being slit open at the belly, and I could barely find the breath myself to continue. "I think Nathan found out who's been causing all the trouble. He caught someone breaking the lock from the cannery, and found another lock before coming to the house to tell you. Meanwhile, someone booby-trapped the bridge."

When I told him the details, he shook his head. "It can't be proved."

"No."

"Who is it, Egret?"

I shook my head, frustrated that I'd been no help. "Anton, what have you done to make someone hate you so much?" I hoped by phrasing the question as an accusation it would jar something loose.

He didn't seem to mind the bluntness. "For some damn reason people expect me to shoulder their problems. I don't have the energy to spare, or the inclination. But I've never purposely hurt anyone, do you understand?"

"I understand that someone feels injured."

"I can't be responsible for people's failure to cope."

"Did you do something to break up the relationship between Julian Hornbeak and Celeste?"

"No!" he said, then added slyly, "Other than I threatened to break the skinny little weaselshit in two. He thought by marrying Celeste, I'd help him with his pathetic bookstore. He took out his disappointment on Celeste, but only once."

"He got physical?"

"You could say that."

Anton went back to work. At the next opportunity I asked if he still planned to unveil his work the next day. He nodded yes.

"Are you prepared for an open attack?"

He held up his broad, thick palms. "Are these protection enough?"

"What can I do?"

"Just be there, Egret. Just keep your eyes and ears open."

All week I'd tried to maintain my focus as a journalist, but now I realized how interwoven I'd become in the story. I cared for these people, and it mattered that some of them cared for me. Now that I'd been invited even deeper into Anton's confidence, the journalist seemed a mannequin, posed in some window back on San Juan Island. Any hold on objectivity had been surrendered when I'd let Blake take me in his arms.

"How was it in the sweat lodge," I asked. "With Blake being there, I mean?"

"Don't you ever run out of questions?" He thought about this one for a while. "It's hard to act normal with a man if you don't know you can trust him."

"If it spoiled the experience for you, blame me. I kinda forced him into it."

He creased his forehead. "No, it was okay."

"I've heard things changed with the family after David died."

"Changed? We grew up. Isn't that what families do?"

"You grew apart. Not all families do that."

He took up a riffler rasp and tested its grit against his thumb. "Well apparently this one did."

When I arrived back at the house, Court pulled me by the arm into the sitting room. His aunt Celeste had organized a Monopoly game and he insisted I play. The thought of it seemed bizarre given the trauma that gripped the household. But when Celeste made a comment about Monopoly being a family tradition—probably an invitation for me to butt out—I understood the game to be a desperate reach for something normal, something anchored in a more tolerable past.

When I declined, Court begged me to be his advisor. He said he'd only played a few times and wasn't very good at it. I could see he wanted to make a good show, even at the expense of using a hired gun. It seemed an okay compromise to Celeste, and Blake said, "C'mon, Egret, be a kid," so I agreed.

Buzz and Charles were out tinkering with the generator, and Eugene Gobi acted like it was beneath his dignity to play, but the others settled onto pillows around the coffee table: Celeste and Rooks; brother Blake; aunt Glenda who'd put aside yet another whodunit; Court; his grandmother Clare. They began by ritual squabbling over the selection of tokens. Blake designated a seashell taken from his pocket, and weathered some protest for not using an 'official' token. Just when the traditionalists had caved, and the game began, his shell grew legs and advanced to Reading Railroad on its own. Blake thumped it with a pencil and told it to behave. Celeste, as I'm sure Blake anticipated, threw a fit and said she would not stand for hermit crab abuse. Quaking with mirth, Blake put the hermit crab under the piano to play with Moon and Sixpence. "You know what's worse than a crab under your piano?" he asked. "One on your organ."

Court laughed although he didn't get it. He wanted to be the banker, but was so unanimously dumped on that he withdrew his offer. It seems his competency in just about everything was suspect. After several laps around the board, the players had shown their stripes. Clare held to a Depression-era conservatism, wanting to hold off any trading until all properties were in play. She would have been content to block every monopoly, then nickel-and-dime her way through the game. Glenda was her polar opposite: the wheeler-dealer, proposing Byzantine deals from the get-go. Three and four way trades sweetened with cash, IOU's, free rides, options, and contingencies. Rooks had set goals about which monopolies she wanted and doggedly negotiated for the pieces. Blake played a weak hand by cleverly spoiling other deals that would have hurt him, pointing out pitfalls and preying on others' lack of confidence in their own judgments. Celeste was the hardest to figure out. She had the luck—the most opportunities to buy—but her rationale for buying

Virginia Avenue and then passing on St. Charles escaped me. Ventnor but not Marvin Gardens.

During the trading-foreplay stage, Court proposed swapping all his properties for two railroads from Blake. I took him aside and talked strategy. Even when I'm not sitting at the board, I play to win. So he traded instead for a flophouse monopoly and the cash started rolling in. With some final advice to Court, I withdrew. I figured he'd be swatted like a mosquito soon enough, but would be pleased to have drawn blood.

In the kitchen, I put some newly dug potatoes and freshly laid eggs on to boil for a spud salad. By the time I checked in on the game, the Monopoly board had become a dangerous place, ringed with houses and hotels. Court had followed the plan and was hanging on by his fingernails. I settled into a porch chair to enjoy the last hour of sun and to try recreating my notes. After ten minutes, I heard a chorus of whoops and Blake joined me, admitting he'd been suddenly and thoroughly stomped. "I put every nickel into houses on Boardwalk and Park Place. Then I hit one of young Courtney's sleazy hotels, which softened me up for Celeste, and that's my sad tale."

"Explain something to me, Blake: in real life you build shelters for indigents; but playing Monopoly, you went for the trophy properties."

He shrugged. "Against my sisters, you either win quick or die. Otherwise, they gnaw away like termites. You know what finished me? Those blasted railroads. I don't know how she does it, but Celeste always winds up with the railroads. It doesn't bother her to lose, but if you won't trade her the precious railroads, she'll mope."

"You should have kept something in reserve in case you hit one."

"I hadn't hit one all game."

"Sounds like a silly risk."

"Maybe I was in the mood for a more challenging game." He leaned forward and took my hand. "High stakes. Something with a prize worth winning." His eyes squinted with mischief.

"Just what kind of prize is worth winning?"

"Oh, I'd want it to come in a pretty package." He brushed the back of my hand so lightly I felt a shiver all the way up my arm.

"I suppose you're the kind who likes to shake the package before you open it."

He laughed freely. "Oh, I'd give it a good hard shake. I wouldn't want anything too fragile."

I hoped the flush of heat on my ears didn't show. "You have to win the game before you get to shake anything."

"It would help if I knew the rules."

My husband-from-afar often said rules are for people too dumb to think for themselves. I almost repeated it because it sounded clever, but didn't really believe it. Not always. "Blake, if you don't know the rules by now, there's no hope." A goldfinch landed on the clematis vine and picked at one of the fluffy seed heads, then a bumblebee began worrying the goldfinch, mistaking it for a flower because of its brilliant color. I patted Blake's knee. "Maybe, if we can just get through your dad's birthday—without any surprise packages."

He nodded. None too eagerly.

"Tell me about the sweat lodge."

Blake gave me a palms-up gesture. "Neither of us said a word."

"And?"

"After an hour I wanted to leave. My legs were cramped, my back hurt, I was tired, sweaty, thirsty—and didn't feel particularly welcome. Then I remembered what you said about not having many more chances to be with Dad, so I decided to stay another hour and felt more relaxed. I got interested in watching energy move around in my body." He paused. "Then something strange: my heartbeat became like a drum and I heard singing to the drum's beat—more of a chant than a song. I thought it must be coming from outside the sweat lodge, so I went out to see. Of course, there was no one outside, and the drums and chanting stopped. I put on my clothes and went back to the barn."

I shook my head. "You blew it."

"I know."

A shrill cacophony came from the house. There would be one less player. Could Celeste possibly be making a living off her railroads? Then the green eyeshade part of my brain figured something out about Blake's oldest sister. "Celeste won't buy any property with a man's name, will she? St. James Place, Marvin Gardens."

Blake chuckled. "I've tried to throw her off the railroad kick by connecting Pennsylvania Railroad with William Penn, but to her it's just a neuter state name."

"Is she really a man-hater?"

"Celeste hasn't learned the art of using men, like Rooks has." He raised a sly eyebrow. "It makes me wonder where you fall in the spectrum."

I twirled a lock of hair. "I worship men... from afar. Now I've got work to do."

Blake glanced at my pad and pencil. "Life and Times of Anton Gropius, Chapter One?"

"Just reconstructing my notes."

"From memory?"

"I have a good memory. Most top tennis players do. After a game, I could recall just about everything that happened, what I did wrong, how my opponent reacted in various situations. To this day I can tell you the game scores of my important matches and a lot of the big points—shot by shot."

"That's almost scary," he said.

Exactly what I wanted him, and the whole family, to think. "Only if you're hoping I'll forget something." I'd also wanted to test Blake's memory of his brother's death. Any two witnesses rarely agree on all the details. I'd studied the film showing David in trouble, being swept downstream past the tire swing. And I'd heard Rooks' recollections. So I asked him.

Blake didn't want to talk about it.

"Really, Egret, you—"

Blake stifled his comment, but I'd already heard the same edginess as when we'd parted abruptly at his secret place. "I wouldn't ask," I said, "but, instead of developing an adult sense of getting on with life, one of you has been nurturing a profound urge to hurt your father. David died about two years before the statues were damaged, and I've heard the family began disintegrating around then. You're not obtuse, Blake. You know I'm looking for a motive." Grasping at straws, I thought.

Blake snorted impatiently. "Know what? We've never been the Osmonds. We always fought and picked at each other's weaknesses. We didn't fall apart because of David. We just became individuals, different interests, and we paid less attention to each other, that's all. We were proud to be sons and daughters of a great sculptor, and a very classy mother, but Dad never took much pride in being our father."

I saw no hate in Blake's eyes, just pain, frustration, emotional exhaustion. And, I could see he cared what I thought.

"If anything changed, it was that Dad spent longer hours in the studio."

I asked again. "What do you remember about the accident?"

This time he answered. "I was below the dam, trying to raise it and plug leaks so it would back up more water. We left a spillway to ride inner tubes over. We'd jump off the bridge into the pool, but the spring runoff had knocked some rocks off the dam. That's probably why David hit bottom when he jumped—the water was too shallow. I didn't realize he was in trouble until I saw him floating toward the spillway. His head pointed downstream and he sort of flailed his arms to keep his face out of the water. I went for him, but caught my foot between two rocks and rolled my ankle. By the time I hobbled downstream, David was face down and Dad came thrashing through the creek, picked him up like a rag doll and climbed the bank in about five huge strides. The rest of us didn't even get out of the water right away." Blake bit his lip. "At that age, it was inconceivable to us that David could be seriously hurt. There was so much life in him. To have it go away so easily..." He stared out at nothing.

Blake might deny the poison running through the family, but I could feel it corroding my life force and I wanted to purge it. "Did your dad ever watch the film afterwards?"

A tiny spasm shot through Blake, a memory perhaps that he'd kept stopped up. "The day it came in the mail from the processor, I heard the projector rattling in the den. I listened at the door. Dad kept rolling it back and playing it over. I finally went in. I just wanted him to stop, but he kept on. Then Mom came and made me leave."

I shuddered at my burned-in memory of the scene at the creek, and I knew there were things I'd never understand, or accept, about Anton. What if it had been one of his other children? In my heart I knew.

Chapter 25

Charles and Buzzy had no luck with the generator, so we fired up the lanterns at twilight. Someone found batteries for Buzzy's poker game so we had a tantrum-free evening while he amassed a digital fortune. Court crowed about his near-miss performance at the Monopoly board, and took it equably when Blake shellacked him repeatedly at checkers. The victor, Rooks, excused herself from kitchen duty contending the Monopoly champion was entitled to privileges. Advance to GO; do not do dishes. Charles dutifully prepared yet another hot bath for her. Glenda complained of constipation. Celeste seized the moment to extol colonic cleansing, preferably with a concoction of cowslip and strongly brewed coffee. If Glenda's mouth wasn't puckered before, it certainly was when she heard the details.

Eugene Gobi, who'd seemed withdrawn at breakfast, and had disappeared into his room to nap away the afternoon, seemed in low spirits and spent a great deal of the evening on the porch watching the tips of his thin cigarettes glow. Between smokes, I asked him to play something on the piano, and Clare said, "That would be nice, Gene."

I had my reasons for asking. Rigid in his leather chair, working through a full shaker of Manhattans, Anton's presence felt like a ticking bomb, undercutting the family's efforts to grasp a few strands of normality and knot them together. Anton stared accusingly, not at anyone in particular, but at all of us, as if that circuit of his brain capable of distinguishing friend from foe was smoking on overload. His extraordinary power of focus induced a palpable current of tension in the room.

With a glance, Gobi appealed to Anton on the question of whether he should play. Anton said, "Please," settling the matter.

Music may have soothed the beast had Gobi not selected such a brooding and malignant piece, a dirge apropos to a Paris sewer. Though the performance was powerful, it deepened the overhanging morbidity. As we waited uncomfortably for the piece to end, Anton scrutinized every face as though the music itself had the power to elicit a spasm of guilt.

Gobi sustained the final chord past the point I could hear it, then whisked away to the porch, shoulders hunched, avoiding eye contact. Where had his studied dignity gone? As conversation resumed, I went upstairs to fetch another box of Anton's archives. The stinky kerosene fumes had concentrated there on the upper floor, so I propped my room window open with a book, closed the door, and went downstairs to read and take notes. Others drifted off to bed over the next two hours, then I, too, took a candle and headed upstairs. Blake stopped me to propose a moonlight stroll, but I declined. With Anton watching, I didn't want him thinking I'd get distracted from full—and objective—attention to his situation.

Sitting cross-legged on my bed, fighting sleep, I worked on my reconstructed notes. But it seemed pointless. I'd found nothing before they'd been stolen and had little hope now. Perhaps the theft had to do with family privacy and nothing to do with concealing incriminating clues. Interesting that we'd found no sign of the missing films in the fireplace. I'd sifted carefully through the ashes after Blake discovered the scrapbook remnants, and felt confident I hadn't missed any lumps of plastic. Possibly the films were too precious a slice of personal history, incriminating or not. I sensed a bonding force in the family, existing in near equilibrium with the forces tearing them apart. Even Buzz and Glenda seemed to regard the Gropius name as a coat-of-arms to be polished and displayed. Eugene Gobi, too, stood behind the Gropius aegis.

Through my drowsiness, I forced myself to think things through from the start. Anton believed someone on the island had defaced eleven of his masterpieces twenty-one years ago. There had been attacks against two additional works in the intervening years. The symbol painted on the marble block convinced him his newer works were in jeopardy, so he wanted to lure the vandal into the open. He'd lost the upper hand almost immediately when the cruel taunting began: the nose in the chowder, the springing of Nathan's otter trap rigged to the headstone, the posting of the vitriolic review from the critic Clement Ely, the sabotaged generator, and the cracking of the cannery lock with the same hammer used long ago to bash the sculptures. Then Nathan's fall to his death. With the motorboat wrecked and the radiophone silenced by lack of power, we were essentially trapped on the island. Except for my kayak. Why? Did someone want to confine everyone but me? Anton himself had ordered the family to stay, and had asked me to.

My brain might be able to pose questions at 11:30 p.m. but it wasn't up to answering them. The room still felt stuffy. I tried raising the window further but it was jammed, and I thought I'd opened it the full height of the book, but must have decided on just the book's thickness after all. I didn't have the energy to work on it, so I doubled the pillow behind my head and lay on top of the quilt. Hadn't I been chilly the night before, or had I slept in the barn? Days were running together. Candlelight lunged out toward the corners of the room but couldn't quite reach. My eyes fixed on the only ornamentation in the austere space: the hand-painted tin plate covering the access hole of the chimney. A boy in a straw hat, fishing. But the water ran catawampus and the boy would surely fall in. Another idea. What if Anton had arranged the nose and the fire and everything else? It seemed like such a clever hypothesis, I assumed for a moment it was true. Then it didn't make sense, and I couldn't imagine why it ever had. Oh well, more answers tomorrow, maybe, on Anton's seventieth birthday.

An odd sense of lassitude had come over me, a sickly pall with a demon at the fringes flicking his tongue, smirking, waiting for me to fall asleep. I forced my eyes open, unaware that I'd closed them. I felt a black eye winking malice at me. I knew I had forgotten to do something before going to sleep, and I tried to think what it might be. Something kept me from thinking, as if the tentacles of midnight had reached into my brain. I sat up, felt my head being pushed off center. My chin hit my chest and I winched my head upright. How had I ever been able to hold my head upright my whole life when it weighed so damn much?

Something jarred me to a groggy awareness. My view of the room was from floor level. How silly of me to have toppled out of bed. What must the person in the room below think? But I couldn't remember who was below me, and when I struggled to think of their names, a muted panic alarm went off. My candle still burned, though the flame was very small, its light surrounded by the most beautiful halo with intricate geometric designs. The black eye winked, witnessing my lapse into idiocy. I crawled toward the door. I had to learn to crawl again, but soon I had it down pretty good and made it to the door. It didn't seem fair. The doorknob turned, but the door didn't open. I wanted something outside that door, but wasn't sure what. I looked up at the winking eye as if it would give me the answer, and at last it did. The eye became a black crescent mouth below the painted plate in the chimney. It told me what I wanted outside the door was air, something to breath, and I tried the door again and scratched on it. In my frustration, I tried to breathe through the space at the bottom. I could smell the wood and the dust but not the sweetness of fresh air. I had a crazy thought about burning a hole in the door. When I looked at the candle, I saw two flames, dressed in gold finery like angels. Where had the second candle come from? Had someone else arrived? How would they have gotten in? My heart tumbled over at the sudden thought that my son, Toby, had come back to me. I crawled closer to see, but it was just a reflection of the flame in the window glass. So I was alone. Or was I?

I pulled myself upright to the sill and breathed but the air wasn't fresh, and I wondered how to get the window open further, knowing I had to find some hidden reserve of strength and will. I remembered how it felt to reach deeper and deeper for strength and concentration.

The candle was dimming. I panted, my heart raced, and sickness made my stomach heavy, but I knew there was no time to be sick. I tried to set my friend, the candle, on the floor where it would have more air to breathe, but clumsily spilled hot wax on my hand. Oddly, no pain, just a surge of luminescence through my body. I used that luminescence to power my arms, knowing I may never muster the strength again. Shattering of glass. Reading lamp thrust halfway through the windowpane. Jagged teeth daring me to go through, then the fresh air cleared my head just a little and I grabbed my pillow to cover the teeth and crawled out on to the little hip of roof. Pieces of glass under my hands and knees and we were all sliding together toward the edge.

Chapter 26

I listened to the babble of liquid pain coursing its rocky banks. To my surprise, the babble resolved into low voices. The rocky banks became my body. A spicy aroma triggered a memory of when a nice man let me pick flowers for my mother. Petunias, cosmos, marigolds. Perhaps the first time I'd ever smelled those things. Something abraded the tip of my nose, a small, but annoying pain among all the others. It got worse so I opened my eyes. Just Dinah, licking, licking. Thankfully someone moved her before my skin was sandpapered off.

Then bursts of pain, the awareness of being probed by stiff, competent fingers along my neck and vertebrae, then collarbone, arms, ribs, abdomen, pelvis, legs. The shoulder I was lying on hurt terribly, and when the hands squeezed my ribcage I about came unglued, though I lacked breath to cry out. In a detached way I wondered if I'd punctured a lung.

"Egret, I need you to push on your toes." Dr. Underwood. Charles.

He made me push and pull. Apparently satisfied with my feeble efforts, he directed someone to carry me into the house. When they lifted me, the pain in my shoulder made me cry out despite the shame of it. I felt broken and crumpled, less than human, and by the time they got me to the parlor, I hurt so bad my eyes were awash with tears. They propped me upright on a sofa, and by lamplight I could see my left shoulder was missing—just a strange bulge the size of a baseball below my collarbone—and I gasped with horror at my disfigurement.

"Oh you've noticed your little lump, have you," Charles said, his words measured and soothing. "That will never do. You'd look ridiculous in a swim suit."

He bent my left arm up at the elbow and pulled it to the side. I grimaced, but I would endure any amount of pain if he could make my body whole. He told Blake where to hold on to me and warned him about a cracked rib. "Better to do this before the ligaments tighten up." He told me it would hurt, kept my arm bent at an angle and swung it forward like a rusted-shut hinge. Just as I could bear no more and released a screech of agony, Charles tilted the arm up and the joint popped back into place. Magically, the pain stopped.

"That should feel better," Charles said. "That's the cool thing about dislocations. You must have grabbed the rain gutter when you fell." He had me lean against some pillows while he unwrapped a towel from my hand and worked on a cut. Someone had covered me with a blanket, but I didn't realize I was shivering until Clare brought a hot water bottle and put it on my chest. The smell of antiseptic made my nausea worse, but watching Charles's deft, hairy fingers, nails trimmed to the quick, kept my mind off it.

"Can you tell us what happened, dear?" Clare said.

The entire household had gathered—even Moon and Sixpence watched from the coffee table where Celeste was grinding something with a mortar and pestle.

Yes, I'd fallen. The glass... sliding... grabbing for something... the shifting equilibrium of the long fall. I jerked involuntarily at the thought of impact.

"Steady," Charles said. He was taking stitches in my palm.

"Fumes," I said. "From the chimney. Couldn't get the door open."

Clare looked at Anton with alarm and gestured with a glance toward the stairs. Anton nodded, but looked fatigued merely at the effort needed to shift forward in his chair. Blake must have noticed too, because he offered to go. Anton nodded and settled back. I heard the F-sharp creak as Blake ascended.

My head continued to clear, but my body stiffened. My hip ached and I couldn't find a comfortable position. New pains declared themselves every time I moved, so I decided not to. Even breathing hurt, though I felt thankful for every breath. I closed my eyes and tried to figure out what had happened in my attic room. Surely I would have smelled gas. And isn't propane heavier than air? How could it have come up the chimney from the gas fireplaces on the second floor. Of course! The gas fireplaces would have been burning. Making exhaust.

Charles read my jugular for pulse. "How are you feeling Egret?"

A pound of carpet tacks had been stirred into my brains, and my stomach had been used as a vacuum cleaner bag. "I'd have to get better just to die," I said.

"Carbon monoxide poisoning. Other than that, some nasty cuts and bruises and a cracked rib, nothing that won't mend. No sign of internal injuries, but we'll check again in the morning." Then Charles said to Clare, "We were using our fireplace. You too?"

I listened closely. Clare said she'd just turned theirs off when she heard the window crash. The two large bedrooms had back-to-back fireplaces, which, I was sure, shared a chimney. Celeste had the small bedroom with no fireplace.

I opened my eyes just in time to see Charles holding a syringe upright. "What's that?"

"Something to help with the discomfort so you can sleep."

As he swabbed my shoulder, I stiffened with apprehension. Needles don't scare me, but this one did. Without knowing exactly why, I pulled away as the tip reached the icy spot on my shoulder. "No!" At that moment my mind cleared enough to realize someone had tried to kill me. I didn't know who. I didn't know what was in the syringe. And I didn't like the idea of someone trying to make me sleep. I hugged the hot water bottle as if it were my only friend and let it absorb my trembling.

"Really!" Rooks said. Even rousted from bed at this hour she looked anything but rumpled: satiny robe over a matching nightgown. "You don't refuse free medical care from Dr. Underwood. He charges so much, *I* can't even afford him." She laughed artificially.

Celeste whispered to me, "So typical of patriarchal medicine. The job isn't complete until you've been violated. They're always trying to jab something in you."

My half-cleared mind could see something of the katydid in the pose of her slender limbs. Her mortar and pestle became mandibles, munching on her mate.

"They used to burn women for practicing herbal medicine, they called us witches. But we're stronger now, aren't we. I'm going to make you a nice pot of cowslip tea, Egret, and in the morning I'll make a rub for your muscles—glycerin and arnica and St. John's wort."

I thanked Celeste, but would feign sleep before the tea was ready. I had no desire to eat or drink anything unless someone else took it first. I did ask for some ibuprofen—good old vitamin I—for my headache.

Blake returned down the stairs carrying something. "The door wasn't locked," he said. "It's aired out now. I found this swallow's nest blocking the chimney."

I looked at the crude adobe nest and the soot on Blake's arm where he'd reached up the chimney. "Did you notice if the cover over the chimney hole was partially off?" I asked.

Blake looked puzzled. "I'm sure I would have noticed."

Clare appeared worried, the muscles of her face bunched up, probably wondering about my claim that I couldn't get out the door, resulting in me tumbling out the attic window onto her petunias. "She's not going back up to that room tonight. And I'll sleep down here in the big chair."

"Thanks," I said. As the others bade me goodnight, I remembered the hour and said, "Happy birthday Anton." And added on impulse, "I hope I survive long enough for the party." Though I'd not intended to be macabre, the comment seemed to have that effect on the family. They shuffled away to their beds. When everyone but Clare had gone, Blake returned with an armful of quilts and blankets. He gave a couple to his mom, spread another over me, wrapped the last one around himself and leaned against some pillows at the foot of my couch.

I lay awake for a long time, remembering the fall from the third story, thinking how easily I might have landed headfirst, broken my neck, been killed or reduced to a wheelchair. Finally I dozed fitfully until daybreak brought birdsong and the clank of the kitchen stove. I gingerly propped myself on one elbow and decided I'd survive. Clare's face still sagged in sleep. Blake brought me coffee.

"Feeling okay?" he asked.

"A good undertaker could make me feel better by half."

"Anything I can do?"

"Yeah. My feet are cold."

Little smile wrinkles appeared at his eyes. He sat on the sofa, my feet in his lap. His hands felt warm and strong as he began massaging, looked deeply tanned against the white of my feet. In profile, his nose looked sharper than it did full on, and he seemed absorbed in thought. I made purring noises every so often so he wouldn't stop. Cramps of tension released throughout my body, somehow wrung out through my feet, and he didn't stop until both were thoroughly warm and I felt half-human again. Clare slept on.

"Egret Van Gerpin," he whispered as we sipped coffee. "Egret. It's a good name. I'll bet there's a story behind it."

"Indeed there is, but you're not going to hear it."

"It's embarrassing?"

"Very."

"What if I promise to tell you a secret?"

"I don't know. It would have to be juicy."

"Ask me anything."

I checked to see that Clare hadn't wakened. "Then tell me about the whaling boat at the Neah Bay."

He chuckled. "I guess I asked for that. Okay, well, my secret is that I didn't scuttle it."

"But you know who did?"

He nodded.

"Then why are you hiding?"

"I didn't want the cops asking about it. The person who did it needed time to cover his tracks."

The idea that Blake had acted to protect the gray whales from slaughter had had an appealing gallantry to it, but I felt relieved knowing he didn't have to face the consequences. "That's not really an embarrassing secret."

"In a way it is," he said. "I've got a taste of what it's like to be a folk hero, and I rather like it. Now how did you become Egret?"

I sighed and tried to think of a way out, but I felt trapped by a foot rub and a shared confidence.

"My dear mom, Firefly, claimed she felt the precise moment of my conception." You'd think a woman so attuned to her uterus would have a wealth of maternal instincts. Not so with Mom. It must have come as a great surprise to her that babies didn't raise themselves, though I practically did. She saw me, I think, more as a little sister than as a daughter, and I didn't begin to resent it until I saw how normal mothers behaved. "At the ripe age of eight she gave me the details. For her, revealing my personal creation myth was the ultimate act of nurturing, making all the everyday stuff unnecessary." I nipped at the inside of my cheek—a bad habit. "At this very moment, I wish she'd spared me the education."

"Your father wasn't a space alien, was he?"

"If I see one more smirk, that's all you're going to hear about it." The way he straightened his mouth was even worse than a smirk. "No, however, I may be the only woman you'll ever meet conceived in a watering trough."

Blake nodded. "So far."

"According to Firefly, it was a broiling hot July evening. My father, who at the time was a DJ from Rapid City, who called himself Gabe Gurion, had scored a kilo of Michoacan weed and Mom baked some into brownies to celebrate. The farmhouse was full of crazies, as usual. Someone had followed a delivery truck with an unlatched rear door, picking up cases of Jell-O—enough to congeal the entire stock tank by the windmill. Naturally, everybody took their clothes off and got in. Mom's favorite song was *White Bird* by It's A Beautiful Day. It was blasting over the barnyard on huge speakers as she and Gabe made love. Mom claimed she felt my spirit entering her during the electric violin solo."

I looked at Blake. He hadn't figured it out. "She wanted to name me then and there, and the most beautiful white bird she'd ever seen was a snowy egret."

"Ah." Blake looked askance at me. If he thought I'd invented the story, so much the better. "What happened to your dad?"

"After Firefly gave birth to me, Gabe went off to found a Tantric cult and plot the takeover of South Dakota. Later to become known as the Rapid City Rasputin. That's the whole sordid truth of it, and if you ever tell anybody I'll rip your lips off."

Blake chuckled. "You should be thankful your mom didn't fancy albatrosses." He tickled the soles of my feet.

I giggled and flinched and groaned with pain. Then, as if a fuse blew, my sense of well-being went out, leaving me hyperventilating, wanting a safe place to hide.

"Did I hurt you?" Blake asked.

"No," I said, and tried to shake the feeling that had come over me.

Clare yawned and stretched, making such a production of waking up that I suspected she'd been listening all along. She fretted over my aches and pains, and I grabbed on to her like a life ring and felt my breath return along with my wits. When she offered some painkillers from her first-aid box, I declined, wanting to gauge the worst of it before masking the pain. One hip felt deeply bruised but I tried standing. I got up too quickly. My head felt like a hairy balloon inflated to the bursting point. Wincing, I hobbled to the bathroom. In the foyer, lying on the small table charred by fire earlier that week, was the swallows nest. I paused to examine its mud and wattle construction, its size and shape. Then, after taking care of business and washing up, I felt like trying the stairs.

"If you need something from your room..." Blake offered, but I shook him off, clenched my teeth, made it up the first step and almost up the second. As I leaned against the banister to take the weight from my hip, both Blake and Clare hovered, ready to catch me.

"You're not going up there," Clare said, half a question, half a command.

"That swallow's nest is flat on the bottom—not like it's been built in a chimney."

One stair at a time, I stepped with my good leg and swung the other up beside it, and in the time it had taken me to run a lap of the island the day before, I reached the attic landing. My door had an old skeleton lock—no key. I felt above the doorjamb—nothing. Looked in the lock of the storage room door—no key. Over the doorjamb, and there it was. I tried the key first in the storage room door and then in my door. It turned both bolts. I slipped it in my bathrobe pocket.

Inside my room, the pure, bracing air dispelled some of the trepidation I'd felt at entering. I examined the chimney. During my feverish sleep I'd pictured over and over the boy fishing sideways by the river. Yet now the scene was perfectly level. Of course, Blake had replaced the cover after retrieving the nest.

I shuddered when I looked closely at the jagged glass remaining in the window—how had I crawled through there without opening an artery? The window had stuck and I wanted to find out why, but now it raised easily, rattling loosely within its casing. I positioned the window to where it had been when I'd gone to bed—resting on the thickness of the book that now lay on the floor. I propped the window as I'd remembered it, then looked for and found a small hole in the weathered casing just above the sliding frame. About the size a finishing nail would make, or a pushpin. But why would someone have allowed the window to open at all, assuming they'd wanted me to suffocate from carbon monoxide?

A shaft of sunlight knifed through the broken window. I'd avoided looking out, but now forced myself to do it. The wickedly long drop made my stomach do flip-flops. I'd been very lucky.

The old vanity had casters so, despite sore rib and stiff shoulder, I managed to roll it near the window where I could angle its mirror to bounce sunlight over to the chimney. I removed the flue cover and used a hand mirror to look up and down the flue. Nothing. I was about to replace the cover when I saw a thread snagged on the rough edge of the flue tile. A course red fiber, probably cotton. I saved it. And then I understood why the window had been open, but only a crack. With the chimney blocked above the clean-out hole with the swallow's nest, and probably a towel for good measure, and the cover replaced loosely to allow fumes to escape, a slightly opened window would allow the fumes to draw more freely into the room, displacing good air with bad. Someone had planned it meticulously and it shook me to the quick.

I stood before the vanity mirror and opened my robe. I don't bruise easily, so the purpled hip dropped my jaw a bit. Charles had done a neat job bandaging the slices on my hand and arm. I'd only vaguely been conscious of him tugging stitches through me.

Someone had done this to me. Had tried to do worse. Stripped of strength, of control, I was at the mercy of someone playing the game at a higher level. I was being hunted.

I collapsed on the bed and wept.

Not randomly, not casually. Hunted with stealth, deliberation, and purpose. While I'd lain broken, someone unlocked my door and removed the towel blocking the chimney, pulled the tack which kept the window from raising. To all appearances, a terrible accident. I fought off a thrust of shivering anger. Cool air coming through the broken window had raised goose flesh all over me, so I snugged the robe tighter and headed down the endless stairs for the kitchen fire.

The family was slow to gather. Clare sawed bread from her homemade loaf, dipped it in batter, and griddled it. I washed down ibuprofens with coffee while waiting for the French toast, and tried getting used to the idea that someone wanted me dead.

Then came a strange wailing noise from outside. Clare grabbed a broom, but too late. Dinah leaped in through a partially opened window, something gray hanging from her mouth, a live mouse which she released at Clare's feet. Clare tried to pin the creature with her broom but it scurried under the refrigerator. Dinah sniffed after her prey once, twice, lost interest, and flopped at Clare's feet for her reward. For just a second, Clare raised the broom at the self-satisfied cat, then sighed. She quoted something. "A leaf, a flower, a fruit, even a little water, given with pure intention, is an offering acceptable in My sight." Dinah always seemed to bring out the scripture in Clare.

"What's that from?"

"The *Bhagavad-Gita*."

"Oh?" I said, surprised, but not surprised. "Lucky for Dinah that you're well read."

She looked at the broom with a little smile of embarrassment and returned it to its place.

"Clare... does it say anything in the *Bhagavad-Gita* about evil?"

The empathy that flowed from her eyes felt warm and palpable. She sat beside me and gently pulled my head to her shoulder.

"It exists, doesn't it?" I asked. "And you can feel it when it's near, because upstairs a few minutes ago I felt it—like something eating away at the space around me." I had to fight little convulsions of terror just to get the words out, and I put an arm around her and dried my eyes on her flannel nightgown.

"The word it uses is *maya*—duality, or delusion. Everything projects from the same light, but without maya, there could be no human drama. You see, my dear, where the light is strongest, there the shadows are deepest."

Her voice vibrated through her shoulder, into me, and I trusted it, yet this duality she talked about seemed too impersonal, like the law of gravity. Nothing like the black spirit that had visited me upstairs.

Chapter 27

I endured an hour of pampering and fuss around the kitchen table. Celeste prepared her herbal remedy and, after seeing her drink some, I sipped at it, hoping it might do some good. The stuff tasted like compost wintered over in a gumboot, and the more it cooled, the worse it got. Celeste said she got the recipe from a Korean woman at a vegan astrology seminar in Hawaii.

Anton looked me over before heading to his studio. "Hope you're fit enough for the party tonight."

"Will there be dancing?"

He studied me worryingly, then struck out in his purposeful stride, abused Stetson in hand.

I paid particular attention to what everybody's plans were for the day. Knowing their whereabouts made me feel more vigilant, if not secure. Charles mentioned an article he needed to write, and Rooks traipsed across the yard wearing a lycra exercise suit and headphones. Glenda wanted to go agate hunting again, and Clare went along for company. Buzzy put on his hardware store cap and vest, mouth set determinedly.

"You look loaded for bear, Uncle Buzzy," Celeste said.

"That generator's not going to fix itself. I'm going to tear it down to its toenails if I have to."

"Must be another playoff game today," I said.

He aimed his radar-dish forehead at me as if detecting a foreign object on his horizon, and it struck me that I'd never once spoken to him until now. He might have been thinking the same.

"Ducknagle is scheduled to pitch," he said, as if that explained everything.

When he'd left, Celeste switched to her cartoonish voice, mouth skewed to one side: "I don't expect to be listening to Ducknagle pitch any time soon."

"What are you doing today?"

She brightened, as close to looking pretty as she ever would. "Court and I are going to build a kite and fly it."

"I'm glad. Court needs to feel wanted."

She nodded, then surprised me. "Egret, you seem to have become part of the family."

I smiled. "Thanks." But for one of them, tolerating me was all show.

"You don't act like a guest. You always pitch in and do more than your share."

"Sometimes I do more harm than good—like when I set your hair on fire."

Celeste giggled and fluffed her unruly locks. She couldn't be the one who'd tried to hurt me. Not this Celeste, at least; but there can be more than one person living inside a skin.

By the time she'd left, I felt body-weary and stretched out on the couch to rest.

And to think.

Someone had tried to gas me. Both propane fireplaces had been used last night. Anyone could have anticipated that, given the chilly evening, and figured that carbon monoxide would rise up the chimney that passed through my room.

I'd made no progress on the question of who, so I concentrated on why. Probably not because I stood to thwart his or her plans. The villain, the killer, had been acting with impunity all week, and seemed clever enough to sidestep any interference I might offer.

Had I been targeted, then, because of what I'd deduced at the bridge? From what I'd seen on the films? Court had blurted out to everyone that I'd been kneeling at the bridge, and someone might have pressed him for details later, how I'd experimented with the rock to make the plank tipsy. I needed to ask him at the next chance.

But even if I'd caught on to the booby-trapped bridge, how could I link that to anyone? It came back to my notes. I must have noticed something, probably in the films, and jotted it down. I mentally reviewed the footage, reel by reel, tried to recall what I'd made note of...

I hadn't meant to fall asleep, but when I awoke, I knew I had slept long and deeply. The house was quiet, and I felt lucky not to have been smothered with a pillow.

Gobi never strayed far from the house it seemed, and though Anton obviously trusted him, my own suspicions were on a rampage.

Then I felt a slip of paper, folded in half, laying on my chest under my blanket.

I opened it and recognized Blake's handwriting from notations I'd seen in his sketchbook. He printed with squarish lines that didn't quite touch:

Egret,
   Have made a discovery.
   We must talk! 2:00 this afternoon
at our place.
                —Blake

I checked my watch. Nearly two, and I wasn't dressed. Thankfully someone had brought my clothes down from my room and left them folded on the coffee table. Just slipping into them took twice the time because of my bumps and bruises. I remembered to retrieve the red thread from my robe pocket. By *our place* Blake surely meant the beach at the north end of the island. How the hell did he figure I was going to get there—crawl? By the time I'd negotiated the steps down the front porch, I knew my hip couldn't handle the walk. I sat on a stair in frustration, checked the time—two o'clock straight up. Damn his eyes anyway. A flutter of red caught my attention. A single red bath towel hung out to dry on the line. I knew—without even walking over to compare—it was missing a thread. Had Blake seen someone washing soot out of the towel? Is this what he wanted to tell me in private?

I'd been looking unwittingly at my kayak for half a minute when it occurred to me I could paddle to the north cove. I tested my left shoulder, which had dislocated, found it stiff and weak, but serviceable for a short paddle on calm water. The rib would ache but I thought I could tolerate it under the circumstances.

In a couple of minutes I had my paddling jacket and life vest on, and slid the boat off the driftwood into the water. Easing into the cockpit made me grit my teeth, but soon I was afloat, free for the moment of Thunderhead Island. The sleek boat responded to my strokes like a dog eager for a walk. Court was flying a kite by the barn and hollered something that I made little effort to hear. I simply waved and paddled out of the cove. I didn't push it hard; couldn't if I'd wanted to. On islands, time is rarely exact. The smaller the island, the more a timepiece becomes a blunt instrument. Blake would wait.

I mentioned being afraid of the sea. But now the sea felt like sanctuary. It cleared the head and restored my sense of control. I had the freedom to leave, to trade my circumstances for those on any of the hazy islands out there. A green and white ferry traversed between them, to be eclipsed except for the twin funnels creeping above the forested silhouette. I paddled north, pausing every minute or so to let the ache in my ribs subside, let the current drift me, then turned into the inlet where, at a distance, the old homestead appeared less ramshackle, the hauled-out trawler less derelict. I rode the incoming tide, looking for Blake at the drift log where we'd napped. Not there.

I knew I had to be more careful than Nathan had been.

Through the clear water I could pick out the canoe runs where rocks had been moved aside, and I paddled to the edge of the tide, left the kayak floating and secured the bowline to a rock above high water. Perhaps Blake had gone looking for me on the path when I'd missed the rendezvous. Then I saw it. Near the drift log, a rock-and-shell cairn and an arrow drawn in the sand. I chuckled. Court had been telling the others about the tracking game. I left my life vest on the log and picked up the plastic bag of carbide pellets I'd left behind. We might need them for the lamps tonight. I walked toward the homestead, favoring one leg, looking for the next mark. The sun's warmth and the cries of the shore birds salved my aches and worries, and it all seemed incredibly precious to me because of my brush with death. I wondered about the 'important discovery' Blake had promised, and picked at the ambiguity of it. Had my fall made him discover something important about his own feelings? Part of me wanted to let go of everything for the sake of learning to know him, to enjoy the delight of finding little treasures in each other. I'm not prone to fantasize, and I checked myself from scripting how our encounter might unfold. Life never seems to travel any course charted in advance by the imagination, as if that pathway gets used up just by thinking about it. But at that moment I felt inclined to explore any overgrown path Blake might lead me down.

The trail of markers was none too subtle and Blake's clever use of crab shells and bull kelp made me laugh. I supposed it would lead to the old house, though I would much rather have remained in the sun. To my surprise, the trail veered left to the old boat with the wounded hull. Three makeshift steps made of creosoted timbers led to a ship's ladder of rope and aluminum for the final two steps aboard. The boat, on its rail trolley, was restrained by a winch and rusty cable that looked none too secure. I paused, jarred back to a sense of caution.

"Blake," I hollered. "Come out, come out wherever you are."

Chatter of a kingfisher over the silent inlet.

I decided to climb up just far enough to peer over the

gunwale.

"Blake?" I called more softly, viewing the clutter on deck: rusted brackets, buckets of parts. The wheelhouse door leaned unhinged over the doorway; wires poked from holes where lights or motors had been salvaged. Something felt wrong, and I held to the gunwale with one arm and tried to sort it out. Then I saw another sign—an arrow pointing aft drawn in grease on the outside of the wheelhouse. It had a creepy quality to it.

I felt torn. Every nerve in me pleaded to return to my kayak and clear out of here. But I felt inches away from knowing the answer to the violence and harassment that had been plaguing Anton for all these years. And inches from facing the coward who'd gassed me. The opportunity to learn the truth weighed heavily... but not heavily enough. Just as I'd decided to retreat, however, I saw a little spot of crimson on the deck, and I held tightly to the boat as my strength failed me.

I thought of Nathan's body wedged in the crevice, head caved in, and I pictured Blake crumpled to the deck just around the corner, bleeding to death while I gave in to my fears and paddled off. I couldn't do it.

"Blake, I'm leaving!" I'd hoped to draw someone into the open, but nothing happened—not the slightest vibration in the boat's planking. I spotted a length of pipe on deck that I could wield, steeled myself against aches, climbed aboard, and quickly armed myself. The boat shifted with my weight and I stepped carefully past cables and debris, following the arrow. Another arrow on the afterdeck pointed to an open hatch next to a stack of old crab pots. I felt that same eerie vibration in my lower spine that I'd felt in the attic room that morning.

"Blake, forget it, I'm not going down there." I looked carefully around, dropped to one knee and shaded my eyes to peer into the darkness. Then I felt the boat shift slightly, and in one swift motion I tightened my grip on the pipe and turned, but only enough to see the wheelhouse door crashing down on me with such force that I barely had time to raise a protective forearm before it struck and unbalanced me. My only chance of avoiding a headfirst plummet into the hold was to stretch out and grab for the opposite lip, but with a sutured, strengthless hand I could only claw futilely at the edge on my way into the void.

I don't know what hit first when I landed, only that a screaming light filled my brain and froze my limbs, and consciousness had narrowed to an opalescent shimmering before my eyes. I lay sprawled with the breath knocked out of me, gasping to restart my lungs. Every nerve seemed on fire. Finally a sharp inhalation came and I gasped for breath, and became aware of one side of my face being in a shallow pool of cold, fetid water, and it helped restore my senses. Above me, a scraping sound, and the square of light I had fallen through became a smaller rectangle. I rolled to one elbow, groaned at the pain knifing through my ribs, and tried to get my feet under me, but the hatch cover budged again and again until it pinched out the last slit of light. With it went my composure. I grabbed one thought out of the chaos: had Blake been struck, too? Together could we save ourselves? I dropped to my knees and grasped wildly about, thinking he must be laying bound or unconscious somewhere, but I found only stinking, algae-thickened water and metal surfaces and something round and heavy—the pipe I'd armed myself with. The feel of a weapon in my grip tripped a breaker in my primitive brain and I wanted nothing but to wield it. I located the hatch at arm's reach overhead and swung with desperate fury, then doubled in pain at the effort it cost me.

And then I knew why Blake wasn't down here with me. But I didn't want to believe it.

I stood erect and cried out, first in wordless anguish, then in a hysterical plea, "Blake, let me out of here!" Under my sobs I added, "You rotten bastard."

No reply, just the thump of heavy weights being piled on the hatch cover. Laboring for breath, I stretched my fingertips to feel around the hatch edges for a place to pry with my pipe, but the cover fit too tightly. I felt the boat sway, heard footsteps. I banged the pipe against the sides of my prison—a fish hold—but only made muffled clangs. "Blake, don't leave me here. Please!" I listened for an answer but heard nothing. Nothing but a rasping sound mixed with the buzz of pain. "How long are you going to leave me in here? It's wet and I'm cold!" My voice reverberated shrill and loud, and when I stopped, still the jerky rasping sound.

"Cowardly piece of shit!"

More rasping. Then the boat jerked sharply, knocking me off my feet. It continued moving, swaying and rumbling, and I knew it had been cut loose from the winch. I could do nothing but moan in despair as the boat rolled down the trolley tracks until it splashed and glided into deeper water. The old boat rocked crazily, and began listing almost immediately from water gushing through the rent in the starboard bow. The slimy water in the hold sloshed to one corner. For a moment the old trawler stabilized with her nose slightly lowered, but then, with deep gulps of escaping air, her bow ratcheted downward. Then a spray of saltwater came from somewhere and the hatch over my head began to chatter with air being forced out, and I realized the full horror of it: the boat would go under. I huddled in a corner away from the spray, feeling the seawater wicking into all the dry places in my clothing, and renewing the cold in the places already wet. A minute later, the trawler timbers groaned as she settled on the bottom.

I began wailing through chattering teeth until the echoes of my whimpering so unnerved me I forced myself to shut up. I had but minutes to live and every second lost to panic counted against me. I tried working to the high end of the slanting floor, but slid back, and I hoped perhaps the weights he'd put on the hatch cover had slid off too, so I tried pushing at the lid with the lead pipe with all my strength, then realized that even if the hatch cover was not secured somehow, the force of several feet of water above it would make it impossible for me to lift. A steady hiss of water sprayed in. The water level had climbed past my knees and my legs began quivering and wouldn't stop and finally gave way, plunging me chest deep in the frigid water. I began hyperventilating and felt I would die from lack of breath. My mouth had a coppery, chemical taste in it. Awful. I'd thought tasting death was a figure of speech, but death does have a taste.

As the seawater sprayed in, I fought to control my fear. My tongue circled my dry mouth, found a speck lodged in my teeth and worked it loose, and in the nervous clench of my jaw, I bit it, releasing the rich flavor of nutmeg. There'd been freshly ground nutmeg on my French toast that morning, and it became a kernel around which I began to gather my wits. A comforting touch before death. God is in the details, I'd heard. My oblique and personal proof of a good-humored deity? Crazy, but it reminded me of grandmother's vial of rose petals on the chain around my neck, and, to stay focused on anything but panic, I pulled it from under my shirt, closed trembling fingers around it, and uttered a prayer of sorts. *If there's anything else you want me to do in this world, you better get me the hell out of here!*

It didn't seem so very lonely anymore with something of grandmother's in hand, and I had the sudden conviction it was within my power to escape. Thoughts piled one on another as if my brain had capacity to burn and I felt almost outside of myself.

I tried the pipe again on the hatch cover, but could find no joint to lever into. I could wait until the hold filled with water, and with the pressure neutralized, perhaps budge the hatch. But it seemed like lousy odds, waiting until all the air was gone. At least my legs felt more solid. I let the pipe go and searched the mesh pockets of my paddling jacket. Only my safety knife—useless against the thick hatch cover—the bag of carbide, and three flares. The flares would give me light, but would also make choking fumes.

The water inched over my waist and my leg bones ached from cold.

Choking fumes.

Carbide. Acetylene gas.

Explosive!

Mind racing, I reached for the carbide. Though wet, the bag's seal had held. How to ignite the gas? Of course, I'd put a butane lighter in with the pellets so I could test the lamp. I held the plastic bag away from the spray and pulled open the seal. My stiff, trembling fingers closed around the lighter but in my haste to close the bag before water dripped in, I lost my grip on the lighter and it fell into the water. In blinding despair, I held the bag above water level and groped senselessly for the lighter before the horrible reality dawned that, being wet, it wouldn't light anyway. I cried out in anguish. As if in answer, the hatch cover chattered laughingly with escaping air, and the water crept rapidly to chest level.

Then, with sudden clarity, I knew what I must do. I resealed the carbide, knowing that to breathe acetylene fumes would be a death worse than drowning, and reached for the safety flares in my jacket. I'd protected them against moisture with a vacuum sealer, and I tried tearing the package with my teeth, but the plastic wouldn't give. I unclipped my safety knife, took great caution not to let it slip from my cold-numbed fingers, slit the package, knowing I must act while sufficient air remained in the hold. I let the knife go, held the three flares in one hand, the carbide in the other, ventilated deeply three or four times knowing these might be the last breaths I'd ever draw, then held my breath, squeezed my eyes shut, opened the bag of pellets, and cast them out on the water. I dared not sniff the air to make sure they were working, knowing I would choke on the searingly toxic gas. By the time I found the pull chain of one of the flares, my chest had already tightened from stale air. I plunged my body under the water, pulled the chain. And...

Only darkness.

Lungs bursting, I flung aside the dud flare and found that in jerking the chain, I'd lost my grip on one of the others, leaving only one left. Too, I realized my natural flotation had kept the top of my head above the surface during the first attempt, so I inserted a finger in the pull ring, resolved to hold the flare above the water while sinking my head below, which required me to lay back in the water and let go of my precious air. I exhaled to lose buoyancy, felt the water climb my face as I sank. In a few more seconds my body would gasp involuntarily for air and draw in killing brine. Praying against another dud, I held the flare above at arm's length and pulled sharply.

Chapter 28

The shock wave tumbled and stunned me. A waterfall of sound, a blossom of light. I struggled to orient myself, not knowing if the sounds and light were from concussed senses. I stretched out my arms and felt one wall of my prison. Something solid under my feet. I thrust off toward the brightest part of the light, kicking, pulling, one stroke after another after another.

Then, like waking from a nightmare, I broke surface and gasped for air, inhaling the seawater streaming off my face, coughing it back out. I swept my clinging hair aside, wiped my eyes clear, looked for something to hang on to among the floating debris and found a plastic jug. The hatch cover floated nearby in a sparse flotilla of flotsam. So the explosion hadn't done much damage, perhaps only enough to force the hatch, but it had been enough. Had Blake, however, remained behind to see the job through? I held on to the jug, keeping low in the water, trying to regain my breath, waiting for an indication I'd been seen.

Endless minutes. Nothing. My teeth rattled from the intolerable cold. Though shore was but fifty feet away, I needed to reach it before losing all feeling in my limbs. I sidestroked with arms stiff and tingling, making no sound, listening, watching for movement. I'd make an easy target, but at least I'd look Blake in the eye and force him to show some guts, and get in some kind of a desperation shot.

I swam without much rhythm, and by the time I scraped bottom and I crawled out of the shallows on to the rocky fringe of the inlet, my body felt made of lead. How much time had passed between the sinking of the boat and my escape? Five minutes? Ten? Time enough for him to have hurried off, confident I'd been dealt with; little enough for him to have heard the muffled blast and returned to watch for a body to bob up. If so, he might be waiting in the woods to club me. My kayak drifted in the inlet like a stray dog. He'd shoved it out, but the incoming tide kept it close. Still, I'd have to swim to retrieve it, and was already shivering uncontrollably. I got to my feet and staggered to the nearest hiding place—the winch above the trolley rails—and crouched behind it. After peering carefully about, I noticed the stub of cable running off the winch. Hacksawed cleanly. With a bottomless feeling, I wondered if Blake had been planning my murder even as he rubbed my feet that morning. How could I have been so wrong about him?

I peeled off my clothes with difficulty, stitches in my left palm torn free, fingers scorched by the explosion. I wrung water from my top and pants as best I could and put them back on. Designed for foul weather, they would dry from body heat. I found a driftwood staff, which could serve as a cudgel in the event I had the opportunity to brain the coward who'd sunk me. The cairns and markers which had led me to the trap had been kicked apart. How stupid I'd been not to leave word where I was going. Had anyone seen me leave? Only Court.

Which gave me an idea.

I piled a cairn near the end of the canoe run and used my stick to draw arrows as I walked across the isthmus to Anton's half of the island, enduring my bruised hip in exchange for the warmth generated by moving. And every step fanned another kind of fire in my gut. Crimes of madness or passion I could understand. But the calculated assaults on me were so inhuman as to seem infinitely despicable, and it struck a flare of fury I'd never felt before.

My jaw set in determination, I diverged onto a game trail traversing the eastern slope and labored southward over a rock outcropping, through a glen of leathery ferns, into a conifer and madrona forest. Every so often the trail would peter out, but soon another would appear. Every few minutes I stopped to let the pain subside, and to blaze an alder sapling with a sharp rock, or barricade a fork in the trail. Once, as I built a cairn on a deadfall, I looked up to see a pair of liquid eyes bracketed by oversized ears, one of the dwarfed breed of island deer, her eyes seeming to acknowledge something wild in mine, and I didn't feel wholly human any more, but an older kind of creature at home in the forest, familiar with beauty and brutality, peace and aggression. With a few dainty steps, she disappeared into the understory, leaving me with the blessing of more graceful movement through the clutter. I emerged eventually at a dome of tawny grasses and manzanita, serpentine branches the color of dried blood. My senses seemed dulled, blunted. Mats of moss grew to the edges of the cliffs in pastel hues—pewter, absinthe, jade. As I skirted a thicket of wild rose, a brace of grouse burst into flight, and my heart trampolined. I loosened my death grip on the staff and continued until the metal roof of the cannery building came into view. In a concealed place where I could watch both the building and the trail behind me, a sunny place out of the breeze, I sank into a bed of dry moss. My ears continued to ring, whether from the blast or the headfirst tumble into the fish hold, I didn't know. My scorched fingers throbbed.

The accumulated trauma brought on a bit of shock and, while keeping watch, I battled lethargy. Should I go searching for Anton? What could he do if Blake denied my accusations? What if I ran into Blake first? Though I wanted to protect the statues, my first priority—beyond staying alive—was to see Blake punished for the murder of Nathan Weeping Moon and the twice-attempted murder of Egret Van Gerpin. I didn't see any way of connecting him to the crimes other than with circumstantial evidence. After all, I'd not even seen who'd pushed the door over on me.

The note!

All that remained of the lettering was blue stains. It had been written with a felt-tipped pen. Even if the words could be deciphered, how could the handwriting be identified conclusively? It needed to be more certain than that, and I had no doubt he would commit himself within a few hours.

My mind tore at itself to reconcile the enormous disconnect between my respect—and affection—for Blake, and the brutal reality of his crimes. Then again, the note could have been forged, a cunning trick. Nathan's murderer had consistently been several steps ahead of everyone else. And, in the barn, at the clarifying hour of midnight, Blake's story had rung true: his work for the homeless; brick stoves in Guatemala.

On the other hand, perhaps the FBI was interested in him for more than sinking a Makah whaling boat. Sinking a boat...

A slamming door roused me from near sleep and I rubbed something gummy out of my eyes. Anton emerged from the cannery. Then another figure—Blake. I got to one knee, thought about standing and waving an arm. Anton could tell me how long Blake had been with him, and it would be settled, and what could Blake do to me with his father there. But the question of proof would remain in everyone's mind... including my own. Frozen with indecision, I watched Blake mount the four-wheeler behind his father, who revved the motor and powered it through the gears up the trail. Four-thirty-four by my watch.

When they'd disappeared over the ridge, I willed my stiff carcass upright and stilt-walked to the cannery. I tested the padlock, then considered alternatives for getting in. The old forklift had been parked outside, out of the way. I thought of using it to rip the door off, but that would defeat my purpose.

I circled the building, pulling at loose sheet metal, searching for a breach I might crawl through. Nothing. I looked in vain for a hidden key, then gave up, crossed my arms to think, and envied the pigeons flying in and out the bank of high windows. Eighteen feet or so off the ground. I couldn't recall seeing a ladder about.

But maybe the forklift... It took me a few minutes to start it and experiment with raising the forks. Extended to full telescoping height, the tines wouldn't reach the windows, but perhaps close enough. And if I entered the building through the north windows, the forklift would be out of sight when people came. Anton or Blake might notice it missing, but it would be dusk and they might not.

Since crawling half-dead from the lagoon, the thought of rising like a poltergeist before my murderer had narcotized my aching body and fueled every step of the long trudge here. Now, what I might shy at when healthy, I undertook with determination, arranging old lumber to create a level spot under the windows, driving the machine into place. I pondered the next problem—raising the lift with me on it.

The forklift's tool compartment contained several wrenches, a coil of baling wire, and a pair of leather gloves. One of the open-end wrenches fit just right to prop the lift lever in the slow operating position. I uncoiled the wire and twisted one end around the wrench.

To my irritation, the forklift automatically shut down when my weight wasn't in the seat. A little trial and error proved the forklift couldn't tell the difference between my butt and two cement blocks.

With the motor running, I pulled on the gloves, wedged the wrench against the lift lever, climbed aboard the closest tine, and fed wire off the spool as I rose. My perch felt increasingly precarious as the lift reached full extension.

Without looking down I yanked the wire, pulling out the wrench, springing the lever back to resting position. The fork attachment shuddered and I clutched the crosspiece for balance, feeling a slight vibration as the machine continued to run noiselessly; I supposed it would turn itself off after idling for a while. I pulled the wrench up, unhooked the wire, and slipped the wrench into my back pocket.

I turned cautiously toward the window, disappointed to find myself only at eye level with the bottom of it. Crouching with arms spread for balance, I baby-stepped along the narrow fork, then leaned forward to grab the window casing.

It was the kind of gridded window that tilted outward from the bottom. With a bit of gentle tugging I got it open as far as it would go.

I tried pulling myself up into the gap, but spears of pain went through my shoulder and ribs and I collapsed back, feet scrambling to find the narrow tine. I collected myself and tried to come up with a better plan. Even if I'd wanted to give it up, I had no way of lowering the fork, and my body couldn't handle jumping down. If I could just get a leg up and over...

I tested the forklift tine for springiness. Not much. I used the wrench to clear the glass from the bottom row of panes. When ready, I held on to the bottom of the window frame, visualized my movements, then before I could chicken out, sprang, throwing my leg up like a pole vaulter to hook it over the ledge.

The window frame deformed with my weight; glass shards showered me and tinkled below. Gritting my teeth against a riot of pains, I got my other leg over the sill and heaved through the gap until safely balanced.

I looked inside, breathing hard. A line of pigeons on a rafter stared back with astonishment. A cabinet stood conveniently near on the old sliming table below, which ran continuously around the perimeter walls. The space had been tidied, with lamps placed at intervals on the steel table and hung from rafters. Anton's statues remained draped with sheets, their placement irregular yet pleasing, like stones in a Japanese garden.

I climbed down on the cabinet, to the sliming table, to the concrete floor. As my eyes adjusted to the dim light, I began working on my two priorities: a hiding place, and a weapon. I recalled the motto taped to my tennis racquet: *Attack!* On my spare racquet, which I switched to in dire situations, the motto said: *Aim for the head!*

Concealment would be easy with so much of the interior in shadows. I could crouch behind any number of crates or pieces of dilapidated cannery equipment. I found a utility knife and kept it, though it didn't feel like much of a weapon. I hefted a crowbar but found it too heavy to wield. There were some big treble fishhooks that Nathan could have rigged into a trap—but, too complicated.

Nothing seemed easy, and I even considered filling a pump-style oil can with kerosene to make a rudimentary flamethrower. I could charbroil Blake without any squeamishness; however, I doubted his on-looking family would share my satisfaction.

Doing a Tarzan swing from the rafters would be impossible with my limitations. The exertion of climbing through the window had re-opened the deepest of my lacerations, the one on my left forearm. I closed my eyes in frustration and felt small and powerless.

In weary indecision I gathered a few items that could be hurled or wielded or jabbed, then retreated to a nest of mousy-smelling burlap and rolled into a ball. I just wanted to wake up in my own bed, drenched with nightmare sweat, and take a long soak in the tub.

After a few mousy sobs, I ordered my thoughts and turned them loose on the question *why attack me?* Because of something in my notes? Some observation that so unmistakably indicted Blake that he assumed I'd eventually recognize it? Or could my suspicions about Nathan's death have panicked him? I'd told Anton and Clare my theory about someone destabilizing the bridge. Had they mentioned it to anyone else? And, of course, Court had blathered to everyone about me kneeling at the bridge. Did it matter, now that I knew who had done it?

Or did I really know?

Certainty had stoked a furious rage and released the energy needed to get me in place to repay the murder attempts. Perhaps now, though, certainty had outlived its purpose. If I focused slavishly on one person to the exclusion of the others, I could be letting myself in for a dangerous surprise.

For once, I needed to be thinking beyond the level of Anton's adversary. My adversary. Someone might, after all, have laid a false trail to Blake. Every act of vandalism or violence had been carefully calculated, perhaps over years, to destroy Anton's peace of mind, to warp him with uncertainty and fear.

Even Nathan's death, a murder of ruthless improvisation, had been embellished by sending the boat off with lashed wheel. Wouldn't the killer be inclined to use the same crafty misdirection in arranging my death? If I had the luxury of five minutes with Anton, perhaps I'd learn that Blake had been with him all afternoon, helping to straighten the cannery and set up lights. My watch indicated I had a little over two hours to figure it out on my own.

I tried to put today's attack out of mind. It told me nothing new. The prior attempt on my life had erased all doubt for me that Nathan had been murdered. I pondered and free-associated and let my thoughts follow strings that led nowhere. I found dark motives: jealousy, revenge, greed, self-righteousness. I could make a plausible case against everyone on the island, even against Clare for God's sake. But no proof.

In frustration, I reined my mind back to the films, to my notes and went over it all again... and only then did I recall a singular detail I hadn't missed, but hadn't seen the full significance of. I sat bolt upright, and went over it repeatedly to make sure I hadn't got it wrong.

A rosebud. A single damned yellow rosebud!

It set off another flight of fancy, this one not sputtering or falling back to earth. I hugged my knees and imagined Rib Armentrout before me, the old editor stripping away the assumptions and poking at the soft spots. But in the end, the theory remained aloft. Not a sure thing, but I couldn't find the flaw.

A dull clatter from the door froze my breath. Someone had shaken the padlock. I listened for a long time but heard only ringing in my ears.

Chapter 29

Whoever tried the lock had to either be coming after the statues or looking for me. Anton would have opened it and come in. I could feel it on my clammy skin, someone nosing around outside, looking around the corner, finding the forklift, looking up at the open window then back down at the broken glass, hands on hips, smiling as a plan came to mind.

The rows of pigeons overhead slept with beaks tucked under their wings. Another stood watch from the window, a silhouette framed in the grid. I crouched behind a crate with only my huffing breath to mark the passage of time. Then I could wait no longer to find out who was there. I crept to the table under the window, climbed up, and mounted the tall cabinet. A flurry of wings, an empty window. I stretched upward to peer out. At that moment a hand grasped the window ledge before my eyes and I nearly flew backward off my perch. But it was a small hand, and a tousled head appeared, strained with the effort of chinning himself up.

"Egret. Are you in there?"

The reedy voice could have come from an angel.

"Court," I answered, my heart racing like an owl-struck pigeon. "What are you doing up here? You'll hurt yourself." I heard him scrabbling with his foot to find a loose corner of tin, then, for the moment, he seemed to have found a secure foothold. "You little monkey!"

A smile stretched across his angular face. "I tracked you."

I couldn't help but return his self-satisfied smile. "You did good." My heartbeat began descending toward normal.

"What happened, Egret? Are you hurt?"

I touched my cords of heavy hair and felt something crusty like blood. "I fell. Now listen to me, I need your help."

"Sure. Did you climb through this window?"

"Yeah, ain't I amazing? Court, I need to ask you a question. Remember how you told everyone how I ruined those pants kneeling at the bridge?"

"Yeah?" he answered slowly as if thinking maybe he'd screwed up.

"Did anyone ask you later exactly what I was doing at the

bridge? About putting that rock under one end?"

Court shifted his hold on window. "Noooo."

"Okay," I said. "Do you need to come in?"

"I'm okay."

"Look, Court, you can't tell anyone you saw me. Not your parents, not Uncle Blake, not Grandma, not anyone. Do you understand?" I considered having Court tell Anton I was here, but decided against it. To preserve my advantage of surprise, I wanted Anton to be peeved that I'd skipped out on his party. If they all believed I'd kayaked off the island, so much the better. The possibility remained that the plan for damaging the statues—if that was the plan—would not be carried out during the unveiling, but afterward, when the family had gone to bed. I'd stay here all night if necessary.

"What's the schedule for your grandpa's party?"

"We're having barbecued salmon. Uncle Charles is going to fix it. Grandma and I made a spice cake because it's Grandpa's favorite. And everyone is getting presents ready. I didn't buy him anything, so I tried whittling an otter out of a piece of driftwood, but it doesn't look much like an otter so I'm not going to give it to him."

"That's a wonderful idea for a gift. Don't you even think of not giving it to him. He'll love it, even if it's not very good." Court promised. "When is everyone coming here to look at the statues?"

"Right after dinner, I think. The cake and presents come after that, back at the house. What are you doing in there anyway?"

"Court, this isn't a game. There's something very bad going on and I'm helping your grandpa Anton to stop it. But we need your help, okay?"

Court gave me a 'get outta here' look, like he was trying to swallow his lips, but then nodded his willingness. It caught him by surprise to be treated like a competent human being. Then I paused with misgivings about what might go wrong. If Court were my own son, would I ask this of him? Yes, I decided. Every child should understand the world can be a dangerous place. I told him what to do, and told him to do it no matter who caused the trouble. "But don't do anything if it seems too dangerous. For example, if someone has a gun."

His jaw dropped with the realization we were not playing Monopoly any more. He listened raptly and nodded and repeated my instructions back to me. I found a rope and rigged a safety line for him before he descended, still, my heart stopped when he stretched a foot to the forklift tine and scrabbled down the forklift mast. But as he reached ground, I felt even worse. Although he'd had the smarts and initiative to track me, he was still an eleven year-old child. So terribly vulnerable.

Thoughts crowded my head as I waited. Confidence in my flash of insight wavered. Had Blake become so special to me that I could ultimately believe no ill of him? Had I manufactured a case against someone else because of it?

I tried to understand why my assailant had tried to drown me instead of simply trapping me until the dirty work was done. Sinking the boat would mark the deed as murder, assuming someone found my corpse, and would trigger a far wider investigation than art vandalism would. Perhaps he or she didn't expect the boat to sink, though with the hull damaged below waterline it should have been obvious. I wondered what kind of attack might be made on the statues, when it would happen, and what I could do about it. So many possibilities. No choice but to react. The risk?—there'd be no safety until the killer was dealt with.

The window light dimmed steadily, the tin building ticked as it cooled. Something odd began to happen: whenever Anton's shrouded creations were in my side vision, they seemed to move—a haunting from the days of Crooked Hoop and his longhouse. Anton had talked about putting stone into motion. I felt his dread vibrating in my breastbone, fear that these creations would fall victim to lunacy, felt his heavy-chested anguish at being terrorized by one of the eight people closest to him. And, yes, despite this, I could almost smell salmon broiling over coals of alder. I covered my shrunken stomach and felt a rumble. Spice cake. And I wanted to be with Anton now, on perhaps the most important day of his life. I wanted to toast his accomplishments, participate in the celebration, morbid as it had become.

Rising wearily from my burlap nest, I approached the nearest statue, pulled the sheet from it and stepped back. My breath flowed away and my body felt infused with grace. Anton had made an Indian girl in the bloom of adolescence, admiring through her parted garment the swell of first pregnancy, fingertips depressing ever so slightly the curve of belly, making the stone yield like flesh. This was no craftsman-like rendering, but a triumph of storytelling. I left the sheet crumpled on the floor, lit a lamp, and dragged the cloth from the next carving: a pair of old women seated on blankets before their weaving, reacting to the pregnant girl before them, one with amusement, the other with longing, perhaps jealousy.

With renewed energy, and a sense of stealing a look under the tree before Christmas dawn, I pulled the next sheet, and the next, looking at each creation with delight and wonder, finding stories within each, not stereotypes or even myths, but lives at once individual and universal. Children tumbling over each other like kittens. Crippled man showing a youth how to fasten an adz head to a handle. Boy presenting a captured kingfisher to a blushing girl. Tribal elders seated in council. And, when all the sheets lay in a laundry heap, I wandered among a community of souls, recognizing those I could confide in, those to beware of, those I could tease and be teased back, those I could befriend or desire. An energy connected the characters as if conscious of each other, belonging to each other as cells of a living thing. As each figure, or grouping of figures, told a story, so, I realized with awe, did the ensemble of some two-dozen works carry an overarching unity. I felt the essence of tribalism, a skein of commitment more subtle than familial loyalty, a reliance on each other to keep life safe and make it meaningful. More than a feeling, it triggered what seemed an ancient memory, a nostalgia for that tight weave of relationships absent in modern life. The kind of tightness that had sometimes worked, but more often failed at the Blue Feather Farm. How had Anton breathed this into stone when he'd seemed oblivious to the internal workings of his own family? Nathan had told of his eleven years' service to Anton, then said, "Now he serves me."

Such profound service indeed. In Anton's own sentiment, serving something greater than himself. Despite his plan for presenting his work, I couldn't bear to cover these figures again. I stowed the cloths, and as dusk became night, I began lighting lamps.

Anton's guts would knot when he saw lamplight coming from the building windows, but when he opened the doors and saw nothing harmed, he would understand. Whether he'd keep my presence to himself, I couldn't predict; I didn't want to imagine what my attacker would make of it. Also, lighting the lamps gave me the advantage manipulating the shadowy areas to create a good hiding place.

Not a minute to spare. I had just pumped up the last

Coleman lantern, lit it, hoisted it overhead with twine, and tied it off, when I heard voices outside. I hurried to place the oilcan near the door as arranged, bent the flexible spout to squirt directly ahead, then ducked behind the crates I'd stacked. To my consternation, thin shadows swept across the floor from the suspended lantern's slow twisting. Would anyone notice and wonder why? I clacked my teeth with indecision, then rushed under the lantern with a plastic milk box, stood shakily on it, reached, heard the dull clatter of a key in the padlock, Anton's anxious muttering, couldn't quite reach on tiptoes, ribs not letting me extend, hand quivering, the unmistakable sound of the shackle being tugged open. I gave up and scuttled back to my redoubt.

Breathing heavily, I watched through a gap in the crates as Anton threw the double doors open and surveyed the room intently, lamplight full on his face. He would have made a credible Moses on the big screen. When assured the carvings had not been damaged, I believe he found the sight more powerful than he could have imagined. I'd arranged the lamps so that all figures were illuminated, placing several kerosene lamps on the floor to fill in the harsh shadows cast by the stronger carbides. He seemed frozen by the spectacle as his family entered on either side of him and fanned out in amazement to look. Their initial gasps gave way to silence, absolute but for the hiss of lanterns. No one seemed to notice the lantern overhead twisting ever so slowly.

"I didn't know you had the lamps going already," Clare said. "How wonderful!"

"Yes, I... fired them up before dinner." Blake looked at him in puzzlement. Anton discretely glanced over the general area where I crouched in hiding. My mouth felt as if I'd gargled with talc.

Then came the exclamations of delight and wonder, the praise and congratulations, the milling through the recreated Indian village, Celeste summoning Blake to look at each new thing she'd found before he'd barely looked at the last, Rooks and Charles, arm-in-arm, she with a finger to her lips as if trying to plumb the genius of it. She'd dressed for a fashionable gallery exhibit: cornflower-blue cape, camel pants, black sweater. Buzzy stood well back, arms folded, while Glenda inched forward to touch the warrior, poised to retreat if the thing proved alive. Then someone began applauding and everyone joined in.

I puffed up with pride for Anton. He'd denied himself an audience these many years, something an artist must crave like oxygen. No more waiting. Clare held Anton close and Eugene clapped him on his broad back, and as I saw the glint of moisture in their eyes, my own vision fractured into stars. Gobi, in evening jacket and silk scarf in lieu of a tie, clowned around, striking poses with the statues as Clare took snapshots.

I blotted tears and heightened my vigilance for what I knew must happen. Just let it happen soon, I thought. Be done with it. Any of them could be concealing, say, a bottle of dye with which to deface the statues. I didn't know how long I could remain coiled like a jack-in-the-box, ready to throw a heavy handful of screws, and I shifted from one knee to the other. When I peered out again, Anton was staring directly at me, though he couldn't have known for sure. Court, too, was nosing around the shadows near my barricade with a knowing look on his mug. Luckily, as usual, nobody paid him any attention. When he spotted me, I shushed him, pointed to the oilcan, and motioned him away.

"The whole world must see these statues," Celeste proclaimed in an ecstatic whisper.

Dr. Underwood agreed. "Surely, Anton, you don't plan to keep them here on the island?"

"But that's what the longhouse is for," Blake said. "A gallery. There'll be nothing like it in the world."

I listened for a false note in Blake's voice, but heard only raw enthusiasm. Then he added, "It's too bad Egret's not here to see this," and, from the irony in his voice, I knew that he knew, and a glaze of sweat popped on my forehead.

"I told you, she paddled off in her kayak," Court said, rather too insistently. "I saw her."

"Probably having a nice hot bath someplace," Glenda said, adding a warbling laugh.

Luckily Gobi took the focus off me by embracing his oldest friend. "Ah Anton. You've done it! You've done it. You've showed what the human heart is capable of. What you've created, it's truly masterful. But people must see this. Will they come this far?"

"They said people wouldn't come to the Black Hills to see Mount Rushmore." Anton's reply began loud and kept rising. "And I could give a fig whether people in Chicken Blister, Arkansas, come here. This is for the red man. For the first People of America, and they will come. Here is their Mount Rushmore."

When the reverberations of his voice had faded, Celeste asked, voice inflected with challenge, "It is wonderful and incredible father, but I don't understand. You've always carved heroes and geniuses: the Isaac Newtons and Benjamin Franklins and Walt Whitmans." She swept a stick-like arm toward the sculptures. "But these are fishermen and basket makers and pregnant girls and warriors, and kids wrestling. And, I've got nothing against Indians, but it's not your culture; it's theirs. So I'm not sure...?"

Celeste's question stuck like a fly in the web of tension. It must have been in everyone's mind, the fear that something would go wrong that evening.

Anton hawked phlegm into the shadows. He moved to a place among the statues with full lantern light, and leaned his hands against the muscular shoulders of a crouching hunter. As he looked down, eyes lost under brambly gray brows, I couldn't tell if the question irritated or pleased him.

"Right after Clare and I moved to Thunderhead Island, we met a young squatter by the name of Nathan Weeping Moon. For different reasons, we all needed to start our lives over. Through his big-heartedness, I found my will to work again. We got to know his people—they'd come visiting, or we'd spend a couple days at the rez. We felt welcome there. We came to know them, and maybe understand them a little. And they became my models." He cupped his hand to the head of one of the carvings, the crippled man, and I recognized something of Nathan in the face. "You know, the European tries to view the Indian according to his own power structure. We single out a few names like Geronimo and Sitting Bull and Crazy Horse, and regard them as kings and generals. But the Indians had no autocrats. They didn't want autocrats; they didn't need them—not before the exterminators headed west, anyway. They were damned independent cusses," he laughed appreciatively, and pointed to the cross-legged men passing the pipe. "The old round-bellies would work things out for the tribe, but if some buck decided he knew better... most likely he'd be ignored. These people had a healthy dislike for arrogance and puffery. What mattered was respect. So people developed their heroic qualities to earn respect. Unlike these days, where wealth and celebrity get confused with heroism, and dropping names of big shot dickheads becomes a proper substitute for becoming a hero yourself."

When Anton's words had settled in, Clare said, "We've come to appreciate there's room for as many heroes as there are people."

Anton hooked an arm around Clare's waist as if to indicate they'd said the same thing. "A thousand years from now, I want people to look at these works and get some inkling of what we've lost by living in separate houses with tall fences all around them. But... if I need to explain, then I haven't done my job, have I?"

He looked as if he had much to say, but realized the inferiority of words. Finally, Rooks spoke tersely. "It still comes down to heroes, doesn't it? Why should one man set the standards for everyone? If you could have been happy with a little less..."

After seventy years, why couldn't everyone just let Anton revel in the limelight for this one hour?

Clare moved to Rooks' side and touched her shoulder. "Dear, what your father is saying—"

"I want to hear the rest," Anton said.

Rooks faltered as if she'd begun something and didn't know how to finish. She planted her knuckles on her hips. "I... I just meant if a person only makes room for the heroic, where does that leave us who don't measure up? If you can honor these Indians for being themselves, why in the world couldn't you have honored us—your own family—for being ourselves?"

Clare said, "Your father has come to see the world as his family. He's poured his heart and soul into these statues to give something to that family. It's his way of honoring us, all of us, don't you see?"

I clenched and relaxed, changed positions to assure my joints and muscles didn't become too stiff.

Anton gave an ironic grunt. "I don't need anyone to tell me I'm an arrogant hypocrite." He spread his arms. "I know I'm an arrogant hypocrite! But I'm seventy and I've done my job and I don't intend to apologize for my inconsistencies." He looked immersed in the world of his sculptures as if nothing could touch him. Euphoric at having completed his life's work. His most vulnerable moment, I worried.

Rooks rocked on her heels with a fixed, withdrawn gaze. Glenda found a pack of smokes in her purse and pulled one out with her lips. She turned to Gobi for a light. Celeste crossed her arms, burrowing each hand up the other sleeve. Blake chewed a thumbnail.

Anton said, "If we're done here, I want to show you the longhouse. Bring a couple of these lanterns and put the rest of them out."

I watched every small movement, looking for something premeditated, something false.

Buzzy wasted no time in killing lamps, muttering, "Somebody ought to carve the 1939 Yankees. There was a bunch of heroes." The others helped, and with each dimming of the light, I sensed the moment of crisis passing. In seconds, everyone would simply walk out the door. But in my heart I knew the crisis would return—perhaps when we were less prepared to deal with it. I burned with the need to have it done.

Now.

In playing tennis at the amateur championship level, I'd learned to walk out on the court as if I owned it. I worked up some thick saliva to wet my throat, then stepped from behind the crates, my cramped and unsteady legs undermining the presence I'd hoped to project.

"But we're not finished here," I said. It sounded, to me at least, like a malevolent croak. Ten astonished faces stared at me. Rooks blanched and took a step backward, jaw sagging. When she kept blinking as if beholding an apparition, I *knew*. My narrow-eyed stare had both fury in it and smug satisfaction, and I pointed a finger. "She's got something more on her mind that needs talking about."

I saw astounded and befuddled faces. In a hasty recovery, Rooks pulled her shoulders back and said, "Really, we thought you'd paddled off to your silly little newspaper." A competent portrayal of indignation.

"Egret, what the hell happened to you?" Anton said.

"Oh, my dear, your ear's all swollen and purple," Clare rushed to my side, raising hands to my head without touching.

"I've had a rough day."

"Well, you've got no business crashing my father's birthday party looking like a... a refugee," Rooks said. The first tactic of the scoundrel: claim the high ground.

I gave Rooks a look intended to convey that I knew all her secrets. "Don't you have a little birthday surprise planned for your father?" I watched her hands carefully.

Charles angled a shoulder in front of Rooks. "I hope you aren't insinuating something, because you'd be making a huge mistake."

Rooks bit down on her lip with a canine. Her cogs turned and mine turned with them. Now that I'd returned from the dead, she could walk away from Thunderhead Island without fear of discovery or prosecution. Nothing could be proved. Would she play out the terror now, or walk away and keep Anton fearing for his statues the rest of his life? Backing off would have the added benefit of making me look like an ass.

"You've decided to wear a black sweater again," I said, "just like that night on Queen Anne Hill. At least you started out wearing a sweater. But then you changed. Remember that cowl-necked sweater? You wore your hair tied back and doubled over into a little handle, just like it is now. And in the third reel you wore a yellow rosebud in your lapel. Funny, though, sweaters don't have lapels, do they?" I raised my eyebrows. "So you'd changed clothes. Why? Maybe you spilled a drink on yourself." I took a quick look around to see everyone waiting for the dime to drop. "Or maybe it was marble dust."

Rooks frowned. "Oh, this is *too* too bizarre!"

"She's always changing clothes," Charles said. "It means nothing."

"It means nothing that the yellow rosebud came from Clement Ely?" Though I addressed myself to Charles, I never took my eyes from Rooks' face.

"Who?"

"The newspaper critic who tried to humiliate Anton."

Rooks maintained a haughty, dismissive tilt of the head. I needed to crack her or provoke her into doing something stupid—and I didn't have many face cards to play.

"You were nineteen years old. Nearly a woman, and your father hadn't noticed. Enter Clement Ely, a man your father held in the highest contempt. He crashed the party and was so flatteringly attentive to you. Later, Ely rubbed Anton's nose in it, and when he hinted about his lewd intentions, Anton threw him bodily from the house. You chased after Ely, and no doubt he saw the bitterness you already felt against your father and he spun you up until you were seething with resentment and self-pity."

"I don't think so!" Rooks crossed her arms, and rolled her eyes as if to say *must we endure this?* But her reaction started a couple of beats too late to have been truly spontaneous.

"Did Ely suggest getting even with your father, or was that your own idea?"

She kept her voice marvelously cool. "What's worse—being

slandered by the likes of you, or being served an overpoached egg?"

Charles began dutifully informing me of my legal risk. I cut him off. I'd been nearly murdered twice in twenty-four hours, and Charles' little threats meant nothing.

"While the Quartet played the Beethoven piece," I continued, "you took a hammer from your father's studio and went to the courtyard and began swinging. You probably went after the *Walt Whitman* first—am I right?—because of the awards it had won. No matter, the curtains were closed and nobody could hear if you kept beat with the music, and you could get them all, the Isaac Newton and the others, pitting them, chipping noses and chins, breaking an arm from the *Stravinsky*. You were powerful and justified, and you swung with both hands until dust hung in the air and your arms were burning and you could scarcely lift the hammer anymore."

Rooks' mouth gaped, wondering, I hoped, at my omniscience. She quickly resumed her superior pose, but I'd found a soft spot.

I glanced at Anton, his brow gnarled, angry. Clare wanted to say something, but Anton held her back.

"You picked up Whitman's nose and went to your room," I said. "You hid the evidence, and looked at yourself in the mirror. Your black outfit had marble dust all over it, and it wouldn't brush off. The uncontrollable rage wore off and you realized what you'd done, and knew you had to go back to the party and pretend to be shocked when the damage was found. So you changed into another black outfit, hoping everyone'd had too much champagne to notice. Clement Ely had given you the yellow rosebud, so, as a symbolic touch, you slipped it in your lapel. You took a deep breath—as you did just now—and looking quite composed, you returned to the party and flirted like a pro. Any details you'd like to fill in, Rooks?"

From the periphery of my senses I felt people backing away as if frightened of Anton's expected fury.

Rooks shifted her weight to one leg and sneered. "They must be showing Perry Mason reruns out here in Dogpatch; how dreary. Shouldn't we be heading back for cake? Charles, you can give her something for concussion or whatever. She must have scrambled her brains when she fell out the window." She forced a laugh.

"Not yet," Anton said in a tone sharp enough to send a

shudder through her. "What about this?" He stared at Rooks with the same force he'd used on Blake at the breakfast table two days earlier; a stare which I hoped could penetrate her lies.

"Jesus Christ, father. I changed clothes at a party twenty years ago and that makes me something out of a Hitchcock movie? Someone bumped my arm and I got crab dip or something on my clothes. Big deal."

Anton held his gaze on Rooks, rubbed his arthritic knuckles. Rooks met his eyes and hung tough. He scowled, then shook his head slowly.

"If there's anything alive inside you, Rooks, by God I can't find it. I've never been able to."

Rooks stuck out a haughty chin. "Your loss."

I didn't know what to say, and looked to Blake for help. He met my eyes briefly, and I read him as struggling to sort things out, not convinced of anything. Or could it be an act? I blinked, and despite being so sure of myself a minute ago, I got a queasy sense of being wrong. Maybe I just couldn't live with the obvious. The note summoning me to Blake's favorite place—near the crab boat—had, after all, been in Blake's handwriting. But most people could forge a note that would pass casual inspection. Rooks had studied drawing. They all had. I hadn't talked about favorite places with Rooks, but Blake could have, or Clare. Hadn't Rooks outmaneuvered everybody at the Monopoly game, bargaining relentlessly, stretching the rules?

A lousy argument and I knew it. I sensed my credibility ebbing along with my confidence.

Buzz cupped his hand over a kerosene lamp and blew it out.

Celeste, avoiding my eyes, buttoned her coat.

"'Doesn't prove anything," Glenda whispered. "No smoking gun."

Rooks put an arm around her mother's shoulders and patted Anton's powerful biceps. "Let's go."

Flat footed, my opportunity slipping away, I threw up a desperation lob. I had but one other accusation to make. Almost entirely guesswork. An accusation certain to horrify the family, and mark me as lathered lunatic. But I had only to recall being insane with fear in the flooding fish hold to renew my determination.

"Wait," I said. Gobi had been about to extinguish a lamp, and he paused. "The real mystery is the red hand on the flagstone in the courtyard. The mark someone drew on the path after the damage had been discovered. Same as the withered hand on the marble block I saw in Friday Harbor. It explains everything, why one of you can't let go of the past. I've been asking myself, what's at the root of this compulsion to destroy Anton?—a compulsion that hasn't diminished by a single particle over two decades. Look at what's been stolen—the party films and the reel with David's accident. And what's been destroyed—the scrapbook David made for his father, burned in the fireplace. What does it suggest?"

I let the question hang before addressing Anton. "You watched it over and over. The film of David's last moments as he drifted toward the spillway. How many times have you visualized that last chance to save him—the arm reaching down from the tire swing, the hand grasping David's, then parting. No matter how many times you watched it, it was always the same. David, lost, as that grip failed."

Anton's face melted. As he pinched the bridge of his nose, tears rolled past his hand, into his beard.

"Stop this," Celeste shrilled. "This isn't helping. It's cruel. This is supposed to be a happy day, and you've ruined it."

I paid her no attention. I remembered the osprey Anton had carved for Rooks, with the fish tenuously held by one talon. "It was your arm, Rooks, that reached down for David. And your hand that let go." I had not meant to use the phrase *let go*, but hearing it come out that way revealed the awful truth. My face must have looked fearsome to Rooks, because she quailed as I drew near.

"You let him go on purpose!"

Chapter 30

Gasps of protest and outrage didn't break my focus on Rooks. The muscles in her face became flaccid and she receded into Charles's protection. No haughty retorts.

The game had turned.

When the murmurs subsided, I struck an understanding tone. "You didn't mean for him to die. But there was David, the show-off, the budding sculptor who got most of Dad's attention."

I moved a little closer and Rooks clutched her arms to her chest.

"Little brother hurt himself. So what? Let him struggle and see what it's like. You'd struggled plenty. Let David get out of his own mess. Make it look good, but let the hand slip away."

Her nostrils flared. Charles wrapped his arms around his wife and moved her away from me. "That's enough!"

Clare intervened in a low but commanding voice, "Charles, keep out of this." He stared back, open-mouthed, then loosened his hold on Rooks, leaving only a hand on her hip.

I mopped cracked lips with my tongue and continued. "It didn't seem like a life-or-death situation, did it?"

Rooks didn't look at me. Didn't look at anyone.

"You couldn't have known he would die."

She blinked at the word *die*.

"You didn't want him to die. He was family."

Rooks mouthed something unintelligible.

"It wasn't fair when your father blamed you." In my side vision, I saw Anton start to say something; I held up a palm to stop him.

"It just wasn't fair, was it Rooks?"

"No!" Her eyes looked hurt, but disturbingly incapable of tears. "I wasn't responsible."

"He never accused you directly, but things changed."

"He despised me!" It came out with the force of a primal scream. "He would have traded all three of us children to have David back."

"It was an accident, but your father had to blame someone."

"He kept watching that awful movie. And he would look at me like I was evil. I wanted him to teach me how to sculpt, but he said—" Her voice faltered. "He said if I couldn't grip my brother's hand, I damn well couldn't grip a chisel."

My sympathy button had been disconnected in the hold of the crab boat. Before she could recover, I needed to complete the crucial link. "And that's what you've been trying to tell your father with the red hand. It was an accident and you weren't responsible."

"He didn't care. He was killing me, killing the whole family. As if he could carve a new one that wouldn't disappoint him, or die on him."

"Haven't we heard enough?" Charles said.

"We haven't heard about Nathan," I said.

Someone gasped. Clare, probably.

"Absurd!" Charles said. "You're saying... Don't you think I would know? I'm telling you... What about the night the pumpkin got smashed? And the lock... the motorboat. She was in my bed, I tell you."

That argument had troubled me too, until something had dawned on me. "Charles, you slept late that morning, remember? Right through Celeste's screaming when she found her jack-o-lantern destroyed. You came downstairs after ten o'clock, groggy and dazed. You don't, by chance, keep any sedatives in your medical kit? And didn't Rooks claim jet lag and go to bed early the next evening? Making up for lost sleep."

I looked at Anton. The veins in his temple bulged. In a voice that resonated in my chest, he demanded, "Rooks, the truth!"

Rooks twisted free of her husband's hand. "The truth is it's too bad you didn't learn your lesson the first time!"

I think we all knew a confession when we heard it. I steeled myself for whatever endplay she'd planned. Rooks stared at me with such abject hatred that only then did I understand how deep the malignancy had rooted. Fearing what might be in her handbag, I moved swiftly to grab it.

She let go too easily.

In the instant it took me to realize I'd miscalculated, she'd reached to the small of her back. Then, from the folds of her cape, I saw the small black hole of a gun muzzle. Like an idiot, I put a hand out to protect myself from being shot. Blake rushed her, but she took a step back, leveled the gun at me with both trembling hands, and ordered him to stop. She pushed the safety catch off with her thumb and we all stood in place, Rooks in the dark circle under the hanging lantern.

My ability to feel terror had been used up. I just wanted to live. I wanted to defeat her. Maybe my refusal to cower kept her from pulling the trigger, or the pleas of her family. Perhaps she simply wanted to exact a greater torment. For whatever reason, she slowly drew the gun back from arm's length, turned to her father, and pointed the gun at her own temple.

"Oh, dear God, no!" Clare cried.

Rooks smiled at her father—a twitchy smile. "I'm going to give you another chance at getting your priorities right."

"What are you talking about? Put that thing away."

"There's a nice crowbar over there by the door."

"What about it?"

"Get it."

"This foolishness is over," Anton said.

"Do you really want to see your pretty white statues splattered with brains? You've got five seconds."

His mouth opened and he seemed powerless to move.

"One... two—"

"Shoot *me*, dammit, if you hate me so much."

"No. Three—"

Clare, face twisted in torment, sank to her knees before Anton, wrapped her arms around his legs, and released a wailing plea from an opened vein of anguish, the cry of the heart when it can bear no more, a clawing that ripped open my own deepest wounds to that raw place that sets humans apart from all other animals who grieve their dead.

"Oh Anton!"

I understood clearly, as if an image had been projected inside me. *My sanity cannot tolerate burying another child!*

Anton rested a gnarled hand on Clare's head; the lids of his eyes fell. He seemed to go breathless for a moment before returning from some place inside him. His voice came choked with emotion. "I told you the stone came first. I... I don't know when it changed, but..." He sniffed. "Not anymore." He tilted Clare's head and kissed her brow.

"Four!" Rooks said.

"I'm going," Anton replied without sharpness.

"Don't, Anton," I said, but he shambled toward the crowbar.

Court sidestepped out of his way. Only then did I think of something other than the statues or my own vengeance. Why did Court have to see his mother self-destruct?

Anton took the bar.

Muzzle still pressed to her temple, Rooks pointed to a carving of a young man on one knee bleeding a bear. "This one. The one with David's face."

I hadn't seen the resemblance, but didn't doubt it. The piece struck me as a transition to adulthood, something Rooks had never managed.

Anton looked to Clare. Clare looked away, her choice clear enough. Anton advanced slowly to the statue and flexed his fingers around the crowbar.

I appealed in a hoarse voice, "It won't save her. She's already lost. The bridge—she made it wobble so Nathan would fall. And she tried..." I couldn't finish my accusation, for lack of breath, and for seeing the agony in Clare's eyes. Eyes that would always see the best in any person; eyes that could never condemn her own daughter. Surely those eyes could also see the tangle of darkness, and know that the loving act would be to prevent Rooks from wrapping that good part of herself in skein upon barbed skein of karmic debt. I could sense this, as if with an inner eye, but lacked the words to convey it.

Anton shook his head. "I did blame her. I blamed everyone. The taint of my own bile is on everything I've done."

"She won't let you stop at wrecking one," I said. "Even then, she'll shoot herself just to make you hurt more." I realized she'd probably shoot *me* first.

Anton hesitated.

In agitation, Rooks shuffled toward the statue. "Now!"

"Rooks," I pleaded, "your son is watching. Think what you're doing to him."

"He just reminds me of David—I can't stand having him around!"

Court's heart must have been crushed, because mine was. I looked to Charles. Why didn't he do something besides hold his arms out like a scarecrow?

Clare rushed to Anton and pressed her face to his shoulder. She seemed to be begging his forgiveness for choosing Rooks over the statues.

"I wanted to make things that would last forever," Anton said.

"You made them, that's what's important," Clare said.

He gently moved Clare aside and looked with defeated eyes at his young hunter, and held out his hand as if in final blessing.

"Do it, father."

Anton closed his eyes and raised the bar. "For my family."

I wailed through constricted throat as he struck a massive blow; a marble arm pinwheeled across the floor.

I felt for the utility knife as Anton swung again at the statue. A large chip clanged against the tin siding. Then I saw Court duck under his father's embrace. He looked to me, the oilcan held with both hands, fingers on the squirt trigger. I shook my head and mouthed the word *NO*. He seemed confused and queried me again with his eyes. Why had I even considered involving Court? I should have realized something like this might happen.

"You're doing good," Rooks said to her father. "Now the face."

As Anton swung a third time, Court ignored me. *No matter who it is*, I'd stressed. He took two more steps toward his mother and squeezed. A diagonal streak of oil appeared across Rooks' camel-colored pants.

She instinctively held out her arms and looked down. "Oh, you horrid little brat!"

I abruptly slashed at the twine suspending the lamp, the blade cutting it cleanly. The lamp crashed to the floor not two feet from where Rooks stood, glass shattering, a fireball of pressurized gas roiling up. Blake and I both pounced at her, but she quickly leveled the gun at me and I ducked behind one of the carvings, dropping the knife when my hand banged against the stone. I heard an explosion, the whine of a ricochet, screams, and felt a dusting of marble on my neck. I looked out to see Blake pin Rooks' arms to her sides before she could take aim at me again.

Charles reached for the gun. "Let go, honey."

Rooks relaxed her struggle just long enough for Blake to loosen his grip a little, then butted him with the back of her head and spun free, whipping the pistol in an arc to clear grabbing hands. She danced away from them, and maneuvered for a clean shot at me.

With dreamlike slowness, I shifted to keep the statue between us. Then Court advanced again. *Somebody please stop him*. But nobody did. I didn't know what Rooks might do, and I wasn't going to be responsible for another dead boy. I charged her, but the stiffness in my hip robbed me of the quickness I'd counted on. Fortunately, Court's next blast of oil strafed his mother's face. While she tried to clear her eyes, I tackled her at the waist and pushed the gun aside. It went off. I came down on Rooks as she hit the floor and heard the air go out of her. But she fought with unnatural strength. My left arm, weak from the dislocation, couldn't control her gun hand. I rolled left to pin the gun under my body, hoping my weight would somehow keep her from pulling the trigger. I reached with my right hand to gouge her eye, to buy time for the others to help, but I found her mouth instead and she bit my fingers to the bone. I shrieked, and when I tried to pull free, she wouldn't let go, so I slammed her head back on the concrete. Where were the others, damn them? Then I knew—one of them must have been shot. Someone held her other arm. Again I pulled my trapped hand and slammed her head back. This time, she let go of my fingers, but jerked a knee into my chest. The pain in my ribs left me breathless. I expected to feel the concussion of the gun under me at any moment, the burn of a slug traveling along my body. Then hands tried to pull me away. Didn't they understand she still had a gun? Rooks delivered another knee that nearly rolled me off her altogether. As she struggled with manic strength, I felt my control slipping. "Get the gun!" I yelled to whoever was trying to help. My fingers were too damaged to grab at Rooks, but with the heel of my hand I slammed her jaw. She must have bit the tip of her tongue because she squealed with pain.

Then more hands somehow kept her down and took the gun and, finally, helped me to my feet. Eugene Gobi and Buzzy each held one of Rooks' arms. She glared at me with the vilest contempt a human face could manage, blood streaming freely from her mouth.

I returned a look of pity.

The crowbar clanged on the floor. I looked to where Anton knelt at the fallen body of his son, Blake, and felt my knees buckle.

Chapter 31

I sank into torpor by the kitchen stove, my hand soaking in an iodine solution, while Charles patched Blake on the kitchen table. Blake kept a chatter going to lighten the mood a little. Dinah kept me company in the next chair, switching her tail slowly. I stared at the birthday cake, forgotten on the counter. Not hungry, just numb.

Charles told Blake the slug had passed through the fleshy part of his left calf, missing the bone and tendons. He'd be on crutches in the morning. Charles had developed a tic under one eye, and probably owed his composure to the doctoring that needed done. It saved him from thinking about how his life had imploded. When my turn came, he dressed the wounds on my fingers and decided on a course of oral antibiotics, muttering about the human mouth being one of the filthiest places known to medicine.

I asked about rabies shots and he smiled grimly, shaking a capsule out of a bottle. I hesitated, then swallowed it. He noticed my reluctance, and tried to say something. A jumble of shock and regret and shame registered on his face, but it came out as a stammer.

"Save it for later," I said.

He nodded and began sponging caked blood from my ear.

"You know, Charles, your son did a courageous thing, and if you don't acknowledge it, he'll blame himself for whatever happens to his mom."

He rinsed the sponge far longer than necessary.

"He probably saved his mom's life, and mine. He's a hero. Don't let him think anything else."

Charles sighed and put something on the contusion that stung, then checked the laceration on my hand where the stitches had pulled open. He numbed the area and went to work. As he finished up, we heard Eugene and Anton and Buzzy coming in the front door. They would have Rooks with them, bound securely I hoped.

"Why did she do this?" Charles asked in a despair-wracked voice.

"Couldn't you see something wrong between her and Anton?"

"I... She wanted me to be more like him. You know, driven.

She always made a point of letting people know who her father was, and it bothered her when they didn't recognize his name any more. She always signed her name Rooks Gropius Underwood."

"And when the harassment started up again here on Thunderhead Island, it never occurred to you she might be behind it?"

He massaged his forehead. "She had me convinced her uncle Buzz and aunt Glenda were doing it, out of jealousy and spite. Rooks is damned clever at making people think what she wants them to think. She can charm the toenails off people, but once someone crosses her, that's it. No reconciliation. She doesn't have any old friends—we're always cultivating new ones."

"Charles, when you campaigned for the AMA presidency, did you and Rooks by chance come to Seattle?"

"We did a loop up the West Coast. Why?"

"Nothing." Charles probably didn't know about the hands being painted on the marble blocks while in storage. "Just curious."

He rummaged in his bag, peeled the wrap off a syringe. "She'll need a sedative." He walked stiffly to the front room, as if unfamiliar with his own body.

With effort, I got up and followed as far as the foyer. I leaned against the entry to the sitting room and listened. Anton jostled the fire, added a log, and eased into his chair. Muted voices from Clare, Glenda, Celeste. Making plans. Someone could paddle the kayak for help in the morning. My kayak—had it washed ashore in the inlet? Rooks would remain downstairs, Buzzy and Blake would split watches. Egret would be more comfortable in the barn.

I could see Rooks' head over the back of a chair. Not a word from her. *Cat got your tongue?*

Charles sent Court after a glass of water and Court stopped when he saw me. I hugged him. I felt him tremble and hugged him harder. "You did good," I whispered. "You saved my butt. I'm so glad you're okay."

With Court out of the room, Charles confronted his wife. "You accused your father of destroying his family, but now you've destroyed ours. For what, Rooks? For what?"

She spat her reply. "I thought you were going places." Her swollen tongue sounded the word as *platheth.* "You'd be sewing up broken-bottle wounds on drunks if not for me. I planned every move, and we'd have made it to the top if you'd had an ounce of drive."

Charles pushed stiff fingers over his scalp. "Why couldn't you have been satisfied with what I am? I feel like a piece of soap you've been carving on."

"As if you were satisfied with me, you hypocrite."

"I tried."

"You despised me for wanting an abortion!"

Her shout gave way to an appalling silence, and I clutched the doorframe for support.

"And you've never forgiven me for refusing."

"Well, what did we have to lose, then?"

Charles gasped. "You don't know?" He turned his back and folded his arms.

Anton stared, unmoving, into the fire; dancing flames reflected in his eyes.

Rooks changed her tone to a childlike plea. "Do I need a lawyer? We can afford the best. If I have to, I'll go to a clinic somewhere. Someplace quiet for a month or two. Then we'll carry on, maybe move to Palm Springs."

"We're not going to Palm Springs. I'll hire you a good lawyer, and a good therapist, but let's not pretend." His lip quivered as he looked into her pleading eyes.

Court had returned with the glass of water and saw this part. Maybe he understood.

Celeste heated water on the kitchen stove, poured it into a galvanized laundry tub, added fragrant oils, and helped me bathe. She loaned me a flannel nightshirt, and offered me her bedroom, but I said I'd rather not be under the same roof as her sister. She escorted me to Blake's barn room, and, for the sake of appearances, offered to stay. I smiled—mostly because I needed to smile about something—at Blake laying on his bed, bandaged leg outstretched. "He's harmless."

When Celeste had gone, Blake asked about what had happened earlier that day. I showed him the smeared note and told him about the signs leading to the boat, the knock on the skull, and the rest of it. He shook his head in astonishment and stretched out his arms for a hug. Though he took care not to press my wounds, he didn't miss all of them. But I didn't mind. I buried my face in his shoulder and tasted my tears and smelled his musk and felt safe.

"Did you really believe I could do that to you?" Blake said, voice soft and choked up.

"Yes." I sniffled. "I hope you can understand. The unthinkable has happened to me before. Maybe I'll spend the rest of my life ready to believe the worst, I don't know."

"Maybe it's time you changed."

I wasn't sure I could do it on my own.

"I'm going to help Dad finish that longhouse. Then, if he truly wants Thunderhead Island to become a destination, he'll need an interpretive center, café, and gift shop—that sort of thing. The point is, Egret, I'll be an hour from Friday Harbor by boat. A lot of people commute an hour."

My emotions seemed to be on a hair trigger. I bit my lip and wiped the blur from my eyes. "I'd like to say yes, Blake, but I need to talk to your father. If we're going ahead with the biography, I don't see how I can have a relationship with someone in the family."

He reflected for a moment. "You sound like Dad: 'The stone comes first in my life.'"

"I know. But I'm not really so sure what comes first in mine."

"Two people can discover these kinds of things together. How long would it take to write? The biography?"

"Two years—at a minimum."

He nodded. "I'll still be sipping Cutty Sark two years from now."

Was I worth waiting for? "Sip this," I said, and planted my mouth squarely on his. When I'd given it all I had, I slipped under the quilt, pulled his hand close and stroked it gently.

"I just want to feel safe tonight," I said, then rolled on my side. Saying nothing, he fit his body to mine. I slept deeply until he left to stand his watch over Rooks—despite injury, he'd insisted on taking his turn—then I slept fitfully, waking often because of aches and pains, and because of claustrophobic nightmares.

At dawn, Clare came to check on me, bringing a basin of steaming water and a fresh washcloth. She wore an unbuttoned flannel shirt over the same pullover she'd worn the last evening. She looked tired, but seemed to float within a protective bubble.

"You've been up all night, haven't you," I scolded.

She didn't answer. This time, she didn't act concerned about me spending the night with Blake, but she had something on her mind. I sensed it. Yet, we didn't talk—it seemed too soon.

Glenda and Celeste were cooking breakfasts to order when I hobbled into the kitchen; no one spoke to me more than necessary, as if I were complicit in adding fresh calamity to their family. I suspected they'd heard of my escape from the boat, as Eugene said that Anton and Clare were walking up to the north cove to recover my kayak, and Court had tagged along. I'd eaten some tasteless eggs and sausage by the time they'd returned. Clare asked me to take coffee with her and Anton on the porch.

The October sun didn't have much punch that early in the morning, but Clare brought Afghans for our laps. Dinah looked at all three laps, but chose mine.

"Disloyal beast," Anton muttered.

His life's work completed, I wondered if he could allow himself to bask in it, or if the shadows would always remain. I sighed into the steam hovering over my cup. "The kayak was safe, then?"

"Quite," Clare said. "Court insisted on paddling it down to our cove and promised to stay within five feet of shore. Then Blake is going for help, if you don't mind lending your boat." As always Clare sat erect, but she picked nervously at a nail. Anton stared past his coffee to the sea. Clare said, "We looked at the cable where that old boat had been winched up, and saw the fresh cut." She shook her head. "We shouldn't have involved you in our problems. What you've endured... "

Anton nodded, and rolled his hand for Clare to continue.

"On our hike, we talked about things. Tried to. I can't seem to think anything straight through. We want the family to be involved here—to the extent they're interested. Shuttle boat; gift shop. We need to pull together."

As she paused, a surge of true warmth came from the sun. A Stellar's jay landed on the railing and Dinah chattered at it.

"Of course, our main concern is about Rooks." Clare kept wetting her lips, then wiping them dry. "You've been a parent... Even when they're grown, a mother's eyes see the child superimposed on them, the child bursting with potential."

Breakfast became heavy in my stomach.

"In a few hours, they'll want a statement about what happened. What you say will change the rest of Rooks' life."

Clare left it for me to fill in the blanks.

"Whether it can be proved or not," I said, "she's responsible for Nathan's death." I didn't go into the worst of my suspicions. They'd find out later. Even without a corpse to autopsy, there might be traces of Nathan's blood or hair on the hammer. "So how does it help Rooks to let her go on being that way? How does it help anyone?"

Anton nodded, but Clare just looked at me. I wondered what she'd do if our roles were reversed. As if in answer, she told a story. "A priest once escorted his elderly abbot through the woods where they were attacked by a notorious highwayman, who'd murdered many travelers. In the struggle, the priest managed to take away the thief's weapon. But as the priest was about to drive the sword into him, the thief spat on the abbot. The priest lowered the sword, and said, 'I cannot kill with anger in my heart.'"

I felt my own heart shudder, as if shedding something heavy, and I realized it mattered to Clare not only what I did, but why I did it. A person could choose to overcome vengeance. Rooks hadn't. Then I understood something about Clare: she was a great sculptor in her own right. She'd chiseled her life to a Shaker-like simplicity, and had helped Anton chip away at his stony crust until, gradually, something lighter and more pure had begun to emerge.

Soon Court arrived with the kayak. When Blake was ready, Anton and I helped him launch. Then I sat in the crook of a madrona, a huge old octopus of a tree, wondering what good it is to be unwaveringly clear about life without some blinding insight to steer by. My palm closed around the vial of rose petals, and I watched the flashes of Blake's paddle blades until they became lost in the dazzle of the sea.

About the Author

After a career in labor relations, Michael Donnelly published *Awakening Curry Buckle*, a young adult adventure novel, with Blue Works. *False Harbor* is the first in an adult mystery series, also set in the San Juan Islands, featuring the wry and relentless journalist, Egret Van Gerpin. Besides writing, Michael makes time for community mediation, growing rare plants and kayaking the Northwest's coastal islands. He may be contacted through his website at www.donnellybooks.com.

About Windstorm Creative
and our Readers' Club

Windstorm Creative was founded in 1989 to create a publishing house with author-centric ethics and cutting-edge, risk-taking innovation. Windstorm is now a company of more than ten divisions with international distribution channels that allow us to sell our books both inside the traditional systems and outside these paradigms, capitalizing on more direct delivery and non-traditional markets. As a result, our books can be found in grocery superstores as well as your favorite neighborhood bookstore, and dozens of other outlets on and off the Internet.

Windstorm is an independent press with the synergy and branding of a corporate publisher and an author royalty that's easily twice their best offer. We have continued to minimize returns without decreasing sales by publishing books that are timeless, as opposed to timely, and never back-listing.

Windstorm is constantly changing, improving, and growing. We are driven by the needs of our authors – hailing from ten different countries – and the vision of our critically-acclaimed staff. All of our books are created with the strictest of environmental protections in mind. Our approach to no-waste, no-hazard, in-house production, and stringent out-source scrutiny, assures that our goals are met whether books are printed at our own facility or an outside press.

Because of these precautions, our books cost more. And though we know that our readers support our efforts, we also understand that a few dollars can add up. This is why we began our Readers' Club. Visit our webcenter and take 20% off every title, every day. No strings. No fine print.

While you're at our site, preview or request the first chapter of any of our titles, free of charge.

Thank you for supporting an independent press.

www.windstormcreative.com
and click on Shop

See next page for title recommendations.

Fiction
from Windstorm Creative

Bad Apple Jack (Gregg Fedchak)
The Big Five-O Cafe (James Wolfe)
Bones Become Flowers (Jess Mowry)
Breed of a Different Kind (Walt Larson)
The Broccoli Eaters (Gregg Fedchak)
Guardian Devils (Rebecca McEldowney)
Heir Unapparent (John Harrison)
Judah's Luck (Walt Larson)
The Junk Lottery (Mickey Getty)
Love Among the Tomatoes (Gregg Fedchak)
Manual for Normal (Rebecca McEldowney)
On a Bus to St. Cloud (Patrick Brassell)
The Sitka Incident (Walt Larson)
Soldier in a Shallow Grave (Gerald Cline)
Soul of Flesh (Rebecca McEldowney)
Storm on the Docks (Walt Larson)
Strong Medicine (Walt Larson)
Visibility (Cris DiMarco)
Willy Charles, Esq. (Walt Larson)
Woman's Sigh, Wolf's Song (Kathryn Madison)

**For more titles in all genres,
visit us online at
www.windstormcreative.com**